TREASURE COAST

DECEIT

TREASURE COAST

DECEIT

Paul E. McElroy

TREASURE COAST MYSTERIES, INC.
STUART, FLORIDA
www.TreasureCoastMysteries.com

Printed in United States of America

Publication date January 2002
1 3 5 7 9 10 8 6 4 2
Copyright © 2001 by Paul E. McElroy
All rights reserved.

Publisher
Treasure Coast Mysteries, Inc.
43 Kindred Street
Stuart, FL 34994

LIBRARY OF CONGRESS CATALOGING-IN-PUBLICATION DATA:
McElroy, Paul E.
Treasure Coast Deceit / by Paul E. McElroy
p.   cm.

ISBN 0-9715136-0-0

1. MacArthur, Phillip (McCray, James - Mack) Fictitious character – Fiction.
2. Undercover agents – Florida - Fiction
3. Florida – Fiction   I. Title.

For my mother and father who instilled my ideals and values.

For Michi who has stood by my side and supported me in the good times and the bad, through sickness and health and all of those times when she knew that I had to do something because I just had to do it regardless of the outcome – like this one.

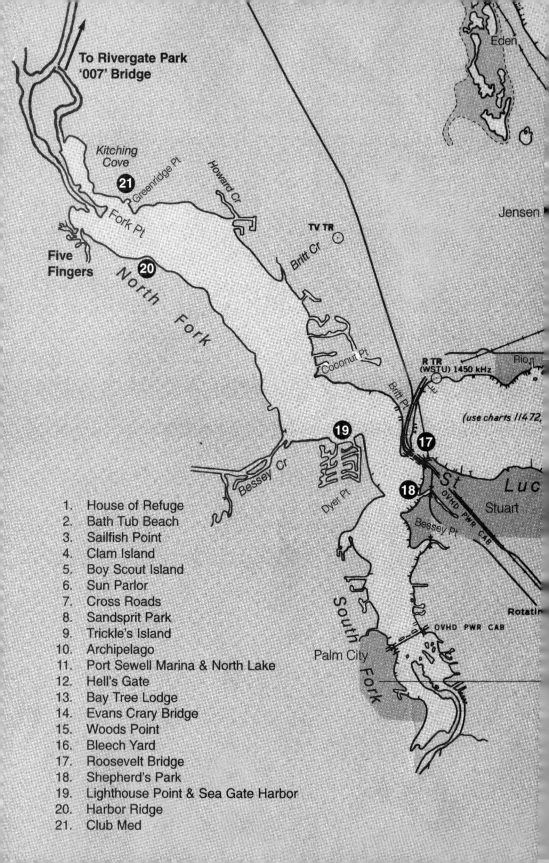

To Rivergate Park
'007' Bridge

Kitching Cove

21

Greenridge Pt

Howard Cr

TV TR

Britt Cr

Fork Pt

Five
Fingers

20

North Fork

Coconut Pt

R TR
(WSTU) 1450 kHz

Rio

Britt Pt

(use charts 11472,

19

Bessey Cr

17

St. Luc

18

OVHD PWR CAB

Stuart

Bessey Pt

Dyer Pt

Rotatin

OVHD PWR CAB

South Fork

Palm City

1.   House of Refuge
2.   Bath Tub Beach
3.   Sailfish Point
4.   Clam Island
5.   Boy Scout Island
6.   Sun Parlor
7.   Cross Roads
8.   Sandsprit Park
9.   Trickle's Island
10. Archipelago
11. Port Sewell Marina & North Lake
12. Hell's Gate
13. Bay Tree Lodge
14. Evans Crary Bridge
15. Woods Point
16. Bleech Yard
17. Roosevelt Bridge
18. Shepherd's Park
19. Lighthouse Point & Sea Gate Harbor
20. Harbor Ridge
21. Club Med

Eden

Jensen

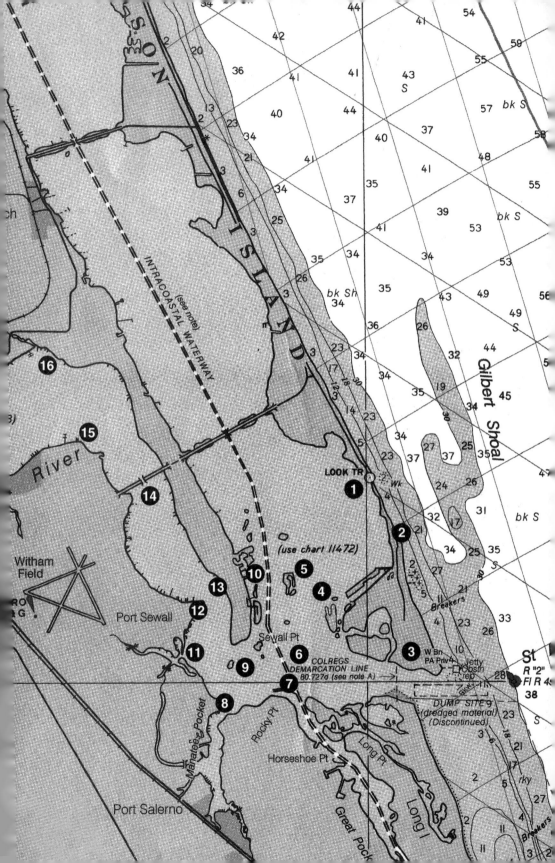

FLORIDA'S 'TREASURE COAST'

Appropriately named for the twelve ship *Spanish Plate Fleet* that sank along it's shores on July 30, 1715 Florida's *Treasure Coast* stretches along the Atlantic coast from Jupiter to Sebastian sixty miles to the north. Tucked in between Highway 1 and the Atlantic Ocean the *Treasure Coast* ambles along luring visitors to its Gulf Stream kissed beaches of fine sand.

Amateur treasure hunters strolling along the sandy beaches with metal detectors in hand attempt to appear disinterested in the trinkets that they scoop up from the sand in wire-meshed baskets.

The *Cartagena* and *Vera Cruz* Spanish treasure fleets arrived in Havana in May 1715 on their way back to Spain. They planned to replenish their meager stores and sail a few days later. The captain of the *Vera Cruz Fleet* had 1,000 chests of silver in the cabin beneath his own and had stuffed the holds of his other ships with gold bullion and silver ingots. The *Cartagena Fleet* was loaded with silver and gold coins from the mints in Columbia, gold jewelry from Peru and 166 chests of Columbian emeralds.

The combined ships, now named the *Plate Fleet* departed Havana the morning of July 24, 1715 to enter the Gulf Stream and proceed northward along the Florida coast. However, on July 30 a hurricane struck the fleet. All but one of the ships had its bottom ripped out on coral reefs and sank resulting in the death of more than 1,000 Spaniards and the scattering of treasure from *Sebastian* to *Stuart*. Historical records indicate that much of the treasure was salvaged, but the *Urca de Lima* has yet to be found.

Hopeful treasure hunters from around the world come to the *Treasure Coast* to try their luck. Why don't you visit us too? You might catch sight of Rat, Mack or Tina and can even wet a line in hopes of catching a record setting *'cat-snapper'*.

EPIGRAPH

"Stare not into the abyss,

lest the abyss stare back at you."

Nietzsche

CHAPTER
1

The gambling boat industry brought jobs and excitement to suburban Illinois. Wherever there was enough water to float a boat a lavish floating gambling palace complete with a uniformed captain and crew, slot machines, roulette, crap and blackjack tables appeared almost overnight.

It's a pleasant, unseasonably warm Sunday afternoon in late March. James McCray, called 'Mack' by his friends and business associates had brought along the long-legged blonde bimbo that he picked up in a bar in Chicago's Old Towne district the night before. She lived in Schaumburg an affluent suburb located twenty-five miles northwest of the Loop. After a leisurely champagne brunch at the Schaumburg Hilton she suggested that they drive to Fox River Grove and spend the rest of the sultry afternoon on a casino boat. He didn't have anything else to do and agreed to go. If an emergency arose his answering service could reach him via cell phone or pager.

Fox River Grove's pride and joy was the truly magnificent paddle wheeler the *GRANDE DAME*. She measured 410 feet long from bow sprite to paddle wheel, was 115 feet wide at the beam, had two full upper decks and was authorized by the Coast Guard's Chicago Marine Safety Office to carry 1,014 passengers.

Mack was playing blackjack one-on-one against a short, balding, middle-aged very bored dealer and betting $500 a hand.

After two hours of play he was two grand behind. Then he got a break! The dealer smiled and dealt him a pair of kings face down - the king of hearts and the king of spades - a good chance for a blackjack! He flipped both cards face up, split the kings by placing the king of hearts to his right and the king of spades to his left and doubled his bet to $1,000 on each hand. Before the dealer could deal him another card the pager on Mack's belt vibrated signaling an urgent message. He glanced at his watch. 5:45 P.M. The pager's digital display read '911 911 911'. That meant that he should call his voice mail immediately for an urgent message. But, now was not the time to quit. The opportunity to catch up, and maybe even win a few bucks, was at hand. He couldn't pass it up and decided that the message could wait until he played out the two hands.

The dealer dealt him two cards face down - one on top of each king. The dealer's hand of two cards showed the ten of clubs face up and he stood on his hand. Casino rules required that the dealer stand on a hand of eighteen or better. The dealer did not take a 'hit' indicating that he had at least 'eight' as a hole card. Mack peeked at the two cards in the hand on his right. The freshly dealt face down seven of spades combined with the king of hearts gave him only seventeen. The hand was a certain loser because the dealer's hand had a count of at least eighteen. Mack had to take a hit and take the risk of going 'bust'. He couldn't win otherwise.

Mack softly tapped the polished mahogany table edge with the knuckles of his right hand for luck and turned his attention to the hand on his left. He slowly lifted up the edge of the card laying face down on top of the king of spades. It was the ace of hearts. Mack flipped it over face up alongside the king of spades and blurted out "blackjack!" The bored dealer smiled and slid $1,500 in $100 chips across the table towards Mack's meager pile of chips. He motioned with his head towards the hand with the king of hearts face up, shrugged his rounded shoulders and raised his bushy eyebrows as if asking Mack what he wanted to do.

It was decision time. Mack cut his losses to $500 with the blackjack and if he won this hand he would be $1,000 ahead. The dealer's hand added up to eighteen or better. Mack's hand held seventeen and was an obvious loser. He had to take a hit - there was no other choice. He cupped the face down seven of spades in his right hand and tapped it on the green felt surface as a signal for the dealer to deal him another card. The dealer obliged with the four of clubs face up. Mack slapped down the seven of spades and shouted out *"Twenty-one!"* The smiling dealer pushed a second pile of fifteen $100 chips towards Mack's side of the table. Because he won both hands Mack was $1,000 ahead for the day. He tipped the dealer a $100 chip, scooped up the neatly stacked piles of chips and headed for the cashier's cage. He still had to make that call to his voice mail!

The bimbo had hit him up for $100 to play the slots when they arrived. Now she was plastered on free booze and happily feeding quarters into a computer controlled slot machine as fast as she could pull the handle. She smiled at Mack, waved frantically and almost fell off the stool as he walked toward her.

"Let's go before you lose everything that I gave you."

"Mack, I don't want to go yet. I'm having fun and I still have some quarters left in my bucket."

Mack frowned, reached down and picked up the round cardboard bucket partially filled with quarters that rested in her ample lap. Mack held open the side pockets of his blue blazer and filled them with the remaining quarters. "Now you don't have any quarters and I'm leaving. Are you coming with me or staying here. I don't really care which."

She stuck out her glossy, crimson lower lip in a feigned pout, folded her arms over her excessive man-made boobs and kicked him in the left knee cap with the toe of her right high heel. "I'm staying. I can find someone better than you in five minutes." Before she could utter a word of protest he flipped the empty cardboard bucket upside down over her head and walked away.

There was one somewhat ominous message on his voice mail.

"Dinner is at Mario's on Peterson Avenue at seven o' clock. Come by yourself and don't be late."

Mario's is a 'mom and pop' Italian restaurant on Peterson Avenue, east of the Eden's Expressway, in the Edgewater Neighbor on Chicago's Far North Side. It's small, and cozy, with black, plastic-covered booths in the back where patrons can talk without extra sets of ears paying attention to what they have to say to one another.

Mack was running a bit late. When he walked into Mario's the clock on the wall above the bar read 7:10. The aroma of garlic and basil simmering in warm tomato sauce wafted in the air. Dino was softly crooning *'Volare'* through four round speakers recessed in the drab white 'popcorn' ceiling. Wicker baskets filled with warm, fresh Italian bread covered with checkered red and white napkins graced every occupied table. Open bottles of *Chianti* nestled in their raffia outerwear breathed in the air and blossomed to their full fragrance. Mack was famished.

Mario's looked as if it had been disassembled in Palermo, moved to Chicago and reassembled. The interior walls were real brick and not the plastic decorative facade available at home supply stores. At each window a green canvas awning stretched over the table. Plastic bulbs of garlic and onions hung down from the awnings. Two pine needle wreaths, each flocked with garlic cloves, occupied the space above the wooden-framed glass entrance door. Three brass-based ceiling fans, equipped with heavy wooden blades, moved slowly over the dining area and wafted the warm aromas from the kitchen downward teasing the diners with a delicious hint of what was in store for them.

Mario, the silver-haired, first generation Italian American proprietor greeted and seated his customers with a flourish. Capri, his wife of forty years, was the cook. His two sons Johnny and Joey waited on the tables and washed the dishes. Mario's was a family business in the 'old country' tradition.

Mack wanted to make small talk with Mario to try to get a hint from him of what was going on. He noticed two identical white plaster statuettes of a girl in flowing robes filling a water pitcher sitting atop wooden pedestals on each side of the front door. "Mario. Do these two statues have any special significance?"

Naw. I got a good buy on 'em at a yard sale. They were for a cemetery in Oak Lawn that went broke." He gestured with his thumb over his right shoulder towards the back of the restaurant and grunted. "O'er dere. De're waitin' for you in the back booth. You're late and de're not happy."

Three men dressed in expensive Italian-cut suits were sitting in the back booth well beyond the earshot of other patrons and they weren't smiling. A distinguished silver-haired man in a gray pinstriped suit looked directly at Mack, tapped the face of his watch, shook his head from side to side and frowned. Mack wasn't concerned. What was ten minutes between business associates and friends? It wasn't life or death. Or, so he thought.

Mack took a deep breath and briskly walked with his head up and his back straight towards the rear of the restaurant. When he reached the booth he stuck out his right hand towards the silver-haired man. Mack smiled partially because he had $3,000 in $100 bills nestled in the right inside pocket of his blazer, but mostly because he wanted to disarm the trios obviously hostile glares.

The silver-haired man glared at him, softly cleared his throat and spoke in a low, stern voice indicating superiority and to impress the two *goombas* sitting beside him. "Mack you are almost fifteen minutes late. This is a very important meeting and you owe me a good explanation."

The *goombas* nodded their heads indicating full agreement with their boss's words. But, they didn't miss a beat in stuffing their faces with forkfuls of grilled, and deep fried calamari from the steaming platters resting on the table.

"Sam, I'm really sorry. I was in Fox River Grove on the gambling boat when you paged me. I got stuck in traffic on my way back at the Kennedy and I-94 junction. What's up?"

"Mack, I apologize for biting your head off. Let's not talk about it now. Sit down, dig into this calamari, drink some wine and enjoy a good meal. We'll talk business after dinner."

Four bottles of Chianti, dressed in dried raffia skirts, shared the table with two baskets of fresh Italian bread and two platters plied high with calamari. Mack ordered an antipasto appetizer of sausage and rapini and chose Veal Marsala for his entrée. The group exchanged meaningless small talk intermixed with grunts of satisfaction from the pair of *goombas*. The food was far too delicious to allow interruptions for meaningful conversation.

Several times during the lavish meal Mario's wife Capri, affectionately called 'Momma' bustled out of the kitchen and came to the side of their table to inquire about the meal.

"How's everything?"

Each patron was expected to praise the food if they knew what was good for them and if they expected to ever come back again. Any other response would no doubt cause her to beat the customer into submission with an ancient, cast iron frying pan.

The silver-haired man reached out, and lightly grasped her wrinkled right hand between his palms. He gently rubbed and patted the back of her hand. "Momma. Everything was perfect. Thank you and your family for such excellent service. Please ask your son to clean off the table, bring desert and then leave us alone so that we may discuss business without interruption."

"Gracia. Gracia. Gracia." The "Momma' bowed slightly from the waist and graciously backed away from the table. She snapped her fingers to get her husband's attention, nodded her head towards the table and hustled into the kitchen. There were orders for many more delicious meals waiting for her to prepare that evening. The eldest son Joey came out of the kitchen quickly cleaned off the table and was gone in the wink of an eye.

After they finished their spumoni and were sipping hot cappuccino topped with whipped cream and grated cinnamon the silver-haired man waved the *goombas* away to the bar. When the loutish pair was well out of earshot he lit up a cigar and began speaking in a soft monotone. "Mack, far too many people are getting close to you. We feel that it's best if you make a move out of town tonight. You were officially terminated from the project at six o'clock this afternoon and your services are no longer required." He gave a flourish of his left hand to show off a diamond-studded gold Rolex and five-carat pinky ring as he passed a large brown manila envelope across the table to Mack.

The nine by twelve inch envelope was securely sealed with clear plastic packing tape and was obviously not to be opened at the table. It brought back flashes of the times that he had seen *'FOR EYES ONLY'* printed in bold red letters on the top margin of documents that had to be destroyed immediately after he had read and digested their sensitive contents.

"Your Chicago bank accounts have been closed and two new bank accounts set up for you in Florida. There's a money market fund in one and a checking account in the other. Both banks are in West Palm Beach and your mailing address is a Stuart post office box. The checkbooks are in the envelope along with your new Florida driver's license, voter's registration card, Social Security card, passport, birth certificate, vehicle title, registration and insurance papers. Mack, I want to give you some friendly advice. Don't ever go inside a bank. They have security cameras and you might be identified. That could big trouble for everyone in the organization - especially you!"

"But Sam, I have obligations here and . . ."

"Sorry Mack. This is not negotiable. I have to go. He rose, motioned to Mario that he was leaving and wanted the dinner tab added to his house account. Mario nodded back in understanding. The two *goombas* took their positions on either side of him and the trio left the restaurant without uttering another word.

Left alone Mack contemplated what had taken place and tried to make sense of it. However, the message was clear. *"Get out of town. Don't call us. We'll call you."* He looked around to see if he was being watched. There was only a young couple in a corner booth playing 'tongue tag' and they weren't paying any attention to him. He glanced at his watch. 9:20 P.M. Mack rose from the booth and walked out into the street trying his best to appear as if nothing unusual had taken place five minutes earlier.

The nippy late March air raised goose pimples on the back of his neck. He took out his cell phone to check his voice mail. The cell phone was dead. They worked fast and had cut him off from being able to communicate. He was relieved to see his red *Porsche Carrera* cuddled up against the curb where he had left it more than two hours earlier. At least he still had transportation. He crouched behind a blue *Chevrolet Caprice* and started the *Porsche* with the remote ignition switch - there was no explosion. He waited ten seconds before he crossed the street and cautiously opened the door. He slid into the red leather bucket seat, cranked over the high performance eight cylinder power plant, made a U-turn on Peterson Avenue, headed west, jumped on the I-90/94 South Ramp and bee-lined it for the Loop. He jumped off at Exit 50B onto Ohio Street and headed for the Hancock Building.

Mack's apartment was on the forty-fifth floor of the Hancock Building and he would have to risk taking the elevator. He entered the parking garage from the East Delaware Place entrance and fumbled with his plastic card key. He raced up all six floors of the parking garage ramp in first gear and slipped into Section C, Space 14. Although a private resident's elevator leads from the parking garage directly to the residence floors he wanted to stop by the lobby and check for messages.

When Mack entered the lobby, Fred, the obese, bald-headed, meek looking, sixty-something private security guard pulled him aside and whispered in his ear. "Mack. I was told to give you ten minutes upstairs and then I'm supposed to call the cops. Ten minutes. No more. No less. Please hurry. I have a family."

Mack rode the resident's elevator to the forty-fifth floor, jammed the 'Open Door' button in and wedged it in place with a wooden toothpick. At least he'd have an elevator car waiting for him if he had to leave in a hurry. His apartment door was slightly ajar. He pushed it open with his right foot and slipped alongside the outer wall. The door swung open to the left and stopped against the wall-mounted rubber stopper with a soft *'thud.'* The apartment's lights were on and the CD player was echoing the hauntingly soft muted sounds of Kenny G. playing *'Sentimental"*.

Mack felt under his left armpit for the reassuring weight of the .25-caliber *Berretta Model 70* semi-automatic pistol that his grandfather brought back from Italy as a war souvenir in 1945. It wasn't registered, the serial number had been filed off and the spot where it had been stamped was etched with acid. The pistol was untraceable. Mack had added a custom silencer that permitted only the sound of *'Pfffttt'* - like the soft sound of a woman trying to stifle a sneeze - to escape from the barrel. The pistol wasn't there! His stomach juices rose upward through his esophagus into his throat and left a sour, acidic taste in his mouth. The hair stood up on the back of his neck and his legs shook. He entered the apartment cautiously and left the door wide open in case he had to beat a hasty retreat to the elevator.

The apartment was clear. Mack entered the bedroom and saw his neatly packed suitcase laying open on the bed. His brown leather shaving kit was nestled between his rolled up socks. The holstered *Berretta* and a thick, white, number ten envelope were lying side by side atop his gray slacks. He started to reach for the envelope with his trembling right hand and halted. It could be booby-trapped or perhaps contain a letter bomb. He 'hunkered down' on the side of the bed and used a straightened out wire coat hanger to flip the bulky envelope out of the suitcase. The envelope landed on the carpeted floor with a soft *'thunk'* and a stack of fifty, crisp $100 bills spilled out onto the carpet.

Mack ran to the clothes closet and threw open the louvered wooden door. His clothes had been ripped from the rack and tossed into a jumbled heap on the closet floor. He gasped for breath and stammered aloud, *"Did they find it? Please God no!"* He kept throwing clothes out into the bedroom until he could finally see the closet floor. The carpet was still intact! He gasped, *"Maybe they didn't find it."*

He reached up with his right hand, grasped the wooden and brass tie rack, pushed on it and turned it one full turn to the right. Silently the closet floor began to rise upward on four stainless steel rods. When it stopped it revealed an opening three feet long and eighteen inches high. The cramped space held a black leather valise that looked similar to the medical bags carried by country doctors making house calls and it was filled with many of the same medications and instruments. It also held a flat, brown leather case about three feet long, a foot wide and four inches deep. Mack carefully lifted them both out, placed the long, flat case inside brown leather suit bag and zipped the bag closed.

He threw the suit bag over his left shoulder, picked up the black valise in his left hand, his suitcase in his right hand and ran for the open elevator. The other elevator was on the way up and had passed the fortieth floor. He might have company already on the way up and he had to hurry. Mack could go directly to the parking garage or stop by the lobby. He opted for the lobby, pushed the 'Down' button and held it in with his thumb. When the elevator reached the lobby floor the automatic door opened and the security guard turned his back to him. It was obvious that Fred knew too much and didn't want to get involved. Mack sensed that Fred had been watching him on the security camera's video monitor as he ran down the hallway to the elevator. But, who else was watching with him?

Mack flipped Fred his apartment key wrapped in a $100 bill held in place with a wide, red rubber band. "Fred. Thanks for the extra five minutes. I needed it and I owe you one."

"Mack, please hurry up. I called the cops five minutes ago. But, somebody else got here first and both of them are on their way up in the other elevator. They gave me no choice. I have a wife and six grand kids."

"No problem. If the two *goombas* ask where I went just tell them that I went out the front door and took a cab to O'Hare."

Mack glanced at the elevator 'floor position' indicator. One car was stopped at the forty-fifth floor. The other one was on the eleventh floor and its way up. Both parking garage elevators were on the lobby floor and patiently waited with their doors open. He reached inside the first elevator, held the door open with his left leg, pushed in the ninety-fifth floor button with his right thumb and jammed it down with a wooden tooth pick. He jammed the 'Close Door' button down with another toothpick.

He didn't have time to take the stairs up the six floors to the parking garage and he really didn't want to take the elevator because the floor indicator would show his pursuers where he had gotten off. But, he had no choice - time was against him. Mack had to take the elevator, but he was very apprehensive. He knew from experience just how easy it was to wait outside an elevator door in a basement, or parking garage, and *'whack'* someone with a noise-suppressed pistol when they got out. Rarely was anyone in the parking garage at this time of night, especially on a Sunday, and even if they were they wouldn't hear the soft *'Pfffttt'* over the normal street and garage noises.

When the door opened he counted to five before walking out into the parking garage. He put down his bags, slipped back into the elevator and jammed the 'Close Door' and ninety-fourth floor buttons down with a toothpick. He picked up his bags and walked as fast as he could towards Section C where the still warm Porsche waited in Space 14.

Mack knew that he had to get out of town fast, but he didn't understand why.

CHAPTER

2

Mack half walked and half ran dragging the heavy suitcase and suit bag along the parking garage's concrete floor. The suit bag hanging on his left shoulder made him tilt lopsidedly to the left. Sweat ran down his face and merged at his chin into a steady stream that ran down the front of his powder blue shirt. A stream that felt as wide as the Nile River ran down the middle of his back into the crack of his butt.

When he reached Space 14, his Porsche was not there! Sitting in it's space was a blue, well-traveled 1988 Ford F-150 truck equipped with a camper shell, trailer hitch, gun rack mounted across the back window and a Florida license plate. In place of a front license plate hung a plate with a painted fish. The silver fish had a black stripe running the length of its side. He didn't know what species it was and didn't care. But, where was his Porsche?

He plopped the suitcase, suit bag and valise down on the concrete. The driver and passenger side door lock knobs were in the 'up' position. He peered through the passenger's side window. A white envelope with MACK printed in bold, black letters was lying on the seat. He examined the door for trip wires. There were none. He opened the passenger's side door, took out the envelope, opened it and read the hand-printed note.

"The cops are looking for you and expect you to be in the Porsche. The truck keys are under the seat.

There's a shirt, jeans and a pair of deck shoes on the floor on the passenger's side. Shed the jacket and slacks. Dress down now! You might want to wear the baseball cap. The cops aren't looking for a white-haired redneck in a pickup truck with a Florida license plate."

Mack stripped off his blazer, long-sleeved shirt and gray flannel slacks and stuffed them behind the seat. The blue and white checked flannel shirt and well-washed jeans fit him perfectly. So did the pair of well broken-in deck shoes. The black baseball cap was emblazoned with the logo of the *'Florida Marlins'* and the inside perimeter was lined with white hair. He jerked open the camper shell to throw in his suitcase. A brown, canvas duffle bag, two fishing rods, a green, plastic tackle box and two red five- gallon plastic containers labeled *'GASOLINE'* were lying in the truck bed. The extra ten gallons of gas would provide 200 extra miles to that already in the tank before he would have to stop at a gas station where he might be identified.

He slid behind the wheel and immediately got a whiff of stale cigar smoke and fish! A road atlas was on the worn fabric bench seat. A jumbo paper clip held the atlas open to Indiana. A yellow line marked the route to Interstate 65 to Indianapolis and points south. There was also a Martin County, Florida map tucked inside the front cover of the road atlas. His watch read 10:20 P.M. He could make the 185 miles to Indianapolis by 1:30 A.M. with no gas stops. He didn't dare pull into a roadside rest area to sleep because state troopers checked them hourly. He decided to drive straight through Indiana and find a motel south of Louisville.

He reached under the seat, felt a lump of keys and pulled them out. There were more than two-dozen keys on a chrome ring attached to a huge chrome dog leash snap. One key was labeled *'truck'* with one those little sticky plastic labels that are made one letter at a time with a hand-held stamping machine and a roll of plastic label tape.

The elevator door slid open just as he pulled out of the parking space. He floored the gas pedal, smoked the tires and headed for the 'down' ramp and the exit. *"How can I get out the parking garage without being stopped by the attendant?"* Mack scanned the interior of the truck's cab and spotted his plastic card key on the dash. He exited left onto East Chestnut took a right onto Wells, headed for Ohio Street and the ramp to Interstate 90/94. At the split he would turn south on Interstate 94 and at Gary, Indiana he would cut off to Interstate 65 south towards Indianapolis. There would be no stops for gas for several hours.

Mack briefly considered taking the *'Chicago Skyway'* to Indiana and thought better of it because the tollbooths were 'manual' and manned. He might be recognized and police radios outrun cars every day of the week! He decided to take the *Stevenson Expressway*. If he kept in the automatic lanes he could toss in forty cents and be out and gone before anyone could get a good look at his face. Feeling queasy in his guts he eased into the far left lane of the first toll plaza. *'Correct change only - Cars and trucks $.40'* read the green and white sign above the lane. But, Mack didn't have any change! He only had $100 bills and they were in his suitcase in the back of the truck. His blazer had $3,000 in hundreds in the inside pocket, but it was in the back of the truck also! What was he going to do for change?

Mack's right hand automatically went under the seat and he groped in desperation for a change container. Something 'solid' was under there! He pulled out a black plastic container with spring-loaded slots for dimes, nickels and quarters - it was full. He snapped out a quarter, a dime and a nickel with his thumb and tossed them into the white plastic basket. *'Ching Ching Ching'* Finally a *'plunk!'* The coins went through. He was on the way!

He waited for the bar to go up, but it stayed down. It was stuck! He looked across the eight lanes to his right hoping to see an attendant. A *'dufus'* clad in khaki pants and matching shirt was shooting the breeze with a female attendant in a manual booth five lanes down. They appeared to be *'in heat'* for one another. A beefy Illinois State Trooper sporting a crew cut was parked on the far right hand side of the toll plaza exit watching the traffic. Mack wasn't concerned. The cops were looking for a red Porsche, not a blue Ford F-150 pickup with a Florida plate and a white-headed *'hayseed'* behind the wheel. He didn't want to draw attention to himself by blowing his horn, but he had to get through the tollgate.

BLAAAT! BLAAAT! BLAAAT! The driver of the silver sports utility vehicle behind him was pounding on his horn and shaking his fist. Mack threw his hands up with a shrug of his shoulders.

BLAAAT! BLAAAT! BLAAAT!

The state trooper shifted his attention to the silver sports utility vehicle, gave a disgusted shake of his head and looked away. Mack felt for certain that the trooper had been studying his face. The khaki-clad *'dufus'* ran over to Mack's tollgate, pushed the white manual trip button and the bar slowly lifted. The starry-eyed *'dufus'* tripped over his feet and fell down on his way back to the side of the female attendant.

It was 10:35 P.M. when Mack finally eased out of the tollgate. The heavy traffic was flowing smoothly and he stayed in the far left lane to keep as far away as possible from the Illinois State trooper's car. He hoped that a pickup truck with Florida plates wouldn't look suspicious. Mack briefly thought about stopping at an ATM and pulling out more cash. But, without a doubt, his credit cards were canceled and all of the ATMs within fifty miles of Chicago were being monitored for transactions on his account. His location would be transmitted to a central location in microseconds and 'they' would know where he was. Roadblocks would be set up at every tollbooth and there would be no escape. But, he had $8,000 in cash and would be okay – for a while.

Feeling extremely confident in his assessment of his situation he tromped down on the accelerator and the truck leaped ahead. *"Must be a V-8. That's good."* But, his heart skipped a beat when he saw the Illinois State Trooper pull out into the traffic and begin to ease across the three right hand lanes towards him. The trooper pulled in behind Mack and lit up the night with his patrol car's flashing, blue strobe lights. Mack's heart leaped into his throat and his heart pounded in his ears. He lifted his foot from the accelerator to slow down so that he could pull over to the side of the road. Suddenly, the trooper swerved across the two lanes of traffic to his right, accelerated and passed him.

Obviously the trooper was not interested in Mack's truck. He was after the red Porsche that had whizzed through the tollbooth without stopping. The white-haired driver was in a big hurry to get somewhere fast and was doing about ninety miles an hour!

Mack eased off on the accelerator and tried to relax - he couldn't! He was shaking uncontrollably from head to toe.

About two miles farther down the road the Porsche was pulled over onto the side and the roof-mounted blue strobe lights of the trooper's car flashed eerily behind it. The trooper stood alongside and slightly behind, the driver's door. His right hand was on his pistol holster and he was arguing with the white-haired driver. Mack thought that he heard the sharp *'crack'* of two gunshots when he passed the Porsche and hoped that it was just his imagination.

Blood pounded in Mack's temples as he accelerated to seventy miles an hour, slipped into the safety of the middle lane and headed for the Interstate 65 split in Gary - only ten miles away. Then he would be on the way to Indianapolis, all points south and safety! His life style was about to radically change. If he had known just how much it was going to change, and in what way, he might have opted to turn north onto Interstate 94 and head for the wilderness of Michigan's Upper Peninsula.

The drive down Interstate 65 through the featureless Indiana farmland was monotonous except for the *'crackling'* of the CB radio mounted under the dash. He relied upon the truck drivers' hilarious conversations and 'bear reports' to keep him awake. When he reached the exit for *'Lafayette - Purdue University'* at 12:15 A.M. he could barely keep his eyes open, was dead tired and desperately needed sleep. Mack pulled off onto the exit to look for a motel close to the campus. Anyone looking for him would expect to find him sacked out in the truck in a roadside rest area, or checked into a motel close to the Interstate. College was in session and a pickup truck with a Florida plate close to campus wouldn't arouse the suspicion of local cops.

He checked into a run-down *'Mom and Pop'* motel two blocks east of the main campus and got a first floor room with a king size bed for $39. He chose a parking space three doors down from his own room and backed the truck in to make it impossible for someone to read the license plate without getting out of their car. A local cop wouldn't make that much effort. Not with the town full of college students and out of state vehicles.

Mack was 'bushed'. He stripped off his clothes, fell into bed without opening his suitcase and was out like a light in less than a minute. Being overtired terrified him – that's when horrific flashbacks came to him in dreams. He attempted to bypass the time period of the flashbacks by forcing his memory back to his childhood. It was similar to rewinding the tape in a VCR. One night the 'mental tape' rewound much too far. He was sitting up in a hospital bed and eating strawberry ice cream. His throat hurt and his mother was sitting in a rocking chair beside his bed. *"Son. Your tonsils are out and the ice cream will make your throat feel better."* Mack didn't recall the excruciating pain that he experienced when his tonsils were cut out of his throat with only *'ether'* for an anesthetic. Since then Mach abhorred hospitals and their smells of medicine and sickness.

He stirred, shifted his position and struggled to open his eyes. They felt like heavy weights were holding them closed. Then a whirling orange spiral with a black center invaded the retinas of his eyes and the core of his brain. The whirling motion pulled him deeper and deeper into the black hole. Images flashed across his eyes into his brain.

Mack gritted his teeth knowing that he could not stop what was about to take place. *'It'* was coming back. He moaned in desperation, *"Oh God. Please make it stop."*

CHAPTER

3

Bam! Bam! Bam!

"Hey! You in there! When are you going to wake up and get your sorry ass out of there? It's almost noon and we need to clean the room."

Bam! Bam! Bam!

The aged wooden door shook and the cheap, brass-plated security chain rattled against the door with each strike of a meaty fist. Mack sat straight up in bed, rubbed his eyes and tried to figure out where he was and how he got there. The room was as dark as the inside of a bear's winter den, except for the small ray of sunlight that leaked in along the side of the ragged window curtain.

Bam! Bam! Bam!

"Hey. You in there! Do you hear me? You've got fifteen minutes to get your sorry ass out of there before I call the cops. They'll come over here and get you out."

Bam! Bam! Bam!

Mack stared at the glowing numerals of his watch through the veil of mist covering his eyes. He squinted and tried to focus on the digital dial. It read 11:45 A.M.

"Okay. Okay. Okay already. I'll be out in ten minutes. Give me a break. I over slept."

Mack pulled back the edge of the curtain closest to the door while trying to avoid the bright sunlight. Now he knew how vampires must feel about the sun. His squinting eyes focused on an unshaven, balding, fat guy in a white tee shirt preparing to slam his meaty fist on the door again. He balanced a cigar large enough to choke a mule between the thumb and forefinger of his left hand. He saw Mack peering through the window and tapped the crystal of the watch on his hairy left wrist with his right index finger. "You've got fifteen minutes to clear out of the room. Stop by the office before you pull out. I want to talk to you."

"Okay. I've got to take a shower and shave. I want to look pretty when I meet you."

When Mack stopped by his office the fat guy asked Mack if he knew anything about fishing in Florida because he and his wife were going to Disney World and Daytona Beach in December. Mack told him that he didn't know anything about Daytona Beach and suggested that he call the chamber of commerce.

After checking out of the motel Mack stopped for breakfast at the Denny's across the street. During breakfast he studied the road atlas and made some mileage calculations on a paper napkin. He figured that if he drove all night at the speed limit, stopping only for coffee and bathroom breaks, that he could make the Florida line in seventeen hours. That would make it about sunrise on Tuesday morning. From the Florida-Georgia line it looked to be four hours to Stuart via the Florida Turnpike. He should be there at noon Tuesday.

At 1:22 P.M. he got back on Interstate 65 and headed south towards Indianapolis. He stopped at a roadside rest area north of Louisville to empty the two five gallon containers of gas into the truck's tank. He didn't want to risk stopping at a service station because still being relatively close to Chicago he might be noticed. The gas tank held nineteen gallons and the needle read '¾'. That gave him about fourteen gallons of gas. At sixteen miles per gallon he had enough fuel for two hundred miles. Including thirty minutes for a dinner break and fuel stop he could be in Nashville before nine o'clock. From there it would be on to Chattanooga, Tennessee. He should be in Atlanta about midnight.

He stopped for fuel and dinner at the Franklin exit south of Bowling Green, Kentucky and got back on the road at 7:15 P.M. He made Nashville at 7:47 P.M. At the junction of Interstate 65 and 24 he took Interstate 24 and headed towards Chattanooga. He made the *'Choo Choo'* city at 9:51 P.M., crossed over to Interstate 75 and headed for Atlanta. He hit Atlanta at 11:48 P.M., fueled up and grabbed a cup of coffee. It would be almost a straight shot south for the next ten hours. He got sleepy a little south of Macon, Georgia and knew that he should pull over for a nap before he dozed off behind the wheel. He still had eight hours of hard, boring driving ahead of him.

At 1:52 A.M. he pulled into a roadside rest area north of the Warner-Robins Air Force Base exit. He had been stationed there in the 1960's. It was a C-130 overhaul facility and hosted a squadron of B-52's. He worked on Electronic Counter Measures equipment among other things. He located a parking space shaded from the bright halogen security lights by a large oak tree. Magnificently curved branches swung down from the trunk in long graceful arcs as if they were trying to reach the ground. Stately looking, chigger infested, gray Spanish moss hung from the limbs tempting daring passersby to reach up for a touch. An act they would regret later when they started itching.

He walked over to the restroom for a *'whiz'*, strolled around the parking area to get the kinks out of his legs and went back to the truck. The bench seat didn't recline and he had to force his 6-foot 4-inch frame to fit across it from end to end. His knees were wedged under the steering wheel and his head was crammed under a metal armrest, but the hard truck seat felt like a feather bed after the twelve-hour drive from Lafayette, Indiana. His eyes closed. As he drifted off into unconsciousness a swirling orange whirlpool with a pulsating black center danced before his retinas affixing its image in his brain. He had seen it many times before. His body shuddered as he silently mouthed a Nietzsche quote, *"Stare not into the abyss - lest the abyss stare back at you."*

Although Viet Nam, Laos and Cambodia weren't in the average American's vocabulary in 1960, the United States had been secretly involved in Southeast Asia since the fall of the French at Dien Bien Phu in 1954. The Air Force and Central

Intelligence Agency were actively engaged in intelligence gathering and covert political actions.

Mack enlisted in the Air Force at seventeen after pleading with his parents to sign for him because he was under enlistment age. Enlisting was better than the judge's alternative that also offered a uniform, three hot meals a day and a cot. He arrived at Lackland Air Force Base for Basic Training weighing 175 pounds. When he left eight weeks later he carried 225 pounds on his 6-foot 4-inch frame. He joked that it was 100 pounds of spring steel covered by 125 pounds of 'tiger meat'.

Mack volunteered for some 'special' laboratory tests and was paid twenty dollars cash for each day that he participated. It was far better than marching in the hot merciless Texas sun all day long. One test involved listening to foreign languages coming through earphones. He was instructed to write down what he thought the word or phrase meant. He wrote a lot of words because foreign languages came easy to him. Another evaluation consisted of interpreting code sent by metallic 'dits' and 'dahs' delivered through earphones.'

The test that caused him significant mental anguish, and nightmares for years afterward required that he wear a baggy suit, padded boots, thumb-less mittens and a hooded helmet. He could not see because his eyes were covered with black blinders and several layers of black cloth and his nose was plugged with soft wax. He was unable to feel, taste, see, hear or smell. He felt like he was inside a cotton ball. He was made to recline and had the sensation of floating on a cloud of air. But, he didn't know if he was vertical or horizontal. Oxygen was piped through a rubber mouthpiece that he gripped between his teeth. He couldn't move, or feel resistance, because his hands and feet were tethered to lengths of surgical tubing that absorbed every movement. He held a small cylinder with a push button on the top in each hand. He didn't know it, but he was floating in a swimming pool filled with warm mineral oil. It was part of a CIA sponsored experiment to determine how long a human being could withstand total sensory deprivation without suffering mental collapse. His instructions were piped through tiny earphones inserted in his ears.

"The purpose of this evaluation is for you to estimate the passage of time. Press the button under your left thumb at intervals of one minute. Press the button under your right thumb at intervals of one hour. There is no way for you to communicate with anyone or stop this evaluation. You will remain here until you have recorded the minutes and hours over a six hour period."

Fear ran down Mack's spine. He had no visible reference to measure the passage of time! He couldn't speak to object because his mouth was filled with the plastic mouthpiece.

After an indeterminable amount of time the earphones began to emit noise similar to radio static. The noise had no rhythm or beat. It was just *'noise'*. It increased and decreased in intensity and volume similar to the sound of ocean waves meeting the shoreline and receding back into the sea. The *'noise'* had no form. It was just there and it wouldn't stop! Later he discovered that the static was *'white noise'* which creates severe anxiety in some people and total relaxation in others because it has no form, substance or definition.

Shortly after the introduction of the *'white noise'* everything went black. He woke up in a hospital bed with no recollection of the dire events. Unknowingly, he had been introduced to *'Ketamine Hydrochloride'* a drug that causes humans to become comatose and erases their short-term memory. Included in the mixture was *'Diazepam'* that alleviates anxiety and instills a hypnotic state in humans. The two drugs are often used together by intelligence agents to induce speech when interrogating tight-lipped, uncooperative subjects.

Years later, during a physical at a Veterans Hospital Mack recalled, and accurately described, several specific tests that he participated in while in basic training. However, the VA doctors told him that there were no records in his file indicating that he participated in any testing programs. Mack was terrified because he knew that he had been involved in several psychological experiments. They returned to him in the darkness of night in dreams that were preceded by the swirling orange whirlpool with the black hole in the center.

Bam! Bam! Bam!

"You in there! Wake up!"

Bam! Bam! Bam!

The metallic banging startled Mack out of deep REM sleep. The bright flash light beam raking across his eyes blinded him and shrank his light-sensitive pupils to tiny pinholes. He tried to sit up and he hit his head on the armrest. Twisting to get his long legs untangled from under the steering wheel he slipped off the seat onto the floorboard. His baseball cap fell off and he realized that his disguise could be compromised if he didn't get it back on before someone saw him. His right arm was numb was lack of blood circulation and he tried desperately to hold the baseball cap in place with his tingling left hand. "I'm okay. I was tired and pulled off the highway for a short nap."

"Son, do you know what time it is?"

"No. I don't. Six or seven maybe?"

"It's ten-thirty in the morning. You've been zonked out since about two o'clock. When I came on duty at eleven last night my shift leader told me to keep an eye on you to be sure that you hadn't died in this here old blue truck. Now that you're awake I'll be pulling out. Wash your face real good in cold water and wake up before you get back on the road. Okay?"

Mack slowly rose up from the floorboard holding the baseball cap in place with his throbbing left hand. When he saw the Smokey Bear hat perched atop a shock of snow-white hair he panicked. As he sat up higher in the seat the biggest neck and widest shoulders that he had ever seen appeared in the truck's driver's side window and they were clad in a light tan Georgia State Trooper's uniform.

He responded in a hoarse voice filled with sleepiness. "Yes sir. I understand completely. My legs are still asleep and I can't get up right now. I'll be up and out of here in a few minutes. You can count on it. Thanks for checking on me."

The wearer of the Smokey Bear hat smiled politely, displaying an array of pearly white store-bought teeth, and spoke in a soft southern drawl. "It's okay son. Us old southern boys have to take care of each other these days. I'll see ya'll around. Drive careful. Hear?" The trooper waved slid behind the wheel of his patrol car, closed the door and gave Mack a friendly *'toot'* on the horn as he pulled out of the rest area onto Interstate 75.

Mack fell to the ground when he slid out of the truck because his legs were numb from the lack of blood circulation. He pulled himself to an erect position with the door handle, took a few deep breaths, shook each leg to be certain that it still worked and limped to the rest room to wash his face and take a *'whiz.'* He was behind schedule and still had an eight-hour drive ahead of him. It had been fourteen hours since he had eaten and he was ravenous! At this point he was so famished that he might consider eating fresh *road kill* - if he could find some that he could warm up on the engine block. Luckily for any prospective road kill in the immediate area there was a restaurant close by.

After bolting down a breakfast of three eggs 'over easy,' pan cakes, grits, bacon and four cups of coffee he was ready to hit the road. It was almost 11:30 A.M. by the time he fueled up and got back on the road. He figured to make Stuart about 7:30 P.M.

The monotonous drive down Interstate 75 was punctuated by the pungent aroma of paper pulp cooking in the near by paper mills. Billowing white clouds of steam and pollution spewed from the mills' towering red brick smoke stacks and clung close to the damp ground like early morning radiation fog. It traversed and engulfed the highway appearing like a gaseous goblin lurking in wait of a victim traveling too fast for the visibility conditions.

He crossed the Georgia-Florida line, and shortly there after Interstate 10, and switched over to Interstate 275 and the Florida Turnpike. He made good time and reached Yee Haw Junction - about sixty miles north of the Stuart exit - at 4:55 P.M. Although there was only a relatively short distance left to go he decided to pull in for gas and a bite to eat. Factoring in thirty minutes for grabbing a snack and gassing up the truck he hoped to make Stuart by 6:30 P.M. He should be in bed, zonked out and dreaming by 7:00 P.M. at the latest.

There were two hours of daylight left when he turned off the Florida Turnpike onto the Stuart exit ramp at 6:22 P.M. He asked the very bored tollbooth cashier, "Is this the exit for Dallas? I think that I might have missed a turn somewhere last night."

"Dallas? No sir. This is Florida not Texas! You are really lost. You should find a motel room in town, get some rest and get back on the turnpike in the morning and head north."

"I see. You're right. How can I find Port Sewell Marina?"

"Port Sewell Marina? I thought ya'll wanted to go to Dallas, Texas?"

"I'm sorry. I was in Dallas a couple of days ago and just got mixed up. Do you know where the Port Sewell Marina is?"

"No sir, I don't. But, if it's a marina it has to be in the Manatee Pocket. That's where all the marinas are located. Just stay on this road, its Martin Downs Boulevard. Go over the Palm City Bridge and keep going straight until you reach Highway One. Turn right and go south until you reach Indian Street. There's a traffic light there and WALMART is on the right hand side of the road. Turn left on Indian Street and go straight until you hit a red light. That's Old Dixie Highway. Ask for directions at the gas station on the corner. Good luck."

"Thanks. I'll be able to find it from here." He handed her a one hundred dollar bill with his toll ticket. "Keep the change." Mack pulled out of the tollbooth and headed towards Stuart. When he crossed High Meadows he pulled into the *Publix* shopping center to look at his own road map. Her directions were correct and it didn't appear that he needed to ask directions at the gas station on Dixie Highway. The fewer people who knew that he was a recent newcomer to the area the better. He realized that he made a serious error in calling attention to himself at the tollbooth, but it was too late to repair the damage.

Traveling east on Indian Street he crossed the railroad tracks at Dixie Highway, passed over the Willoughby Creek Bridge and turned right onto gravel-covered Old St. Lucie Boulevard. Just past Whittaker's Boat Works the banyan tree lined road made a sharp bend to the left and straightened out. Down about one hundred yards on his immediate right he saw it! The weathered wooden sign read, *"PORT SEWELL MARINA. Members only."*

He was there! The gray Cape Cod style cottage perched atop the boathouse looked like a postcard. *"What more could a man ask for in this lifetime?"* He was about to find out. The vacant lot in front of the marina needed mowing badly. Mack wondered who was supposed to take care of that mundane task. When he turned into the gravel driveway the tiny stones crunched in protest under the wheels of the faded blue pickup. He turned off the ignition and patted the dash lightly. *"Good girl. We made it and we're going to have some good times together. I promise."*

Not expecting a reply from an inanimate object he didn't wait for one - opting instead to open the door and slide out. He bumped the horn ring with his right elbow and the truck let out a soft *'blat'." I knew that you understood. Get some rest. We'll have plenty to do over the next few days. You have to show me around town."*

There was only one car in the parking lot - a silver-blue *BMW Z-3* convertible. That seemed strange because it was early evening and there should be lots of boaters still at the marina. He decided to check that out tomorrow. Now it was time for some well-deserved sleep! He dragged his suitcase, suit bag and black valise up the four wooden steps and unceremoniously plunked them down on the front porch. He held the patched screen door open with his right knee as he searched the key ring for the 'right' key. He found one labeled *'Marina Cottage'* on blue sticky-backed label maker tape. The lock worked as smoothly as a kitten's soft purr and the door swung inward by gravity as if to welcome him home. He dragged in his bags and flipped on the light switch just inside the door with his left elbow.

He dropped everything on the floor when he saw 'her!' She was tall, red headed, green-eyed and exquisitely beautiful. She was lying back in a green lounge chair and holding a glass of red wine in her left hand. Pink flesh peeked out of her fluorescent orange bikini in just the 'right' places. Her shoulder-length red mane curled up on the ends, bangs covered her forehead and framed her emerald green eyes. His own eyes were drawn to the vivid black and white tattoo of a panda bear on the outside of her left thigh half way between her knee and her voluptuous hip. When she spoke her voice came out in a soft, but authoritative, moist, southern drawl that almost made him wet his pants.

"Yankee Boy. It's about time that you got your sorry Yankee ass down here! I took off work today just to welcome you to sunny Florida. You could have been here by eight this morning if

you hadn't sacked out in that Indiana flea trap. Plus, you slept in the roadside rest area in Georgia like an itinerant migrant worker. I thought that you had more class than that. It's only a nineteen-hour drive if you drive straight through. I guess that you couldn't handle such a long ride - could you Yankee Boy?" She put the emphasis on 'Yankee Boy' with a sneer of her upper lip. "What do you have to say for yourself - Yankee Boy?"

"Yes ma'am." He hadn't ever heard himself whine out loud before. He didn't know why, but he felt that he had to explain. "But, I was tired." His words weren't actually spoken. They dribbled out and landed in a mushy heap on the wooden floor. "I didn't know that anyone was expecting me at any particular time. I didn't know."

"If that Georgia Smokey Bear hadn't watched over your sorry Yankee ass last night you might not have woke up at all this morning."

"Yes ma'am. I know."

"I don't know if you noticed when you drove up, but the grass out front needs cutting real bad and my car needs washing. You can do that first thing tomorrow. First thing! Did you hear me clearly Yankee Boy?"

"Yes ma'am. I noticed the grass."

"Yankee Boy. I'm extremely tired and I'm ravenously hungry. After I change my clothes I'm going to take you out to dinner. Then we are going to go over the things that you have to do to keep this marina running the way that I want it to run - and keep me happy. I own the place." She stuck out her glossy scarlet lower lip in a feigned pout and looked at him with a pair of glowing emerald-green eyes that reminded him of industrial lasers that could melt stainless steel. "Ya'll do want to keep me happy - don't you Yankee Boy?"

"Yes ma'am." He stammered out the words as drool ran down the side of his mouth.

She waved her left hand in the general direction of a doorway on the left side of a small hall. "Toss your crap in that bedroom on the left. Then take a shower and put on some fresh clothes. You smell like a wet mule. I'll change clothes on my boat and meet you down at my car in five minutes. Don't be late. I've got reservations for dinner and I do not like to be late."

"Yes ma'am." Now he knew for certain exactly who was going to cut the grass and he'd better do it right!

CHAPTER
4

He didn't know her name, or who she was, but he realized that she was in complete control. She didn't utter a word and concentrated her attention only on the road as she drove the silver-blue *Beamer* convertible to the restaurant like it was a *Daytona 500* racecar. After they were seated and ordered a round of drinks she continued the one-sided conversation.

"*Yankee Boy* allow me introduce myself. My name is Tina Louise McShay and my family has lived in this area since the early 1900's. My friends call me *'Red'* and my enemies call me *'bitch'* with a capital 'B', but only behind my back. I'm a natural red head, stand five-foot ten-inches tall, weigh one hundred twenty-five pounds and wear a size thirty-six bra 'C' cup. Any questions?"

"None and I am all ears. Please feel free to talk away and let it all hang out. I'm a good listener and it appears as if I have all night. You literally have a captive audience."

"My parents built Port Sewell Marina in the 1940's and I grew up there. They were killed in an auto accident in 1990 and the house burned down a week later. That was five years ago and I have no plans to rebuild the house. I come up here from Palm Beach to spend weekends on my boat and relax. I intend to keep the marina in operation as long as I can. Although it's not a moneymaker the slip rentals cover the taxes and upkeep. A lot of good memories go with the place and I can't let them go - not just yet. Your job is to keep the marina clients and me happy. Especially me! It doesn't take much effort. Just keep the grass cut and watch over the boats. Everything else will take care of itself. The boathouse under the cottage is for your boat. You do have a boat don't you?"

"Obviously not. I just got here an hour ago."

"Get down to *Billy Bob's Boat Sales* on Old Dixie Highway first thing tomorrow and pick up the new boat I ordered today. I called him this afternoon and told him that you're coming. It's a twenty-two foot, center-console *PURSUIT* equipped with a super-charged two hundred-fifty horse *YAMAHA* outboard. You can't be a marina manager without a boat. Plus, I like to go snook fishing. *Yankee Boy*, have you ever been snook fishing?"

"Yes ma'am. I grew up in Fort Myers on the West Coast. I did a lot of snook fishing when I lived there. I'm sure that I remember how, but I have to check out the area."

"Wait just a minute now. I can't call you *Yankee Boy* if you grew up in Florida - now can I?"

"You can call me anything that you want."

"I'll just call you Mack."

After four drinks she was beginning to slur her words.

"I'll just call you Mack. Plain Mack. Okay?"

"That's just fine."

"What else do you want to know about me?"

"Whatever you want to tell me. I'm obviously not going anywhere because you're driving."

"Okay. Here goes. I live in an ocean-side condo close to *The Breakers* on Palm Beach. I've been divorced twice. Both of my husbands were drunks and we had no children. I graduated from Martin County High School, but I'm not going to tell you in what year, attended Florida State University in Tallahassee and went to Stetson law School.

I'm an assistant state's attorney in the Felony Division in the West Palm Beach Office. I've been there for fifteen years. My parents left me with a generous trust fund and I don't have to work. But I enjoy putting bad guys away in the 'slammer'. What do ya'll think about that?" She slurred her words.

"Very impressive. Please continue."

Mack was bored with her self-important rambling and began to study her. She wore pierced diamond solitaire earrings in gold settings, a thin gold necklace on which hung a jade butterfly in a gold mounting and a gold *Rolex* adorned her left wrist. A small silver charm, a little larger than a dime, dangled in solitary on a thin silver chain encircling her right wrist. Her perfume was *White Diamonds.* Her perfect teeth were no doubt the successful byproduct of several painful and embarrassing teenage years of wearing wire braces.

"Now that we are on a first name basis I might just reveal a few naughty secrets about myself." She smiled demurely and motioned the nervous waiter over to the table with a crook of her right index finger. "Waiter. Get me another *Vodka Gimlet* 'pronto'. Tell that lazy-ass bartender to put some vodka in it this time or I'll revoke his probation tomorrow morning." She stuck out her over-glossed lower lip in a sexy pout and rested her chin in the palm of her left hand. "Now where were we? I know. We were taking about me."

"You were going to tell me some of your secrets."

"Okay. Here we go! I have perfect vision and very fair skin. I burn easily and have to literally lather on SPF 50 sun block if I'm out in the sun for more than ten minutes. Sometimes I drink a little too much and I absolutely love Vodka Gimlets. Did you get it? I said absolutely! *'Absolut'* is the name of a vodka."

"Yes ma'am. Absolutely! I got it! No doubt. Absolutely!"

"After graduating from law school I interned in Washington, DC at the Department of Justice for a year. I made some excellent contacts some of which I still use today.

I even interviewed for a job at the *CIA*. Would you believe that their employment application is thirty-four pages long? It took half a day to fill out. I love sail boating, casino boat gambling, wild parties, paperback romance trash books, disco music and an occasional dirty movie. But, it has to be on video. A female state's attorney can't be seen going to a porno flick. I don't get along well with women. Don't take this personally, but men strike me as just plain stupid! I have a saying about men hanging on my office wall. Can you guess what it is?"

"I can't imagine. Is it the Burt Reynolds nude centerfold?"

"No silly boy. It's a poster that says in great big letters *Boys are dumb! Boys are dumb! Boys are dumb!*"

"I think that I understand. I'll work on not being dumb."

"You can't be very dumb. You are with me and I'm buying your dinner. That's smart."

"I guess it is - if you say so. I won't quibble about it."

"Let's talk about what we might be able to do for each other. When your uncle, Sam I think his name was, called from Chicago to tell me that you were on the way down to Stuart he mentioned that you had electronics experience in the military and liked to tinker with that stuff. The extra bedroom has a lot of electronics junk in it and I don't understand any of it. You can play with it if you like. He also told me that you also did some intelligence work in the military. Maybe you can do some things for me on the QT?"

"Sure. I like to mess around with electronics, but my uncle tends to exaggerate. He may have told you a few things that weren't completely true."

"Like what?"

"I don't know what he told you."

"Okay Mr. James McCray. Let's stop playing cat and mouse with each other! I know exactly who you are and you know that I know! But, no one else needs to know. Part of my job is to provide you with a good 'cover' and to protect your new identity. If the wrong people find out who you are, and where you came from, you are a dead man. Some very dangerous people want to kill you. They are looking everywhere for you're furry little behind. Do you understand?"

"I think so. But, I have to work on the not being dumb part."

"That's for sure! Be careful. You're safe at least for a while anyway. But you are a new face in this area. People will start asking questions. Keep your trap shut! Nobody knows who you are, or where you came from. Keep a low a profile. We may want to use you as a CI to gather evidence for prosecuting tough cases. You would be perfect for that."

"I don't understand. Perfect? Why? What's a CI?"

"I'm sorry. I used shop lingo. CI is short for *'confidential informant.'* It's someone who provides information that can be used as evidence in court, or for a search warrant. The CI's identity is kept secret just like in the witness protection program. We suspect that large quantities of high quality cocaine are passing through here at night during the week from the Bahamas. I want to 'nail' them real bad! Don't ask me why because it's a personal thing, but you can help."

"Why am I perfect?"

"Because you are faceless. No one in the area has seen you before. You can go into places, gather information and not be obvious. No one would remember that you were there.

"Isn't that dangerous? I'm not very good at violence. I could get killed and I bleed easily."

"Of course its not dangerous. Are you some kind of a wimp? It's perfectly safe. We'll train you, provide you with security and protect your identity. You have my personal guarantee. After just the little bit of you that I've seen I wouldn't want anything bad to happen to you. You do trust me don't you?" She stuck out her lower lip in a false pout daring him to say no.

"What does it pay?"

"You get to stay alive, maybe make a few bucks and keep me company if and when I need you."

"I'll take the job. Do I get a company car, full medical plan and expense account with it?"

"Of course not. But, you do get to keep the pickup truck."

"The truck smells like fish! What happened to my Porsche?"

"I'm so sorry. The Porsche was in a terrible accident. But, be very thankful that you weren't in it! The Chicago Police Marine Unit found it in a parking lot close to Navy Pier Monday morning. There was blood on the front seat and six bullet holes in the driver's side window."

"What are you talking about? It can't be so! Prove it!"

"And, the Chicago Police Marine Unit recovered a body floating in Lake Michigan outside Monroe Harbor. Here. Read about it yourself. It was the headline in yesterday's *Chicago Tribune*." She opened her clasp-topped, red sequined purse and passed him a folded newspaper page. "Waiter we absolutely need two more Vodka Gimlets over here. Pronto!"

Mack opened the page. The forty-eight point headline read:

Floating body found outside Monroe Harbor

Although the head, hands and feet had been cut off the body was identified as James McCray by the MIA tattoo on the upper right arm. Police feel that it was a rival gang hit over a botched drug deal. The victim's red Porsche was found in a parking lot close to Navy Pier. There were six bullet holes through the driver's side window and blood on the seat.

A Hancock Building security guard said that the victim entered the lobby about 9:30 P.M. Sunday evening and appeared to be in a daze. He boarded the residents' elevator and took it to the forty-fifth floor. Fifteen minutes later the victim exited from the elevator and ran through the lobby dragging a large suitcase and a suit bag. The last time the victim was seen alive he was running towards the residents' parking garage entrance. The guard said that he did not see anyone unusual in the lobby that evening.

"That wasn't me. I'm right here!" Mack shoved his right sleeve above the deltoid muscle. "My MIA tattoo is on my left arm – not my right! Here. Look at it! This is a big mistake."

Tina straightened up in her chair, brushed the flaming red hair out of her blazing, emerald-green eyes and looked directly into his eyes. She was suddenly sober. "Okay big boy. Let's take off the gloves and get serious! It's no mistake. You no longer exist as James McCray. You are a dead man! I verified it by running your name through the NCIC and the Social Security computers this morning. But, you've got some friends in very high places and they want you to stay alive. Your name is Phillip MacArthur, you are here and I'm in charge - have no doubt about that!"

"I don't. But, . . ."

"Shut up and listen to me carefully! I'm going to give you a couple of important hints that may keep you alive. Try to get yourself established in the community, but very slowly. Stay low key. Many families have lived here for several generations and some of us aren't warm to newcomers. Especially *Yankees*! Go to school and get yourself a Coast Guard license so that you can be a fishing guide. Go fishing and have fun. Keep your nose clean and don't snoop around. When we need you we'll call you. Understood?"

"Yes ma'am. I like the fishing part. I can do that. Do I have to be in for bed check too?"

"Only when I'm in town. Here's a pager in case I need to reach you. Wear it twenty-four hours a day. You will know that it's me if it reads *6-6-6*. My pager number is printed on that blue label. After it answers enter *9-9-9*. I'll get back to you as soon as I can." She glanced at her watch and flinched. "Oh crap! It's eleven-thirty! I have to be in Criminal Court in West Palm in the morning at nine sharp. Waiter, bring me the check and a Vodka Gimlet in a cup to go. Now!"

The drive back to the marina was as frightening as anything Mack had ever encountered in his life. He figured that she was as drunk as a skunk. She drove down deserted alleys, doubled back, sped up to seventy miles an hour and slowed to a crawl. She made the evasive driving instructors at Camp Peary look like beginners. When they reached the marina and the silver-blue *Beamer* finally screeched to a stop Mack was drenched with sweat.

"Mack. I guess that maybe I should apologize for the rough ride and the detours of the 'beaten track.' I wanted to do a little *'dry cleaning'* before I dropped off my own dirty laundry. You don't know who might have followed you down here. Now don't fret even a little bit about the car parked right behind us. It's an undercover officer from the Palm Beach County Sheriff's office. He follows me everywhere I go to be certain that I don't get pulled over by a 'local yokel' or "county mountie' for a silly traffic stop. See ya'll later. *Yankee Boy*."

Mack stepped out of the *Beamer* convertible directly onto a giant toad, lost his footing and took a header onto the dew-covered grass. He got up, brushed himself off and strode up the gravel driveway in the direction of the marina cottage without looking backwards, or saying a word.

She took the opportunity to yell a final insult in his direction out of the open convertible. "Bye *Yankee Boy*. Ya'll do your homework on Martin County before you get into trouble. Ya'll hear? She gunned the engine, spun the tires and loose gravel flew in all directions. The tiny, brown pieces of gravel and quartz rained down like hail stones when they returned to earth.

Mack mumbled to himself as loose gravel crunched under his shoes and the brown hail of stones rained down on his head. *"The first thing that I have to do tomorrow is find out who she is and how much of her story is true."* Tiny white lights, triggered by hidden motion detectors buried in the sod, lit up the driveway ahead of him as he walked along. The porch and living room lights automatically came on just a split second before his foot touched the steps. He muttered as he fumbled the newly made brass key into the lock. *"Devil woman. This must be a nice touch when you come home stoned in the middle of the night."* The door opened inward as smoothly as a bead of condensation running down the outside of a cold glass of beer on a hot day. He stood in the doorway and took inventory.

The front door opened directly into the living room. The quaint cottage was about 800 square feet, more or less. A stand-alone home entertainment center equipped with a television set and CD player with speakers at least four feet high dominated the northeast corner of the left wall. A fake brick fireplace, with a wooden mantle, was framed between the two windows on the east side. Above the mantle hung a painting of a white haired man wearing a straw hat, a long-sleeved blue cotton shirt and khaki shorts. He was standing up in a green skiff and the open cast net leaving his outstretched arms hovered in a perfect circle over a school of silver mullet. The walls were knotty pine.

The right side of the room was a continuous bookcase constructed of polished dark wood, possibly mahogany, that ran from the southwest corner to the short hallway leading to the bathroom and two bedrooms. The bookcase rose gallantly upward from the bare pine floor to the vaulted ceiling ten feet above. A green, round throw rug formed the centerpiece of the floor. Two pea-green fabric-covered recliners and an oblong glass-topped coffee table mounted on a spindly-legged, gray driftwood base completed the living room's sparse furnishings. The recliners formed a divider between the living room and kitchenette. There were no air conditioner ducts, or wall-mounted units in sight. A solitary, ceiling-mounted, slow moving, brass fan equipped with four wooden paddles stirred the stale, humid air around the room.

An avocado-green refrigerator stood as silent, tall sentinel in the corner next to the hallway. Next to it was an avocado-green electric range, followed by a short length - maybe three feet - of green counter top that led to the corner and an avocado-green ceramic sink. The white microwave snuggled in the corner niche between the sink and the range, looked 'out of place.'

The kitchenette's south-facing side featured a sliding glass door that opened onto a small deck that overlooked North Lake and the St. Lucie River. An early 1950's vintage chrome-legged, plastic-topped oblong dinette table and four matching chairs completed the furnishings. Cupping his hands around his eyes, Mack peered into the darkness through the dinette window that faced east. Squinting so hard that his brow drew into deep furrows on his forehead he forced his eyes to see in the faint moonlight. His eyes slowly became accustomed to the low light and he made out what appeared to be a high island and south of it a smaller one. The next day he would learn that he had an outstanding view of 'Sewell's Point' and 'Trickle's Island'.

Mack locked the front door, walked to the hallway leading to the bathroom and took a 'whiz'. In the bedroom he stripped down to his briefs, flopped into bed and glanced at his watch. 12:35 A.M. He was over-tired and a little 'boozed up' to boot. Sleep, but not rest, would come quickly.

When he flipped off the small bedside lamp and closed his eyes everything went 'black' for only an instant. Then swirling orange whirlpool, with the pulsating black center, appeared and began its tantalizing dance holding his retinas captive. Moving slowly at first, it quickly picked up momentum, and began forcing its image into his brain. He was helpless to stop it! Over the years he had tried unsuccessfully to blot out the poignant memories of the violent explosions and agonizing pleas of the wounded. Tonight, the agonizing screams would return.

"I've been hit! Please, for the love of God somebody help me! Don't leave me here!"

Pinned down by mortars and strafing from machine guns deeply imbedded in the jungle morass of northern *Laos* no one on the eight-man insertion/extraction team could move a muscle to help. Forced to listen - Mack shuddered and cringed. Screams gave way to soft moans and then to uncontrolled sobbing. Then came only eerie silence except for the buzzing of the green flies that appeared instantaneously at the moment of death.

Assigned a mission of absolute secrecy the team members had been *'sheep dipped'* to remove any possible vestige of their country of origin. They were outfitted in non-official battlefield gear, carried Swedish compasses, wore Swiss watches and were armed with Swedish K nine-millimeter submachine guns and Belgian-made Browning nine-millimeter pistols. No one carried any personal identification. Dog tags were not allowed because the metallic *'clink'* provided an audible signal. Plus, sunlight, or a flashlight beam, reflected off metal would give away a man's position to a sniper. His instructors at Harvey Point, North Carolina taught him to aim at anything that reflected sunlight in the chance of hitting the enemy in the throat.

During the early 1960's four eight-man covert teams were assigned to northern Laos. Their only identification was a *South African One Rand* coin. Each team's coin was inscribed with a numeral stamped in a different location on the side of the coin containing a *Springbok*. The numbers from '1' to '8' identified specific team members. Mack's team's numbers were stamped between the Springboks front feet. Mack's number was '1'.

Each man understood that if he was killed or captured that he would be considered to be a *mercenary*. Thus, avoiding embarrassment to his country and providing assurance that their families could not be harassed. Those who managed to get out would account for the others in closed-door debriefing sessions.

The insertion/extraction teams had to be mobile and could not be burdened with the dead or wounded. All volunteers, each team member knew that if they were killed that their body would remain where it fell. The wounded would be left with a cyanide capsule between their teeth to be used when the pain became unbearable or capture was imminent.

Mack touched the inside of his right thigh with his left hand for the assurance that a packet about the size of a matchbox was still in place. A hard slap of his hand would activate a small cylinder of compressed carbon dioxide. Instantaneously a needle would puncture the femoral artery and the carbon dioxide would expel a fifty-milliliter dose of *toxin*. He would lose consciousness immediately and the toxin would stop his heart in five seconds assuring that no enemy would be able to use his knowledge against his fellow warriors or country.

His greatest fear was that a team member would be so badly wounded that they could not be able to activate the toxin packet. It would be necessary for the safety of the team and the mission for someone to assist them. Mack recalled how difficult it was to put an animal away on the farm when old age or disease struck them. Vets were far away and very expensive. A bullet only cost a few cents and the animal didn't feel pain for long - if at all. It was the sight of those trusting eyes looking at him and seeming to understand that he was taking away their pain that often haunted his dreams. Could he do it to a fellow team member in order to protect the integrity of the mission? He must. They would understand.

Wheee! Blam!

The mortar shell hit fifty yards to the left of the dug-in team. They needed air cover badly and they needed it now! Mack furiously cranked the stubby handle of the ancient *EE 8 Field Telephone* that connected him to the backup team trailing one mile behind. He picked up the handset and listened for a reply. Nothing! He crammed the handset in the cradle.

Brrrrrrrr! Brrrrrrrr! Brrrrrrrr!

The field telephone didn't ring with a bell - it buzzed with a soft *brrrrrrrrr*. A bell was not used in field telephones because the ringing of a bell would attract attention. The backup team had responded. Mack grabbed the handset and pressed the 'push to talk' button. *"Alpha One. Please send your traffic. Out."*

Mack strained to hear over the noise of the small arms fire. There was only the *hiss* of static. He tried again. *"This is Alpha*

One. Please send your traffic. Over."
There was no response except for hard breathing and laughing in the background. He shoved the handset back into the olive-drab canvas field pack and snapped it closed.

Brrrrrrrr! Brrrrrrrr! Brrrrrrrr!

Mack ignored the ringing. It was *'Charlie'* was on the other end. They had tapped into the field telephone line and were letting him know that they were cut off from the main force.

Wheee!

The high-pitched whistle indicated an incoming mortar round! Experienced veterans said that you never heard the round that hit you. Mack covered his head with his arms and silently prayed for the best. He didn't hear the explosion, or feel its concussion. He just felt tired and wanted to sleep.

Brrrrrrrr! Brrrrrrrr! Brrrrrrrr!

Mack just wanted to sleep.

Brrrrrrrr! Brrrrrrrr! Brrrrrrrr!

His body's life giving plasma slowly seeped into the dark loam of the tropical jungle floor and became part of the earth.

Brrrrrrrr! Brrrrrrrr! Brrrrrrrr!

CHAPTER

5

Brrring Brrring Brrring
The ringing wouldn't stop and he couldn't muffle it or blank it
out. It even pierced through the feather pillow covering his head.
It was merciless and wouldn't stop! *"It must be a female phone!"*
Brrring! Brrring! Brrring!
Mack cracked his eyes open just a 'sliver' and immediately
snapped them shut. The bright sunlight streaming into the room
felt like red, hot pokers to his light-sensitive retinas.
Brrring! Brrring! Brrring!
He groped desperately with his right hand for the offending
avocado-green plastic screaming demon and with a blind swipe
knocked it off the nightstand onto the bare wooden floor. Silence
at last. *"He knew that he had killed the damn thing. It was dead!"*
The handset had fallen off the cradle and he heard the shrill
screaming of a woman's voice emanating upward from the floor.
'It' pierced through the pillow covering his ears.
*"Mack! Get your lazy, no good Yankee butt out of bed! Do
you hear me? You've got things to do! Do you hear me?"*
He remembered that voice not so much by it's sound as by it's
tone. It was the red headed female egomaniac from Hell! He
hoped that he was having another really bad dream!
"Hello?"
"Hello my sweet pink ass! *Yankee Boy*, do you have any idea

at all what time it is?"

"No ma'am I afraid that don't know. I think that I might have overslept just a little bit. What time is it?"

"Just a little bit? A little bit my ass! Your sorry-assed, wimpy *Yankee* butt was supposed to be at *'Billy Bob's Marina'* first thing this morning to pick up the boat I ordered yesterday. That's why the truck has a trailer hitch on it! Don't you remember anything about our conversation last night?"

"I'm not sure about anything right now. I can't even open my eyes. Is the sun always this bright early in the morning?"

"Early in the morning? Morning my sweet ass! It's ten thirty-four! It's afternoon! I got up at six thirty and kicked the sun's ass out of bed! That's what you call morning! Not ten thirty-four! I've been in court since nine o'clock and have already put three bad boys in jail. That's a full day's work. What time do *Yankees* usually get their butts out of bed? The middle of the afternoon?"

"No Ma'am. But, I was really tired from that long drive and I had a really bad dream last night."

"My poor little old *Yankee Boy*. He's all tuckered out from a little old drive down from Georgia. I apologize for waking you up so early. Can you forgive little old me? I guess that I should have taken that long drive into consideration when I kept you out way past your bedtime at seven thirty. Can you ever forgive me?"

"Yes ma'am. It's okay. I forgive you. Now can I go?"

"Bad dream my ass! *Yankee Boy* I'll give you a bad dream that you'll never forget! I'm going to be your worst nightmare ever and starting right now! Do you understand me?"

"Yes ma'am."

"Now get your lazy, no good, wimpy *Yankee* butt out of that bed and shag it down to *'Billy Bob's Marina'* and pick up my damn boat. It's registered, gassed up and ready to go. I want it hanging off the davits in the boathouse by three o'clock this afternoon! Do you understand?"

"Yes ma'am. But, do you mind if I get dressed and eat something first?"

"Hell yes I mind, but I don't have any choice. Ya'll will need your strength to cut the grass after you pick up my boat. Go to the *'Queen Conch'* restaurant on Old Dixie Highway in Port Salerno.

It's on the corner and about a block north of *'Billy Bob's'*. Tell Mary, she's the owner, that I sent you over and she'll put your breakfast on the marina's account. The riding mower is in the shed next to parking area. After you finish cutting the grass go to the Martin County Library on East Ocean Boulevard. I want you to check out every book they have on Martin County. You need to do some homework before I get up there this weekend. There will be a test! Do you understand me clearly *Yankee Boy*?"

"Yes Ma'am. I do. Pick up your damn new boat, cut the grass in the front of the marina and go to the library. Anything else?"

"As a matter of fact there is. Stop by the chamber of commerce on Kanner Highway and see Louise. She has a 'marked-up' Martin County map waiting for you. I want you to get familiar with the area this afternoon. Take that old truck for a ride down Kanner Highway to *Port Mayaca*, cut up Highway 610 to *Indiantown* and come back on the old Martin Grade road and Highway 714 to *Palm City*. Then take Federal Highway, that's US 1, north to Jensen Beach Boulevard. Cross over the Jensen Beach Causeway to *Hutchinson Island* and drive south to *Sailfish Point* and *Bath Tub Beach*. Get out of the truck at *Bath Tub Beach* and walk around a little bit so that you get the local flavor. I'll meet you for dinner at six-thirty at the marina. Be rested up and be ready!"

"All of that by six-thirty? I'm not Superman!"

"That's for certain. But, if you had gotten your lazy *Yankee* butt out of that damn bed at a decent time you would have had plenty of time to do what you had to get done. Now get up and get going. I've got to file some papers, grab some lunch and get back to court by one o'clock. I've got to put some more bad boys away this afternoon."

Click

Feeling much more awake after the merciless butt chewing that he had just received Mack rolled out of the sack. When his bare feet hit the floor the floor moved and felt furry! His feet withdrew to the safety of the edge of the bed. He peered at the floor through the mist covering his eyes and held the telephone above his head in his right hand ready to smack the trespasser.

"What the hell was that?"

Meow

His moving, furry floor mat was a cat! It was emblazoned with splotches of black and white fur and had white feet. The cat had a black mask across his face similar to a raccoon and a blaze of white fur that stretched from under its chin to its underbelly. Its long fur and reminded him of an Angora cat that his great grandmother owned many years before when he was a kid. The cat purred like a high-performance racing engine running at high rpm's and trying to rub up against his bare ankles that were hugging the edge of the bed for safety!

Brrring

He grabbed it before the second ring. He learned his lesson.

"Mack. Is your sorry *Yankee* butt out of bed yet?"

"Yes ma'am I'm up and getting ready to take a shower."

"Did you feed the cat yet?"

"How did you know about the cat? Whose cat is it?"

"It's my cat lard butt. The cat food is in the fridge. Give him three tablespoons of food in a saucer, there's a clean saucer in the sink, and nuke it in the microwave for exactly fifteen seconds. No more no less. If it's too hot or too cold he won't eat it. Put a piece of wax paper over the saucer when you 'nuke' it or the food will splatter all over the microwave. Can you handle that?"

"I think so. Does he need a napkin? Do I burp him too?"

"You can drop the sarcasm. The cat's smarter than you are any day. He will want to take a shower before his breakfast and again afterwards. Then you can let him out for the day."

"A shower? What are you talking about? A cat shower? Does he need a towel?"

"There you go again being a dumb *Yankee*. Southern cats are very clean and he likes the shower. Now go turn on the shower, the cold water only, and leave the shower stall door open so that he can get in. He's not really taking a shower, but he likes to drink out of it. The vet told me that the cat thinks that the shower is rain and that he is drinking out of a running stream. It's kind of a *'back to nature'* thing for him."

"So, the poor cat's neurotic. Do you take him to a shrink too?"

"Of course not! He's an animal and wouldn't understand. But, he is several steps in the food chain above you!"

"What's his name? *Sylvester* seems to fit. Will *Tweety Bird* show up next?"

"Don't get smart with me. His name is *Sparky*, but he doesn't like it so just call him *Kitty*. Can you pronounce '*Kitty*' all by yourself? I realize that it has more than one syllable, but if you break it down it's easy. Try it. *Kit - ty. Kit-ty. Kit-ty.* Got it?"

"No, but I can pronounce *Smart - ass. Smart - ass. Smart - ass.* Try it. It's easy. *Smart - ass. Smart - ass. Smart - ass.* Got it?"

"Okay *Yankee Boy*. You are making fun of me. Ya'll are mocking me, *Yankee Boy*! Just remember that paybacks are hell."
Click

"Well, *Kitty* old boy, things are tough all over and I understand where you're coming from. Maybe you can't express it in words, but I've only been in town for less than twenty-four hours and I can tell why you are neurotic. Let's go take a shower then we'll have breakfast."
Meow

After the pair had showered, *Kitty* ate breakfast and showered again. Then they each went their separate ways. The cat went out to do whatever cats do all day. Mack headed for the *'Queen Conch Restaurant'* for something to eat.

The restaurant parking lot was packed and there were no open parking spots on the street. He parked the blue pickup truck in a vacant lot next to the fish house. Mack didn't expect to be able to find a seat, but he had a feeling that he was expected. He opened the door and looked around. Every table was filled. He turned to walk away and try to find a restaurant less crowded.

"Hey Mack. Where do you think you're going? We've been waiting for you. I understand from a good source that you had a rough night and slept in a little bit. Shame on you - *'sleepy head'*. We get up before noon around here." The deep, booming voice came out in a resonating southern drawl. Startled Mack turned around to face a large man with a head full of white hair, a neck the size of a rhinoceros with a torso to match. He grinned and his bright white store-bought false teeth sparkled. He looked familiar, but from where? Mack had never been here before.

"Come on in and sit a spell. Some of the boys and I have been waiting for you. *'Red'* told us that you were coming over and that we should introduce ourselves.

I'm David Thatcher. People call me *'Thatch'* because of my thick hair. I understand that you had some electronics experience in the military and like to 'piddle' with the stuff. I own an electronics manufacturing company, but I don't know much about the technical side. The engineers tell me what the stuff does and how it works. Our biggest customer is Uncle Sam and we do a lot of business with him and his nephews up at the *'Cape'*. If you are interested I'll let you piddle with anything that we have in our catalogs and maybe with some of the stuff that Uncle Sam doesn't want the public to know about.   Come on back and have a seat with us. We might be a 'tad' ugly, but we won't bite."

'Thatch' threw his meaty left arm around Mack's shoulders and guided him to a table in the back of the restaurant where four casually dressed men were waiting. They all stood up when Mack and *'Thatch'* reached the table.

"Mack, each one of the boys is going to introduce himself because we don't want someone else telling you things that you might not need to know. Ralph you go first, then Bear, then Rat then Mel. Okay Ralph, take it away. It's show time!"

A tall, thin, red haired, slightly balding middle-aged man wearing blue jeans and a white crew shirt with a pocket on the left side stuck his hand across the table to Mack. "Hello Mack. I'm Ralph Thomas. I've lived in *Port Salerno* all of my life and I'm one of the last remaining commercial fishermen. My family has been commercial fishing these waters for years and we're going to fight the proposed gill net ban with a vengeance. We're going down fighting with our gill nets in our hand."

"Hold it Ralph just a *'cotton-pickin'* minute. You're not on a soapbox. The man hasn't even been in town for a full day and you're already preaching to him about how to vote on the net ban proposal. Give him a chance to find out who you are and where you stand. Then you can preach to him. Now go ahead."

"I apologize. You don't know much about us yet and I made some pretty big assumptions. That was dumb on my part. When you have a chance we'll get together and talk fishing. I hear that you are from the West Coast around *Fort Myers*. Ever do any commercial fishing?"

"No, I haven't. I've been away from Florida for almost thirty years. I need time to get my bearings. We'll talk soon. I'm certain about that. Maybe you can show me some spots for snook?"

"No problem on the snook spots. We have to know where they hang out because we try to avoid getting them caught in our nets, except for Bear. Snook are illegal for gill netters to possess because they are supposed to be 'sport fish'. Whoop-dee-do!"

"Bear. It's your shot. Make it brief. Mack doesn't have much time. Red wants him to pick up a boat at *'Billy Bob's'*, cut the grass at the marina and drive to *Indiantown*. If he doesn't get it all done she'll be on him like ugly on a wild hog's butt."

A short, compact man, built like the ideal football team guard and wearing a shaggy black beard that stretched half way down his massive chest nodded his head as a greeting. "Okay, my name's Bear. I've got a real name, but I prefer that nobody 'round here knows what it is for personal reasons. I commercial fish just like Ralph and I ain't ever been caught with no *snuuks* (snook is pronounced by locals with an exaggerated "u") in my boat yet and they won't neither. I'm to smart for 'em. You'll see me fishing most nights in the North Fork up around *Club Med*. I think that I might know you. I grew up in *Punta Rassa* and my folks owned the fish house 'till it burned down in 1960. I knew a guy called Mack from *Fort Myers*. If you're him you have changed a lot in thirty years. You really growed up ugly."

"What? You're *Bear* from *Punta Rassa*? It certainly is a small world. No one heard from you after the fish house burned down and you left town with the commercial fishing tug. I joined the Air Force and left town right afterwards and haven't been back since. How've you been?"

"I'm doing okay. When I left town I moved here and stayed with my grandparents for a while. It was obvious that somebody over there didn't want me, or my family around. I sold the fish house land and I understand that there's a big condo on it now. I haven't been back since it burned down. I was drafted into the Army in 1962 and spent two tours in *'Nam*. I don't like to talk about that - if you don't mind. Please don't ask me about it."

"I understand completely. Maybe we can get together and talk about old times. Have you kept in touch with anyone since you left Fort Myers."

"Nope. After the fire I had no kin folks left there and it was time for me to move on."

"Okay *Rat*, or perhaps I should address you as Rodney William? It's your turn. Our guest doesn't know anything about you and it might seem strange to him that we have a *Bear* and a Rat at the table. Tell him who you are and be brief. We don't have all day. I'm hungry and he's got a lot of things to do today!"

"Okay. I will in good time. Don't push me. Just because I don't look so pretty anymore doesn't mean that I am that much different than the rest of you. I am a very sensitive person and have feelings just like everyone else. Do you understand?"

"Yes. I understand and I apologize. I'm sorry."

"It's okay. Just be nice to me in the future."

"Yes. I will be very careful to address you as *Mr. Rat*. Sir."

"Okay, that's better. My name is Rodney William Mathers. I was born in Kentucky. I have lived here since 1992 and live on my sailboat anchored in the St. Lucie River at Shepherd's Park. I attended Florida State on the GI Bill after I came back from my second tour of *'Nam* in 1971 and got a Master's Degree in Criminology."

"Why do they refer to you as *Rat*?"

"That's because in *'Nam* I was what they called a *'tunnel rat'*. It was my job to crawl down into the tunnels and roust out any *'Charlies'* that might be hiding in the tunnel. I got hurt pretty bad and was sent back stateside to recuperate. It's impossible for me to get an office job because of my face. I get a VA disability pension every month and do a few odd jobs for pocket money."

"Okay. Okay. Okay. We didn't need your life story. Mel. It's your turn. Please try to be brief. I'm hungry!"

"I'll try my best. My name is Mel Mangini. I am a detective in the narcotics unit of the Martin County Sheriff's office. That's a *'narc'* in street lingo. I've been there for five years and am still looking to make the 'big one.' I'm not sure why I allow myself to be seen in public with this bunch of oddballs, but we seem to have a lot in common. Let's eat."

"What do you mean that you're looking for the 'big one'?"

"That means that I'm looking to bust a really big drug dealer.

He's here and close by. I can feel it, but I can't seem to get a handle on him. But, I will. He's here and I know it! I can feel it."

"That's a big ambition. Do you have any leads?"

Okay guys. That's enough 'shop-talk' at the table. Mary's here with lunch. Let's eat."

After lunch 'Thatch' pulled Mack aside outside the restaurant. "Mack. I want to give you a 'heads up' before you do something stupid. 'Red' is in charge and she can make your life miserable. Do exactly what she tells you to do. She doesn't know how to ask for anything. The word 'please' is not in her vocabulary. She tells you what she wants – she doesn't ask. There's a reason for you being here and you will find out soon enough what it is. Do your homework and learn as much as you can about the area so that you can fit in quickly."

"Fit into where? Why?"

"Did you ever hear the expression, 'Ours is not to wonder why, but to simply do or die?'

"Yes I have. But what am I supposed to be doing? What exactly am I looking for and where should I be looking for it?"

"You should have picked up a couple of hints at lunch, but it's not my place to tell you. 'Red' will tell you when she's ready. Think about what you've heard so far. Just listen."

"I am listening, but I guess that I'm not hearing. It's almost one o'clock! I've got to find out where to pick up the boat and get it back before three o'clock or she'll have my butt in a sling!"

"You are a fast learner aren't you? You've been in town for less than twenty-four hours and can already smell the 'wrath' of the 'red head from hell'. Good! I sensed that you were pretty sharp when I babysat you all night long at that rest area in Georgia. But, you couldn't hold that baseball hat on your head for nothing. I was about to die from laughing when I pulled out."

"I thought that was you! Who are you really and why were you watching me?"

"Yep. It was me all right. I had to pay that trooper a hundred bucks to borrow his uniform and car for the night. But, it was worth it. You got here safely and in one piece. There was only one close call and that was back in Indiana at that 'flea-bag' hotel. If I hadn't rousted that half-wit manager out of his office to wake your lazy butt up it would have been all over for both of us. The cops found the Illinois State Trooper's car about an hour before and were going from hotel to hotel along the interstate exits looking for you. It was close. Almost to close."

"What do you mean they found the state trooper's car and they were looking for me? I didn't do anything to a state trooper. The only one that I saw was on the side of the road stopped behind a red Porsche. I thought that I heard pistol shots when I passed him, but I kept on going."

"That was the one. He had a terrible accident The Chicago cops found his car over by Navy Pier, but not him."

"Oh no! Are you telling me that you *'whacked'* the trooper, drove his car to Indiana and set me up for whacking him? Was that his body in Lake Michigan?"

"I'm not telling you anything more and I've have said too much already. Let's just say that you had better never go back to Illinois, or even Indiana for that matter. He had a good cremation.

"Oh my God! Now I'm wanted for whacking an Illinois State Trooper? What's next?"

"I don't know how you could be wanted for anything. You're dead! Your body was found floating in Lake Michigan, identified by a friend and cremated. There is no James McCray! Perhaps you should check your driver's license and find out who you are. If I recall correctly your name is Phillip MacArthur and your friends call you Mack. Now that you know exactly *'who'* you are I suggest that you get over to *Billy Bob's* and introduce yourself. I asked him to deliver the boat and put it in the boathouse to save you time. She's got a two hundred-fifty horse *YAMAHA* outboard mounted on a stern bracket, plus GPS, that means Global Positioning System and all the bells and whistles. I'm jealous."

"I'm confused. I'm a thousand miles away from home. I don't know who I am and I'm being told what to do by a red headed witch! What has happened to me? "

Thatch smiled smugly and turned to leave. He took three steps, paused in mid-stride, as if he had forgotten something, and spun around to face Mack. "Hey Mack. I almost forgot. Red thought that you might like to have this. See ya' around." He flipped something silver in the air that caught the light as it spun.

It hit the ground, rolled towards the curb and paused upright momentarily before it fell over on its side. It was a coin! Mack picked it up and turned it over between his fingers. It was a *South African One Rand*. Stamped between the front feet of the proud Springbok on the reverse side was the number '1.' Mack shuddered, began sobbing uncontrollably and frantically looked around for *'Thatch'*. He was gone. Shaken to the core, Mack ran to the blue pick up truck for the security of its metal cab. He sat in the truck for almost an hour rolling the coin between his fingers and staring at the water of the *Manatee Pocket* while trying to regain his composure. After he managed to get his act together he stopped to see Billy Bob about the boat and talk for a few minutes. Then he was off to the *Martin County Library*.

It had been thirty plus years since he had been in a library and he couldn't remember what the *'Dewey Decimal System'* meant much less how to use it. He relied upon the assistance of an understanding woman in the Research Department. Janet was originally from Pennsylvania and she guided him in the proper direction. At the time she didn't realize how many times he would return for assistance on other subjects and moral support. The thought came to him that if someday he attempted to write a book that perhaps she would once again provide guidance and assistance as a *'mentor'*.

Mack's arms were filled with books when he left the library at 3:30 P.M. The next stop was the chamber of commerce, then the drive to *Indiantown*, back to *Palm City*, then to *Jensen Beach*, over the *Jensen Beach Causeway* to *Hutchinson Island* and back to the marina. He pulled into the marina driveway at 6:03 P.M., bounded into the cottage and threw the library books on the floor. He expected to see the silver-blue *BMW* convertible pull into the gravel driveway at any second. He was running out of time and still had to cut the grass!

The cat was rubbing against his ankles and purring like a steam engine obviously buttering him up for a shower and dinner. He ran into the kitchen, snatched the can of cat food out of the refrigerator, dumped the contents into a saucer, threw a paper towel on top of it and put the whole mess in the microwave. He punched in fifteen seconds and hit the 'start' button. The microwave went *'ding'* while the cat was waiting for the shower water to reach the correct temperature. Mack tossed the loudly protesting cat into the shower and raced back to the kitchen. He snatched the saucer of cat food out of the microwave and put it on the floor. Then he remembered that the shower was still on, made a dash for the bathroom and rescued the soggy and highly pissed off feline. While he was drying off the very disgusted cat with a towel the phone rang. He glanced at his watch. 6:13 P.M. He still had time to cut the grass.

Brrring

"Hello?"

"Mack. It's Tina. I'm sorry that I yelled at you this morning, but I was stressed out. I'm going to be a little late getting up there tonight. Oh, and don't worry about cutting the grass. I forgot that the lawnmower was in the repair shop. They called me this afternoon to tell me that it was fixed and they are dropping it off on Monday. *Yankee Boy,* are you mad at little ol' me?"

"Me mad? Of course not! Why should I be mad? I got to meet a *bear* and a *rat* for lunch."

"Now don't get mad at little ol' me. I have your best interests at heart. I'm just trying to help you get out of the big mess that you left back in Chicago with that poor Illinois State Trooper and all. Don't you appreciate me just a little bit?"

"Appreciate you? I'd like to wring your damn scrawny neck!"

Now Mr. MacArthur, please control yourself. I gave you a reason for not cutting the grass. We still have a dinner date and much more business to discuss. Don't you remember the test about Martin County history? You are supposed to be studying."

"The test isn't until this weekend. You've had me running all over the county all day and I haven't had time to study anything."

"*Yankee Boy,* I'm very sorry, but a woman does have the prerogative to change her mind. Plus, you did sleep in a little bit extra this morning. But, you sound exhausted and are a little 'crabby'. Lay down and take a nap. You should be rested by the time I get there about seven-thirty and I'll wake you up."

"I'm not tired, or crabby and I don't want a nap. I sure as hell don't want to go out for dinner with you. I want to be left alone."

"*Yankee Boy!* Who told you that you had a choice in the

matter? This is a not a democracy as far as our relationship is concerned. Don't be persnickety. I'll be there about seven-thirty."

Click

Left holding a telephone receiver emitting a *'buzzing'* dial tone in his hand, and a cat rubbing at his ankles asking for an after dinner shower, he felt impotent. He slammed the handset on the cradle. He ran the shower water until it reached the correct temperature for the cat. When the cat was done showering Mack remembered to turn off the water. Maybe Tina was right and he needed a nap. He dropped the window blinds and crawled onto the bed. His eyes fluttered briefly and he drifted off into the unconsciousness of deep sleep. The swirling orange whirlpool with the pulsating black center appeared and forced its image into his brain stem.

Thwack! Thwack! Thwack! Thwack!

Mack awoke to the sound of a man screaming in agony and felt excruciating pain in the soles of his feet. It took tremendous effort to raise his head because he was upside down and lashed to a bamboo pole by his wrists and ankles like a hog on a spit. He looked towards the source of his pain. A white-haired oriental man clad in black pajamas and wearing a straw hat was slashing at the soles of Mack's bare feet with a bamboo pole. Each time the pole contacted his feet the excruciating pain pulsed to the top of his skull. He then realized that the screaming was his own voice reacting in time to the tempo of the pole strokes.

The aged, white-haired old man wielding the bamboo pole didn't seem to be in any hurry. He administered the strokes at a constant pace with no display of emotion. It was if he did this every day and it was just a job to him. No matter how loud Mack screamed and begged for him to stop he continued the beating. What did he want from him? The bamboo rod was covered with blood that ran down onto the old man's hands and wrists. He seemed to be unaware of the blood and continued the beating. Mack continued screaming in time with the strokes.

Thwack! Thwack! Thwack! Thwack!

Mack awoke in a deep, foggy haze of pain and standing in water up to his upraised armpits. The soles of his feet felt as if they were in a blast furnace. The pain was excruciating. He could feel the black, bloodthirsty river leeches boring their suckered mouths into the cuts in the soles of his feet, but he was powerless to stop them. When he managed to crack open his swollen eyes he saw that he was confined in a bamboo *'tiger cage'* sunk in a river and precariously tethered to a nearby tree by a light piece of weather-beaten, extremely frayed piece of manila rope.

Mack's hands were tied together at the wrist, stretched above his head and secured to a black steel ring that hung from the top of the cage. He needed sleep. The swirling orange whirlpool with the pulsating black center appeared and forced its image into his brain stem. The cherub fairy goddesses *'Blessed oblivion'* and her twin sister *'Unconsciousness'* wrapped Mack snugly in their warm cloak of darkness and took him away to the safety of a 'happy place' where he would no longer feel pain.

CHAPTER
6

Thwack! Thwack! Thwack! Thwack!

The pulse of the predictable sound was almost cathartic. Sheer terror filled his body as it anticipated the horrible pain that followed the sound. However, Mack was far beyond the sense of normal pain - he was in a 'happy place'. He was floating, pain free in the humid air and he could see his trussed-up body strung on the bamboo spit below him. The relentless sound continued.

Thwack! Thwack! Thwack! Thwack!

Mack's throbbing bare feet recoiled upwards in reaction to the intense pain and he heard himself scream.

"Mack! Wake up. It's okay. Mack! Wake up! It's okay!"

He heard the shrill voice, but he couldn't move to respond. His head reeled with a deep pain that throbbed with each pounding heartbeat. His mental senses were deeply immersed in the thick cobwebs of semi-consciousness. Mack shook his head and tried to sit up, but someone, or something, roughly pushed him back down. He tried to open his eyes and sunlight rushed in causing his pupils to constrict. Even squinting he couldn't see through the bright light and dull throbbing pain. His head throbbed, his joints ached and he felt the dampness of the soaked bedding beneath him. He felt drugged.

"Mack. Are you awake? It's Tina! Mack. I'm here. Everything is okay. You were having a bad dream. Please wake up. Talk to me! You're going to be okay. Please wake up. Mack. Please."

The incoherent words pushed through the misty veil of semi-consciousness and tried to register in his brain. But, everything was spinning around him. He had lost his mental equilibrium. "I'll be okay. Just wait a minute for me to get my bearings. Where am I? What time is it?"

"It's seven-fifteen in the morning and time for you to get up. Mack you are safe and sound in *Port Sewell Marina*. You've been zonked out since late yesterday afternoon."

"Seven-fifteen in the morning? I have got to get up. I have things to do." He attempted to rise up on one elbow, felt a stab of pain in the middle of his forehead and in his feet and fell back.

"I spoke with you about six-thirty last night and you sounded really 'crabby'. I told you that I would be up for dinner about seven-thirty and suggested that you take a nap. But, I got held up in court and didn't get here until almost eight o'clock. You were out 'cold as a cucumber' and I felt sorry for you. You had the pillow in a headlock and were snoring so hard that the windows were shaking and I couldn't bear to wake you up. I pulled the blanket over you, closed the door and spent the night on my boat. After I got up this morning I came over to check on you. I was tapping you on the feet with a wooden ruler trying to wake you up and you started screaming. That's when I got scared."

"Did I say anything intelligible while I was asleep?"

"You were moaning and pleading with someone to 'stop' doing something. You kept mumbling *'stop stop stop'*. That's all I could make out."

"Okay. My head's starting to clear and I think that I can get up. I have to take a shower."

"Here. Take my hand and I'll help you get up."

He reached out for her outstretched right hand with his left hand. He used his right elbow as a lever to lift his shoulders and help raise his torso to a sitting position. His head was spinning and he closed his eyes to steady the room.

"Are you going to be sick? Do you want a pan or can you make it to the bathroom? I can help you."

"I'll be okay. Just give me a minute to get my bearings. I'm just a little dizzy and my feet hurt like hell."

"Mack. I'll be in the kitchen whipping up some breakfast while you are getting ready. Hurry if you can! I have to be out of here by seven forty-five because I have to drive back to West Palm, take a shower, get my face on, change clothes and be in court by nine! Judges have no sympathy for assistant state attorneys that are late for court - even on a Thursday morning."

Mack's head was throbbing and he felt like he was going to collapse. He steadied himself by leaning his left shoulder against the wall as he slipped around the corner and down the hall into the bathroom. He pulled back the thin, avocado-green plastic shower curtain and stepped in.

Meow.

"What the hell are you doing here? This is my shower! Get out you bag of fur!"

Meow.

The cat looked up at Mack with green eyes that seemed to be the size of saucers.

Meow.

"Okay. You can take your shower first. Just let me get out of the way." Mack stepped out of the shower stall, turned on the water and adjusted the temperature to make it 'just right.' The cat just sat there looking at him and made no effort to drink. "What's wrong now? The temperature is just like you ordered."

Meow.

"Tina, can you come in here, please? I don't understand what the cat wants from me. He's sitting here meowing and just watching the water run in the shower."

"He wants you to take a shower first. After you're done he'll jump in and lap up the water while it's still running down the drain. The vet says that he must like the taste of the body salt in the water, or the lye from the soap. Don't argue with him. He'll sit right there meowing at you until he gets what he wants."

"What's next? Does he want me to wipe his butt after he uses the sand box?"

"No, he doesn't use a sandbox. But, you do have to flush the toilet for him. He can't reach the handle to flush after he's done his business and you don't have to wipe him."

"What do you mean that I have to flush the toilet for him?

Since when does a cat use a toilet? They use sand boxes and cover it up don't they?"

"Not this one. I taught him to climb up on the seat and do his thing. It's a lot cleaner and doesn't smell like a sand box. Don't forget to leave the lid up or you're apt to have a mess on your hands. He doesn't know the difference between open or closed."

"Any more surprises that you haven't told me about?"

"None that you need to know about right now. The rest of them can still wait for a while longer. Hurry up. I have to go!"

Mack and the cat arrived at a compromise -at least in the cat's mind. Mack finished his shower, stepped out of the shower stall and the cat jumped in for his turn. He paused, turned his head, looked directly at Mack and gave him a soft *meow*. Perhaps it was a cat 'thank you'? When he returned to the bedroom Mack found a pair of beige shorts, briefs and a blue, short-sleeved sailcloth shirt lying on the freshly made bed.

"Mack. I put out some appropriate fresh clothes for you and even changed the sheets. I hope that you don't mind."

Obediently Mack donned the shorts and shirt. A pair of brand new brown deck shoes sat beside the bed.

"Mack! Don't put on any socks! Here in Florida men always wear deck shoes without socks."

"No socks? I'm going to fit in just fine with the local hicks and have blisters too."

The aroma of bacon, eggs and hot coffee drifted into the small bedroom from the kitchen. Mack was famished and was amazed that she could cook! He ran a comb though his hair, dashed on some *Old Spice* and went out to the kitchen.

"My. My. My. Don't we smell good today? We even look like a Florida boy! You pass inspection just fine. Now you eat your breakfast and take your time. You have all day to look around the place and get situated. The other bedroom has a few electronic toys in it that you might enjoy tinkering with. *'Thatch'* had them set up for you. He left a business card in case you want to call him for lunch or whatever. He can fill you in on what's going on and introduce you to the right people. Oh crap! It's seven forty-five. I have to run. I'll be back Friday night. We'll talk then. Don't forget your Martin County test on Saturday. Study those books. Drive around town. You have to get acquainted fast! See ya'll tomorrow night! Bye." With a light brush of her soft lips against his cheek she was gone.

The *Beamer's* engine roared into life and was followed by the sound of gravel spinning under the tires as she peeled out of the driveway. A few loose stones pelted the tin roof, wobbled down unevenly like unbalanced marbles and spattered on the front porch. She was gone! Peace at last - at least until she comes back.

Mack polished off breakfast, poured another cup of coffee and decided to survey his quarters in the daylight. With coffee mug in hand he began his self-guided tour with a stroll around the living room. The floor-to-ceiling bookcase was filled with classics. Many of them were 'first editions' including works by, *DeFoe, Hemingway, Poe, Twain, Steinbeck,* et al. The *History of Western Civilization* and a recent edition of the *Encyclopedia Britannica* were included among the reference works. The magazine rack held the current issues of *Newsweek, Time, International Relations National Geographic, Organized Crime Digest* and oddly enough *GLOBAL SPY NEWS*.

Mack walked over to the east side of the cottage. Dazzling sunlight streamed through the sheer, white lace curtains covering the double-paned windows on each side of the fireplace. He lifted a curtain by the left bottom corner with his right thumb and forefinger and pulled it off to the side. A spectacular view of the *St. Lucie River* and *Sewell's Point* greeted his swollen, bloodshot eyes. Mack dropped the curtain, watched it lightly fall back in place, turned and walked through the kitchenette to the door leading to what he hoped was a porch or deck.

With only a slight push the door swung open onto an open deck that ran from east to west across the back wall. Two white plastic chairs and a matching round, white plastic table, with a round, ribbed, green umbrella sprouting out of its center on a metal pole completed the decor. The deck was enclosed by a waist high wooden railing supported by risers turned in the shape of bowling pins. The deck was supported on black, creosoted wooden pilings that rose about twenty feet above the water.

Mack placed his elbows on the railing and leaned over to survey the majestic panorama in front of him. The view almost took his breath away. The cottage overlooked the entrance to *Willoughby Creek* on the west, *Sewell's Point* was to the east and the *Manatee Pocket* was directly to the south. A narrow, sand peninsula curved from left to right and sheltered the marina from the *St. Lucie River*. A lone, female osprey perched on her nest built of branches and Spanish moss lodged in the top branches of an Australian pine tree was surveying the river for breakfast.

The cottage and boathouse formed the center of the marina. A seventy-foot wooden 'finger pier' ran along each side of the boathouse and extended forty feet into the *North Lake* and the marina basin. Ten feet of open space between each pier and the boathouse provided room to bring in boats with an eight-foot beam, but not much bigger.

Three sailboats were moored on the west pier and there was one vacant slip. That seemed strange because Tina had told him that the marina was full. Four powerboats ranging from twenty to thirty feet in length were moored along the east pier. No doubt the *'rag baggers'* and *'stink potters'* didn't get along and had to be kept separated from each other. That wasn't unusual.

Mack's coffee was gone and he went back inside to check out the other bedroom. When he reached the hallway *'the smell'* invaded his nostrils and made his eyes water. Undaunted, he covered his nose and mouth with his right hand and forged ahead into the bathroom. There *'it'* was floating on top of the water in the toilet bowl. Mack had forgotten about the cat! With his nose and mouth covered by his right hand he flipped the toilet lid down and tripped the flush lever with his left. He raised the bathroom window, dashed out and slammed the door shut behind him. He needed fresh air and lots of it!

After his eyes stopped watering Mack crept down the hall to check out the other bedroom. A large brass padlock hung loosely from the hasp and a key poked out of the lock. A note taped to the door at eye level read, *'Lock the door when you leave'*. He slipped the lock off the hasp and gently pushed the door open. The room contained a virtual electronics lab! 'Military standard' nineteen-inch wide, gray metal racks filled with electronic equipment lined the walls and the windows were covered by dark green shades. A 'control console' with four video screens, four rows of buttons and slide controls took up the center of the room.

One bay of equipment contained meters labeled; *Salinity, Ph, Temperature, Water Height, Current Speed, Current Direction, Relative Humidity, Dew Point, Wind Speed* and *Wind Direction.*

Mack made a mental inventory of the equipment; a multi-channel digital CD video recorder, a sixteen channel multiplexer capable of producing a photo of any frame of a video; a half-inch video editor; *Extremely Low Frequency, High Frequency, Very High Frequency* and *Ultra High Frequency* radio receivers and scanners; satellite telemetry receivers; a *Global Position System* satellite receiver interfaced with a color video plotter; *UHF* and *VHF* radio direction finders and several things that he could not identify. Neatly nestled under two racks of satellite receivers, was a workbench fully equipped with soldering irons, voltmeters, an oscilloscope and a multi-band frequency counter. A rack across the top of the workbench was filled with tools.

Bewildered and confused, Mack left the electronics lab, filled up his coffee mug and went out the front door onto the porch. The gravel drive was straight ahead and the porch dropped off three feet to the ground. A doorway on the right side of the porch opened to a flight of twelve wooden steps that led down alongside the boathouse to the dock. He went down the four wooden steps that led from the porch to the walkway, walked out into the 'pea gravel' driveway about fifteen feet and looked back at the cottage. It looked like a picture postcard from Cape Cod.

The sides of the cottage and boathouse were native cypress that had weathered to a soft gray and the windows were accented by white trim. The silver metal roof was slanted at a steep pitch and reflected the sun's withering rays. Mack looked forward to hearing raindrops beat their soothing 'tattoo' on the roof during a rainy night. The walkway that led up to the steps was flanked on each side by a concrete Greek Classical style urn that contained a flowering tropical plant that he was not familiar with.

Mack walked out into the uncut vacant lot that formed the marina's parking area, turned and looked back to get a better view of the cottage and boathouse nestled underneath. The tin roof was festooned with a myriad of antennas and satellite dishes, but the eight-foot in diameter parabolic dish enclosed behind a wire link fence enclosure got his attention. He hoped that it was for a satellite television receiver. He was puzzled by the two very large *rhombic antennas* suspended over the marina grounds from insulators attached to trees at the corners of the lot. *Rhombics* are directional and used for very long-range *high frequency* radio reception. These antennas faced east to west and north to south. *"This place looks like a porcupine in 'heat' with all of those antennas. Do the neighbors often complain about the television interference?"*

Walking back to the cottage Mack noticed a small television camera mounted under each corner of the roof. Each camera was inside a clear, round housing that looked like a fish bowl. *"No doubt they're equipped with night-vision irises, wide angle lenses and are triggered by motion detectors. 'I'll even bet that they are connected to a VCR and digital multiplexer somewhere."*

Wooden stairways of twelve steps each led down to the wooden finger piers extended along each side of the boathouse. Mack noted that the boathouse could be accessed only by a separate covered stairway that led off the front porch. He stepped up onto the porch and the boards let out a *squeak.* *"Now that's what I call old fashioned security."* He looked overhead and saw the two sets of dual-bulb halogen floodlights mounted under the eaves. *"The place is wired for television. All we need is a director to yell out action!"*

Mack went down the stairs that led to the boathouse wondering what 'surprises' he might find inside. The door was unlocked and he let himself in - it was dark. He fumbled and felt around for the light switch and discovered that it was on the right hand wall instead of the left. The new boat was on its lift, suspended about a foot above the water and smelled of fiberglass resin. The boathouse contained what a boathouse would be expected to contain. Two five gallon gas cans sat on the wooden walkway, an ancient white, canvas-covered cork life ring hung on a nail on the wall, four fishing poles stood upright up in the corner and a green, plastic tackle box nestled between them. The boathouse access door was connected to an automatic door opener and the 'master control unit' was mounted on the wall beside the light switch. He pushed the 'manual' button on the control unit and the door slid open effortlessly.

"Nice boat. Let's take it for a spin and I'll show you around."

Mack spun around and dipped into in a low fighting crouch to face the deep, male voice behind him. There stood *'Thatch'* with a grin on his face as wide as the St. Lucie River. He had a portable cooler in his left hand and a rolled-up nautical chart in the other. He was wearing a hot pink, short-sleeved sailcloth shirt, a pair of robin's egg-blue shorts and white deck shoes.

"A little jumpy aren't we? Who did you expect? Guido or Luigi from Chicago? Don't worry. Nobody knows where you are. You are officially deceased, cremated and plunked in Lake Michigan somewhere between Monroe and Diversey Harbors. Now relax and let's go for a boat ride. Put up the top because it's going to be a scorcher and I burn easily."

"Dave! You scared the 'crap' right out of me. Plus, I think that I messed in my pants. Why did you sneak up on me like that? I could have hurt you, or myself, for that matter."

"Mack. I didn't sneak up on you, or make you 'crap' in your pants. You must have poor 'anal sphincter control' and you should have it checked. I know a good proctologist. When we get back I'll give you his phone number. I marched right down the stairs clomping all the way. Your mind must have been somewhere else. Push the 'down' button on the lift and let's get the bottom of this brand new boat wet. It's like a fine thorough bred race horse and needs daily exercise to stay in shape."

"What about Tina? Isn't she expecting me to be here?"

"She called, told me to pick you up and show you around. She also told me to remind you not to leave the cat in the house or you'll come back to another mess in the toilet."

"What did she mean another mess? How did she know about the first one?"

"That's easy. The cat was in the house when she left and she figured that you would forget to throw him out."

"Oh crap! Give me a couple of minutes to run upstairs and find him. I can't go through that again!"

"Mack. Lock up the lab and put the key in your pocket. After you close the front door turn the bent over nail head in the wood frame above the door so that the head faces up. That activates the monitoring and alarm system. If anyone approaches the place we'll be beeped."

"You people think that you have it all figured out don't you?"

"Yes. And, just for the record - we do!"

Mack raced up the stairs taking them two at a time. When he reached the porch he hit the front door at full stride hoping against hope. He was to late! The *'crap happy'* cat had struck again! Covering his face and nose with his right hand he dashed into the bathroom, flushed the toilet and fled into the kitchenette for safety. Gasping for breath he opened the back door for ventilation and fresh air. At the same instant the phone rang.

Brrring

"Hello."

"You forgot about the cat didn't you?"

"Yes ma'am. I did, but I won't ever forget again."

"I knew you would and I'll bet you will again. *Dumb boy!*"

"No ma'am. I won't ever forget again. I learned my lesson."

"Good. Has Dave arrived yet?"

"Yes. He's in the boat house waiting for me."

"He's going to show you the area by water. Listen to him carefully because he is going to explain a little more about what's going on here and why I asked for you."

"What do you mean you asked for me?"

"You had better find the cat and throw him out before you leave. Look inside the wicker clothes hamper in the bedroom."

Click

Left alone to mull over her words, Mack was awash with frustration tinged by a trace of anger and a hint of rage. He wanted answers and he wanted them now. But, first he had to find the *'crap happy'* cat. Mack went to the bedroom and flipped up the lid on the brown woven wicker clothes hamper with the end of a broom handle. When the lid flew off he jumped back expecting a hissing King Cobra to leap out at him.

Meow

The cat was nestled in Mack's dirty underwear and looked as innocent as a baby.

"There you are! I should wring your damn neck!"

"I don't think so. It's my cat."

"Tina! Are you here?"

"Nope."

"Where did your voice come from?"

"Right over here - the picture over the fireplace. The same place where the miniature television camera is hidden. Look in my father's eyes and smile. Now gently lift *Kitty* out of the hamper and set him down gently on the front porch. He is a very sensitive animal and doesn't react well to violent yelling. That's animal cruelty."

"What's next? Do you have micro-chip in my neck so that you can track where I go?"

"Honey child - it's not in your neck."

Click

"Okay *'crap happy'*. Its time for you to go outside and do whatever cats do all day. I've got to be careful with you because your older sister is watching me. She hisses and scratches too."

"Mack. I heard that."

"Meow to you too cat woman!" Mack tossed the cat on the front porch, locked up the electronics lab, went out the front door and locked it behind him. He found the little nail above the door and turned it so that the head faced up. Immediately the security cameras went into operation and began scanning from side to side. Furious and boiling mad, Mack tromped down the twelve wooden steps to the boathouse. The boat was in the water, the top was up, the engine was humming and spitting a stream of water out of the exhaust port. Thatch was obviously ready to go.

"Looks like the engine is warmed up. Mack, jump in. I'll drive because I know the water. Are you ready for a cold one?"

"A cold what?"

"I thought that you were smart? A beer - you dummy. An 'ice cold' beer. There's a cold 'twelve pack' in a cooler inside the live well. Just lift that hatch cover and pull a couple out."

"A beer? It's only eight-thirty in the morning?"

"Let's not be picky shall we? Sure, here it's only eight-thirty in the morning. But, it's five-thirty in the afternoon somewhere."

"No thanks. My head is still pounding from this morning. I can't even think straight."

"I understand completely. Reach in and grab another cold one for me. This one's a 'dead soldier'. You had a real good time last night from what I hear. Absolutely a good time was had by all."

"What do you mean a good time? I was bushed and fell asleep about six-thirty. I didn't wake up until almost seven-thirty this morning!"

"Is that right? You slept straight though? No dinner or nothing to drink? That's odd. Then why do suppose you have such a bad headache this morning? To much sleep I suppose?"

"That's right. I overslept. Yesterday was a long day."

"How do your feet and legs feel? Any stiffness in them?"

"Yeah, they're sore alright. I feel like I ran five miles across the desert in my bare feet."

"It's more like ya'll danced five miles in your bare feet. Most people usually feel pretty darn tired the next day - especially with only four hours of sleep and a hangover to boot."

"What are you talking about? I slept for almost thirteen hours and I had nothing to drink last night. Ask Tina. She'll tell you. We were supposed to go out for dinner about seven-thirty last night, but when she got up here about eight o' clock I was already asleep. She felt sorry for me and let me sleep. She woke me about seven this morning. She'll tell you where I was all night."

"I don't have to ask her. I know where you were. At least until about eleven-thirty when I went home. You were flying high. Absolutely flying high. Absolutely! Why don't you ask Tina where you were? That is if you really don't remember."

"I don't remember anything except laying down on the bed about six-thirty last night and Tina waking me up this morning. I couldn't have gone out? Could I?"

"Hello? Wake up and smell the roses. Enjoy the red-headed rose garden, but watch out for the thorns!"

"What happened to me? Did she drug me?"

"Now would a sweet, professional, red-headed, twice divorced ex-Federal agent do that to you? Plus, take advantage of you in a weakened condition? That's a crime!"

"What do you mean ex-Federal agent? How could she drug me? I didn't drink anything before I went to bed. Oh, I did have a glass of ice water from the fridge."

"Did you lay your head on the pillow?"

"Of course I did."

"Come on Mack. Didn't you take *'Drugs 101'* when you were at Williamsburg? It's a basic course."

"Of course I did. So?"

"It must have been quite some time ago. Didn't they teach you about *Ketamine Hydrochloride*? It's been around for a long time. It comes in liquid and powder, plus a spray that dries on contact and turns into a fine dust that is inhaled during respiration."

"She spiked my pillow and my water?"

"You'll have to ask her. I suggest that you buy bottled water and keep a 'special' pillow and pillowcase stashed away where she can't find it. Now let's go for that boat ride and do some serious talking." Dave shifted into reverse and the boat slipped backwards with only a whispered low hum emanating from the engine. Mack pushed the down button on the garage door controller and the boathouse door slid into place.

Dave handed him a black plastic packet that looked like an electronic pager. "Clip this on your belt and pay attention to it. If it beeps, or vibrates, it means that we have a visitor at the marina. Push the top button on the right side and a small screen flips up." Dave pushed the button and a screen, perhaps three inches square, flipped upright and began flashing.

"This is a digital screen. It doesn't require any warm up time and comes on instantly. The keyboard let's you select any camera by numbers 'one' through 'ten'. Camera 'one' is on the northwest corner of the cottage and scans ninety degrees each side of northwest. Camera 'two' is also on the northwest corner, but its primary position is due north. It also scans ninety degrees and overlaps camera number 'one' to provide full coverage. Number 'three' is on the northeast corner, faces north and also scans ninety degrees. The numbering system continues around the cottage ending at camera 'eight' on the southwest corner."

"What about cameras 'nine' and 'ten'? Where are they?"

"Look back at the boat house. Can you see the camera bubble mounted in the center just above the automatic door?"

"Yes, I do."

"That's camera number 'ten'. Camera 'nine' is over the front door. Watch! I'll key in camera 'ten' and 'presto' there we are in full living color on the screen. Isn't that neat?"

"It sure is, but how about the cat-woman? Does she have a monitor like this?"

"Of course. Plus, her master unit also controls the cameras inside the cottage."

"She's always watching isn't she?"

"She listens too."

"What do you mean she listens too?"

"The cameras are interactive and contain very sensitive, directional microphones that record audio from whatever the direction the camera is pointing towards. They are so sensitive that they can pick up the *'click'* of a cigarette lighter five hundred yards away."

"Wow!"

"Everything is recorded. Even what we are saying and doing now is going through the digital multiplexer, being recorded on a disk and can be reviewed at high speed. The digital camera can print out a color photo containing the frame number, the time and date in five seconds. It provides a permanent record.'

"I suppose that the next thing you are going to tell me is that she can talk to us through that thing in your hand."

"Yes. She can. It's a complex and very effective system. You can direct your own voice and image out of a 'high-definition' television monitor mounted next to any of the camera pods. Weatherproof microphones and speakers are mounted in strategic locations around the marina, driveway and the cottage in case you want to talk to someone on the grounds. Or, just listen in."

"Hello boys. Have a good trip and play good together. I've got to be in court in five minutes. Bye. Bye." Tina's voice came out of the plastic monitor in Dave's left hand.

CHAPTER

7

The 250-horsepower *YAMAHA* outboard purred softly as Dave guided the boat through North Lake at idle speed. The bow wave softly caressed the water sending a ripple towards the shoreline where it lapped softly and melted into the porous brown sand.

A female osprey whistled a shrill warning from her perch in an Australian pine tree and dove head first towards a school of finger mullet foraging in the shallows. At the very last second, she dropped her tail, flipped over and arrived talons down onto the back of a mullet just below the surface. Without breaking the momentum of her dive she swooped skyward with her wriggling six-inch silver catch firmly pinned in her talons.

"Isn't that amazing? *Mother Nature* at her best."

"You'll get used to it. Ospreys have been nesting in that Australian pine tree for at least fifty years. Next spring she'll have a pair of fuzzy chicks up there in her nest. Then you'll see her really hard at work feeding them - plus herself."

"Living in big cities for so many years I'd almost forgotten just how beautiful the natural environment can be. It'll take me some time to get used to it."

"You'll get used to it. Watch for her about five-thirty in the morning. She'll be waiting for Bear to come around *Hell's Gate*. The local folks refer to her as Bear's Bird."

"Why is that? It's a wild osprey isn't it?"

"He raised her from a chick. He found the mother hanging from a limb of her nesting tree in the North Fork. Monofilament fishing line was tangled around her feet and legs. She had been dead for several days and the two starving chicks were raising a ruckus. Bear couldn't climb the tree, but he teased this one into jumping down by tossing finger mullet up in the air. She wasn't feathered out and couldn't fly, but she must have been real hungry to jump fifty feet down into the water. He took the chick home and hand-fed her for weeks."

"What happened to the other chick?"

"It refused to budge from the nest and kept screaming its head off for its mother. Bear told me that several turkey buzzards attacked the chick and killed it after this one made its escape."

"That's horrible to imagine."

"Yes it is, but it's Mother Nature's way. Look at the positive side. This one was the boldest and the strongest. *Michi* endured Nature's gauntlet of survival and lived to pass on her genes."

"What do you mean, *Michi*? Is that her name?"

"Yes. Bear named her after a beautiful girl that he met during his recuperation in a hospital in Japan. She was strong, beautiful and free-spirited just like this osprey. The bird reminded him of the girl, so he named her *Michi*. As a chick she went along on his nightly fishing trips to the North Fork, sat on his shoulder and supervised his every move. Bear taught her how to fly by pushing her off the roof of his house just like a mother osprey would do in the wild. After she learned to fly and began fishing on her own she staked out that tree for her roost.

At dawn you can count on seeing her on her perch waiting for Bear to come by and toss her several finger mullet for breakfast. If he's late she gets anxious and takes off for the North Fork looking for him. After she finds him she'll raise hell with him for being late. But, they'll arrive back at the *Pocket* together in Bear's boat. She'll be sitting on his shoulder eating chunks of fresh mullet that he carefully slices off one at a time. That's the nice thing about *Martin County*. It's still pristine and relatively unspoiled by development. The chamber of commerce slogan is *'Enjoy Our Good Nature.'* Those of us who have lived here for many years dread the idea of sacrificing trees and open space for concrete and shingles. People come here because it is relatively undeveloped. After they get here they build houses, strip malls, self-storage units, gas stations and on it goes. Maybe we should erect blockades at the Georgia line and the Dade County line."

"When I was growing up in Fort Myers it had twenty thousand people. Now they have almost that many in one development."

"Mack. We can sit back and dream about how it used to be way back when, but keep in mind that our parents heard the same thing from their parents. We should take the time to enjoy what little bit of nature there is left and do our best to keep it this way as long as we can. Now, let's go for a boat ride and see what this baby will do." Dave shoved the throttle as far forward as it would travel and the boat leaped up on plane.

Spray flew into the air and slapped Mack across the face. He grabbed his hat with his left hand and held onto the seat with the right. "Going a tad fast aren't we? I think we passed *Mach One* and the speed of light."

"Nope. According to the speedometer we're cruising about forty-five and the tachometer is running at forty-five hundred rpm. Just perfect. I'll cut it back a little so I can point out a few things to you as we go along. You need a quick history lesson. Did you pick up those books on *Martin County* at the library?

"Yes. But, I haven't had a minute to look at any of them."

"I'll give you a fast history lesson. I'll turn around at the *Crossroads* and we'll head back up the *St. Lucie River* towards Stuart. The chart for this area is in the other cooler. Pull it out."

"Aren't you worried that it might get wet?"

"Nope. It's waterproof. So keep it out and pay attention. The *Manatee Pocket* is up ahead on the port side. There are several marinas, a big charter boat fleet and some excellent restaurants in there. Tina's favorite one is open air and sits right on the water."

"She didn't take me to a restaurant on the water. She took me to a fancy place with linen tablecloths, waiters wearing tuxes and the whole nine yards. We seemed to drive forever, although she drove like a race car driver and scared the hell out of me."

"Did she cross over two bridges to get there?"

"Yes, at about eighty-five miles an hour."

"Did she order *Absolut Vodka Gimlets* and threaten to revoke the bartender's probation?"

"Yep."

"I know exactly where you were. It's a fancy five star resort on *Hutchinson Island* with a lot more class than where you were last night. Before last night I didn't know that people could line dance in their bare feet. Everybody else was wearing cowboy boots and you almost lost your toes."

"I don't know how to line dance. I've never been in a country western place!"

"Oh no? What's that mark on the inside of your left wrist? It looks like a purple horseshoe."

"What the hell? How did I get that? Where was I last night?"

"That's a mark the *Silver Saddle* bar in Indiantown uses to let the doorman know that you can leave and come back in without paying a cover charge. Did you check your butt for a brand?"

"She's got some explaining to do when I see her! She drugged me. I know it!"

"So what are you going to do? Call the law? I don't think so. Don't worry. Be happy!"

"It wasn't fair. I was tired and she took advantage of my condition."

"It wasn't fair? Ha! It sure looked to me that you were having a good time. I didn't hear any protesting."

"How could I? I was out of it! *Ketamine Hydrochloride* makes you catatonic!"

"Stop bitching. You had a good time. The best part about it is that's you don't remember what you did and I'm sure as hell not going to tell anybody. It's embarrassing enough."

"What do you mean it's embarrassing? What did I do? Tell me. I have to know."

"Let's just say that if I were you I wouldn't go back to the *Silver Saddle* until things quiet down and people have a chance to forget. Considering the circumstances and what happened five years would be about right. I think that Tina talked the newspaper out of running the photos, but they still might run the story."

"What story?"

"Let's just say that it all started after you had your first ten *Tequila Sunrises* and decided to jump on the mechanical bull.

You did pretty well at first and held your own. Things really went downhill fast after it tossed you over the bar. You got pissed at the operator and spit on him. But, he's not going to press charges. Elmo, the Sheriff's Deputy that came out, is Tina's first cousin."

"Was I blasted out of my mind? She gave me drugs and Tequila together? What was she thinking?"

"Forget it. Let's get on with the tour. I heard that the trip back to Stuart was hilarious."

"What do you mean you hear? Where were you? If you were there why didn't you stop me from making a fool of myself?"

"I left about eleven-thirty. I'm no dumb boy! I know Tina."

"What did I do that was so hilarious? And, if you left so early how do you know what I did?"

"I saw the video tape that the deputy made of you and the bull with his patrol car camera. They were showing it on a monitor at the jail just after the seven o'clock shift change."

"What do you mean a video? How could the deputy get his patrol car inside a bar?"

"The video was shot in a cow pasture on Highway 714 just the other side of *Palm City*."

"A cow pasture? What was I doing in a cow pasture?"

"You called it 'cow tipping'. You said that you did it once after drinking all night with some charter boat captains in *Kewaunee, Wisconsin*. You said that the objective was to find a cow standing up deep asleep in a pasture, then run across the pasture at full tilt and try to knock it over with your shoulder. I guess that's late night entertainment in Wisconsin?"

"Yeah, I did that once and felt like crap for a week. I ripped my pants, lost a shoe and smelled like cow crap for a month afterwards. I swore never to do it again. Ever!"

"Then what do you suppose you insisted on doing on the way home last night when you saw a cow sleeping in a pasture?"

"Oh no! Not cow tipping! Who saw me? Please tell me that it wasn't the newspaper reporter?"

"The newspaper reporter wasn't there. Only Tina and her cousin Elmo, the deputy who shot the video, were the only eyewitnesses. But, there was a very interested reporter at the Sheriff's Department this morning watching the video. He didn't know who you are, and your face was in the shadows, but he said that he might write a *'human interest'* piece. The headline would no doubt read, *'Man tips over bull'* or perhaps *'Bull meets man.'* Something similar to that."

"What do you mean 'bull meets man'? Is that supposed to be a pun or something?"

"Well from what I hear, and this is only hearsay, because I wasn't there. You spotted a cow standing up in the pasture and insisted that Tina let you out so that you could show her how to tip it over with your shoulder. You managed to get over the barbed wire fence after ripping the seat out of your pants and took off running across the pasture. When you hit the cow, or bull, as we now know it to have been, you bounced off and landed on your butt in a big, fresh, juicy cow pie. I reckon you pissed him off because he knocked you thirty feet across the pasture with his head. Fortunately for you he had been dehorned and only had short stubs on his head for horns."

"You have to be pulling my leg. Tell me that you are joking."

"Okay, if that's what you want. I'm joking. But, there's a copy of the tape on top of the television set at the cottage. The video, there was sound with it, shows you running across that pasture as fast as your legs would go. You were screaming like a goosed goat! When you hit the fence, you bounced back like a paddleball right back into the bull. He flipped you *'ass over tea kettle'* over his head and caught you on top of his back. You wound up facing his butt and grabbed his tail for support. You pulled his tail up over his back and 'yanked' on it real hard.

That really got his attention! He took off running full blast and cleared the top of the fence by five feet. You were hanging on for dear life and jerking that bull's tail as hard as you could. His tail was flopping sideways so badly that I figured that you had broken it clean off and that only the skin was holding it on.

When the bull hit the roadside drainage canal water flew over the road clean across to the other side. You flew over the bull's head and landed five feet deep into a compost pile beside the road. They took so much time digging you out of that compost pile that the bull drowned. The ambulance driver said that if the deputy hadn't done mouth-to-mouth CPR on you that you would have died. That's all that happened. It was really nothing to write home about. I'd call it a normal night in Martin County."

"Is there going to be no end to my torment? What have I done to deserve this?"

"Just lucky I guess. Remember she's coming back tomorrow night. Lucky you!"

"Can you hide me out somewhere? I'll pay you anything. Name your price!"

"You don't have enough money and this is fun. The entrance to *Willoughby Creek* is coming up on the left. Its great snook fishing there on an outgoing tide during a full moon. There's *North Lake, Point Sewell* and the marina. I've still got 'camera ten' locked in on the monitor and we're looking good Smile!"

"You really do enjoy this, don't you?"

"Yep, guess I do. Now let's get back to your orientation. On your left is a house that *Al Capone* used when he was not in Miami. His boats brought booze across from the Bahamas, through the *St. Lucie Inlet* right up to *Willoughby Creek*. They unloaded their cargo right here. After unloading they ran down the coast and checked in with US Customs at West Palm Beach.

On your right is *Sewell's Point*. Years ago, when *Stuart* was still called *Potsdam*, the Post Office was located on the end of a long wooden pier that stuck off the end of the point. The mail boats pulled up there and dropped off the incoming mail and pick up the outgoing. After the end of WW II *General Douglas MacArthur* was given several acres of land right over there, but after a few months decided that it reminded him to much of the Philippines and he left. Some very famous families live on *Sewell's Point* and they rightfully prefer to remain very low-key.

"Who are they? Can you give me some names?"

"Nope, that's part of your research and why you got the books from the library. Now we're coming up to the *Evans Crary Bridge*. That old, iron bascule drawbridge will most likely be replaced by a high, arched modern concrete bridge in a few years. I really hate to see history disappear like that.

Look straight ahead and to the right and you'll see what appears to be a big sand dune. It's the highest point in *Martin County* and has some interesting history behind it. Back in the

1700's pirate ships sailed up the St. Lucie River and anchored just off the hill. They washed their ship's sails in the fresh water and spread them on the sandy hill to dry. The old pirate maps call it *'Ye Olde Bleache Yard.'*

Back in the early 1900's there was a commercial fish house on the other side of the hill and their loading dock stuck out into the river. The boats unloaded their fish on the dock. But, to get them over the hill they had to pay a ten-cent toll to the operator of a donkey tram who had a set of rails running over the hill. That's how it got the name *'Ten Cent Hill'*.

"You seem to know quite a bit about the area. I'm impressed."

"Don't be impressed. I've lived here for quite awhile and did my research. Now it's your turn. On your left is *Wood's Point*. That cove offers an excellent view of the traffic going up and down the river. There are some more places further upriver that I want to show you. Hang on to your hat. It's going to be windy. Here we go!" Dave shoved the throttle forward. The boat leaped out of the water like a porpoise after a school of mullet.

The wind stung Mack's face and his eyes watered. The boat skimmed over the water like it was rocket propelled. Mack glanced at the speedometer. It read fifty-two mph. He wanted to plead with Dave to slow down, but when he opened his mouth to breath the wind caught his lower lip and tried to pull it over his chin. He prayed silently that they wouldn't hit something hidden below the water and drown.

Dave pulled back on the throttle and the boat settled back in the water at idle speed. He pointed to a white building. "That four story white building off the port side is *Martin Memorial Hospital*. It makes a good landmark when you are running the river at night. Straight ahead is downtown Stuart. The large white water tower is also a good landmark. *City Hall* is straight ahead just beyond that wooden pier. When you run this area in the dark keep well to the north because of those pilings sticking out of the water. A sandbar runs north and south parallel to the *Roosevelt Bridge*. It's not marked on the south side, but there's a wooden 'dolphin' with a green flashing light on the north end. At high tide you can run over it at full plane if you trim the motor up a little. The depth of water over the bar averages less than a foot at low tide. Be very careful."

"Why should I ever be up here at night?"

There are two possible reasons. The snook fishing is best at night and the old *Roosevelt Bridge* is a *'honey hole'* for monster snook. The most important reason is because the people we are trying to catch run through here only at night. That's why you are going to be a fishing guide. You can sit here all night fishing without causing any suspicion. But, it's crucial that you know where your boat can go and where it can't. It would be extremely embarrassing to rip the lower unit off an outboard engine at three o'clock in the morning. Especially if someone with a gun is chasing you."

"What do you mean we are trying to catch? Do you have a mouse in your pocket?

"Why do you think we went to so much trouble to get you here? You were Tina's first choice. Of course, we had to sanitize you with the fake death, new identity and all."

"I need to understand what's going on. You almost had me killed, made me run for my life and faked my murder to get me here. I was Tina's first choice? That doesn't make sense."

"Sure it does. You got through to some of the biggest dealers in the Midwest. They didn't suspect you for a minute. A lot of them were put away because of your information. You were so convincing that when the 'big boys' got the word that the cops were going to 'whack' you for double-crossing them they wanted to throw a dinner party for you. But, someone 'dropped a dime' and let it out that you were a government informant and they wanted to 'whack' you themselves. Both the cops and the mob were after you. That's why you had to disappear the way you did.

The cops are happy because they think that the mob 'whacked' you. The mob is happy because they think the cops did it. Everyone is happy except the over zealous trooper who wound up in Lake Michigan. But, that's life in the big city."

"So, you have a problem that you can't solve. But, why me?"

"Well, let me count the ways. You have experience in intelligence, counter intelligence, electronics, explosives, drug interdiction, self-defense, fire arms, speak fluent Spanish and grew up in Florida. There must be a few more that I forgot. Oh, and Tina likes you."

"So. What else?"

"There isn't anywhere else that you can go other than here without the risk of being identified. The right people think that you're dead. Let's leave it that way. Plus, you are still on Uncle Sam's payroll. This is an assignment, not a retirement position."

"You aren't subtle in the least. Guess I don't have any other choice than to play ball."

"I don't have to be subtle. Now let's talk 'brass tacks'. That's the *Roosevelt Bridge*. The only way to get from the St. Lucie Inlet to the *North Fork* is by going under it. There is a tender in that little house twenty-four hours a day. They open the bridge on demand for boats that can't fit under the draw."

"What's the *North Fork* and why is it important?"

"Cocaine is coming from the Bahamas at night in a mother ship, transferred to high speed powerboats at a rendezvous point offshore and brought through the St. Lucie Inlet. We suspect that's it's stashed, awaiting distribution, between Jupiter and Stuart. We feel that it's being ferried to Port St. Lucie at night via high-speed boat. It's flown out the next day from Fort Pierce by private plane to Atlanta where it's transferred to private aircraft going to New York and Chicago."

"If you know that much why can't you catch them?"

"We don't know who, where and when. But, we have suspicions and need verification."

"How did you get that much information?"

"Several sources. Bear and Ralph are commercial fishermen and they spend a lot of time on the water at night. They reported seeing black speedboats, without any navigation lights showing, running up and down the river well after midnight. Bear's had several encounters with them in the *North Fork* because they ran into his nets and got their props fouled. They threatened to shoot him if he continues netting in the *North Fork* and getting in their way. But, he's stubborn as a mule, or should I say Bear?"

"What about local law enforcement? Where do they fit in?"

"Not much of anywhere. They don't have much in the way of resources or manpower. We are treating this as a Federal case because the cocaine is coming from a foreign country into the

United States and crossing state lines for distribution. Also, it's being moved between counties. This makes it difficult to coordinate all of the local agencies. Customs and DEA are also out of the loop - at least for now. The Florida Department of Law Enforcement has an undercover agent assigned to the project. But, we don't know who it is. Any more questions?"

"Was anyone else working the case before me?"

"That's the other thing that I wanted to talk to you about. I'll pull into *Shepherd's Park* and we'll talk. We might see Rat. He sleeps all day and prowls at night. That's his sailboat over there. It's the red and white one with the mast lying on top of the cabin. It hasn't moved since he pulled it in here and dropped anchor after *Hurricane Andrew* blew through in nineteen ninety-two."

"What does Rat do for a living? He has to work somewhere doesn't he?"

"Work? Don't make any rash assumptions about Rat working. I've heard about it, but haven't actually seen him working. He washes dishes for change, lives off what he scrapes off of dinner plates and does some dumpster diving. His forte' is *road kill!*"

"Road kill! You must be joking. Nobody eats road kill!"

"Rat does. We're here. This is *Shepherd's Park* - home of Rat. Grab the wall, wrap the front line around the cleat, run a couple of figure eights and tie it with a half hitch. I'll get the back one. "

"Why do they call it *Shepherd's Park*? Did they raise sheep here or something?"

"A good question. In 1923 William Shepherd and his wife Lucy moved here from Cleveland. They built a home here on seven acres and called it *South Harbor*. When their estate was settled in 1943 it became Shepherd's Park."

"That's interesting. I've got much more Martin County 'homework' to do. I have a quiz on Saturday."

"Let's sit on that bench and talk. It's wide open all around it, we can see people coming and no one can hear us. Shoot me your questions. I'll do my best."

"Was anyone else working the case before me?"

"That's a tough question and it deserves an answer. Yes."

"That's not an answer! Who was it? Where are they now?"

"No it wasn't, but I answered it correctly. As for your follow-up question - I can't tell you who it was and I don't know where they are. They're just gone."

"Were they killed? Were they assigned somewhere else? Maybe to my job in Chicago?"

"We don't know what happened to him. He was here one day and gone the next. Did notice that there was an open slip on the sailboat pier at the marina?"

"Yes, but I didn't think anything of it. I figured that the boat was out for the day."

"That was his boat, or at least the one assigned to him for the case. He was a '*rag bagger*' and as curious as a cat at heart. That might have been his downfall."

"Why?"

"He had a tip that a 'shipment' was coming over from the Bahamas. Most likely he sailed offshore to wait at the rendezvous' point and be there when the drop was made. He figured that he could use night vision lenses and watch the deal going down. But, he didn't tell us when, or where, so we couldn't provide backup. He liked to sail at night so nobody thought anything about it when his boat was not in its slip the next morning. After three days we scrambled a Coast Guard search and rescue crew out of Miami. They didn't even find a life ring.

The Gulf Stream sets due north at about three knots an hour. If you fall overboard in the stream - in twenty-four hours you'll be seventy-five miles away. In three days you're gone.

"Where was he living?"

"At *Port Sewell Marina*. He lived in the cottage."

"Do you think that he was 'made' as an agent and whacked?"

"No. He was in the wrong place at the wrong time and they didn't want any witnesses."

"How long ago was that?"

"Last week. We reported him missing last Wednesday morning. They gave up the search and rescue mission Friday afternoon. Tina called for a replacement on Saturday."

"They called me in for a dinner meeting on Sunday afternoon. That was touch and go!"

"I know. It was even hard for me to make conversation at the bar with the two 'almost literate' goombas for an hour."

"You were there? Baloney! I didn't see you! You're pulling my leg aren't you?"

"Nope. Didn't you notice the good-looking bartender? Before I got to the restaurant I stopped by your place and packed your suitcase to save you some time. I followed you home in the truck and even brought you a change of clothes. I guess that I'm not appreciated."

"You're the one who told the security guard to give me ten minutes?"

"Guilty as charged."

"You baited the trooper with the Porsche to get him off my tail and whacked him?"

"Guilty as charged. Well, almost. I take the Fifth on whacking the trooper."

"You were the trooper in Georgia who woke me up?"

"Guilty as charged."

"Where was the trooper? Did you whack him too?"

"Naw. He was my cousin. I gave him a hundred bucks to use his patrol car. He picked it up at the Florida line."

"How about Lafayette, Indiana? Were you there too?"

"I was in the next room. I was driving the state trooper's car."

"How did you find me?"

"That was easy. The blue pickup truck has a GPS tracking transmitter connected to the CB antenna. You couldn't have talked to a trucker if you had tried. Plus, you had an agent in an eighteen wheeler on your 'donkey' from the time you got on I-95. He never left your back door open an inch."

"You win. Tell me about Tina, Rat, Bear and Ralph and anyone else in the menagerie."

"There's not much to tell you about Tina. She told you just about everything. But, she most likely left out that her first husband was killed in Laos. He was a member of an extraction team and got caught in ambush. She doesn't like to talk about it."

"She told me that she was divorced twice and that both of her husbands were drunks."

"Effectively divorced twice. But, in reality only once."

"What do you mean by in reality once?".

"Call it twenty-five years of denial. Her first husband was her high school sweetheart. She was the head cheerleader and he was the captain of the football team. After graduating from Martin County High School they went to Florida State. After graduation he enlisted in the Air Force and got involved in covert operations in Southeast Asia - Laos mostly. She took an internship with the CIA in DC so that she could track his movements."

"How could she track his movements?"

"He was tagged with a microchip transmitter that sent a homing signal to a satellite."

"She was in the CIA? She told me that she interviewed with the CIA, but conveniently left out the part about being hired. Just wait until I see her again."

"She wasn't hired by the CIA as an employee - she was an unpaid intern. No doubt she left out a few other things as well, but she might tell you more when she's ready."

"What happened to him?"

"On his last mission into Laos his team was ambushed and he was captured. Satellite photographs located the compound where he was being held captive. A scouting team found four American prisoners detained in the camp. They were kept in bamboo 'tiger cages' tied off to trees and submerged in a river. A rescue attempt was made when the main contingent of troops from the camp was on a raid into South Viet Nam. It failed miserably.

The rescue team didn't realize that the each cage was booby-trapped with a delicate trigger that would release the cage into the river if it was touched. All of the cages slipped into the river before anyone could get a line on them. Three of them were swept downstream by the current. The fourth cage caught on a tree limb sticking out from the riverbank and the man in it was rescued. The last man out of the compound snatched a box from the headquarters hut that contained the men's personal effects."

"Tina told me that her husbands were drunks and that she divorced both of them."

"A true case of denial. Neither of them was a drunk. I just told you about number one."

"Why would she mislead me like that?"

"In her mind she did divorce both of them. If you go to the Martin County Court House you will find uncontested divorce papers filed against each husband. There was no response to either of them and the divorces were automatically granted. That's her escape from reality."

"Is she nuts?"

"She's perfectly sane. But, aren't we all just a little bit nuts? She's had a very hard life with her parents being killed in a car accident and all. Plus, losing both husbands."

"What do you mean losing both husbands? You just told me that she divorced them."

"I can't address that - I'll leave it up to her. Let me finish filling you in on the details of her first husband's capture and the rescue raid that went bad. He was on an extraction mission to capture some village officials that were suspected as being collaborators and bring them to a Provincial Interrogation Center for questioning. Her husband and three others were captured and tortured. The others were killed, beheaded and their heads pointed on poles overlooking their decapitated bodies."

"How do you know this?"

"High resolution satellite photos. You don't think that it's new technology do you?"

"I did - until now."

"The pre-dawn rescue mission was carried out by two eight man teams dropped into positions up and downstream of the camp by helicopter. Each team launched an RB-8. That's rubber boat, eight-man, in military lingo. They attacked simultaneously from upstream and downstream. Two Huey choppers stood by five miles away until the all clear was given to come in and pick them up. There was minor resistance because the camp's main force was on a raid ten miles away. They came running back when they heard gunfire, but it was too late. Our team had fired their huts and was in the air on their way back to base.

The team couldn't bring back the bodies because of the state of decomposition. Only one man came out alive. That was you. Tina's husband was in one of the cages that sank. She wears his identifying One Rand coin on her right wrist. Didn't you see it?"

"I saw something dangling on a chain on her right wrist when we were at dinner, but I thought that it was just a lucky charm."

"That little coin is much more than a lucky charm to her. All of her hopes, dreams, fears and loves are embodied in that single coin. It's all that she has left of her husband."

"Was her husband one of my team members?"

"No. He was part of an earlier team that was captured before you. Three of your team members and yourself survived the attack. Bear was a member of the team that brought you out. He doesn't know that you were the man saved. It's better that he doesn't know because two of his buddies were killed during the raid on the compound. Because you grew up with him in Fort Myers it could be very traumatic for him."

"I can't wait until I see him and kick around old times."

"He doesn't need to know about the rescue. Let that be! He's messed up enough as it is. After he came back he spent several months recuperating in the West Palm Veterans' Hospital. He doesn't talk about what he did and saw in Southeast Asia. He has blanked it out of his mind like a bad dream and it needs to be left that way, at least for now."

"What about Rat?"

"I almost forgot. The rescue team also snatched up a man who had escaped from the camp several months before and had been living in the jungle. The 'Charlies' didn't try to catch him because they figured he had gone nuts and wouldn't bother them. That man was Rat. He was a 'tunnel rat' in Nam and that's how he got his name. I don't know the details, but after his capture he was tortured for days. He escaped and was found hiding in a tunnel in the jungle by the rescue team that brought you out.

He doesn't know who you are and I suggest that you keep it that way. He is one messed up boy! Play it cool if he gets on the subject of Southeast Asia. We are concerned that he could go postal one of these days."

"What about Ralph, the commercial fisherman?"

"His is a truly sad story. Ralph and his brother received their draft notices on the same day. When they went for their physicals Ralph was rejected because he is almost blind in his left eye. When he was a kid he got hit in that eye by a fishing weight thrown by his brother. It broke his heart that he couldn't go because they were very close. He stayed home to watch over the family and try to eke out a living from the water.

His brother volunteered for Special Forces. He was assigned to one of the first Studies and Observation Group teams to enter Laos in 1963 on rescue attempts to get our pilots out of the prison camps. He was reported as missing in action and presumed dead after a routine patrol was ambushed. None of his team members made it back to base camp. Rumor is that they were captured and tortured for several days before they died.

"How about Mel, the 'narc'? Where does he fit in all of this?"

"His brother is the agent that is missing. You replaced him."

"How about you? You seem to be running the show. Where do you fit in?"

"I'm not running the show. I'm just a coordinator."

"Were you in the military in Southeast Asia?"

"I wasn't in the military, but I was in Southeast Asia. I was a civilian employee of *Air America* and assigned to *Udorn Air Force Base* to develop a satellite photo-recon program. Later I was sent to *Long Chien* in northern Laos to help coordinate the establishment of the *Provincial Interrogation Centers*. We called them *PICs*. After that I was assigned to Saigon and helped to set up the *National Identification Card Project*. Every South Vietnamese over the age of fifteen was required to carry one of our ID cards. The motivation was simple. If they were stopped, and didn't have an ID Card with them – they were assumed to be North Vietnamese infiltrators and they could be executed on the spot. No questions asked.

"Don't you see how all of this fits together? All of us, Tina, Ralph, Bear, Rat, you and me have links to one another."

"Dave, where are you really from? What's your background? Where do you fit in this whole mess?"

"My vital statistics are obvious to the astute observer. I'm fifty-four years old, stand six feet two inches tall and weigh two hundred and sixty-five pounds. My thick, blonde hair is slowly turning a distinguished gray at the temples and over my ears. My hair is why some of my jealous friends call me *'Thatch.'* I'm in perfect health and don't smoke, but I do drink a *Brandy Manhattan* once in awhile. I play tennis and golf as you can tell by my tan. I enjoy *Bach* and *Beethoven* and read *Hemingway* when I want to relax.

I've never been married and don't plan to take the plunge. Life is too much fun this way. Plus, there are a lot of single women out there who need affection and a shoulder to cry on once in awhile. I'm an excellent listener and can make myself available on a moment's notice. I like to dress well and enjoy good food as my waistline demonstrates.

I was born in Sturgeon Bay, Wisconsin and attended *Yale* on a tennis scholarship. I dropped out of law school to join *Air America* in 1961 for excitement. My father founded an electronics manufacturing company in the 1940's. Uncle Sam is our best customer. I live in *Eagle Creek* in Palm City. It's a small, gated community off Highway 714. I don't need a paying job because my trust funds and endowments take care of me. I think that I covered everything. Any questions?"

"Where do you fit in?"

"As I told you. I'm just a 'coordinator'. I make all of the pieces fit together. Tell me what you want, how many, what color and when you want it. I'll see that it's delivered to your front door within twenty-four hours. I'm a good guy to know." I have a few contacts here and there that I can call if you need assistance.

"I can tell. I'm a bit overwhelmed. Anything 'special' that I should know about the area?

"Yes. When you get back to the marina take out a Florida map, study where we are and consider why we are here. Stuart is strategically located on the Eastern side of the Florida peninsula thirty miles north of West Palm Beach. It's an excellent location because the Orlando and Miami International Airports, and a flight to anywhere in the world, are only a two-hour drive away. Cape Kennedy's resources are sixty-five miles north of here. A lot of things take place at there that the public has no clue about. 'Joe Public' thinks of it as a rocket launching and space technology center. Did you ever hear the analogy, *'Make it so obvious that no one can see it'*, or *don't try to hide it or they'll find it for sure*. Or, how about, *people can't see the forest because the trees get in the way?"*

"Yes. I understand. Say no more."

"Good. Untie the lines and we'll get on with our tour. First, we'll make a swing down the South Fork to the *St. Lucie Locks*.

There aren't very many places down here that someone in a boat can go and not be seen. Plus, it's a dead end. Only one way in and one way back out."

"Where does that cut east of red marker number forty go?"

"On a long, winding, meandering route down the South Fork to the *Humpback Bridge*. Boats much over eighteen-feet can't get under the bridge. Mack, I've decided not to take the time to go all the way to the locks. I'm turning around and we'll run up the North Fork. Hang onto your hat." Dave pushed the throttle forward and the 250-horsepower super-charged outboard roared to life. The boat skimmed over the surface of the water so fast that it seemed to Mack that only the engine was in the water. Dozens of silver mullet leaped into the air ahead of the boat as if to take a peek at the crazed occupants of the speeding boat. Dave appeared to be lecturing him, at least his mouth was moving, but the roar of the super-charged air passing by Mack's ears made it impossible for him to hear anything.

Mack's eyes watered, an unidentifiable liquid ran out of his nostrils, rolled down the sides of his face and skipped off his cheeks into the wind. The boat whistled past a trailer park and rounded the curve into a straightaway. Dave pointed the bow at the center of the fifty-four foot high arch of the *Palm City Bridge* like it was a guided missile. When the boat reached the twin sets of black, creosote soaked, wooden pilings marking each side of the bridge opening Dave throttled back so fast that Mack's head and neck couldn't keep up with the rest of his body.

"Dave, slow down! I think I have whiplash. Don't you know any speed in between 'stop' and 'supersonic'?"

"Mack. Stop your whining and wipe the 'snot' off the side of your face. It's not very becoming."

"Why did you finally slow down? Where are we going now?"

"Why do you ask so many questions? The next thing that I expect you ask me is how high is up? I slowed down because the Marine Patrol and Sheriff's Marine Units patrol both sides of this bridge. It's an easy way for them to write tickets. I don't need to get their attention and neither do you. You'll meet them soon enough. We're going to have lunch at a little restaurant that sits over the water. You can cook your own steak on the grill just the way you like it. After lunch we're going for a ride up the North Fork. Okay Mack. Hang on tight! Here we go again!"

After the boat passed under the bridge and cleared the 'no wake' zone Dave shoved the throttle forward as far as it would go. The boat leaped forward so fast that Mack's plea for 'mercy' was left hanging in the air. He had no choice except to hang on and hope that the testosterone charged 'wannabe' jet pilot knew where he was going and could see to navigate between the channel markers at a speed of *Mach One*.

CHAPTER

8

After they had finished lunch Dave continued the tour by taking Mack up the *North Fork* of the *St. Lucie River* and pointing out the most relevant features of the waterway.

"That's *Dyer's Point* on the left. A couple of those docks have a light shining on the water all night long. There're great spots to catch snook, if you use a white, feathered jig head. *Light House Point* and *Sea Gate Harbor* are a little further up. They each have their own entrances and a maze of canals leads deep into the development. They're a good place to slip into if you are being followed. Watch out for the gators and stay out of the water at night. A few years ago a gator dragged a boy right off the canal bank in back of his house."

"No way! This is the twentieth century and not the jungle."

"It's apparent that you don't watch very many television news programs, or keep up with current events around the world. Riots, kidnappings and murders are out of control. I dare say that we are far less- civilized today than we were one hundred years ago. At least back then, you could shoot a thief in your home without being sued for violating his civil rights.

If we were to go back to hanging murderers and thieves within twenty-four hours of being convicted I'm certain that our crime rate would drop significantly. Plus, if we cut the balls off of rapists women would feel a lot safer. Sure, we might make a mistake once in awhile and that's to be expected. But, the jails wouldn't be as full and we wouldn't need as many lawyers, or judges either, for that matter. Plus, our taxes would go down significantly. It would be savings all the way around, plus the crime rates would drop."

"I assume that you are for capital punishment?"

"Of course, but I'd drop the electric chair. It uses too much electricity I favor drawing and quartering criminals in the public square in front of the courthouse. It's fast and there wouldn't be as many last minute appeals to waste taxpayers' money."

"Were you a judge in the *Inquisition* in a prior life?"

"I think so. Hang on tight. Here we go!"

The boat was going so fast that Mack couldn't do anything except hang onto the seat and watch the trees along the shore melt into a green blur. There was no seat belt to hold him in place if Dave hit something. Mack wondered, *"How far will my body fly through the air before it hits the water. Will it hurt very much to die that way? Will I drown, or will the impact kill me?"* At last, and not a minute to soon for Mack, Dave finally throttled back and allowed the boat to settle in the water. Mack was ecstatic. He could still breathe, see and even hear Dave talking to him. At least he didn't die and wasn't maimed for life.

"Here we are. This is the North Fork. That point on the left is called *Fork Point*, some charts refer to it as *Coon Point*, is actually an island that separates the North Fork from *Kitching Cove*. About a mile up river there's a narrow, mangrove-lined channel that separates them. Only very small boats can squeeze through it. On your right is *Club Med* and straight ahead is *Kitching Cove*. Do you see that cove on the left just behind those mangrove and Brazilian pepper trees? You can slip in there, anchor up in the mangroves and nobody would be able to see you. My little brother's body was found there about a year ago."

"What do you mean your brother's body was found there?"

"A sport fisherman found his body floating beside his boat. It was tangled in a gillnet."

"What happened to him?"

"No one knows for certain. If they do, they aren't talking. The coroner's report said that he fell overboard, hit his head, got tangled up in his net and drowned. I don't think so. I suspect that someone figured that he had seen too much and that he might talk to the wrong people."

"What makes you think that he was killed and didn't just fall overboard and drown?"

"He was an excellent swimmer and the water where they found him was only three feet deep. If he fell overboard he could have just stood up and walked to shore. Plus, his arms were run straight through the mesh of the gill net. His hands had to have been forced through with the fingers held together because the mesh of a gillnet is smaller than the width of a hand."

"What was he doing up here anyway?"

"He was a commercial fisherman. Because he was up here fishing almost every night the Florida Department of Law Enforcement asked him to report any suspicious activity that he observed. They suspected that drugs were being run up this way by small boat. The day before they found his body he told me that a black boat ran south through the backside of the island about eleven-thirty every night and came back the other way about five in the morning. He thought that it was strange because the boat didn't show it's red and green navigation lights and was always going like a 'bat out of hell' when it passed by him."

"Were there any signs of a struggle?"

"Not that you could tell. But, he had a good-sized knot on the back of his head. The coroner felt that he slipped and hit his head on the side of the boat when he fell."

"If he fell out of the boat face first wouldn't the knot be on the front, or the side of his face, rather than the back of his head?"

"That is logical isn't it? I figure that someone snuck up on him in a canoe, or kayak, belted him on the head with a club and held him under water until he drowned. Then forced his hands and arms through the net mesh and left him floating beside his boat."

"What did the FDLE do about it?"

"Nothing. They won't even admit that they asked him to watch the area. Case closed."

"What are you doing about it?"

"Just watching and waiting. They'll make a mistake. That's why you're here."

"What am I supposed to do that you can't?"

"Watch them, wait for them to make a mistake and nail them to the wall. Most everyone around here knows me by sight. But they don't know you - at least not yet. You'll nail them sure. I have a lot of confidence in you. But, I want to be there when they go down. He was my brother."

"If I can do it - you've got it!"

"Let's take a ride up the back channel to *River Gate Park*. We think that they launch a boat off a trailer there, run down river and make the pickup somewhere between *Stuart* and *Jupiter* or *Stuart* and *Fort Pierce*. Here we go. Hang on tight!"

Dave shoved the throttle full forward, the boat surged ahead, then careened sharply to the right, straightened out and headed directly for a group of mangrove trees that spanned across a narrow opening that didn't seem to go anywhere. The narrow channel appeared to be all of six feet wide from mangrove root to mangrove root. But, that didn't slow Dave down in the least. Branches slapped Mack across the face and he threw his arms up for protection. Leaves and bits of branches covered the bottom of the boat, but Dave didn't seem to mind. It was Mack's boat and he could clean it up later.

A fork in the channel appeared ahead and Dave made a sharp turn to the right throwing water spray several feet into the air. Then he made a sharp cut to the left and throttled the engine back to idle speed. "We have to take it slow here. There's a very low bridge around the bend and there's usually a few people fishing off of it. You don't want a fish hook in your head do you?"

"No thanks. Isn't this channel awfully narrow? Are you certain that the water is deep enough to float this boat?"

"Let's see. According to this fancy digital depth finder there's nine feet of water here. This boat will float in nine inches of water if you raise the engine up. Don't worry. Be happy."

"I see the bridge. Hey, it's really low. Are you certain that we can get under it?"

"Yes. I checked out the clearance myself at high tide before Tina selected this boat. But, you'd better duck because we didn't account for your extra body height in the calculations!"

"Thanks a bunch."

"You're welcome. Locals call this the *'007 Bridge'* because a couple of *James Bond* movies were filmed here. They mounted cameras on the bridge to take shots of the boats speeding up and down the river. Once we get out from under the bridge there's a 'no wake' area for a mile or so. I'll have to take it slow for a while. Then, we'll be at *River Gate Park*."

"That's fine with me and my stomach. It needs some quiet time to crawl back down from my throat. What's at *River Gate Park*?"

"It's has several public boat launching ramps. We figure that they launch their boat from here because it's close to where they live. When they get here they load their boat on the trailer, jump in their vehicle and 'boogie' down the road for home."

"If you know so much, why haven't you caught them?"

"It's not my job, or yours either. The apprehension of suspects in a criminal investigation is the role of local law enforcement. Our role is only to document any suspected criminal activity that we observe and use it to develop evidence for use in prosecuting the case. When the time is right, the evidence will be submitted to a Federal Judge for review and the issuance of Federal warrants for suspect apprehension.

The 'take down' raid will be coordinated between the local law enforcements agencies for maximum media exposure. Our little group will stay in the background when the actual bust goes down. We'll feed them whatever information we can to strengthen their case, but we'll fade away as the case nears the trial stage. However, we do not want to be involved in court hearings, depositions or trials. That could compromise our position in the community as normal citizens and place some of us in jeopardy. Especially you! Do you understand? *Kapish*?"

"I suppose that I do. But, I thought that you wanted to be in on the bust because of what happened to your brother?"

"I do and I will. You'll see to that. The local law enforcement agencies will be very buy somewhere else. They'll be notified just a little too late to do much except pick up the pieces and take the credit for the bust. Understand? *Kapish*?"

"Yes, I understand completely."

"Mack. Look to your right. Do you see what looks to be an opening in the bushes?"

"Yes. So what?"

"That's the entrance to *River Gate Park* and the boat ramps. I'll run down past the ramps so that you can 'eyeball' the place and then I'll turn around. There's a set of color photos of the area, including aerial shots, waiting for you back at the marina. Plus, a video tape."

"It looks to me like you have almost everything scoped out. You are thorough."

"Not almost everything. Everything! But keep in mind that I'm only a coordinator. I provide you with the tools and resources to do the job. You're the *'mechanic'* in this caper." Dave passed the launching ramps and continued up the waterway to the low overpass under *Midport Road*. When he reached the overpass, he swung the boat around sharply and reversed course back toward the launching ramps and the entrance to the *North Fork*.

The trip back down the *North Fork* to *Port Sewell Marina* was at a speed that could only be described as 'balls to the wall'. Mack hung onto the seat with white-knuckled hands and blinked away the tears streaming down his face from his violated eye sockets. Mucous flowed from his nostrils and flew off the side of his face into the void of the violent air stream ripping at his fiber. He wanted to scream at the top of his lungs, but he felt that if he opened his mouth that his lips would be ripped loose from his face and join the mucous-filled air stream behind the boat.

When they finally exited the 'whirling vortex' and the boat slowed down, Mack slowly opened his eyes, but without loosening his 'death grip' on the seat. His face felt like it was on fire from windburn. Mucous from his nose ran down his chin onto his pants. His eyes ran like they were staring down a gigantic Bermuda onion and his lips were numb. Through the veil of mist blurring his vision he made out the Australian pine that stood as a silent sentinel at the entrance to *Port Sewell Marina*.

"Mack. We made it back in record time. It only took us fourteen minutes to make the eleven miles from *River Gate Park* to the marina. Not bad. Are you okay? You look terrible. What's that stuff running out of your nose? Are you feeling bad?"

"I'm fine. Give me a couple of hours in a decompression chamber and I'll be good as new."

"Mack. I was really worried about you. I suppose that I might have been going a little too fast. You should have hunkered down behind the windshield like I did. That would have kept you out of the wind."

"Hunker down my ass! You fat *turd*! How could I hunker down if I couldn't move? You exceeded the 'speed of sound' by at least a factor of two. You scared the crap out of me!"

"I'm sorry. I should have been more considerate. It's your boat and I should have let you drive. I'll be more careful the next time we go out."

"There won't be a next time *'bourbon breath'*. Our dual joy-riding days are over. From now on I drive if, and that's a very big if, we go anywhere together by boat. Understood? *Kapish*?"

"Yes. Mack. You have a right to be upset. I apologize. But, at least we're back safe and sound. It's only three-thirty. You still have time to clean up the boat before it gets dark."

"What do you mean that I have time to clean up the boat? You made the mess!"

"It's your boat. Hit the garage door opener and I'll pull her into the boathouse. After I leave rinse it down with the hose. The leaves and dirt will run out the scuppers and the automatic bilge pumps will pump it dry. Connect those metal hooks to the rings on the bow and stern then lift it out of the water with the power davit. She'll air-dry in an hour and be clean as a whistle when you are ready to go again. I've got to run. Got an appointment."

After 'Thatch' left, Mack rinsed off the boat, raised it on the davits and left it suspended three feet above the water. He pushed the 'down' button on the master control unit and the boathouse door slid in place with only a whisper. He slunk up the wooden stairs to the marina cottage, turned the nail head over the front door so that it pointed 'down' and went inside. He slipped off his deck shoes and slid into one of the inviting green recliners. The room was spinning around him, his face burned and his nose was still dripping yellow mucous down his chin. He was too tired to care and fell asleep.

BRRRING BRRRING BRRRING

Mack shook his head, opened his eyes, tried to get his bearings and identify the shrill noise coming from behind him.

BRRRING BRRRING BRRRING

He twisted around, saw the green telephone mounted on the kitchen wall, but he couldn't reach it from the chair. He tried to get up, caught his foot on the chair's footrest, took a 'header' onto the wooden floor and crawled into the kitchen on his elbows and knees. He raised himself up to counter level on his knees and managed to reach the handset with his left hand while holding onto the counter top with the right.

"Hello?"

"Mack. It's Ralph. What cha' doing for dinner?"

"Ralph? The commercial fisherman at the restaurant."

"Right. You sound really tired. 'Thatch' said that he rode you hard today. How about coming over to our house for dinner? We're having *snowy grouper*. I caught it this afternoon bottom fishing off *Push Button Hill*. It's real tasty and we've got plenty"

"Sure, I'd like that. Ralph. I fell asleep in the chair and I'm a little groggy. What time is it?"

"It's five-thirty. Throw some cold water on your face and I'll come over and pick you up in fifteen minutes."

"Okay. Are you sure that I'm not imposing on your family?"

"I invited you didn't I? They're thrilled to get to meet you. Plus, Bear is there already. See you in fifteen minutes."

"Okay. Bye."

Mack slid the handset onto the cradle and rested his head on the edge of the counter top. He felt 'whipped'. It had been a rough and tumble couple of days. It was Thursday and he had only been there since Tuesday. In that short time he met *Rat* and *Bear* and learned more than he needed to know about them. He was expected to determine who was bringing drugs over from the Bahamas and killing people to boot - 'piece of cake'. And, there was Tina! Yes. Tina!

RAP RAP RAP The front door rattled as someone tapped on it hard with his bare knuckles. "Mack! Are you awake? It's Ralph. I came to pick you up for dinner. It's six o'clock."

"Ralph: I apologize. I fell asleep again. Give me a minute to wash my face and I'll be right there." Mack slid down the counter top towards the refrigerator, grasped the door handle, pulled up to a 'semi-crouch' and lurched towards the bathroom. The pungent, caustic odor met him halfway and drove him back into the kitchen. The 'crap cat' was back and he forgot to flush the toilet!

Gagging and just short of vomiting, Mack grabbed a hand towel from the kitchen counter and soaked it with water from the faucet. Holding the wet towel over his face he made a dash for the bathroom hoping to reach the flush lever before his air gave out. The big toe of his right foot caught the curled-up edge of the braided throw rug in the hallway – it slipped. Mack flew headlong into the bathroom and slid across the tile floor. His head slid under the toilet's water tank and wedged solidly in place.

The blow against the green ceramic water tank wasn't hard enough to graciously knock him unconscious. It only stunned him and caused him to lay helpless as a baby on the floor while he slowly regained his senses. Mack cautiously opened his eyes and looked up at the dripping water tank wedged over his head. He thought that he was going to die on the spot. But, 'fate' decided that 'death' would be far to easy and forced him to lie prone and semi-conscious in a pool of cold water. It was a 'fate' far worse than mere 'death'. It was 'cruelty to humans'.

"Mack. Are you okay? I heard a terrible scream and a crash."

"Ralph. Please, Come in and help me get out of here. I'm wedged under the toilet bowl and I can't get up. I'm paralyzed."

"Okay buddy, I'll be right there." Ralph jerked the screen door open, busted the safety latch off its aluminum mounting and raced towards the hallway leading to the bathroom. But, his senses warned him of a foreboding trauma ahead if he continued in that direction. He tried to stop, but the throw rug in the hallway 'jumped up' from the floor and snatched his feet right out from under him. Ralph's feet went up and straight out ahead of him. His body, carried by it's own momentum, became 'horizontal' and continued the 'flight path' into the bedroom. His left foot caught the wicker clothes hamper and lifted it straight up into the air towards the spinning ceiling fan. A professional soccer player couldn't have made a better penalty kick.

Ralph hit the floor and at the same time the wicker clothes hamper bounced off the rotating ceiling fan, flipped upside down and it's smelly contents became airborne directly over his head.

The 'crap cat' was peacefully napping in the wicker hamper

and was now totally traumatized by the bizarre' events. He bounced off the blades of the ceiling fan and magically flipped right side up in mid-air on the way back down. Ralph's hairy abdomen was bare because his shirt had slipped over his head. The sharp, fully extended claws on all four of the cat's feet landed directly in the center of Ralph's protruding belly. The cat, reacting to the trauma of the landing, instinctively sunk its sharp claws deeply into what they touched first. It was Ralph's sunburned, bright pink, 'oh so soft' and tender belly skin.

Ralph instinctively reacted to the intense pain of the sharp claws puncturing his abdomen. His closed right fist caught the cat behind its left ear and sent him 'airborne' towards the living room. Fortunately for the cat the front door was hanging off its hinges. When the cat hit the door it flew open allowing the cat to make a hasty, but undignified 'escape' into the surrounding trees.

"Ralph. Are you okay? I heard some horrible noise in there."

"I think I'll live. That is if I can get up and am still able to walk. I'm not sure about the cat though."

"Can you come into the bathroom and help me get up? Wet a towel in the kitchen sink and put it over your face before you come in or you won't be able to breathe. Flush the toilet fast."

"Mack. How about you?"

"I don't think I'm breathing at all. I think that I might be dead, but I'm not certain. I can't move my head because it's wedged under the toilet tank and I feel cold water dripping in my ear."

It was very difficult to pry Mack's head out from under the tank. Ralph lathered his head up with shampoo in order to get it to budge. Once he got out from under the tank, Mack was able to stand up and walk with some assistance to Ralph's orange truck.

After a dinner of snowy grouper fillets and hush puppies and consuming a six-pack of beer in the back yard Ralph tried to relate the day's events. "Bear. You wouldn't believe how far I knocked that damn cat into 'next week'. You should have been there to see it. His green eyeballs were the size of saucers. He used his tail like a boat rudder to keep from hitting the walls on the way through the living room. He smacked into the front door, rolled over three times and headed for the trees. He won't be back - ever! I guarantee it. "

"Ralph, that cat has to come back. It's Tina's cat. She'll have my head on a platter!"

Bear grinned. His broken off yellowed stubs of teeth, stained by years of 'bacca chewing, were framed by his black beard. He spat a nasty-looking, thick brown stream of *'bacca* juice through the wide gap where his front teeth used to be and knocked a sleeping green dragon fly off a tire that was leaning up against a palm tree at least ten feet away.

"Mack, I'm sorry to be the one to break your bubble. But, it's not your head that she'll cut off. I know her pretty well."

"It wasn't my fault. If Ralph hadn't come running through the house like a bull in a china shop he wouldn't have slipped on the rug. He knocked the clothes hamper over, not me."

"Do you think she'll really care who did what? You had better worry about how you're going to explain the busted toilet tank and the water all over the floor."

"Ralph, tell him what really happened."

"I can't. Mack, you made me promise never to tell what happened to you. But, you didn't make me promise not to talk about what happened to me. I'm proud of how far out into left field that I knocked that cat."

"Okay, it's a draw. Ralph, let's tell Mack about the black boat. That's what we *'brung'* him over here for in the first place."

"Bear, you're right. We've got some very important business to talk about. Mack did 'Thatch' tell you about the black boat and what happened to his brother up in the North Fork last year?"

"Yes. He told me that his brother was a commercial fisherman and that the FDLE asked him to make reports about anything strange that he saw up there. His brother's body was found by a couple of sport fishermen tangled up in a gill net. He said that his brother told him about seeing a black boat speeding through the narrow cut between Fork Point and Kitching Cove between eleven-thirty at night and five the next morning."

"Yep, that's it. Did he add that they never found out who killed him and nobody seems to be trying very hard to find out?"

"Yes, and he didn't seem very happy about it."

"He told you what he wanted you to know. We're not sure about where he fits in and what he's doing. He doesn't seem to have a job, but he has a lot of money and likes to show it off. Somebody is running drugs over from the Bahamas with a mother ship and unloading the stuff offshore into small, fast speedboats. Those speedboats run through the St. Lucie Inlet and up the North Fork at night with no running lights showing. We figure that's what the black boat is doing."

"What makes you think that the black boat is involved?"

"That's easy. I spent a couple of nights in the North Fork with Dave's brother last year helping him gill net *'silver mullet'*. When the moon's full and the tide's up at a full high stand the mullet run up the North Fork to feed in Kitching Cove.

We ran our gill net across the narrow channel that leads behind *'Coon Point'* towards the *'007 Bridge'*. That black boat ran right through our nets and cut the float line to pieces. Usually they just kept going, but one night they got their props tangled and had to stop and cut the net out. The last time that I went with him they raised holy hell with us and said that if they got caught in our nets again that we would be *'sleeping with the fishes'*."

"When was that?"

"The night before Dave's brother was found dead. They made good on their promise. Bear, tell Mack about what's been happening to you in the North Fork since you've been fishing it."

"I kinda' took over where Dave's brother left off. Commercial fishermen are particular and we don't move in on someone else's spot. After he was gone I started fishing it. I've been having a lot of problems with them lately, but I'm not talking to nobody especially the cops. I know that Dave's brother was talking to the cops, because he told me so, and I'm sure that's why he got killed up there."

"What makes you think that he just didn't fall out of the boat, whack his head and drown?"

"Ralph, you tell him. Don't be bashful. Tell him the truth. We can trust him. I think."

"Okay, but if it gets back to Dave he'll freak out."

"I know how to keep my mouth shut. Don't worry."

"The St. Lucie County coroner is my uncle on my mother's side. The 'official' report said that he hit his head on something, fell over the side, got tangled in his nets and drowned."

"Ralph, that's exactly what Dave told me."

"Maybe he doesn't know the truth. There was no water in his brother's lungs. That indicates that he was dead before he hit the water. The lump on the back of his head was made by low-velocity .22-caliber bullet. It bullet penetrated his skull. Because it had a low powder charge it never exited. It stayed in his skull and there was no exit wound. But, nobody knows he was shot."

"Your uncle knows. He's the coroner! But, his report says death by drowning doesn't it?"

"That's what he was ordered to put down in the 'official' report. Someone much higher didn't want the public to know what really happened in the North Fork. It might scare them."

"Can't his body be exhumed and another autopsy done?"

"Nope. It's gone. Dave ordered it cremated."

"So, what does this all mean?"

"We're not sure except that Dave's brother was killed and Bear's been threatened."

"Mack, they got caught in my nets again last night, shot me the *'bird'* and told me that they'd take care of me the next time it happened. I don't want to end up like Dave's brother."

"What do you expect me to do? I'm not law enforcement."

"We know. That's why we're talking to you. Did Dave tell you about the sail boater that disappeared last week? He had your job at the marina for two months. We figure that he was either involved in drug running or saw too much and got whacked."

"Guys, tell you what. My head is exploding with information and I have to go back to the marina and sort it out."

"Did Dave tell you about Tina's husbands?"

"He told me that she was married and divorced twice. Her first husband was a CIA agent in Laos. He was captured and died in a rescue attempt."

"That's true. Bear was part of the *'Special Forces' SOG* rescue team that went in to get him out. He doesn't talk about it because he doesn't want Tina to know that he was there."

"That's not the only reason. I don't like to talk about being in Southeast Asia period. It was not a good time of my life and I've managed to blank most of it out. I get bad dreams once in awhile and I have to take medication to help me sleep."

"What can you tell me about it?"

"We were on a rescue attempt to try to save four Americans that were being held in bamboo *'tiger cages'* sunk in a river. When we raided the camp four of us ran for the cages to get the guys out while the others kept the *'Charlies'* busy. But we didn't know that the cages were booby-trapped with trip wires. When we touched them they just let go and fell into the river. They sank so fast that the guys didn't have a chance to get out, except for one guy. His cage got caught on a tree stump sticking out of the bank and we managed to drag him out before he drowned. He gave me this coin as a souvenir and told me to never take it off."

Bear lifted his beard and pulled out a leather cord that hung around his neck from inside his shirt. A large bear claw was strung on each side of a small silver coin that hung between them from a short length of silver wire."

"I know a little bit about coins. Can I take a closer look at it?"

"Okay, Mack you can look at it, but don't try to take it off."

Mack held the coin between the thumb and index finger of his right hand and tilted it so that it caught the yellow glare from a street lamp. The figure of a *South African Springbok* caught the pale light and Mack saw the numeral "1" stamped between it's forelegs. He dropped the coin allowing it to fall back around Bear's neck. "I guess that I don't know as much about coins as I thought I knew. I don't recognize it."

"It's a *South African One Rand* coin. That's what he told me."

"Bear, how did you know that Tina's husband was one of the prisoners in the camp?"

"I didn't. That was over thirty years ago. I didn't even know who Tina was back then. A few years ago the *Stuart News* ran a story about her and what happened to her husband. When I read the article I knew it had to be him - there's no doubt. But, she doesn't know that I know."

"Which one was Tina's husband? The one that you saved?"

"No. He was one of the guys that fell into the river and drowned in a bamboo cage."

"Tina thinks that he was a drunk and that she divorced him."

"Ralph. Can you fill him in on that?"

"Tina had a 'nervous breakdown' after the story about her

husband hit the papers. She was hospitalized for several months in DC and it was rumored that she went through hypnosis, electroshock and drug therapy to help her forget. She thinks that she divorced him because she is in denial that he died."

"What about her second husband? Was he a drunk? Did she divorce him?"

"That's a subject that I don't know anything about."

"Ralph. Tell him about your brother. He deserves to know everything."

"Did 'Thatch' tell you anything about my brother?"

"He told me that you and your brother were very close and that he went into the Army, but you couldn't go with him because of your eye. He joined 'Special Forces' and was killed in a raid."

"My brother was on the same rescue attempt in Laos that Bear was on to save Tina's husband."

"I'm sorry."

"There's nothing to be sorry about. He wanted to serve his country. His team brought his body back in the chopper and he's with us in the family plot in *Miles Grant Cemetery*."

"Mack, what do you think about all this stuff? Can you help us out? We're scared that we could be next."

"Bear, I honestly don't know. I have a lot of thinking to do. I came down here to get my Coast Guard license and be a fishing guide. That way I can fish every day and get paid for it. I don't have any expertise in this kind of stuff. But let me think about it."

"Mack. Why don't you go to captain's license school with me in Stuart next week? The state is paying for us to get our Coast Guard license because of the gill net ban we're being put out of business. I can use some help studying 'cause I wasn't a very good student in school."

"Bear, I'll think about it. I've got to get going. It's past eleven o' clock and I've got to get some sleep."

"Mack, how about if Bear and I pick you up in the morning about seven? We'll have breakfast at the *Queen Conch*. Then we'll take you on a ride down to Jupiter in one of our boats. We'll take the outside route down, have lunch in Jupiter and come back up the *Intracoastal Waterway*. It makes a nice ride"

"How fast do your commercial fishing boats go?"

"Fifteen knots at full speed. We can't go fast enough to blow the snot out of your nose. We'll go real slow - I promise."

"Okay Ralph. I don't have anything else to do until Tina shows up on her broom Friday evening. Tomorrow is Friday?"

"Yep, all day long. Maybe the cat will come back by then. Come on I'll take you back."

Mack shook hands with Bear and jumped in Ralph's 'ratty' orange truck for the five-minute ride back to the marina. His head was spinning with information overload.

"Mack, I'm sorry if we talked 'out of bounds' tonight. But, I'm worried about Bear. He's not the kind of guy to back down from anyone and he's apt to do something stupid. Please think about helping us solve this problem. I think that we can trust you and you can trust us. But, I don't know whom else you can trust. There are too many weird things going on. Especially with Mel's brother disappearing last week without a trace. Here we are. See you tomorrow."

"Okay, see you at seven o' clock. Call me on the phone first to be sure that I'm awake."

Mack slipped out of Ralph's truck and walked up the gravel driveway. Tiny white lights activated by motion detectors buried alongside the driveway lit up and ahead of him like magic. When he reached the porch he felt a little wobbly and started to sit down on the top step. Then he thought better of it because he was tired and might fall asleep. When touched the screen door handle, it fell off of its broken hinges and smashed onto the porch.

Meow

"Kitty. You're back. Let's go in and have some cat dinner and a shower. I missed you." Mack and the cat slipped through the front door together.

After he fed the cat, gave him a shower and tossed him outside Mack poured himself a full water glass of Merlot. He walked out onto the deck, sat down in a cheap, white, plastic chair and put his feet up on the railing. It had been a busy three days and his head was spinning. He had a lot of thinking to do. He was very tired, felt drowsy and it was past midnight.

A soft salt breeze from the ocean drifted towards the marina and wafted through the long fringed fronds of the coconut palm trees. It made a sound that reminded him of rustling crenalines under a poodle-decorated hoop skirt. The engines of boats speeding up and down the St. Lucie River hummed in a soft drone as they passed the marina. Their red and green running lights softly poked through the darkness like glowing 'spirit' eyes. Sleep came and wrapped him in her warm velvet cloak.

The soft *'whup whup whup'* of the rotor blades of a helicopter passing overhead made Mack glance upward. The white strobe light mounted on its belly flashed every two seconds in sequence with its red and green navigation lights.

The *'whup whup whup'* became deafening. It was followed by gunfire and the sound of desperate men shouting to one another.

"Sergeant, get those four men out of those cages 'pronto' and watch out for land mines and booby traps. Hurry! We don't have much time! Their main force is on the way back! Hurry!"

"Corporal, grab that cage before it goes under. Lieutenant! The bastards booby-trapped the releases! We're losing them in the river and three of them are gone. Corporal! That one's stuck on a tree. Grab it! Corporal - grab it now!"

"I've got it. Sarge! I need those bolt cutters over here quick! I've gotta' cut the chain off his arms."

""Lieutenant! Get those choppers in here now and let's go. We can't do any more. We lost three of them."

"Yeah, Sarge. We lost three of them, but we got this one. I sure hope that his sorry butt was worth it."

"Me too corporal. Me too. Son, run for the chopper – now!"

CHAPTER

9

"Good morning sleepy head. Did you sleep well? You've been out for almost two days."

Mack tried to focus his eyes, but strain as he might everything remained out of focus. He couldn't move his arms and legs. He strained to raise his head off the pillow, but his neck muscles wouldn't respond. His neck felt like useless rubber. He didn't know where he was, but he smelled antiseptic and disinfectant. He remembered those smells from many years before. He was in a hospital! His guts started to boil, he felt nauseous, his pulse raced and he tried to speak. The words slowly drifted out of his mouth like he was in a slow motion movie. It was surreal.

"Where am I? What happened to me? Why can't I move?"

"You are in *Bethesda Naval Hospital* in Maryland. You will be just fine in a few weeks. You've had a rough time of it and you need to recuperate."

"Why can't I move my arms and legs? I'm paralyzed! Help me! Please!"

"The paralysis is only temporary. You will regain the use of your limbs very soon."

Mack's eyes began to focus and he could make out two people dressed in white standing alongside the bed. The tall, red headed female was apparently a nurse. The tall blonde male wore a stethoscope around his neck and was no doubt a doctor.

The sides of the bed were enclosed by a three tier high, light green, metal railing. His hands and feet were tethered to the railings with thick, padded leather restraints. A wide, brown leather belt stretched across his chest. A tight leather band across his forehead held his head down. A needle was in place under the skin of both his left and right arms on the inside of the elbow. Above his head, on each side of the bed, stood a chrome stand that held a clear plastic bag fill with an amber liquid that dripped into the plastic tubes leading to his arms. He could hear the pulsating beep of a mechanical device above and behind his head.

"What's going on? Get me out of here! Help me! Please!"

The female placed a warm hand on his forehead and spoke in a soft purr tinted with a southern accent. "Is your name Mack?"

"I think so. But, I'm not sure of anything right now. What am I doing here?"

"You've been having some very bad dreams, delusions and hallucinations. We're here to help you get rid of those bad dreams because you are imagining things that never happened. These things can be very dangerous if they are not caught early and corrected. Do you understand?"

"I don't know what you're talking about."

"Just relax and let me ask you a few questions. We need to determine if our treatment of your condition is showing any measurable progress. Is that okay with you?"

"Yes! Yes! I'll do anything to get out of here. Anything!" He strained at his leather tethers as if to make his point.

The nurse connected electrodes to his arms and Mack heard the *'click'* of a switch being activated. The interrogation began.

"Were you ever in the military service?"

"Yes."

"What branch?"

"The United States Air Force."

"Where did you attend basic training?"

"*Lackland Air Force Base* in San Antonio, Texas."

"After basic did you receive any technical training?"

"Yes."

"What type of training and where?"

"Electronics at *Keesler Air Force Base* Biloxi, Mississippi."

"How long was your training period at *Keesler?*"

"Fifty weeks, I think. It was almost a full year."

"Did you receive any other type of training, or participate in any voluntary medical tests at either *Lackland* or *Keelser Air Force Base* during this period?

"Yes. I volunteered for some language tests at *Lackland*. I sat in a dark room with earphones on my head and listened to tapes of strange languages. I was told to try to make out words and write them down on a pad. I also participated in some memory recall tests and including attempting to read a newspaper that was upside down on a table about fifty feet away."

"Were you paid for participating in those tests?"

"Yes. I was paid twenty-five dollars a day. It was better than marching in the hot sun."

"Is there anything else that you can recall about them? Were you ever injected with anything?"

"It's all coming back. I remember being zipped up in a white rubber suit. I couldn't see or hear anything and they made me float on my back in some warm liquid. That was scary."

"Mack. You don't really remember these things do you? You are hallucinating again."

"I'm not hallucinating. I remember everything. It's all coming back to me. Let me tell you."

"That's very unfortunate. That means that we must continue with your treatments until you stop hallucinating. Doctor, please open his mouth and insert the rubber mouthpiece. We don't want him biting off his tongue during treatment now do we?"

"Do you really think that we should zap him again? He needs at least twenty-four hours to regenerate the brain cells that were burned out. He's had enough for today. Let's sedate him and let him rest overnight. We can pick back up tomorrow."

"Shut up you wimp! You know that it has to be done. We apparently didn't get the right ones the first time now did we? Increase the *Ketamine Hydrochloride* and *Diazepam* drips to fifty milligrams. Dial up fifty milliamps at one hundred-fifty volts. Give him three four-second bursts, with a two-second pause in between, over a period of fifteen seconds. Then give him thirty milligrams of *Benzedrine* to wake him up. We'll check his memory and test his recall again when he wakes up."

"Don't you mean if he wakes up? Those current and voltage levels might be too much for him! It can do some serious damage to the *medulla oblongata* and *cerebellum*. He might become a vegetable, or even die!"

"Do it! Both our butts are on the line if he remembers anything. Zap him! Do it now!"

The horrific pain started at the soles of Mack's feet, rushed up through his legs, ran roughshod through his torso and exploded in his brain! His body convulsed, thrashed from side to side and rose off the bed. The leather strap across his chest held him down. The terrible pain could not ever be imagined by, or described to another person. When the pain subsided his body relaxed. The electroshock cycle began two seconds later with even greater intensity.

"Good morning Mack. Did you sleep well? You were having serious hallucinations and bad dreams when we last saw you. Do you remember our last visit and what we talked about?"

"No. I don't remember anything. Where am I? Who are you?" A single bright ray of sunlight gingerly dancing through the white lace curtains projected a false aura of tranquility. Bouquets of flowers sat in vases on stands in each corner of the room. It smelled like a florist shop. A pastel blue wool blanket rose from the foot of the bed and stopped at his chest. A white sheet was folded over the top end of the blanket. His folded hands rested on top of the sheet. The *smell* of disinfectant told that he was in a hospital room. *Terror* ran up his spine.

Mack's eyes began to focus and he made out the fuzzy figures of a man and woman standing alongside the bed. They each wore a white smock. The stethoscopes hung around their necks identified them as physicians. The woman was perhaps five foot ten and wore her long red hair in a neatly pinned bun. The man was six foot two or better, had thick blonde hair that swept back along the sides and peaked in a pompadour above his forehead.

Mack was sitting up in bed. His shoulders and neck rested upon a pair of fluffy pillows. He felt totally relaxed and at ease.

"Mack. Are you awake? My name is Tina and this is Dave. We have been right here by your side through your long ordeal.

We'd like to ask you a few questions. Is that okay?"

"Sure. Ask me anything that you want. Where am I and how long have I been here?"

"You are in *Bethesda Naval Hospital* in Maryland. You are going to be just fine and will be going home very soon. That is provided that our last treatment session took properly."

"What kind of treatment? Was I hurt in an accident?"

"Yes. You were in a car accident, got banged up pretty good and have been in a coma for almost two months. You sustained a extremely serious head trauma that bruised your brain. It caused a blood clot and a lot of swelling. We operated and inserted a shunt to relieve the pressure on your brain. You may have some loss of memory because of the clot, but your brain will regenerate itself to make up for the cell loss. You should be just fine.

Mack, now I am going to ask you a few simple questions. Were you ever in the military? If so, what branch and when?"

"I was in the *Air Force*. I was an electronics technician.

"Good. Did you receive any other type of training, other than in electronics, or participate in any voluntary tests, at either *Lackland* or *Keesler Air Force Base*."

"Not that I can remember. The electronics school was enough. I was in class eight hours a day. Can you give me any specifics?

"No. But, your answer was perfect. I'm sorry. That was a poor choice of words. I meant that your answers were correct. In fact, you did not receive any training other than fifty weeks of electronics school at *Keesler Air Force Base* and you did not participate in any voluntary tests or experiments. Mack, what do you do for a living and how long have you been doing it?"

"I'm an electronics technician. I work in the central office of the telephone company in McLean, Virginia. I've been there for two years and my specialty is microwave radio."

"Do you ever have nightmares? If so, what are they about?"

"No. I sleep like a log. I may dream about something after a heavy dinner, but I never have nightmares. It's strange because, even if I do have a dream, the next day I can never remember anything about what I dreamed about. Isn't that strange?"

"Not at all. It's quite normal. Dreams are caused by *neurons* in your brain that build up an electric charge during the day and randomly discharge it when you are sleeping. It's like the static electricity that builds up in a rain cloud. When two electrically charged clouds bump together the built-up electricity is discharged to the ground as lightening.

The specific brain cells that make up memory can only recall events that actually happened and are stored in a permanent place in the brain. Dreams are usually about events that didn't actually take place, thus the brain has no reason to store the electrical charges that made them occur. Do you understand any of that?"

"No. But, I'll take your word for it. Can I go home now?"

"Not yet. There's still some significant swelling in your brain. After the swelling goes down we'll do some brain wave tests called electroencephalograms. They enable us to evaluate your cognitive motor skills to determine if there was any permanent brain damage. We'll also do some tests on your short and long term memory functions. You should be out of here in a week."

"A week! How about my job at the phone company? I've got to get back to work."

"Mack, your supervisors have been kept fully informed of your progress and they are very concerned about you. They assured us that your job is still there. It's my understanding that the company plans to provide you with some significant retraining before they put you back to work."

"Retraining? Why? I still tell a *klystron* from a *thermistor*!"

"You've been here for several months and technology changes every day. You should consider yourself very fortunate to have such an understanding employer. You were in a very serious accident and you must allow your brain some time to get itself together. It has a lot of cells to regenerate. It can't do that if you're active and talking.

After you are released we expect you to check into a VA Hospital once a year for a full evaluation. If you have any bad dreams, or nightmares, we want you to call us immediately. That would be a sign that some of those random firing neurons need to be adjusted through additional treatment. Now I want you to lay back and relax. I'm going to give you something to help you sleep. It won't hurt a bit. I'll be right here when you wake up."

"But, I don't want to . . ."

"Shush. Mack. Just relax and go to sleep."

A muted, metallic *'click'* came from above and slightly behind his head. The horrific pain started at the soles of his feet, rushed up his legs, ran through his torso and exploded in his brain! His body involuntarily convulsed and thrashed from side to side. The thick leather strap across his chest held him down on the bed. The pain slowly subsided and his body relaxed. The cycle of pain began two seconds later with even greater intensity.

"Good morning sleepy head. Did you sleep well? That chair sure can't be very comfortable."

Mack heard a voice emanating from behind him, but the words didn't register. He shook his head and tried opening his eyes. The sunlight blinded him and he snapped them shut.

He was slumped in an arc in the plastic chair and felt numb from the waist up. His neck throbbed and he couldn't move! His body felt as if it was locked in a steel vise that held no sympathy for his plight. His legs were propped up on the deck railing and were completely numb. He pried his unfeeling legs from the railing and his feet hit the wooden deck with simultaneous thuds. Excruciating, white-hot daggers of pain shot up both of his legs signaling that blood circulation was being restored.

"Mack. What happened? I told you that I'd stop by this morning at seven o' clock to take you to breakfast. Bear is waiting for us at the *Queen Conch*. I called you on the phone at six forty-five and even let it ring twenty times. When you didn't answer I figured that you might have overslept. So, here I am."

"Where's the cat?"

"He's in the shower. I popped his breakfast in the microwave for fifteen seconds and it'll be ready in a jiffy. I'll feed him and toss him out while you are taking a shower. Shave too."

"Am I still alive, or am I dead? I feel like death warmed over."

"You're alive, but you look like 'crap'. Why did you sleep out here on the deck in a chair?

"It wasn't on purpose. After you dropped me off I poured a glass of wine, came out here to sit and enjoy the view. There must have been a big boat accident off shore because helicopters were flying around here all night long. I couldn't sleep."

"Mack. You were sleeping all right. I could hear you snoring clear out to the driveway. But, there weren't any helicopters around here last night. Bear and I stayed up mending nets until about two-thirty this morning and it was pretty quiet then. You must have been dreaming."

"Ralph I know that it was real! Two choppers hovered right over the marina. I could see their red and green running lights. The white belly strobe light lit up the deck when it flashed."

"Mack, please believe me. There were no helicopters around here last night. Go take a shower and get cleaned up. Bear is waiting for us at the *Queen Conch*. He'll be bitching up a storm."

"Okay Ralph. If you say there were no helicopters then there were no helicopters. But, I know that I heard them and I saw them too. I really did."

"Mack. You're apt to get locked up for talking crazy like that. People will think that you're nuts."

"Okay. I hear you. I'm heading for the shower. Watch the cat! I'll be out in five minutes."

After breakfast the trio walked to the fish house dock where Ralph and Bear moored their commercial fishing boats. After some good-natured haggling about whose boat was faster and more comfortable the trio voted to take Ralph's boat. The reason given by the winning duo was that Ralph's boat didn't smell as bad as Bear's. Because his boat ran a close second in the vote tally Bear was elected to be the tour narrator.

"This here's the *Manatee Pocket*. Years ago it was chock full of commercial fishing boats. There was three fish houses and a shark processing plant here at one time. Now we only got one fish house and there ain't enough sharks left to make it worthwhile to catch 'em. Look at all them fancy sport fishing boats! Most of them stay tied up to the dock without ever going out fishing but once or twice a month. Some of them cost more than a million dollars. If I had me a boat like that I'd be out every day and I'd catch me a mess of fish. I'd be rich."

Ralph took his eyes off the water and looked at Bear. "You have to be rich to buy a boat like one of those. The people who own them have full-time captains and spend more money on boat upkeep, fuel and dockage than we make together in a really good year of commercial fishing."

"Ralph. It's because of them *'sporties'* that the gill net ban got passed. They go offshore to catch sailfish - just for fun."

Mack tapped Bear on the shoulder to get his attention. "Yes, Bear, that's very true. But, the owners of the sport fishing boats contribute a tremendous amount of money to the local economy through what they spend for fuel, dockage, hotels and restaurants. I haven't seen any statistics, but I'll bet that the sport fishing boats account for several million dollars in annual local expenditures. They pay for their enjoyment big time."

"But, Mack, we spend money for fuel too and we get paid for our fish. That brings money into town."

"Sure you do, Bear. But, look at the difference in the amount of money that they spend for their enjoyment and they don't take anything out in return. They release most of the fish they catch."

"They do so keep some fish! Just like we do."

"But Bear, they eat what they catch, or give it away."

"Stop your squabbling! We're out here for a tour not to argue the pros and cons of sport versus commercial fishing. That battle was fought and we lost. It's over. The net ban is in effect. We have to find something else to do to feed our families."

"Ralph, I'm still hot about it because they was saying that the fish population is down because of the gill nets. The fish population's down because of the pollution from septic tanks, fertilizers and bug killers that they all spray on them pretty green lawns of theirs. They've destroyed the mangroves and grass beds that the fish use for spawning grounds and nurseries. About the only place that a fish can find to hide these days is alongside a concrete sea wall that was built after the mangrove trees were ripped out to make room for it."

"That is probably all true. But, Bear, stop your bitching. It's over and done with. We lost."

"Ralph, you know that I'm going to keep on netting in the North Fork just like always."

"But, what if they catch you with a gill net in your boat? Are you willing to pay the price?"

"First, they'll never catch me with a gill net in the boat. They aren't up that late at night. Second, I always carry a couple of big cast nets with me. There're legal. Plus, I have a fishing rod in the boat that I use to catch *'snuuks'*.'"

"You wouldn't know how to use a fishing rod even if you needed it to save your hide."

"Ralph, the Law don't say that I have to know how to use it. But, I got one in the boat just in case they stop and ask me."

"Mack. Would you tell him to stop? He's wound up tight."

"I agree. I've only been here for a few days, but I already know more that I should. How about that tour? You've both been yammering like a couple of old women and have over looked telling me very much about where we are, or where we're going."

"You're right. Bear, shut up! You haven't missed much because we're just coming out of the *Manatee Pocket* into the *St. Lucie River*. That's *Sandsprit Park* on the left. Look north, up there by *Hell's Gate,* and you can see *Port Sewell Marina*. That island over there, just off the end of *Sewell's Point*, is *Trickle's Island*. A deep channel runs through there, but be careful at night because there's no lighted channel markers.

That little island is where the original *Stuart Post Office* used to be years ago. That's way back when Stuart was still called *Potsdam*. Mail boats would come up the *Intracoastal Waterway* from West Palm and drop off the mail there. There's a big sand bar on the east side of *Trickle's Island* that runs all the way to the *Cross Roads*. It comes out of the water at low tide and leaves some deep tidal pools that hold bait fish."

"What's the *Cross Roads*? I don't see any street signs here."

"Can you see that square green marker on the top of that metal *dolphin* that's standin' kinda' lopsided? That's the *Cross Roads*. It's where the *St. Lucie* and *Indian Rivers*, the *Intracoastal Waterway* and the *St. Lucie Inlet* meet. When the tide's ebbing out 'hard' on a full moon there are strong cross currents here that will be going every which way. Be careful. Straight ahead, where the waves are breaking over the rocks is the *St. Lucie Inlet*."

"Is it safe to run a boat through there?"

"The inlet can be very dangerous and there's some real nasty spots where you can run aground. Come out and spend some time getting to know the water on both the incoming and outgoing tides. That's *Sailfish Point* over yonder. It's a very ritzy place. That sandy area on your left, sticking up out of the water, is called the *Sun Parlor*. Don't try to run through there until you've had lots of practice. I've lived here all my life and still avoid running through it."

"Where can I buy aerial photographs of this area? It would really help me to get around."

"Ask Dave. He can get anything. I'm going to cut through here, run up *Smuggler's Cove* to *Clam Island* where we're going to catch lunch. Over there's *Boy Scout Island*. If you know these back channels you can run all the way to the *Stuart Causeway*."

"Why did he names of *Smuggler's Cove*, *Boy Scout Island* and *Clam Island* come from?"

"Years ago the *Boy Scouts* used the island for weekend camp outs. I did it when I was a kid. *Clam Island* is a great place to dig up clams and oysters for lunch - if you know where to dig. During prohibition whiskey smugglers came through the St. Lucie Inlet in big boats, snuck in here and unloaded the whiskey into smaller boats for distribution. That's why it's called *Smuggler's Cove*. Okay. We're here. Mack tie off the bow line to that mangrove tree, jump out and come with me. I'll show you where to dig for oysters and clams. Bear, you get out there on the flats with your cast net and catch us a dozen silver mullet."

"Why do I have to do all the hard work? Why can't I dig for clams and oysters too?"

"Because you're better than me with a cast net. I'm slow."

After Bear caught a dozen mullet, and Ralph dug up enough clams and oysters for lunch, the trio continued on their tour. They went out the *St. Lucie Inlet*, turned south and ran the coast along the *St. Lucie State Park* and *Jupiter Island* to the *Jupiter Inlet*. They turned north into the *Intracoastal Waterway* and pulled in for lunch at *Peck's Lake*. During lunch Ralph and Bear took the opportunity to bring Mack up to speed on their suspicions.

When the exhausted trio pulled into the Port Sewell Marina Bear's tame osprey 'Michi' whistled at him from her safe perch high up in the Australian pine tree. "Mack, we hope that you had a good time and maybe learned something about the area."

"Ralph, and you too Bear, I learned so much today that my head's throbbing. It's four-thirty and I have work to do before Tina comes up from West Palm. She's probably on the way."

"Mack, we are very glad that you could spend some time with us. Remember what we told you."

"Mack, don't forget we've got captain's license school next week. The school is on Kindred Street off Colorado Avenue. You can't miss it. They've got a sign in the window. I'll pick you up."

"Okay Bear. You win. I'll go. I've got to have a license anyway. We'll help each other."

"All right! I'll pick you up right here on Monday mornin' at seven-thirty and we'll go to breakfast before we go to school."

"Thanks guys. Bear, I'll see you Monday."

Ralph and Bear pulled away from the wooden pier, turned around in the marina basin and headed towards *Willoughby Creek*. *'Michi'* whistled and dove out of the Australian pine tree directly towards Bear's head. At the last moment she flipped her tail down, slowed to a stop and gently landed on his shoulder. She whistled softly and pecked him on the cheek to welcome him back. Bear was ready for her. He had cut several mullet into bite-sized chunks that she could gulp down and regurgitate to feed the two partially feathered out chicks in her nest. All seemed to be right with the world.

Mack needed rest. He crawled up the twelve wooden steps to the cottage, turned the nail above the front door to the 'up' position and slunk through the door. There was no sign of the cat. He crept cautiously towards the bathroom with his left hand close to his nose. He wasn't going to take a chance on being bushwhacked again. It was all clear and he collapsed on the bed.

"Hello sleepy head. Are you going to sleep all day? I'm here and I'm tense. Let's play!"

Mack could smell *'White Diamonds'* and felt a soft, warm palm caressing his forehead. He smelled fresh lipstick as something soft brushed across his cheek. He shook his head and opened his eyes. A pair of bright green eyes, framed between red bangs and glossed ruby lips, were looking directly through his retinas into the base of his soul. He knew that he must be 'dead'.

"Come on *Yankee Boy*. Get up. I spent all day in a courtroom putting bad boys away in the 'slammer'. I'm tense and I need some relaxation. There's only two ways that I can work off tension and relax. One of them is in bed, with a good book, and the other is to go out for a good dinner and some dancing. Get up. Let's go. It's six-thirty and my motor's running."

"Tina? You're here early. I'm pooped. I spent all day on the water with Ralph and Bear."

"I can be early if I want to be. It's my marina. I know exactly where you went and what you did. That was by water. Now I'm going to show you around by car. Get your 'furry' little butt up and take a shower. Don't forget to shave. I don't like whisker burns when I'm dancing."

"But, I want to . . ."

"Drive my car? I don't think so. Get in the shower. I'll lay out fresh clothes for you."

Obediently Mack 'slunk' down the hall to the bathroom. He hesitated at the door, took three precautionary sniffs to check the air before entering, went inside and closed the door. The hot shower made him feel almost like a human again.

With a fluffy, emerald green towel wrapped around his waist he stepped out into the short hallway. The cottage was dark, except for a tall, pine-scented, red candle on the dinette table that flickered like a wet log. Soft, muted strains of *Lionel Hampton* drifted across the room. The pair of long legs that stretched across the recliner's footrest tapered down to thin ankles and red spike heels. A glass of red wine, no doubt Merlot, stood erect on the arm of the chair and was rotating in a slow circle on it's glass base guided by two long fingers that terminated in crimson nails. He started to walk closer.

"Okay *Yankee Boy* you can stop right there. Don't ya'll get excited - at least not yet -it's too early. Get yourself dressed and let's get going. Time's a wasting and the sun's going down fast. We're going to take a trip and I'm driving. Hurry up."

By the time Mack got dressed and got outside she was already waiting in the silver-blue *Beamer* convertible. The engine was running, the top was down and she was tooting the horn. The second he sat down she 'started in' on him. "Put this Martin County map on your lap and follow along as I narrate. You have to know your way around here by water and by car - especially at night." The tires spun, loose pea gravel flew up from the driveway and bounced off the tin roof. They were off!

She took *Old Dixie Highway* south to Cove Road, cut across to U.S. 1 and after fifteen minutes of sheer terror pulled into the parking lot of *Captain Jack's Crab House* in Jupiter. The befuddled hostess recognized her and led the pair to a cozy corner table beside the stone fireplace. Two *Absolut* vodka gimlets were waiting on Tina's side of the table. She opened the conversation. "What have you learned the last two days?"

"That I have more questions about you. You told me that you were divorced twice and that your husbands were drunks."

"That's correct. So what else is new?"

"Why didn't you tell me that your first husband was in the CIA and in Laos, and that you were also CIA?"

"My. You are a little 'testy' tonight. I'll bet that a little bird's been chirping - hasn't he? None of those things are any of your concern. Maybe you already know too much? Next question?"

"Why did you take me to Indiantown and embarrass me?"

"You embarrassed yourself. I didn't force you to drink ten *Tequila Sunrises* and ride the mechanical bull. You made a fool out of yourself all by your little old lonesome. But, I truly enjoyed every minute of it and the video tape came out real good. I watched it again last night. I especially like the part where you flew over the bull's head and landed in the compost pile. The judge laughed his ass off over it this morning in court."

"Don't tell me that you showed a judge the tape!"

"I'm really sorry. Honest I am. It got mixed up with a couple of evidence tapes that we were reviewing before jury selection. I'm glad that he laughed about it because that was his ranch and his bull that you killed. But, he doesn't know it yet. Don't worry the deputy who saved your butt is my cousin Elmo. He's the only one who knows that it was you and he's on our side."

"But, he showed the tape at the Sheriff's department during the morning shift change."

"He did? I bet him a hundred bucks that he didn't have enough balls to show it. I'm proud of him. He's real kin. That show was worth a hundred bucks any day of the week."

"You made me the laughing stock of a courtroom, and the sheriff's department, and your cousin makes a hundred bucks. What did you get out of this?"

"Nothing except to see a man make a fool of himself. Remember, all *boys are dumb!*"

"What evil do you have planned for tonight? Do you have a spray bottle in your purse?"

"None. No tricks tonight. Besides that old one only works once. Most people get wise to it. Tonight we're going to hit *Clematis Street* and *'boogie'* 'til closing time. Are you up to it?"

"What's Clematis Street?"

"Just a quiet corner of *West Palm Beach* with a few bistros, restaurants and bars. Let's go."

By 2:30 A.M. the last bar had closed and Tina was ready to go back to the marina. She *'boogied'* so hard that she wore the feet out of her panty hose. Mack, fearing reprisal for his questions, drank bottled soft drinks all night. Tina was bombed out of her gourd and Mack had to drive her car. During the drive back on U.S. 1 to Stuart the convertible top was down and Tina rested her head on his shoulder. A little south of *Cove Road* the aroma of bacon coming from a Denny's across the highway woke her up.

"Let's stop for breakfast. I'm starved. If I don't eat I get really mean and grumpy."

Tina ran her toes up and down his pant leg from the time they left Denny's until they arrived at marina at 3:45 A.M. Mack, hoping for a continuation of the after shower episode, put his arm around her waist as they walked up the driveway to the cottage.

At the porch steps she paused, tilted her head up and looked him in the eyes. He brushed the hair out of her eyes with his fingers. She smiled demurely and walked away. "I'm so sorry Mack. I practice *'tease and release'* when I go out on the town. I let the little ones get away so they'll grow even bigger. I'll be up to take a shower in the morning. Bye."

Dejected, he slunk into the cottage feeling like a complete fool. She had baited him and he took the bait. She hooked him, played him like a trout just for the sport of it, and released him. Knowing that he couldn't sleep, he poured himself a glass of warm Merlot and walked out on the deck to sit, watch the water, smell the salt air and relax.

The cabin lights of her sailboat moored in the slip below glowed like white embers. Were the lights a belated invitation?

No! He was 'hooked' once tonight and played like a fish. He decided not to take the bait again. Tomorrow would bring round two of their chess match and Mack would play to 'win'. He would watch carefully for her opening 'gambit' and counter it with a 'check-mate'. He leaned back in the white plastic chair, put his feet up on the railing and closed his eyes.

The silence was shattered by the whine of a boat engine operating at high rpm's. Mack dropped his feet from the railing and sat up. Moonlight reflected off the wake of a boat passing through the *Cross Roads* at high speed. It turned northwest and cut through the narrow channel between *Trickle's Island* and *Sewell's Point*. When it rounded *Sewell's Point* and changed course towards *Hell's Gate* Mack made it out clearly. It was a black speedboat, about twenty-five feet long, and it wasn't showing any running lights.

He glanced at his watch. 4:20 A.M. The black speedboat was right on schedule. Should he wake Tina and chase the black speedboat to find out where it was going? He thought better of it. There would be other days. The black speedboat's route and schedule were both predictable. She wasn't - at least not yet.

Mack finished off his glass of warm Merlot and went to bed. Tomorrow was another day and it was already here.

CHAPTER
10

"Good morning 'sleepy head' its time for you to get up and out of bed. You are getting older by the minute"

"Huh? What time is it?"

"It's almost ten-thirty in the morning. The day's half gone already. We've got places to go and people to meet."

"Come on let me sleep. I didn't get to bed until four-thirty."

"So? You've had six hours of sleep. Consider yourself lucky to have gotten that much. I kept the lights burning for you until four-thirty, but you couldn't even bother to walk down a flight of stairs. What's a bashful girl supposed to do these days when she's horny? Hang out a shingle? I'll be damned if I'm going to hang up a red light on my mast."

"What are you talking about? You told me good night and added that you played *'tease and release'* when you go out on the town. I distinctly remember saying that you let the little ones go to grow up and get even bigger."

"Who said that you were a 'little one'? You made a very big assumption. But, you certainly didn't try very hard, did you?"

"I didn't even think about sniffing around your door like a dog in heat. I went to bed and didn't give you a second thought."

"Then why did you sit out on the deck drinking wine until four-thirty this morning? Maybe you needed a cold shower. You were watching for the black boat weren't you?"

"How do you know where I was and what I was doing? Were you spying on me?"

"Motion detectors and camera number six. There's a direct feed from the security system's video multiplexer into my boat's television set. I need it for security when I'm up here all alone."

"I'll bet that's pretty often."

"Yes. I'm up here almost every weekend."

"That's not what I meant."

"What did you mean?"

"That you're usually on your boat alone and I can see why. Did you know that the female tarantula bites and kills the male after mating? They can't make it two weekends in a row."

"That's true when the female bites a male tarantula. But, when she bites a human the bite is very painful, but rarely fatal."

"Touche'. But, why are we having this inane conversation?"

"You started it! I came up to take a shower. When I finished, I looked in on you. You were sleeping peacefully and I gently woke you up. No fatal bites! At least this time."

"Why do I have to get up? Where are we going?"

"We have places to go and people to meet. Get your hairy butt up and get going. I can't explain everything while I'm standing around half-wet in a bathrobe. We'll talk later."

"Tina. I really like your slippers. Pink bunny faces are cute. Do your *'jammies'* have little feet in them too?"

"Don't be a smart ass *Buster Brown*! I'll change you from a rooster to a *'capon'* in about ten seconds if you continue to push your luck with me. And, believe me - I'll make it hurt real bad."

"Yes sir! Okay, you win. I'm getting up. Don't you think that perhaps your testosterone level is just a little high this morning?"

Whap!

She caught him along the left side of the face with a *'round house right'* that knocked him right off the bed onto the floor. He opened his eyes and saw that her left fist was cocked and 'ready to fire' in the direction of his right eye at the least provocation.

"Come on *'smart-ass'*. Say something else smart-mouthed! Do you want to try the other side of your face so that you have a matched set? Your extra-large *'alligator mouth'* overloaded your puny *'canary ass'*! Come on – say something smart! Come on!"

He thought better of saying anything at all because she had the advantage. She was standing over him *'straddled-legged'* ready to swat him into 'next week'. Her pink, bunny slipper-clad right foot was off the floor and cocked back about two feet behind her. He realized that if he opened his mouth and said anything, regardless of what it might be, that he would never be able to father children and would be wheelchair bound for the rest of his life. That is, if she let him live.

"Cease fire. I give up. You win."

"*Yankee Boy* you are very observant and correct on both counts. You give up and I do win."

Whap!

Her cocked left fist recoiled like a highly *'pissed-off'* King Cobra towards his left cheek. He tried to duck and deflect the some of the punch's momentum, but it was too late. She caught him squarely on the cheekbone below his right eye.

"Now Mr. Smart-ass - we'll entertain a cease fire. But, there will be no negotiations, or conditions. You lose and you will surrender unconditionally. Do you understand me you male *'scum bag'*? Mr. Yankee Boy!"

"Yes ma'am. I understand. This isn't fair! I'm wedged under the windowsill and I can't move. Please, don't hit me again."

Just to make her point Tina swung her right foot towards his unprotected groin – but stopped it in mid-air – just a split second before he would have been emasculated. She smiled sweetly and softly purred in a silky-smooth southern drawl, "Well, *Mr. Yankee Boy*, I guess that my testosterone level is back to normal. How's yours? Get ready!" She spun on her pink 'bunny-slippered' right foot, threw her shoulders back and strutted out of the room like a Bantam rooster that had recently gone through a 'sex change' and just won 'its' first cockfight.

Tina shouted back to him from the living room, "Mack. You had better be dressed and out at the car in ten minutes. I don't want to have to come up here and roust you out again. If would be right down embarrassing for you if some of the neighbors saw me kicking your *Yankee butt* all around the marina parking lot."

"I'll be ready." Mack rubbed his throbbing cheekbones and hoped that she didn't split the skin. Chances were that she was skilled enough to pull her punches to avoid any serious injury. He shaved, showered and got out to the car in eight minutes flat.

Tina was sitting in the silver-blue *Beamer* with the top down looking at her watch. She shook her head, frowned, and motioned with her head for him to get in. "You certainly took long enough. Did you have to shave your legs and trim your nose hairs before you could get dressed? Get your sorry, worthless *'Yankee butt'* in here and sit down. We're going to brunch. It's a long drive and I'm famished."

"Where are we going?"

"To one of your favorite haunts. *Indiantown.*"

"Indiantown? I'm not up for any bull riding. I did that once and I'll never do it again."

"We're going to the historic *Seminole Inn* for brunch. It was built back in 1926 and has a very colorful history. Their Sunday brunch buffet is out of this world. It's ten-fifty now. It'll take us forty minutes to get there which will put us in the parking lot at eleven-thirty exactly when the buffet opens for business. Now just sit back, relax and pay attention. There's a lot to see."

She shifted the *Beamer* into low gear and tromped the gas pedal to the floorboard. The tires spun and loose pea gravel flew onto the front porch rattling like hail stones. With the gas pedal pressed to the floorboard she jerked the steering wheel hard left to make the turn on to *Old St. Lucie Boulevard*. The little car 'fish-tailed' from side to side for almost fifty feet before the tires caught on the pavement and it straightened out. Mack's head snapped first to the left then to the right.

"Tina! What the hell are you doing? You are going to kill both of us if you don't slow down."

She tossed her head in response and shifted into second gear without lifting her foot off the gas petal. The little car leaped ahead. Mack's head snapped back and slammed into the soft leather headrest. At the junction with *Old St. Lucie Boulevard*, she glanced to the left, then to the right, completely ignored the stop sign and roared through while simultaneously shifting into third gear. Loose gravel flew in all directions. When the spinning tires finally made contact with the asphalt they squealed like a shoat pig caught in the jaws of a toothed, steel bear trap.

Mack's head slammed into the headrest and he grabbed the top of the windshield for support with his left hand. "What is wrong with you? What are you trying to prove? You'll kill us!"

"What's the matter *Yankee Boy*? Are you afraid to ride with a woman driver with an extremely high testosterone level?" Tina grinned devilishly and jerked the steering wheel hard to the left and then back hard to the right. Mack slid to the left and back to the right slamming his shoulder on the door. But, he didn't say a word. He closed his eyes and hoped that when she crashed into something that he wouldn't feel very much pain when as he was decapitated by the windshield.

"Okay *Yankee Boy*. You can open your eyes now. You don't have to play 'possum with me. Everything from here on out is going to be just fine. I'll be good and behave like a lady. I just had to get rid of that 'extra' testosterone.

This is Indian Street and it feeds across U.S. 1 to *Kanner Highway*. When we reach Kanner Highway we could turn left and take it all the way to the junction with State Road 10 at *Port Mayaca*. But, that's the long way. We'll take the scenic route through *Palm City* and over the *Martin Grade* road. That way you can take in the scenery. Any objections?"

"Would it really do any good for me to object?"

"No, it really wouldn't. But, I just wanted to make you feel like you had something to say about it."

Mack crossed his arms across his chest, slumped down into the seat and tried to get his head below the level of the windshield. If she hit a flock of birds that at least the top of his head and scalp wouldn't be ripped loose from his skull.

She made it across U.S. 1 in spite of running a red light and reached the intersection of Indian Street and Kanner Highway.

"Pay attention *Yankee Boy*! Here you can turn left and follow Route 76 all the way to *Port Mayaca* and turn north on Route 710 to *Indiantown*. It's the long way, but it's a faster than the scenic route through *Palm City* that we're taking this morning." She made a hard right turn and floored the gas pedal.

"If the other way is faster, and you're so darned hungry, why are we going this way?"

"Because I want you to know what the rural area of Martin

County looks like. And, I want to see if they got that bull that you were riding out of the rim canal. Elmo told me that it sank like a rock and that the tow truck driver refused to get into the water to tie a line on it because it smelled so bad."

"I don't remember anything about riding any bull. You're just putting me on aren't you?"

"Haven't you looked at the video tape yet? I left it on top of the television set."

"No. When have you given me time to even sleep?"

"You got six hours worth last night and should be well rested and ready to go. This is the *Palm City Bridge*. On the left is the *South Fork* of the St. Lucie River - also called the *Okeechobee Waterway*. It leads to the Corps of Engineers locks that open up to *Lake Okeechobee* at *Port Mayaca*. It makes a nice boat ride."

"I know all about it. Dave took me down to the locks on a boat ride at a speed of Mach I."

"I doubt that it was Mach I. That boat tested out at a 'top-end' speed of only sixty-two miles per hour at fifty-five hundred rpm."

"It was going so fast that I couldn't breathe and snot flew out of my nose."

"Perhaps you were just having an anxiety attack. That happens. Straight ahead of us is the *Florida Turnpike*. This is the exit that you took when you got off the turnpike on Tuesday. The road to the right, that's the one we are taking, is Route 714. We call it *Martin Grade* because it was an unpaved gravel road until this year. Now it's paved with blacktop. Sit back, relax and take in the scenery while I drive."

Mack glanced at the *Beamer's* speedometer. It read '65'. That was a safe speed and hopefully it wouldn't attract attention. The sides of the black asphalt road were lined with pine trees and palmetto studded fields. The many unpaved gravel roads leading off the highway to unknown destinations were marked by silent, weathered mailbox 'sentinels' mounted on wooden posts which sported round red reflectors. The several riding stables and plant nurseries alongside the highway were framed with weathered, wooden split rail fences.

"Tina! Watch out for those dogs on the right hand side of the road. They might run across the road in front of us!"

Tina hit the brakes as a trio of mongrel dogs ran across the road in pursuit of unseen prey. A quarter mile further up the highway a female German shepherd stood in the grass alongside the road with her nose high in the air seeking the scent of her pack mates. "I doubt that any of those dogs will find its way home tonight. Their owners should be neutered in a public square and strung up in a tree for their lack of concern for their pets."

"I agree. Don't you have leash laws in this county?"

"Of course. But, how do you enforce ignorance?"

"I guess you can't. Sometimes I feel that people should have to take a course in animal husbandry, take a test and be licensed before they can own a pet. At least for the animal's sake."

"First, you have to give them a test to see if they can read."

"And, spell responsibility!"

"That's *Boat Ramp Road* on the right. It's not paved and it'll jar your teeth out if you go too fast. There's a launching ramp at the end of it that feeds into the *C 23 Canal*."

"What's the *C 23 Canal?*"

"It drains excess water off the farms, ranches and orange groves during the rainy season and stores it for use in irrigation during the dry season. This is the intersection with State Road 609. We're going to turn left and take it south to Indiantown."

"What if we continued going west on this road?"

"You'll wind up at the *Lake Okeechobee Rim Canal* in about five more miles."

The narrow, two-lane asphalt country road had a wide white stripe running along each side and a dashed yellow line down the center. A canal, maybe fifty feet across, bordered the east side of the road and hundreds of orange trees. An ancient two-strand electric power line, mounted on skinny, creosote treated wooden poles, ran north and south between the canal and the orange grove. A blue Kingfisher, with a feathered crest on top of its head, swooped down from its vantage point on the power line to snatch a small fish from under the shadow of an oak tree. Fishermen outfitted with long cane poles lined the canal's banks hoping to catch a *'bass'*, *'speck'* or *'brim'* in the brown water.

The west side of the road was lined with Brazilian pepper trees. A female osprey, startled by the *Beamer's* engine, screamed a shrill whistle of alarm as she rose from her perch in the dead pine tree beside the west side of the road.

The smell of cow manure and urine entered the open car the instant they passed the row of pepper trees and came into an open area. A herd of several dozen *'Brangus'* cows (half *'Brahma'* and half *'Angus'*) grazed in the open pasture on the west side of the road. It was a scene for a picture postcard – except for the microwave radio tower equipped with three parabolic dishes and the high-voltage power lines mounted on concrete towers on the east side of the road. After a sod farm and just before the junction with State Road 710 sat several tiny flat-roofed duplexes - obviously *'migrant worker'* housing.

A convenience store and gas station 'combo' were directly across the intersection on the south side of State Road 710. A green and white Martin County Sheriff's patrol car sat alongside a van on the west side of the convenience store. The deputy appeared to be monitoring traffic.

"I'll bet that's my cousin Elmo! Let's find out." The *Beamer* streaked across the intersection leaving about twenty feet of black tire tread marks on the highway behind it. Tina 'slammed' on the brakes and twisted the steering wheel hard to the left just before she collided with the deputy's parked patrol car. The *Beamer* slid across the gravel parking area sideways, threw gravel in all directions and left a dust cloud hanging in the air equivalent to a herd of a five hundred cows on a *Chisholm Trail* cattle drive.

"Hey cousin Elmo. How's it hanging?"

"Tina! What brings you and that *Yankee* cowboy out here to the Wild West? We've got some real mean riding bulls out here."

"He needed to know how to find his way around the county. We're going to have brunch at the *Seminole Inn*. Do you want to join us? I'll buy."

"Nope. I'd love to go with ya'll, but I've been on duty since eleven last night and I've still got to write up my reports. Plus, I'm waiting for a tow truck to pick up this abandoned van."

"Did they ever get the judge's bull out of the canal? He doesn't know about it yet."

"Nope. The ranch manager decided to leave it there. Between the gators, the alligator gar fish and the turkey buzzards it'll be gone in a week. But, it sure does smell like hell. You can see the buzzards circling it about a mile down the road."

"I believe you. We don't need to see it. The judge saw the video tape and I thought that he would 'split a gut' laughing. He doesn't know that it was his bull. I didn't tell him either."

"He won't miss it. He has four more. He only uses the ranch for his card games 'wild weekends' anyway."

"How are the owners of the *Silver Saddle* making out? Did you get them calmed down so they won't sue him?"

"Yeah. I told them that you would send them a check for the damage to the electric bull and the mirror behind the bar. But, the owner's wife is real pissed off over her broken big toe."

"She'll get over it. It was her fault anyway for trying to teach him how to line dance bare footed. I understand that you played the tape at shift change. I owe you a hundred bucks."

"Forget it. Just watching him fly *'ass over tea kettle'* into the manure pile was worth it."

"Elmo, it's eleven twenty-five and we've got to get over to the *Seminole Inn* for the buffet before it gets too crowded."

Before Mack could get a word in edgewise Tina the dropped silver-blue *Beamer* into low gear, spun out of the parking lot onto State Road 710 and showered the deputy's car with loose gravel. The dust cloud resembled a World War II smoke screen.

"Tina. Why didn't you give me a chance to say something to your cousin to explain?"

"Actions speak louder than words. Yours certainly did. He knows who you are. That's enough. Here we are. This is the *Seminole Inn*. I hope that you appreciate ambiance and history."

"I'll try."

"Look around and feat your eyes on seventy years of old Florida history. The *Seminole Inn* was built in 1926 by a banker from Baltimore a Mr. S. Davies Warfield. He planned to make *Indiantown* the southern headquarters of his *Seaboard Airline Railroad*. Look at those six high-backed wooden rockers sitting on the porch. They're waiting for someone to come along and sit a spell. The inn advertises that *'there's no charge or reservations needed for porch rocking'*. That ceiling is made from *'pecky cypress'* and it will last forever. Let's go in and have brunch."

The white trimmed, double French doors swung open and they walked inside into the lobby. Mack felt as though he had just stepped out of a 'time capsule' into the 1920's. Twin elegant winding staircases that lead to a 'sitting room' above the lobby framed the brick fireplace. The wall fixtures were solid brass and elegant bronze chandeliers hung from the twelve-foot high *'pecky cypress'* ceiling. The hardwood floors, polished to a soft gloss, mirrored the sunlight from the lace-trimmed windows.

The small wooden table in an antechamber across the room and framed by an arched door caught Mack's eye. He walked over to examine the contents of the tabletop and was pleasantly surprised. It contained a 'treasure trove' not unlike that in the shoebox that he kept hidden under his bed when he was a boy. There was a bleached out white turtle shell, sans the turtle of course, a set of deer antlers, a deer skull equipped with a set of antlers, a dried corn snake skin, a piece of the jaw bone of a cow, a piece of a wasp's nest and some garden snail shells.

"Hey there *Yankee Boy*! Are you coming, or what? The buffet line is open. Let's go!"

"Okay. I'm coming. Hold your horses."

After they were seated, and had started to eat, Tina opened the conversation. "What do you think about Dave? Did you guys have a good conversation yesterday?"

"He's okay I guess. I think that he tried to scare me to death and display his lack of basic boat piloting skills."

"Do you think that he's straight? Is he a straight shooter? Can we trust him?"

"You would know that better than me. He said that you were in charge of whatever is going on around here and that he was just a coordinator. He told me that his brother drowned in the North Fork, but he thinks that he was murdered. He doesn't know by whom, or why, except that he might have been working undercover for the FDLE. He has a suspicion that the guys in the black speedboat killed him. Ralph told me that Dave's brother was shot - not drowned, but that Dave doesn't know it."

"That's all true. But, did Ralph tell you that his uncle was the St. Lucie County coroner?"

"Yes."

"Did he fill you in on Rat and Bear?"

"Yes. But, I haven't had a chance to spend any time alone with either one of them."

"Did he advise you to stay low key on the subject of Laos when you talk to them?"

"Yes. Do they know who I am and why I'm here? Although I'm not sure that I even know for certain."

"No. They might just go *'postal'* if they knew. They are both very unstable and unpredictable."

"Aren't we all just a little bit unstable? It depends on who is doing the evaluating."

"Mack. Let's just drop the subject. Neither one of us is a psychiatrist. They'll both look you up in time and on their terms. You need to check them out carefully. What did he have to say about Mel the *'narc'*?"

"Not much except that his brother was living in the marina cottage and disappeared one night. He suspects that he had a tip on a drug drop offshore and tried to make the bust solo."

"That's also correct. He was an agent and you took his place. I suspect that someone 'fingered' him as an undercover agent and 'whacked' him. I also think that he was set up by someone who had access to information about the investigation."

"Why am I here?"

"Because you are very different. We took great pains to 'sanitize' you completely. There may be some suspicions about you are and what you are doing here, but you have to play the 'hired hand' and 'fishing guide' routines to the hilt."

"Yes ma'am. Reckon that I can do that.

"Mack, it's almost the end of March. If you get your Coast Guard captain's license soon you should be in the flow of things by the end of May or at the latest the first of June. It will take a couple of months for you to build up a steady clientele and repeat customers. You need to be doing a lot of night fishing to get the 'lay of the land' so to speak. I'm going to try to stay out of your hair for the next few weeks and treat you like an employee. No socializing at all. Do you understand?"

"Yes ma'am. Reckon that I do. You can't fraternize with the lowly 'hired help'. Yes ma'am. I understand completely."

"Mack, what do you recall about your last assignment?"

"Nothing. I remember waking up in a 'fleabag' motel in Lafayette, Indiana with some 'goon' trying to beat the door down. I don't know what I was running away from, or why, but I knew that I had to get out of Chicago and get my butt to Stuart."

"Do you have any recollection whatsoever about what you might have been doing in Chicago?"

"No. Why?"

"Often people in situations such as yours have a tendency to hallucinate about things they have done, or places they have been. We try to identify the symptoms early and provide them with suitable treatment before it gets completely out of hand. Hallucinations can be very dangerous and can make someone neurotic, or even psychotic, in some severe cases. Do you ever have any strange dreams about covert military activities that you might have thought that you were involved in at some point?"

"Why do you ask that? If I do it's my own private 'purgatory' and I can deal with it in my own way."

"Mack. Don't get defensive. I'm only trying to help you."

"Tina, I don't need any help. I'm just fine."

"When were you last hospitalized for any type of illness, physical or mental?"

"When I was a teenager. I broke my shoulder playing football on the beach."

"Are you certain?"

"Yes."

"Have you ever received any counseling, drug therapy, or electroshock therapy for hallucinations?"

"Of course not! Why would you ask such a stupid question?"

"There is no such thing as a stupid question. But, there are stupid answers."

"Are you done asking questions? I'm tired of this 'cat and mouse' game."

"I'm quite finished. Mack it's past one o'clock and we have been sitting here gabbing for an hour and a half. Let's go."

"Where are we going?"

"Your tour isn't over yet. We're going to keep going west on Route 710 until we hit Route 70. We are going to take it east to

Fort Pierce. There is an antique shop up there on the west side of U.S. 1 that I want to stop at. I want to see if they still have the *Roseville* cookie jar that I looked at last week. They were asking two-fifty for it. If it's still there they might be willing to drop the price. I really want it."

"Two bucks and a half for a cookie jar?"

"Not two dollars and fifty cents you dummy! Two hundred and fifty dollars. That's a real bargain for a green *Roseville* cookie jar in the *magnolia* pattern."

"What the hell is *Roseville*? Solid gold?"

"If I have to explain it to you then it's much to complicated for you to understand anyway. You are just a *'dumb boy'*."

Put firmly in his place by Tina because of his lack of expertise in the antique cookie jar market Mack decided to sit back and shut up for the rest of the trip. He might see something that he could put to future use. But, he wished that she would stop running her mouth. The monotonous drone and soft purr of her voice blended in with the sound of the rushing air and he dozed off. He awoke to the simultaneous shrieking of tires and a sudden jolt to the right that threw him hard against the car door. The *Beamer* skidded to a noisy stop in the dirt parking lot of the antique shop and raised a cloud of brown dust that enveloped the car in a choking mist.

"They've still got the cookie jar. I called them on the cell phone while you were snoring like a gorilla and they agreed to take off ten percent if I bought it today. I'll be right back."

"How can I go anywhere? You have the key and I'm strapped in. I'm hesitant to move in fear of what I might have left in my pants - I don't want to smear it."

Mack took stock of the place. The antique shop was a quaint Victorian-style house sitting on top of what appeared to be a high sand dune. Unfortunately for him Tina had parked under a tree filled with squabbling blackbirds all of which very upset that she had invaded their territory. The birds took turns dive bombing Mack's head and picking at his hair. He fended them off with a rolled up map and clobbered two of them into 'next week'.

"Hey bud. Those birds are a protected species. Leave 'em alone or I'll swat you with this."

Startled by the voice, Mack turned around in the plush, blue-leather bucket seat. Directly behind the silver-blue *Beamer* stood a short, squat, bald-headed man wearing yellow Bermuda shorts, black knee-high socks, open-toed brown leather sandals and a Hawaiian-style short-sleeve shirt. He gripped a dried out palm tree frond like it was a baseball bat and looked ready to hit Mack's head over the right field wall of *Shea Stadium*.

"Hey bud - take it easy. I was trying to protect myself. The crazy birds were dive bombing my head."

"Then why did you park under a tree where they're nesting?"

"I didn't park here. I wasn't driving. She was." Mack directed his adversary's attention towards the tall svelte redhead wearing a lime-green mini-skirt and matching top who was briskly walking towards the *Beamer* and gingerly carrying a small box.

"Tina. What are you doing way up here in *Fort Pierce*? It's a long way from *West Palm Beach*."

"Well judge, I could ask you the same question. But, I'm antique shopping. I didn't know that your wife was interested in antiques. Is that her sitting in your car? I should tell her hello."

"That's okay. She's very tired. We spent the night at the ranch because some *dumb ass* tried to ride my bull like it was a horse, ran him into a canal and he drowned. I think that it's the same guy that was on the video tape that you showed in open court yesterday. Why didn't you tell me that it was my bull?"

"I didn't know. But, you thought that it was funny yesterday."

"It was funny yesterday, but I didn't know then that it was my prize *Brangus* bull."

"Maybe you will find out who it was someday. Judge, where did your wife change her hair color to blonde? I'm going over and tell her how nice her hair looks."

"Tina. Stop right there and go on about your own business. I'll see you in court on Monday."

"Okay judge. See you on Monday."

"What was all that about?"

"That wasn't the judge's wife. It was his girl friend. She's an exotic nude dancer at a club in *Fort Pierce* and he takes her out to the ranch for private dance lessons. He was looking at your face real hard and I think that he knows it was you on the bull. I got the cookie jar for fifteen percent off. Let's go home. It's two-thirty and it'll be three-thirty when we get back."

"I'm ready. I've seen all that I need to see for one day and I need a nap real bad."

"I feel a little sleepy myself. A nap sounds real good on a lazy Saturday afternoon." Tina smiled demurely, shifted into reverse and mashed the gas pedal to the floorboard. Dirt and stones flew wildly as the *Beamer* tore down the driveway in 'reverse' gear. Mack grabbed the windshield for support and scrunched down in the leather bucket seat. Still in 'reverse', she swung into the southbound lane of U.S. 1, jerked the floor mounted gearshift handle backwards into 'low' and tromped the accelerator to the floorboard. The spinning tires screamed in protest as the *Beamer* leaped ahead barely averting a rear-end collision with a southbound moving van. Mack tried to duck under the dashboard, but his seat belt held him in place and he hit his head on the gear shift knob. Tina smiled sweetly, patted him on the head with her right hand and softly mouthed something that he could not hear over the screaming tires.

Mack leaned his aching head back in the soft, leather headrest, closed his eyes and hoped that she wouldn't rear end the moving van. The thought of the intense pain of decapitation by the windshield ran through his mind. But, he dismissed it. Even if it hurt tremendously the pain wouldn't last for long. The tires slid to a stop in the loose gravel of the marina driveway. A dense dust cloud formed over the car and it's two occupants like an omen.

"Mack. Wake up! We're here."

"Where are we?"

"Back at the marina. You said that you wanted to take a nap."

"What time is it?"

"A little past three-thirty. Come on and get up. Grass is going to grow on your rear end if you sit there long enough."

"Okay. I'm coming."

Tina reached across the car, patted Mack on the left knee and gave it a little squeeze of assurance. He looked up and saw that her eyes were glowing like bright green emeralds under a jeweler's black light. She was smiling from ear to ear. "Come on big boy. Get up. It's 'nappie-poo' time. Let's go to bed."

"Tina, give me a minute. My right leg has gone to sleep."

"Mack, we don't have all day. I've been beeped twice in the past thirty minutes."

"You got beeped? This is Saturday. State employees don't work on the weekend. What's going on? Who beeped you?"

"Our illegal alien task force. We're having a problem with smugglers bringing Cubans and Haitians over from the Bahamas. They drop the refugees off on remote sections along the beach or force them to jump off the boat into water that is over their heads. A lot of them can't swim and they drown. Something big must be going down or they wouldn't have beeped me twice. Oh crap, there it goes again. Go in the cottage, change into something 'real comfortable' and make me a *Vodka Gimlet.* I'll be up as soon as I return this call."

"Okay."

Tina dashed down the twelve wooden stairs to the sailboat dock and Mack entered the cottage. He put a *Kenny G.* album on the CD player, sprayed air freshener in the bathroom and dashed on some *Old Spice.* He had two *Vodka Gimlets* ready and waiting when she burst through the front door.

"Sorry, Mack. Everything is off. I have to run to West Palm right now! There was a major drop of Haitians on *Singer Island* early this morning and my office has been trying to reach me for hours. But, I had the beeper turned off until we left the antique store. The boat captain is in custody and they need me there to write out the charge sheets. I have to appear before a Federal judge in the morning to present the charges. Looks like it will be an all-nighter for me. I'll call you when and if I have time. Bye."

"But . . .

"No ifs, ands or buts. Bye." The *Beamer* 'roared' out of the driveway faster than an *Indy 500* racer leaving the starting line. Loose pea gravel flew across the parking area, 'dinged' off the cottage windows and 'spattered' on the porch. In a matter of seconds there was nothing left except a heavy cloud of dust.

Mack shrugged his shoulders and went into the cottage. He decided to drink the *Vodka Gimlets* himself. After he polished off the two *Vodka Gimlets,* and the glass of warm Merlot that he had poured for himself earlier, he sat down in the recliner, pulled out the footrest put his head back and dozed off.

Brrring Brrring Brrring

Mack's nap was disturbed by the obnoxious green telephone hanging on the kitchen wall. It might be Tina coming back!

"Hello?"

"Mack. Is that you?"

"Yeah. Who's this?"

"It's Bear. Got any plans for dinner?"

"Nope."

"Come on over. I'm frying up a bunch of fish that I caught last night. Plus, I've got three cases of very lonesome cold beer that need a friend. Interested?"

"Sounds good to me. How do I find your place?"

"I live on the east side of Grouper Street. You can't miss it. There's an old green pickup truck propped up on concrete blocks in the front yard. Park your car in the driveway and walk around the north side of the house to the back.

Watch out for the dogs. The black one growls, but doesn't bite. It's the sneaky, white female 'Pit Bull' that lives under the front porch that you gotta' watch out for. She won't attack you from the front. But, when you walk past the porch she'll sneak out and bite you on the calf of your leg. Be real careful, because once she grabs hold on your leg she won't let go. She's my 'ear' dog and I use her as a 'catch' dog when I'm out hunting wild hogs up by *Yee Haw Junction*. Mack, can you make it over for dinner?"

"Sure. Can you stand by the side of the house and watch the white dog for me?"

"No problem."

"I'll see you in five minutes. But, first I have to feed the cat."

CHAPTER
11

Bear invited Mack over for dinner because he was planning on deep frying fish in the backyard and knew that Mack enjoyed fresh fish. Dinner's over and the 'stuffed' duo are relaxing in white, plastic patio chairs alternately burping beer belly gas and breaking wind. Each of them is trying to out do the other in demonstrating male dominance and ultimate bragging rights.

Mack burped and opened the conversation. "Tonight is just perfect for snook fishing. The combination of the full moon and outgoing tide are just right. I'm going to run out to the red nun buoy just before dark, catch a few greenies for bait and anchor up under the Roosevelt Bridge. The tides at a high 'stand' at ten forty-five and it will be running out strong about twelve-thirty. I like to fish for snook during the last two hours of an outgoing tide and that'll be between two-thirty and four-thirty."

"Yep. I agree with ya'll. I'm going to slip up to the North Fork a little ways past *Club Med* and do some fishing myself tonight. I usually 'poke by' the Roosevelt Bridge about eleven-thirty. That gives the 'water cops' time to put away their boats and be on their way home to poke 'mama'. If I see ya'll on the water tonight I'll holler. Keep an eye out for Rat. He likes to prowl around on the full moon."

"What do you mean prowl?"

"He usually hangs out by the *'Silver Tarpon Restaurant'* dock.

Its at the foot of the Roosevelt Bridge just north of *Shepherd's Park*. He throws out food scraps and when them old, scruffy *gafftopsail cat fish* come a boiling to the surface and he nails 'em with a long-handled steel gaff!"

"Catfish? Nobody eats saltwater catfish."

"Rat eats anything that crawls, swims, flies or walks. You haven't lived until you've eaten a *gafftopsail catfish* deep-fried in hot peanut oil. It's yummy for the tummy."

"Yuk! I'll take your word on it. Beat, it's six-thirty. I have to leave if I am going to catch any bait before dark. That fish was really good. What was it? Pompano?"

"Naw. it was just some old grubby *gafftopsail catfish* that Rat caught last night and brung over to the house about sun up."

"Catfish? You fed me catfish? No! It was pompano? Right?"

"Wrong. It was *gafftopsail* catfish all right. The heads and tails are right over there in the trashcan. Do you want me to dig 'em out and prove it to you?"

"No thanks Bear. In my mind I am convinced that it was pompano and it's going to stay pompano."

"Mack. Have it your own way. Just don't ask me ever again what you're eating for dinner when you're at my house."

"Okay. I won't ask if you promise not to tell me."

"Agreed. If you want to catch some *'greenies'* for bait tonight slip over to the House of Refuge. I call 'em *'snuuk candy.'* (Bear pronounced the double o's as a series of long u's.) The tarpon have the *'greenies'* backed up close to the rocks. The school of 'em up by the red nun buoy were scattered by kingfish and are too skittish to catch. If you are by the Roosevelt Bridge when I come by about five, and you don't have any *'snuuks'* I'll drop off a couple when I see you. If you can manage to stay up that late."

"How could you have any snook? You don't carry a fishing pole and even if you did you wouldn't know how to use it. Are you catching snook in a gill net? That's illegal!"

"Me use an illegal gill net? Of course not! I won't have any *'snuuks'* in the boat except the two that I caught on my hand line. Two's legal to have - if they was caught on hook and line."

"Hand line? Come on Bear. Who are you trying to kid? You can't catch snook on a hand line. You know better than that."

"I catch 'em every night. I'll show you when I see you about five in the mornin' by the Roosevelt Bridge."

"Bear, I'm certain that you will have some snook. You are nothing but an incorrigible old poacher. But the snook won't be in the boat will they? You'll have them tied off to a back cleat with a piece of mono and a weight to pull them down to the bottom if you are stopped by the marine patrol. I remember how it's done. But you won't catch them on hook and line."

"Mack. See to it that you don't ever forget how to poach 'snuuks'. It might just come in handy for you some day."

"I'll never forget. Bear, I have to be going if I am going to catch any bait. I'll see you about five at the Roosevelt Bridge."

"Ta Ta."

Mack stood up to leave and spotted a white nylon gill net strung between two palm trees. "What are you doing with a gill net hanging up in your back yard? They're illegal."

"Drying it out. It got wet in the rain last night."

"Because it got wet in the rain? Who are you trying to kid?"

"Not you, that's for sure. Now Mack git' along now and catch your 'greenies'. And, don't get 'hot and bothered' about what you see in my yard. You never saw no gill net here. Understand?"

"I think I do. I'll see you in the morning. Don't get caught."

"I won't. Don't you fret none about it neither".

Mack waved goodbye to Bear and his wife Emogene. She had taken Mack's seat and was busy demonstrating that she could belch and fart as well as any man.

When Mack got to the boathouse he topped off the boat's fuel tank with the two five-gallon cans of gas that he kept there. He kept the tank full because at full throttle the 250-horsepower outboard gulped twenty gallons of gas per hour. He slipped the two six-foot spinning rods that were kept rigged for 'greenies' (thread fin herring) into the vertical, white plastic rod racks mounted on the front of the steering console.

A 'greenie rig' consists of a series of eight to ten small gold-plated hooks tied to a twenty-pound test monofilament leader. A two-ounce lead sinker attached to the bottom end of the leader gives the weight needed to get the rig to the bottom quickly. When a school of 'greenies' is spotted breaking the surface a cast into the middle of the school usually yields four or five of the silvery green fish on the tiny gold hooks.

Mack located a school in twenty feet of water opposite the *House of Refuge* just as Bear had suggested. He filled his two live wells to capacity in less than fifteen minutes. The sun was setting over the trees in a giant red ball and the ocean was as calm as the water in a child's backyard wading pool. Mack turned off the outboard engine and allowed the boat to drift. Gently caressed by the 'flooding' incoming tide the boat was carried south towards the inlet. He leaned back and inhaled the fresh salt air.

Giant silver tarpon in excess of one hundred pounds had pinned a school of silver mullet against the coral cliffs below the *'House of Refuge'* and thrashed the water into foam with their tails during their feeding frenzy. Screaming gulls and squawking brown pelicans dove head long into the melee unafraid of being devoured by the 'blue sharks' feeding on the dead and dying mullet drifting towards the bottom. The tarpon ignored the dead mullet preferring to attack and engulf their prey alive.

Mack twisted the ignition key to the right and the giant outboard engine roared to life. He shoved the throttle forward to engage the gears and the boat jumped ahead. He throttled back slightly, leveled the boat to a horizontal plane with the hydraulic trim tabs, and headed for the inlet. The boat's bow cut a pie-shaped slice out of the green saltwater and the engine ejected a foaming white rooster tail five feet up into the air behind it. Spray flew in all directions.

He arrived back at the marina at 8:23 P.M. connected the battery charger to the live wells' water pumps, fed the cat, heated up a can of corned beef hash, threw two, over-easy eggs on top of he hash put a *Kenny G.* album on the CD player and sat down to eat. *'A man needs dinner if he's going to be out fishing all night."* After 'scarfing' down the hash and eggs Mack set the bedside alarm clock for 10:00 P.M. and laid down on the bed for a nap.

BRRRING

Startled by the alarm Mack flew out of bed, brushed his teeth, threw out the cat and headed down the wooden stairs to the boathouse. The sun had set two hours earlier and the full moon gave off enough light to make it appear almost daylight. He unclipped the battery charger, slipped the bow and stern lines off the cleats, backed out of the boathouse and pressed the garage door opener 'close' button. The boathouse door slid into place.

Mack was almost to the mouth of *Willoughby Creek* when he realized that he had forgotten to initialize the security system. He made a U-turn and idled back to the marina. He docked the boat in the empty slip on the sailboat pier, raced up the twelve wooden steps alongside the boathouse to the front porch and twisted the nail head above the doorframe to a vertical position. The ten security cameras began rotating in their clear glass fishbowls.

Mack raced down the steps, threw off the lines and for the second time idled towards the mouth of *Willoughby Creek*. He arrived at the *Roosevelt Bridge* at 10:17 P.M. in plenty of time to catch the scheduled turn of the tide at 11:05 P.M. He idled under the draw, turned left, went down four pilings and dropped the ten-pound aluminum *Danforth* anchor over the side. The anchor line hung limply through the starboard bow cleat. The high tide was slack, at a high 'stand' and had not started ebbing towards the inlet and it's jagged rock *'rip rap'* barriers. Mack decided that there was no sense in baiting up until the tide started to move. He put his feet up on the gunwale and stared at the moon. It was difficult to imagine that men had actually walked on its silver surface more than twenty years earlier. He closed his eyes and drifted off into oblivion.

The solid *'jerk'* of the boat against the taut anchor line signaled that the tide had begun its stealthy retreat towards the inlet. It was time to 'bait up' for the giant snook that lurked along the shadow line of the old bridge lying in wait to ambush any foolish mullet that dared to swim into the light given off by the bridge lights above.

Mack selected a 'medium action' seven-foot fiberglass boat rod equipped with a hefty ocean-size reel spooled with fresh thirty-pound test monofilament. Mack used fifty-pound test mono leader because a crafty snook would run around the oyster-studded concrete pilings in its frantic attempt to fray and break the line. He tied on a new 'number two' bait hook and clipped on a quarter-ounce split-shot sinker three inches above the black ball bearing swivel that connected the leader to the line. The small sinker was adequate to keep the bait below the surface, but not heavy enough to pull it to the bottom where the ever ravenous 'cat-snappers' lurked.

Mack dipped into the 'live well' with a short-handled, nylon dip net and scooped up a plump threadfin herring. He hooked the wriggling fish through the thick band of clear cartilage that formed its snout so that it would swim facing into the current. He put the reel on 'free spool' and let out just the 'right amount' of line to hold the frightened fish at the edge of the dark shadow line that ran the length of the bridge. He prepared the second rod in exactly the same manner and was 'ready'.

'Cat snapper' is a code word for 'gafftopsail catfish' that his fishing buddy Kenny made up several years earlier. It wasn't proper for a serious fisherman to report over the marine radio that he was only catching lowly catfish. Everyone listening to the marine radio would know of his disgrace immediately. However, admitting to catching big 'cat-snappers' would cause the radio to buzz with the excited conversations of other unwitting fishermen.

"Billy Bob, what the hell's a 'cat-snapper'?"

"Hell if I know. Must be some new kind of hybrid fish. I think that I read an article about it last week. It's half snapper and half catfish. Supposed to taste as good as a freshwater catfish and fight hard like a snapper."

"Let's find out where those other boys are and go catch us a mess of them 'cat-snappers'."

Mack's reel screamed as line ripped off in a frantic frenzy. The rod bucked in its holder as if it was trying to escape by diving into the water. He snapped back to reality from his imagined 'moon walk' and reached for the rod with his right hand. When he lifted the rod out of its holder he had to grab it with his other hand. The 'sea monster' on the other end of the line was on its way to South Africa with full intentions of taking the pole with it.

Mack leaned back into the rod 'hard' as he could to set the hook without snapping the line. His grandfather referred to that essential process as 'crossing the fish's eyes with love.' His grandfather's words echoed in his ears. *"Hit 'em again boy. Hit 'em again. Cross its beady little eyes for 'em. Hit 'em again."*

Mack fought the underwater titan for a good twenty minutes. His arms ached and his head was pounding. Giant beads of 'man sweat" formed on his forehead, merged into a pool and ran down his nose in a steady stream. Each time that he gained a foot of line the 'sea monster' took back two. It hadn't jumped, or broke water, so he assumed that it was a shark or a monster stingray. For certain it wasn't a *snook*. At last the steady pressure eased. As Mack slowly cranked line back onto the smoking reel the white 'under-belly' of a huge fish appeared under the bridge. Then he saw it! A thick, nasty, mucous-like 'white slime' coated the line above the water thirty feet away. The slime was the tell tale signature of a humongous 'cat-snapper'! Mack reared back on the hefty rod in an valiant attempt to break off the fish

A 'twangy' nasal voice rang out from under the shadows of the bridge. "Hey bud. Are you tryin' to break off that 'cat-snapper'? If you don't want it I'll take it off your hands." A long aluminum-handled, green nylon dip net snaked out from under the shadows of the bridge, enveloped the fish in its deep folds and disappeared back into the shadows. Mack's line went limp. "It's okay. You can reel in your line now. I got him off for ya'"

From out of the shadows of an 'oyster-encrusted' concrete piling emerged the strangest face that Mack had ever seen. The first thing that he noticed was the pair of dark glasses, followed by a long, stringy, unkempt black beard and a mane of black hair tied up in a pony tail and it was 'topped off' by a World War II German infantry helmet painted florescent orange. A long purple ostrich plume, similar to those worn by medieval knights engaged in jousting tournaments, trailed along the right side of the garish helmet. The plume was held in place by a tanned snakeskin band. The gaunt, bearded face featured a long, pointed nose that twitched from side to side, but the head had no ears! There were only dark, recessed shadows where ears belonged. The head nodded from side to side as the 'twangy' nasal voice emanated from its general direction. "Mack. Is that you? It's me, Rat."

"Yes, its me. Bear told me that you might be out tonight. But, he said that you would be over there by the *Tarpon Restaurant* trying to catch catfish."

"Normally I would be, but some inconsiderate stragglers

sitting in the waterside tables don't seem to be in any hurry to pay their check and leave. But, they're throwing scraps to 'my boys' and that'll fatten them up for later. I'll slip over there when the place is closed up. Mack, what cha' doing out here tonight?"

"I thought that I would try my luck on snook. There's a full moon and the tide should start running out soon. I brought along a couple dozen live greenies for bait."

"Only thing I saw you catch was that 'little' *cat-snapper*. That's about all you'll catch over here. The snook are stacked up on the other side of the bridge waiting for the tide to turn. Anchor up under the bridge and let your bait drift between there and the railroad bridge. It'll be at least an hour before the tide's running right. You've got time to sit a spell. Wanna' talk awhile?"

"Sure. Where do you want to go?"

"Why don't I just tie off to your boat? We'll just sit out here and shoot the breeze."

"Okay. Throw me a line and come along this side." Mack got a better look at his visitor under the soft glare of the lights from the Roosevelt Bridge. What he saw amazed him. Rat's boat, if you could call it a boat, was an inflatable kayak, powered with the smallest, and no doubt the oldest, outboard motor he had ever seen. The boat was painted a horrible shade of green and the brush strokes gave the surface a ripple effect. His visitor was about 5' 6" tall and might weigh all of 150 pounds if he was fully dressed and soaking wet too boot.

The wide, yellow ribbon tied into a large bow on the end of the long braided ponytail and the thin leather thong strung around Rat's neck caught Mack's attention. A long thin bone, about two inches long, was strung on each side of a silver coin. The coin was suspended from the thong by a piece of silver wire about three inches long. When Rat slithered over the side of Mack's boat and slipped into the seat alongside him Mack noticed that he was missing the index and middle fingers of his left hand. The hand looked like a giant lobster claw.

"Mack what brings you to town?

"What do you mean brings me to town? I came here to live?"

"Right. What cha' running away from up north? Money problems? Child support? Divorce?"

"I'm not running away from anything. But, thank you so much for caring about my personal life. I moved down here to lay back, fish and take it easy for the next thirty years or so."

"Why are you living in the marina? The last guy disappeared."

"I don't know anything about who stayed there before me and I don't care. I'm there because there was an ad in the paper for a resident marina manager. I took it. Enough said."

"What paper? I didn't see anything in the *Stuart News*."

"The ad wasn't in the *Stuart News* it was in the *Chicago Tribune*. Are you sure that you can read?"

"I can read very well, thank you. I'm a college graduate. I went to Florida State on the GI Bill after I came home from 'Nam. I got a degree in Criminology and spent ten years working narcotics undercover in the Keys for the FDLE. That's short for Florida Department of Law Enforcement. Finally I'd seen enough and quit. Life's too short for that."

"What do you mean seen enough and quit?"

"It's the same everywhere. Law enforcement gets its hands tied by liberal trial lawyers who get their clients off on technicalities. The only people going to jail for drugs are the blacks caught with a rock or two of crack in their pocket and the white kids dumb enough to grow pot in their bedroom under artificial lights and run up a five hundred dollar a month electric bill. My life is worth more to me than getting blown away for a couple thousand bucks a month and a pension - that is if I could last twenty years without getting killed or maimed. I got shot at in 'Nam for only three hundred bucks a month, and that included combat pay, for nothing. It ain't ever going to happen again."

"What are you doing in Stuart? Don't you like the Keys?"

"Sure I like the Keys. But, I was made as a *'narc'* all the way from Key West to Miami. I can't do undercover work anymore because it isn't very hard to pick me out of a crowd. I'm not the type for 'white collar' office work. I can't stand to wear a suit and put up with all the political crap that goes with it. After I left the FDLE I got a Coast Guard license and tried running sailing charters out of Miami on Rickenbacker Causeway. I booked a lot of trips over the phone, but when the people came down to the boat they usually got sea sick and left.

"I can't imagine why. You have a nice personality."

"Right. And, I dance good too. Blind dates never did much for me. Back in 1992, when *Hurricane Andrew* was headed for Miami, I packed up and took off north up the *Intracoastal* as fast as I could go. At the *Evans Crary Bridge* a plastic bread wrapper got sucked into my water intake, the engine overheated and froze up solid as a meteor. I limped into Stuart under sail. When I got to the Roosevelt Bridge the bridge tender dropped the draw to soon and it ripped my mast off. When I got out from under the bridge, my mast was laying on the deck. I used the kayak and five-horse 'kicker' to tow the boat into *Shepherd's Park*.

After Andrew passed, the Marine Patrol told me to get out of the park and anchor out here. That's my boat over there. I can see everything coming and going up and down the St. Lucie River."

"How did you manage to anchor and stay here for so long?"

"It was easy. I pulled the engine out and dumped it over the side. It was frozen up solid anyway. I'm using the engine for my permanent mooring."

"How are you living? What do you do for money and food? Do you have a job?

"A job? Take a look at me. I'm missing my ears, two fingers on my left hand, the tip of my nose and four front teeth. I've got no big toes, I'm deaf in my left ear, walk with a limp and I can't run. Do you think that I got this way by playing in the roller derby? There were gifts from *Uncle Sam* and two tours in *'Nam*. For all of this I get a disability check from the VA and another one from Social Security every month. It's not enough to live on as I'm still paying child support. But it's okay. I'm making it.

"What do you mean child support? You were married?"

"I got married while I was in college and had two kids by the time I graduated. After graduation I got a job with the FDLE in Tallahassee. Then I was drafted. When I came home from *'Nam* I spent four months in the VA Hospital in West Palm. While I was laid up my wife ran away with her lesbian hairdresser and filed divorce papers. When I got out she, the kids and the house were gone. I went back with the FDLE and was assigned to the Keys."

"What a story. Bear told me that you prowl - oops I'm sorry, that wasn't a good choice of words, are most active at night."

"I can't go out much during the day in the bright sun because my eyes are extremely light sensitive. I was a *'tunnel rat'* in *'Nam* and a stun grenade went off in my face. Most of what happens around here goes on at night and there's a lot of stuff to eat out here - if you know where to look."

"A lot to eat? Like what and where?"

"The Roosevelt Bridge tender who works the late shift comes on at eleven. He let's me work the bridge picking up the fish that people leave laying around after they go home. Jacks, ladyfish, catfish, stuff like that. I bring him hot coffee and lots of donuts and he doesn't let people fishing in the bridge bug me."

"Where do you get the coffee and donuts? Do you buy them? That could be expensive."

"Nope. I *'dumpster dive'* for 'em after they close the donut shop. It's okay with them because they have to throw out the ones they don't sell any way. We collect the left over coffee in a Styrofoam bait bucket. The insulation keeps it hot all night long.

"Does the bridge tender know that the donuts that you bring him come out of the dumpster?"

"Why should he know? It ain't no big deal. He likes 'em."

"He can't possibly eat all of the donuts that you drag out of the dumpster. What do you do with the rest of them?"

"We have two other bridges - the Evans Crary and the bridge over to Hutchinson Island. They both have bridge tenders and they all like donuts."

"Why do you give donuts to the other bridge tenders?"

"For the fish, dummy. For the fish and for protection!"

"What do you mean for the fish? You can't eat all of the fish left on the bridges."

"What makes you think that it's only me eating the fish? There are lots of homeless guys living in the woods along the creeks that run through town. They have to eat too!"

"You mean to tell me that you are feeding the homeless stale donuts and old fish?"

"Sure, but that's not all. Do you wanna' hear about how we the pick up road kill and make the restaurant plate scrapings?"

"Road kill? Restaurant plate scrapings? That sounds gross."

"It's not gross. There's lots of good food left on peoples'

plates when they send them back to the kitchen. Often they can't eat everything on their plate and would be embarrassed to ask for a *'doggie bag'*. The guys who wash dishes in restaurants all have a plastic bag hanging on a nail beside the sink. They scrape off meatballs, pork chops, baked potatoes, - it's all good stuff. About midnight when everybody's off work we stoke up the charcoal grills at Shepherd's Park and have a cookout. You should join us some night. You'll like the boys. We eat real good!"

"Not in the near future. I've got a lot to do. Tell me about the road kill collecting. You can't be serious!"

"Of course I'm serious. There's nothing wrong with fresh road kill. *Meat's meat after it's cooked.* Ask any Chinese restaurant owner. Take your cat, dog, moose, horse, beef and pork. Once it's cooked people can't tell what it is. At least most of our guys can't. Some might have an idea, but they don't care."

"How are you doing this collecting? Do you go around in a car picking up road kill?"

"Not in a car. I've got a neat system that took me several years to get perfected for maximum efficiency. I have an Italian *Vespa* motorbike that I salvaged out of the trash. I painted it robin's egg blue with some enamel that I found in a dumpster. The paint has a few streaks in it, but no one notices them in the dark. I bolted a super market shopping cart basket to the handlebars. That makes it easy to just toss in what I find. There's a lot of road traffic out that at night and often there isn't time to stop and pack the stuff away in the saddlebags. I call my system *'snatch and run'*.

My motorbike is equipped with black, plastic saddlebags that I fill up with ice from the ice machine at the Holiday Inn before I go out. I punched some holes in 'em with a screwdriver to let the melted ice and whatever else to run out while I'm driving down the road. More than once I've been chased down a back road by a pack of yelping dogs sniffing at the saddlebags.

"This is really bizarre. You are pulling my leg, aren't you?"

"Nope. It's for real. Come with me some night and I'll give you some pointers. You'll be proud of me for the *'American ingenuity'* that I use in my road kill collecting. I've got a four-foot long, wooden-handled fishing gaff sitting upright in a chrome fishing rod holder bolted to the left handle bar. A nylon fishing net, with a four-foot long aluminum handle, sits in a rod holder on the right side. When I'm huntin' for fresh road kill - I'm always a lookin' and a watchin'. When I spot something that looks really *'primo'* I grab the most appropriate tool. It could be the gaff, or the net. I snatch it up in one swoop, toss it in the basket and I'm on my way. I use the gaff for stuff that has obviously expired. I use the net for the ones that still have a little life in them and are trying to crawl off the road.

"My God! You are serious! You need professional help. Have you told this tale to the VA?"

"I tried. They sent me to some shrink who told me that I was having hallucinations."

"I can't imagine why anyone would believe you. But, strangely enough I do."

"Thank you for saying that. You don't know how much I appreciate your sincerity."

"You're certainly welcome. Is there any more to *Road Kill Collecting 101?*"

"Here's the best part. It's my best idea and I was thinking of having it patented. I wear baseball shoes with metal cleats just in case I come across an overly lively potential roast that tries to get away from me. The metal cleats pin 'em to the road while I whack 'em in the head with a tire iron from a '49 Chevy'. It's American-made and patriotic. I like that."

"How do you get the motorbike over to your boat?"

"I don't. I chain it up to a twin-trunk mango tree in Shepherd's Park. The other live aboard boaters chain their bikes to a metal bike rack on a concrete pad. But. I like the mango tree. It has personality. Just like me."

"You certainly do have personality. Why do you take care of the others?"

"I'm kinda' like a shepherd with my own little flock. Most of the boys are really messed up in the head and need help! They don't have any families, and if they do, they usually don't want anything to do with them. I'm about the only one that doesn't have a head problem."

"I could tell immediately that you are just fine. How many members are there in your flock of lost souls?"

"It varies. Most of them drift away up north in the summer and hang around their hometowns, but we have a few like me who stay here year round. I'd guess fifteen to twenty."

"I detect a slight nasal twang in your voice. Where are you from originally?"

"I was born and raised in Turkey Foot, Kentucky, off Route 587 west of New Zion - right smack dab in the middle of the Daniel Boone National Forest. I grew up with a rifle in one hand and a shotgun in the other. The last time that I went home was in seventy-five and my people didn't want anything to do with 'Nam vets. Look at me. I should be in a side show."

"I understand completely. Is that how most of the others in your group feel as well?"

"Yep. We don't fit in with society and quite frankly we don't give a damn. We do our own thing, live from day to day and don't interfere with anyone else. Mack. Would ya' like a drink?"

"A drink of what?"

"Homemade 'hooch'. It'll rock your socks and tickle your innards. Made it myself." Rat waved an open wide-mouthed glass container under Mack's nose. "Take a good whiff and catch the bouquet. It's to die for and the best you ever tasted. I promise."

"My God. What is that smell? Be careful and don't shake the jar. It might explode in your face!"

"There's nothing' to worry about. It's safe. I told ya' I made it myself. I drink it all the time and it relaxes me so that I can sleep all day. After three shots of this I sleep like a baby for hours."

"Like a baby! You mean a zombie. Is that embalming fluid? Did you raid a funeral home?"

"No, but that's not a bad idea. If we could get our hands on some we could strain it through old donuts to purify it."

"What is that stuff made from? It even smells dangerous."

"Nothing special. The boys pick up a few bottles of cheap aftershave at the corner store on the 'five finger discount plan'. That forms the base. We collect Sterno containers from the park trashcans and mix it all together in a bucket with some rubbing alcohol. Then we strain it through a sieve filled with smashed donuts and bagels to clean it up. It really packs a wallop! Oh, I almost forgot. We toss in a few pieces of lemon for flavor. "

"I think that I'll pass. The last time that I drank anything 'homemade' it was a farmer's potato *sake* in a little village on Okinawa. The other guys at the 'party' told me the next day that I crawled back to the base's main gate on my hands and knees. They also said that I 'growled' at the sentry, pissed on his leg and then bit him on the leg when he tried to handcuff me. I woke up in jail two days later with a really bad headache."

"Suit yourself. It just leaves more for me. You'll regret it later. It's really good and 'warms' the innards."

"Rat. Can you talk about your *'Nam* experiences? Do you ever have bad dreams?"

"Of course I can talk about it. I used to have nightmares and couldn't wake up from them."

"Are you okay with it now? Do you still have nightmares? Do you also have flashbacks?"

"Yes, to all three questions and I managed to work through it."

"You said that you were a 'tunnel rat.' Were you Army or Marine Corps?"

"Officially, none of the above. I worked with a group that was completely sanitized. Our job was to infiltrate North Viet Nam from our base at Lon Bien in Northern Laos and capture village officials for interrogation. It was called *'Project Phoenix'*."

"I'm familiar with it."

"It may sound nuts to you, but I enjoyed going hand to hand, *'mano to mano'* with 'Charlie' underground and in the dark."

"What happened to your hand? Can you talk about it?"

"I made a stupid mistake in a tunnel and my fingers were blown off by a 'satchel charge'. My hearing is bad because of the same explosion. My partner was killed and I was captured, but I managed to escape twice. The last time I escaped and the caught me they broke my left leg over a log for punishment. They figured that breaking my leg would keep me from escaping. It didn't and I got away anyway. The leg healed crooked while I hide out for three months in the jungle. That's one of the reasons why I walk with a limp and don't have good balance."

"One of the reasons? What's the other one?"

"I don't have any big toes because they were pulled off during torture. *'Charlie'* didn't like us tunnel rats because we got to 'em where they lived. After I was captured they tried to get me to talk and I wouldn't. To teach me a 'lesson' they put wire loops on my big toes and hung me upside down over a pigpen. When my toes ripped out I fell head first into the pigpen. The guard thought that it was funny, but they didn't laugh when I killed one of their pigs with my hands. That really made 'em mad and they beat me with their rifle butts – that's when my front teeth got knocked out. Then they drilled holes in my toes and hung 'em around my neck to punish me." Ray lifted the leather cord around his neck and held it up in the light so that Mack could see it clearly. "Mack. Do you see these two bones? Them two bones are my big toes."

"Your toes! You lost them in *'Nam* - didn't you?"

"I still had 'em around my neck when I escaped. There're mine and I kept 'em."

"What happened to your ears?"

"My ears and the end of my nose were chewed off by rats during what they called the *'bag over the head'* torture. They put three field rats in a burlap rice bag, tied it over my head and hung me upside down in a tree. My beard hides the rat bite marks on my neck and face. This here's a rubber nose that covers the cavity in the end of my nose." Rat pulled off the end of his nose and held it in the palm of his hand for Mack to admire.

"Rat. This takes the adage of *'cutting off your nose to spite your face'* to a new level. How did you get away? Why didn't they catch you again? How could you run with a broken leg?"

"I guess they figured the rats would kill me, but I struggled so hard that the rope broke. When I hit the ground two of the rats cushioned my fall and were smashed by my head. The third one got trapped behind my neck and I smashed him on a rock. The guards just left me lying on the ground. I could hear them laughing at me and that really made me mad."

"Why would they leave you on the ground? Didn't they know that you would try to escape?"

"Maybe they figured I had enough and deserved to get away"

"I'll bet that they were going to let the wild dogs drag you away into the jungle during the night and eat you alive."

"So that's why I heard dogs howling. They were waiting for the sun to go down to attack me."

"That's right. How did you get away?"

"The rope on my feet had come loose and although my hands were tied I could still run. The fiber rice sack had some holes in it and I could see through them. So, I got up and started running for the jungle. I ran until I couldn't run any more, tripped and fell down. I found a rock and rubbed the rope around my wrists in two. When I got the bag off it was dark and a pack of dogs was sitting in a circle around me."

"Did they try to attack you?"

"No. They were real friendly. They must have been pets in one of the villages and were lonesome. I think they knew that the *'Charlies'* would kill and eat 'em if they could catch 'em. They all just lied down in a circle around me and went to sleep. There were two lead alpha males - a white one and a black one. I called the black one *"Putter'* because he was always nosing around. I called the white one *'Slider'* because he liked to run through the mud and slide all over the place. Both of 'em snored and farted all night long. But they protected me from the other ones."

"How did you survive? What did you eat?"

"I stayed in the jungle eating what I could catch. Sometimes the dogs brought me things to eat. I lived in an old tunnel. It wasn't bad. I knew that I couldn't ever find my way out through the jungle so I stayed close to the camp figuring that someday someone would come looking for us."

"How long were you a prisoner before you escaped?"

"About a month. Most of it was spent in a bamboo cage half sunk in the river. Those river leeches were pure hell. Oh, there were several other guys soaking in cages with me, but they were so drugged up and out of it that they couldn't lift their heads."

"How many? Civilians or military? What type of uniforms?"

"Four guys besides me. None of them had uniform shirts and they only had on green pants."

"What kept them from breaking out of the cages?"

"'The cages were booby-trapped so that if there was a rescue attempt, or anybody touched 'em, they'd drop into the river and sink. The *Special Forces SOG* team, that stands for *'Studies and Observation Group'* that found me was on a raid to rescue those other guys. They came from both up and down river in rubber boats at the same time. They had a pair of choppers standing by a few miles away. When they raided the camp one of the *'Charlies'* ran out and tripped the releases on the cages. They all sank except for one that got hung up on a stump sticking out of the riverbank. They saved just that one guy."

"How do you know all of this?"

"I told ya'! I hid in the jungle in one of their tunnels. I watched the whole thing go down."

"How did you get out of the jungle and back to the states?"

"The group that came to rescue those guys saw me. They thought that I was a *'Charlie'* because I was dressed in black pajamas. They chased me into a tunnel and forced me out with tear gas. I was lucky that they didn't kill me. They took both of us back to Lon Bien by chopper. After we got cleaned up and had a hot meal the guy gave me this coin. He told me it was an extra one and for me to keep it as a reminder. I've had it right here on this cord ever since. I'll never take it off."

"I know a little about coins. Let me take a look at it. Hold your toes back a little bit." Mack tilted the well-worn silver coin back and forth to catch the light of the full moon. The *Springbok* stood out and stamped between its front feet was a "1."

"Rat, I'm sorry. I don't know as much about coins as I thought I did and I can't tell you anything about this one.

"Mack, what time is it?"

"It's ten fifty-five."

"I gotta' go. The donut shop closes at eleven o'clock and it's my turn to get the coffee and donuts. Keep a sharp eye out for Bear. He should be coming up the river in about in about a half hour. See ya'." Rat slithered over the side of Mack's boat into his green canoe and disappeared into the darkness under the bridge.

Left alone in the silence of the shimmering moonlight Mack closed his eyes, attempted to sort out the events of the past twenty minutes and dozed off into tranquility.

CHAPTER
12

It was almost 11:30 P.M. Saturday night and Bear was passing under the old Roosevelt Bridge on his way to the North Fork to gill net silver mullet and maybe even a couple of *'snuuks'*. He hoped that the Florida Marine Patrol wouldn't be out and were saving their energy for Sunday's day shift. The 'crazies' would be on the water tomorrow and half of them would be *'snockered'* on beer before noon.

If he was stopped by a nosy Florida Marine Patrol Officer Bear would toss any illegal snook over the side of his boat - but they wouldn't be lost. They would be secured to the boat by a piece of thirty-pound test monofilament fishing line tied off to a stern cleat. A quick jerk on the line would undo a slipknot and the fish would sink to the bottom. A small cork float tied on the line five feet above the fish held the line up vertically in the water. Later, when it was safe, Bear would return to retrieve the illegal catch with a weighted treble hook attached to a hand line.

Mack was anchored up on the west side of the Roosevelt Bride and had dozed off about a half hour earlier. When the black speedboat raced past him its violent wake 'smacked' the side of his boat and caused it to rock violently. Instinctively he grabbed the steering wheel to keep from being thrown into the water. The boat pitched upwards, paused in mid air for what seemed to be an eternity and immediately dropped down. Mack lost his grip and left with nothing to hold onto for support except air. He hit the deck face down in a full-length sprawl that knocked the wind out and blacked out. He awoke in a 'sleep-fogged' daze when he heard a familiar voice call out a greeting.

"Mack. Wake up! That was the black speedboat I was telling you and Ralph about yesterday. It's solid black and runs through here *'balls to the wall'* almost every night about eleven-thirty with no running lights showing. It'll be coming back up the river about four-thirty in the morning. Why don't you stay around here and wait? I'll be coming back through here about then and I'll show you some really big *'snuuks'*. How about it?"

"Bear. Is that you?"

"Yep. Its me alright."

"Those guys don't care who they wake up do they? I almost fell out of the boat and killed myself."

"They know that the water cops are home in bed 'poking' mama. Go back to sleep. The *'snuuks'* aren't biting anyway. I'll wake you up when I come back about four-thirty. We'll go have breakfast at the Queen Conch. They open at six. See ya' then." Bear pulled out from under the bridge and pointed the bow of his blue, flat-bottomed, wood commercial fishing boat north towards the North Fork of the St. Lucie River.

Mack managed to generate a weak, half-hearted wave from his awkward face down prone position in the bottom of the boat. "Okay. I'll stay right here and see you about four-thirty. Wake me up gently when you get here. Please, no big wakes. My ribs hurt like 'hell' from hitting the deck two minutes ago."

Mack was bone tired and needed some rest. He pawed an orange life preserver out of the storage bin below the seat and dragged it under his chin for a pillow. It had been a long day. He had a catfish dinner at Bear's, drank far too many beers and met Rat on his own turf. What an experience! It brought back many memories from long ago that he had managed to place in a memory cell and cover with the hard epoxy of denial. *'If he had no memory of it - then it couldn't have happened.'* But, there was something very familiar about Rat and the coin bothered him. How did Rat get the *South African One Rand* coin?

The droning of the traffic overhead and soft sea breeze took advantage of him. The boat rocked gently in the ebbing tidal current and playfully tugged at it's well secured ten-pound aluminum anchor. The *'whir'* of rubber car tires passing over the iron grate of the Roosevelt Bridge opening became a dull monotonous hum. It was peaceful. The temping siren *'Sleep'* was calling him - he could not resist her call any longer. Mack's mind eventually merged with the night.

Screams of pain rousted him from deep sleep. Mack shook his head and attempted to clear away the 'fog' of sleep. The harsh sunlight reflected off the water's mirrored surface, burned into his eyes and forced him to squint. Mack tried to shake the cobwebs out of his brain and reason where he was. He took a deep breath through his nose and felt the soft blood clots lodged in his nasal passages slip down the back of his throat. He gagged, coughed and spat out several bright red clots. They floated lazily on the water, framed by the bubbles in his saliva, and looked like miniature red lily pads. Tiny yellow fish emerged from their hiding places and nibbled at the foamy edges of the red clots.

The horrible screams continued. Mack raised his head and squinted towards the four thatched huts about fifty yards away that formed the compound. A man hung upside down from a rope tied to the branch of a tree directly over a pigpen. His hands and arms were tied behind his back and a brown, coarsely woven sack covered his head. He screamed and twisted savagely in his attempt to escape his bonds. Long, slender brown leaves shaken from the tree by the man's agonizing throes floated effortlessly on the wind and came to rest on the ground around the pig sty.

Four bored guards sat on their haunches on the porch of the largest hut about fifty yards away from the pigpen. They poked one another with their elbows, pointed at the man in the tree and laughed as if they had just heard a good joke. The man hanging from the tree limb continued to scream in pain and he guards passed around a tin canteen cup from which they drank their own home made version of *'happy juice'*.

The sharp *'crack'* from the direction of the tree sounded like a rifle shot and was followed by *'whump'* and the squealing of excited pigs. Mack squinted through his swollen eyes and saw that the rope suspending the man from the tree limb had broken.

The pigs snorted and squealed with excitement as they ripped at the man's clothing and flesh with their razor-sharp sharp hoofs and curved yellow tusks.

With the bag still over his head the 'violated' man crawled through the black mire and green slime of the pigpen and slid through an opening in the bamboo fence. He stumbled, fell to the ground, screamed and began beating the back of his head on a large rock. The guards doubled over with laughter and made no attempt to apprehend him. With his hands still tied behind his back the unfortunate soul struggled to his feet, stood erect, paused, seemed to take a deep breath and took off running towards the jungle screaming like a 'banshee'. A drunken guard discharged his automatic rifle in the man's direction, but only managed to 'knock' a sizeable chunk of bark out of the tree.

Still screaming at the top of his lungs the hooded man pitched head long into the depths of the jungle foliage and disappeared. His screams blended with the barking of a pack of wild dogs and resounded from the dense foliage for what seemed to Mack to be an eternity. The bored guards made no effort to move from their comfortable frond-matted porch and continued to pass around the tin canteen cup, poke each other in the ribs and laugh hilariously.

Mack drifted in and out of the uncharted depths of semi-consciousness, but managed to ignore the pain of the river leeches digging into his legs and the blood-sucking 'blue bottle' flies attacking the corners of his eyes.

The 'sputtering' of a cranky outboard motor brought him around. He tried to shake the fog and sleepiness out of his eyes and peered towards the direction of the sound. A boat with no running lights visible was heading south from the North Fork of the St. Lucie River and passed the triangle-shaped, red number "2" marker at *Coconut Point* on it's port side. When the boat turned east towards the Roosevelt Bridge the *Florida Marine Patrol* officer lit up the night sky with his boat's blue lights. He had been waiting for Bear in the long, dark shadows of the bridge for several hours. It was too late for Bear to turn back!

Bear slipped 'something' silver over the starboard side of his boat into the water. If he had illegal 'snuuks' to hide, a concrete block would pull them under and a length of thirty-pound test monofilament fishing line tied to his stern cleat would hold them to the boat. Bear tied them off there because the Marine Patrol had rubber boat bumpers on their starboard side and they liked to come up from behind and tie off on a vessel's port side.

From his position in the bridge's shadows Mack could see Bear grinning like a *Cheshire Cat.* Bear and Mack both knew the officer from their high school days. It was Bill Mason! The trio had poached gators together in the sloughs behind *Page Field Airport* in *Fort Myers* back in the 1950's.

"Hey there Bill. I sure am glad to see that's it's you. When I seen those blue lights come on the skin around my 'butt hole' got as tight as the top of a snare drum."

"It should have based on what I see in your boat. Bear, it looks like you got yourself a turtle dressed out and ready for the grill. What kind is it?" Several species of turtles were legal to take and several were not. Being from a commercial fishing family himself the Florida Marine Patrol officer was willing to give Bear a break if he gave him the answer he was looking for.

Irritated over being stopped Bear squirted a thick brown stream of brown *'bacca* juice out of the side of his heavily bearded face into the water. "Bill. This ain't no turtle! This here's a little *manatee* calf that I found floatin' dead up in the North Fork. It must have gotten hit by a boat and drowned. I figured that it would be a shame to waste the meat. We're going to roast him on a spit over some green mangrove branches on Memorial Day. I wanted a pig and last week we tried to catch a young wild hog out by *Yee Haw Junction.* But, the old sow pig gut gored my *'ear catch dog'* so bad that she let go of the pig and I had to shoot her." The decayed stubs of Bear's front teeth, yellowed by years of chewing tobacco, formed a grin through his 'ratty' black beard. "We didn't get no pig. So, this here 'lil *manatee* will have to do for our holiday dinner."

The veteran Florida born officer chose his words carefully because he had a *'gung-ho'* rookie officer on the boat with him. The rookie had moved down from Michigan a few months earlier and couldn't tell a *manatee* from a turtle. Over coffee at the *Queen Conch* the day before several commercial fisherman expressed their feelings to him about the rookie. They were concerned that the rookie didn't understand the ways of native Floridians who attempted to squeeze a meager living out of the water in the manner of their forebears. The consensus was loud and clear. *"That skinny, white faced Yankee pup can't tell his ass from a hole in the ground."*

"Bear. Are you sure this isn't a leatherback swamp turtle from the *Kitching Cove* area up past *Club Med*? I saw a lot of them there yesterday. Some of the folks that live on the water are scared of the turtles so we were going to go out up there and thin them out anyway." He hoped Bear would pick up on his tone of voice and inflection. But, he didn't.

"Look here Bill." Bear lifted up part of the cast net exposing a smooth gray flipper and grinned. "You and me was both raised in Florida. We both know that's a *manatee* and that it's damn good eatin' if it's cooked real slow and easy over green mangrove wood. It was dead and lying back up in some mangrove roots when I found it! It's like a *'road kilt'* deer. It shouldn't be allowed to go to waste. There's a lot of good meat here."

The enthusiastic white-faced rookie spoke up. "That cracker knows that it's illegal to kill, or possess a *manatee*, and to cut mangroves for any reason without a permit from the State. He even admits that he knows it's a *manatee*. Let's take him in!"

"*Yankee!* You hold your pants on for a minute. I've known this man for over thirty years. He wouldn't do anything that he knew was against the law. To him that manatee, that is if it's even proven to be a *manatee* and not an old snapping turtle, is just like a road-killed deer. It's better to use it than to allow it to rot in the water. Use your head, boy."

"Are you both nuts? Nobody eats *manatees*!"

"Didn't I just tell you that we aren't even sure if it is a *manatee*? If he found it dead, and we can tell that by examining the carcass, as far as I'm concerned it's road kill and he can have it. If we confiscate it we have to tow it to the marina and fill out a bunch of paperwork. Roasted *manatee* meat makes darn good eating and I haven't tasted any for at least thirty years."

"Bill, do you remember the Sunday afternoons out on *Fisherman Key* when our poppas would build a fire, let it burn down to red coals and add green mangrove branches for flavor?

They'd catch some silver mullet, split 'em in half down the back side, place them on forked green mangrove sticks along the fire to cook. They'd dig a few dozen oysters from the oyster bar at the south side of the island and slip 'em in the edges of the coals. When they popped open, with that steam just a gushin' out, they were ready to eat. We washed it all down with ice cold Dr. Pepper. That was heaven on earth to a teenaged *'cracker'* boy."

The older officer took the opportunity to stress his own native Florida heritage to the wide-eyed, almost hysterical, rookie. "Son, at this point in your career a little Florida history is good for you. Listen up and get some appreciation. The term *'cracker'* came from the *'cracking'* sound of the short braided leather whips used by Florida cowboys to round up range cows for market. They would start out at *Fort Pierce* and drive the herd across the state to *Fort Myers*. They'd stop at each ranch along the way and buy whatever head the rancher was willing to sell. Just to the west *Cape Coral* is *Cattle Dock Point*. The wood burning, smoke-belching steamboats used to come in there and pick up the cattle. Look on a detailed Florida highway map and you'll see the *Florida Cracker Trail* shown just above *Fort Pierce*."

"What has that got to do with possessing a *manatee* and planning on eating it?"

"Didn't you tell me that back in Michigan that you enjoyed sitting down to a good helping of *pickled chicken feet* and a six pack of cold beer."

"I love to snack on *pickled chicken feet*. Pig's feet are good too. What's wrong with that?"

"He happens to like *manatee*. What's wrong with that?"

"*Manatees* are protected. Chickens aren't. Let's take him in!"

The older officer's ears got red, his eyes misted up and his mind drifted away. "Bear, do you remember how we'd drag that pair of old black cast iron tripods up the beach from the boat, rub sand on them to get off the rust and old fat? Then our papas would bring over the gutted *manatee* calf, with its head and flippers cut off, and run it onto the spit from the neck to the rear. They'd wrap it up with baling wire to hold it together and baste it with peanut oil while we turned it on the spit. It looked just like a 'suckling pig' without an apple in its mouth.

"I do! I do! Do you remember how we'd take turns turning the spit ever so slowly while the fat bubbled out? When the fat hit the coals it gave off a snarling hiss and burst of flame. When it was cooked to perfection the meat was sliced right onto your plate with a fillet knife to join the okra and sweet taters crowned by gobs of butter. Oh Lordy those were the days."

"Yes, I remember. But it was a long time ago. Things have changed since then, Bear. That was back then. Today is today and tonight is tonight. I stopped you because your red and green running lights weren't showing. I knew it was you because there wouldn't be anyone else on the water at four in the morning. Pass over your boat registration. I'm going to give you a citation for reckless operation under Florida Statute 327.50, paragraph 2, and US Coast Guard Navigation Inland Rule 23for not displaying your running lights at night."

"Bill. Come on - give me a break. What about that black speed boat that comes racing through here 'balls to the wall' almost every night about eleven-thirty and again about four- thirty in the morning? He never has his running lights on neither! "

"We haven't seen him. Maybe we'll catch him tonight. After we're done with you wait under the bridge and watch for him. We've got to be out here until seven in the morning anyway. Bear. I sure wish that I could give you a break over this, but I am trying to train this rookie properly. Part of his training is to get to know and hopefully understand some of the local folks like you. Just sit still and let me write up this citation for no running lights. Keep your big mouth shut."

"Those Yankees won't never understand us none. They're just interested in buying them fancy boats and tearing up the sea grass beds on the weekends."

"Now you've made me mad. I was waiting for you because I thought that you might be gill netting some snook in the drop off behind the oyster bar in front of *Harbor Ridge*. I'm going to check your fish box for snook." The officer lifted the warped plywood top of the fish box and cautiously illuminated the inside with his flashlight. He was concerned about what other illegal catches Bear might have stashed away that the rookie might see. "I only see about a dozen silver mullet, a couple of sheephead and a few sand perch in the box. You could use some ice in there to keep them fresh. Bear. You are okay this time."

The officer pulled his pad out of his back pocket and snapped his ballpoint pen to begin writing a citation. "Bear. I'm going to give you a ticket for not displaying proper running lights and . . ."

"What about the *manatee*? We've got him dead to rights!" The anxious rookie loudly blurted out his concern and interrupted the older officer's thought process.

"What *manatee*? I only see a skinned out snapping turtle."

"Bill, I already told you that it's a *manatee* not a turtle. Don't you listen? But, it was already dead when I found it. It's like a *'road kilt'* deer. Just like you said, it shouldn't go to waste."

"See! He admits that it is a *manatee*! I'm going to take a picture and ask our lieutenant about it when we report in to the Jupiter station tomorrow morning at seven."

Caught between a proverbial rock and a hard place the officer was left with little choice, but to take a possible career ending chance. He leaned over the side of his boat out of the rookie's earshot so that only Bear could hear his whispered passionate plea. "Bear. Toss that smelly carcass over the side before he gets that camera out and I'll forget the whole thing. Its strong evidence and if he gets a picture of it you'll be in big trouble. Killing a *manatee* is a felony and a Federal charge too boot!"

"You're worried about the *manatee*? Bill, I thought that you wanted these five *'snuuks'* that I got tied off to the stern cleat." Bear pointed to the thirty-pound test monofilament line tied off to the stern cleat that looked like it was going to snap any second.

FLASH!

The brilliant light from the camera's flash startled Bear and he jerked the line. The slipknot pulled loose and the five silver-sided snook, long dead from their capture in the strangling meshed noose of the gill net, sank to the bottom to become crab food.

"I got the picture! Now I can prove that it's a manatee! Let's cuff him and take him in."

The marine radio in the Marine Patrol officer's boat crackled into life. *"Mayday. Mayday. Mayday. Somebody help us. We're sinking and my arm is broken in two places. Help."*

"Give me that damn camera and sit down! I've had it with

you. Now let's answer that distress call."

Bear heard some scuffling and out of the corner of his one good eye he caught the blur of a uniformed arm in motion. The camera arced upward through the air towards the opening in the *Roosevelt Bridge* and landed in twenty feet of saltwater. The officers' twin two hundred-fifty horsepower outboards sprang into life and they were gone in a flash!

"Hey there Bear. I thought that you could use a little help." From out of the darkness beneath the glided a green kayak piloted by a driver wearing a fluorescent pink Nazi helmet decked out with a long purple Ostrich feather. "Bear old on a minute while I give those boys a little better directions. They've got a long boat ride ahead of 'em."

"Mayday. Mayday. Mayday. Calling the Florida Marine Patrol. Please help us! Our boat is sinking and I'm hurt bad."

"Vessel in distress. This is the Florida Marine Patrol. We are on the way to assist you. What is your location?"

"We're in the ocean about five miles south of the St. Lucie Inlet in front of Peck's Lake. We hit a rock or something and ripped the bottom out of the boat. Please hurry."

"Vessel in distress. This is the Florida Marine Patrol. Hold on sir. We're on the way. We should be there in fifteen minutes."

Rat pulled alongside Bear's boat and offered a toothless grin. "Guess that'll hold 'em for awhile. Bear pull into *Shepherd's Park* and I'll help dress out that turtle. The boys would enjoy a steak, or a roast, if you can spare it. Looks like you got about a hundred pounds of meat there and you can't eat all of it."

Mack slid his boat from under the darkness of the bridge and idled up alongside Bear's boat to join the bizarre conversation.

"Hey Mack. How about joining me, and the boys for a cook out on *Memorial Day* on Monday? We're having turtle steaks."

"Bear. You had me worried there for a while. I thought that the rookie was going swimming after his camera."

"Mack. Why didn't you do something?"

"What could I do? You had everything under control until you lifted up that stringer of snook. Mason was going to let you off with a simple citation for not showing your running lights."

"Bear, how about slicing off a little hunk of that manatee,

turtle or whatever it is?"

"Rat. I still have to dress it out, cut it up and get it in the refrigerator. That'll take a couple of hours. I don't know how long it was lying up in the mangroves. It's pretty stiff. Stop by the house this afternoon and I'll slice off a few steaks for you."

"Okay. It's been a busy night and I'm pooped too. Mack. What time is it?"

"It's about four forty-five."

They each sensed the danger before they saw it. The black speedboat wasn't showing running lights and it 'flew' under the *Roosevelt Bridge* directly toward the three boats tied off together. The boat's bow threw spray in all directions making it difficult for the driver to see. At the last instant the driver saw them and jerked the wheel hard to port. The boat tilted onto its port side at about a forty-five degree angle and threw a four-foot wave in the trios' direction. When the 'humongous' wave crashed into Rat's kayak it flipped it upside down and threw him into the water. Mack grabbed the sides of his own boat and hung on for dear life. His boat was lifted four feet up in the air and came crashing down on the side of the wooden piling holding the red marker.

Bear saw the giant wave coming, gunned his engine, steered to meet it head on and it 'crashed' harmlessly over his bow. He circled back to check on Mack and Rat. "Are you guys okay? Rat. Where are you? Are you okay? Rat where are you"

Mack hugged the creosoted wooden piling that supported the red day marker with both arms to keep his boat from crashing into it again. Rat floundered in the water. His rubber kayak was upside down and his fluorescent orange helmet was drifting at a 'fast clip' down the river with the outgoing tide.

"Mack. Are you okay?"

"I'm fine. I'm trying to keep this piling from ripping the side out of my boat. Hurry up and get Rat out of the water."

"Rat, grab hold of this paddle and I'll pull ya' back in."

"I'm okay! My helmet! Get my helmet!"

"Your helmet's doing just fine. It's floating upside down and zipping down the river at about five knots! A good trolling speed, but a big tarpon might try to eat that purple feather. Git' your skinny butt in the boat first! Then we'll worry about the helmet."

"I'm coming. How about my kayak? It's gonna' sink!"

"That damn kayak is filled up with air and it isn't going to sink. Mack will watch it for you."

Rat looked like a drowned rat. He crawled up the wooden paddle, slithered over the transom and fell into the bottom of into Bear's boat. He was immediately overcome by the horrific, putrid smell emanating from the long-dead *manatee* stashed under the cast net in the bottom of the boat. "Bear. I changed my mind. That old turtle smells really bad. You can keep all of it."

"Are you some kind of candy ass? That *manatee* smells just fine. It's just aged a bit and that makes it tender. When it's dressed out and cut up it'll look like beef. But, it'll taste a whole lot better than beef. You'll see. Meats only meat."

"Thanks, but no thanks. Can you run me down the river to pick up my helmet? Please?

Bear and Rat took off to pick up Rat's helmet. Mack waited for the residual waves to subside before he dared to let go of the piling. After the water calmed down, he snatched Rat's canoe with a boat hook and flipped it right side up. Bear and Rat returned from down river and pulled alongside Mack's boat.

"Mack, them's the sons of bitches that I told you and Ralph about. They run through here almost every night about the same time. If I got my nets set out up there by Kitching Cove they'll run right through 'em and laugh about it. They gave me the 'finger' and threatened me the other night. They're up to no good. I just know it. They're really bad news."

"There's nothing that we can do about it tonight. It's after five in the morning and the sun will be coming up soon. I want to get back to the marina, take a shower and get some sleep."

"I gotta' hang around here and locate my stringer of snuuks. When that flashbulb went off I jerked the tag line and they all went to the bottom. Then I've got to get these mullet to the fish house. Wanna' meet for breakfast at the *Queen Conch*? I'll buy.

"No thanks. I've got to get some sleep. Rat, what are you going to do?"

"Look at me! I'm soaked to the skin and smell like a rotten manatee! I'm going to go back to my boat, take a shower and go to bed. I've got some serious sleeping to catch up on."

"Rat, what do you think happened to the Florida Marine Patrol guys? Do you do you suppose that they are they still searching?"

"I doubt that they have even gotten out of the inlet yet. By the time they get outside and run down to the *Kingfish Hole* the sun will be up. They'll look around for a while and figure out that it was a hoax and leave. They have to check in at the *Jupiter* station at seven in the morning anyway. The exercise is good for them."

"Looks like we have a consensus. The night's excitement is over and its time to go home and get some sleep. Bear, you have fun cleaning the *manatee, swamp turtle*, or whatever it is."

The three soaked and disheartened *compadres* cranked up their engines and went their separate ways. Mack poured the coals to the 250 horsepower *YAMAHA* outboard and was back at the marina by 5:30. Bear poked around with a weighted treble hook until he located his stringer of five 'snuuks', dragged it back aboard and putted back toward the Manatee Pocket. When he came around *Hell's Gate* his half-tame osprey *Michi* screamed and flew down to enjoy the final leg of the trip by riding on his shoulder. He fed her chunks of mullet that he cut on the way.

Rat was soaking wet and mad as a wet hen over being dunked. He had revenge on his mind and planned to settle the score with the occupants of the speeding boat. He putted back slowly to *Shepherd's Park* and tied his kayak up to the concrete sea wall.

When the kayak was safely secured he slipped into the public restroom on the hill, stripped down to his underwear and took a bath in the sink. He also rinsed out his pants and shirt in the sink. Dressed only in his stained underwear, he traipsed back down the hill to his kayak, untied his lines and putted out to his sailboat. He hung his wet clothes out to dry over the mast just as the faint pre-dawn light began to peek over the trees. It was time for Rat to disappear for the day. He slithered through the cockpit into the narrow cabin, crawled into his bunk and pulled a black mask with no eyeholes over his face.

He felt a deep, throbbing pain in his back, shoulders and neck, but he tried to ignore it. He figured that he must have hit the water with a real 'jolt'. Unconsciousness came quickly and with it the return of the horrible, continuous nightmare.

KABLAM!

The violent explosion ripped through the tunnel and the flash was as bright as a welder's arc. *"I'm blind! You bastard!."* Rat screamed as he was pulled feet first out of the tunnel.

The leader of the *SOG* unit sent in for the rescue attempt threw a concussion grenade into the tunnel to flush out any enemy that might be lurking inside. Unfortunately for him, Rat had also chosen that particular tunnel as a hiding place and the bright flash of exploding phosphorus made his eyes permanently sensitive to light.

At the time of his rescue Rat was more animal than human. He had subsisted for three months on what he could catch in the jungle and find on the battlefield. Days after fierce 'fire fights' in the area American forward scouts reported back that many of the enemy dead left on the battlefield had their ears and noses sliced off. The puzzling enigma became clear when an Army intelligence officer debriefed Rat at Danang after his rescue.

"I had to eat somethin'. Ears and noses cook up real good in a pot with a little water added for broth. As far as I'm concerned any kind of meat is still only meat after it's cooked. Beef, pork, horse, moose, coon, rat, snakes, or what ever it doesn't make a difference to me anymore. All meat's only meat in my book!"

When he was captured Rat was on a mission in Northern Laos and his team was ambushed in a fierce firefight. A sniper shot a man and disappeared into a tunnel hidden in the jungle. When the tunnel was located several rounds from automatic weapons were fired into the entrance followed by grenades and tear gas. But, no one came out. Rat and his partner *'Thin Man'* were ordered into the tunnel to determine if there was any enemy still alive inside. Rat went first with a safety line attached to *'Thin Man'* who followed ten feet behind him.

The battery-powered miner's lamp on Rat's baseball cap softly illuminated the tunnel ahead as he inched along on his elbows. He was incensed and not as cautious as he should have been because the soldier killed by the sniper was a close friend and a fellow 'rat'. He had to be very careful because the tunnels were often booby trapped with trip wires and time delayed mines designed to explode twenty seconds after the trip wire was crossed. When the tunnel walls collapsed the 'tunnel rat' was trapped inside with no possible escape. An enemy tunnel rat would crawl towards the helpless rat from the other end, blind him with a flare and slit his throat.

Rat watched for trip wires and he was also concerned about blind corners and poisonous snakes tethered by their tails in overhead ledges above eye level. A strike in the face by a snake meant a certain and painful death. Rat inched ahead dragging *'Thin Man'* along behind him. Their nylon safety line led to the tunnel entrance. If they got into 'trouble' the team above ground would hopefully be able to pull them backwards to safety.

Rat's arms were extended out in front of him and the tunnel was so narrow that he could not bend his arms back to reach his belt. A cocked .45 caliber automatic pistol was in his right hand ready to fire at the slightest movement or sound. His left hand grasped a plastic probing knife that he used to test the earth ahead of him for mines. The stale tunnel air reeked of rotten fish and cigarette smoke. Smoke in a tunnel was a serious concern for tunnel rats because the enemy would light a fire in a tunnel and seal off the outside air vents trapping the tunnel rat inside to suffocate from smoke inhalation.

The tunnel was a tight fit and Rat couldn't move his shoulders from side to side. His head scraped the top showering down dirt that drifted into his eyes and filled his nostrils. The tunnel suddenly dropped off downward at a forty-five degree angle. Another leg skewed to the right, but appeared to stay level. It looked to be a blind corner and a possible cache for a tethered poisonous snake. Rat stopped and listened for the tell tale dry 'rasping' of scales against the sand or a soft *'hissing'*. There was only eerie silence. Perhaps a little too much silence to be safe! He heard a muffled cough in the tunnel segment to his right and emptied the pistol in the direction of the sound.

The roar deafened him. His head reeled and the acrid smell of gunpowder filled his nostrils. Fear struck because he couldn't reload his pistol because he couldn't reach the ammo pouch on his belt. He was helpless to defend himself, except for the knife. He groped in the dirt for the knife - it was gone! He had dropped it in order to hold the pistol with both hands. It had slid down the forty-five degree incline and was out of his reach. Rat felt a sharp 'tug' on the safety line, heard an explosion followed by a scream.

'Thin Man' screamed from behind him. "Rat! Help me! For God's sake, help me! Please shoot me. Oh God, it hurts."

In a panic and not realizing that his own body sealed off the tunnel walls and that his voice would not carry behind him, Rat yelled back to his partner. "Hang on. They'll get us out."

The *'Charlies'* had built a parallel tunnel alongside the main tunnel and skewered *'Thin Man'* through the tunnel wall with a metal rod! He was pinned to the tunnel wall like a pig on a spit. Another explosive charge collapsed and sealed the tunnel behind him. There was no escape for either of them! Rat could not move forward or backward. He was trapped! He could feel warm blood and urine flowing under his body and smell the sickening sweet stench seeping in from behind him. The nylon safety line jerked frantically as his partner screamed in pain.

A flash of brilliant light exploded in Rat's face blinding him. Fragments of the 'stun grenade' ripped into his left hand and the sound deafened him. He could not see, or hear, except for the loud ringing in his ears. Hands grabbed his forearms, pulled him forward and down deeper into the tunnel into nothingness. The tunnel to his right had been a decoy, a false front, not a snake pit.

Rat awoke standing upright in a bamboo cage submerged in water up to his chest and his wrists lashed to an iron ring above his head. Giant, black, river leeches had attached themselves to his legs, arms and neck. He felt the blood draining from his body and probed his cotton-dry mouth with his tongue seeking moisture. There was nothing where his front teeth should be except bloody gums and gaping holes that ached when he sucked air through his swollen lips. He tried to open his eyes, but they were swollen shut. He gasped for air through his broken nose, but the smashed nasal passages had collapsed and he felt like he was trying to breathe with a plastic bag over his head. He finally yielded to blessed unconsciousness.

The bright sun forced it's way between his swollen eyelids and he awoke. He couldn't feel his feet, his wrists ached and his shoulders felt as if they were pulling out of his body. He felt weightless and as if he was flying. He cracked open his swollen eyes and looked up to find that he was suspended in the air by his ankles from a tree limb. His feet were swollen, discolored a dark blue and dangled about a foot above the ground. There were only bloody holes where his big toes used to be.

When Rat's eyes became accustomed to the light he cautiously opened them and saw a circle of perhaps a dozen uniformed soldiers surrounding him. Intermixed with the uniformed soldiers were six men garbed in what appeared to be black pajamas. An officer wearing a major's insignia, and holding a brown, woven fiber bag tied shut with a piece of cord, approached Rat and spoke to him in perfect English.

"Mr. Rat. How are you feeling today? Yesterday you were most uncooperative. Your weak toes pulled off and you fell into the pigpen. Regretfully you killed one of our favorite pigs and my men are very unhappy with you. Perhaps today you will choose to cooperate with us or we will have to use extreme measures. I am losing patience with you. Will you please tell us about your unit and the methods used by your fellow American tunnel rats?"

"Hell no!"

After the rescue Mack and Rat went their separate ways and did not see each other for more than 25 years. Until this night neither of them knew that the other was still alive.

At Lon Bien, before he left in an *Air America* C-47 *'Gooney Bird'* for debriefing in Saigon, Mack gave Rat a *South African One Rand* coin. The coin was used as a code marker to identify 'special agents' in Southeast Asia and a '1' was stamped between the *Springbok's* front feet.

CHAPTER

13

It was a typical Saturday afternoon in south Florida and *Memorial Day* was on Monday. The temperature hovered in the mid-nineties and the afternoon shower came right on schedule between 3:30 P.M. and 4:30 P.M. After the rain clouds of steam rose from the heat-saturated asphalt roads and the humidity rose to above ninety percent. It was *'just another day in Paradise.'*

The weeks between March and late May flew by quickly. Tina left on a special assignment to Washington in April and wouldn't be back until June. Mack passed his exams, got his Coast Guard license and started a fishing guide service. His specialty was 'wall-hanger' snook over twenty-five pounds. But, because they exceeded the legal 'slot size' of thirty-four inches they couldn't be kept. However, the temptation to keep a big one was always there. But, the penalty for being caught was very stiff - he could lose his Coast Guard license.

Bear didn't care about the heat, or the humidity. He was a Florida 'cracker' born and raised in South Florida. For him the intense summer heat was a relief from the bone chilling winter cold. He couldn't understand how the northern 'snow birds' could swim in the ocean in January when the surf temperature was only seventy-five degrees. When he trolled for mackerel in January off of *Peck's Lake* the air would often be so cold that 'chicken skin' rose up on his arms and neck and make him shiver from head to toe.

Bear and Emogene were going to celebrate *Memorial Day* with a *'cracker'* dinner of deep-fried silver mullet, gator left over from last fall's hunt on *Lake Okeechobee*, wild hog ribs, heart of palm cabbage and lots of ice-cold beer. Because Bear knew Mack when they were in high school he invited him over for dinner. Mack and Bear both enlisted in the military right after graduation and they didn't see each other again until they met in *Port Salerno* twenty-five years later - just two months before.

Mack didn't talk about the branch of the military that he joined, where he went, or what he did. He told Bear was that he had been living in *Chicago* before he moved to *Port Sewell* and had used his GI Bill benefits to get a college education at Florida State. Although they had been good friends during their high school days in *Fort Myers* they didn't have much in common because they were at different ends of the fishing community spectrum. Mack was a popular fishing guide and active in the 'ban the gill nets' movement. Although they didn't agree on the gill net issue, Bear still looked upon Mack as a good friend. Memories that went back thirty years were hard to give up.

Bear was a 'dyed in the wool' commercial fishermen just like his papa and his papa's papa before him. His papa had told him, *"Fishing runs in our blood. We were meant to catch fish and don't you ever forget it."* This sunny afternoon Bear had fishing on his mind. There was a big demand at the fish house for silver mullet for holiday cookouts. The thought of silver mullet deep-fried in hot, bubbling peanut oil made Bear's mouth water. Gill netting was illegal, but Bear had to make a living the only way that he knew how – gill netting fish. He knew where a school of prime silver mullet was schooled up in the *North Fork* of the St. Lucie River just past *Club Med*. He had been gill netting jacks, drum and snook every night for the past week and had deliberately avoided bothering the mullet because he wanted to save them for the prime market time - this weekend!

Bear was fuming. The night before, the black speedboat ran over his gill net's cork line and slashed it into several pieces. The driver and his passenger gave him *'the finger'* when they raced past him at full throttle. Their boat threw a three-foot high wake that almost flipped Bear's flat-bottomed fishing boat over. He grabbed the sides and held on for dear life. When the 'rocking' stopped Bear pulled in his cork line to view the damage - it was cut clean through in several places.

That's why this afternoon he had some net mending to do while he had enough light and could see to weave the delicate monofilament line. The mending was easy. The difficult part was replacing the cork line that ran the top length of the net and secured it to the floats. Plus he was installing a 'special' modification in the net that would solve his problem tonight. Last night was the third time in as many nights that his nets had been cut and he was pissed and talking out loud. *"The bastards must have put on stainless steel props with rope cutters on their boat."*

Before this week, when the occupants of the black speed boat saw that his nets were across the channel, they slowed down so that he could guide them around them. However, the past three nights they were ran right though them and cut the float line to shreds. When Bear got back to the fish house early Saturday morning, after having his nets cut again, Bear called Ralph and asked him to meet with him that afternoon at his house.

"Ralph, I'm havin' big problems trying to fish the North Fork. Some 'smart-ass' in a black speedboat keeps running over my nets and cutting my cork lines. Last night was the third night in a row. I gotta' do something about it and right now."

Ralph was concerned for Bear's safety because of the remoteness of the area, the time of night, and the unknown identity of the occupants of the black speedboat. "Bear why don't you simply avoid confrontation by keeping your nets out of the channel so they can get through. They won't get their props tangled and you won't get your nets cut up in the process. They aren't going to report you to the Florida Marine Patrol for illegal gill netting because they don't want the Marine Patrol to know that they are coming through there either."

Avoiding confrontation was not in Bear's plans. "I've been fishing the North Fork for years and I've got *'dibs'* because I was there first. They should go around *Fork Point* and run up the channel to *River Gate Park*, or where ever they're going. How 'bout if I a take a shotgun with me and give 'em a good scare?"

"Because they might shoot back and they might not intend to scare you! They must have a good reason for not taking the main channel west of *Fork Point*. If I were you I would stick on the east side of *Kitching Cove* and stay out of the channel. There's some nice sand bottom there and it's a safe place to set your net."

"Ralph, I'm going to stick with my place in the North Fork and I have a couple of ways to teach them a lesson or two." Bear tilted his head and lifted his beard to display the bright scarlet scar that ran from ear to ear. "Do you remember this?"

"Sure I remember. I took your silly ass to the hospital and you almost died. Bear, don't you even think about running a cable across the mouth of the channel. You might kill one of them and that would be murder!"

"Did I tell you that their boat is all black, including the engine cover, and they don't turn on their red and green running lights. Their engine must have a special muffler on it because you can't hear a sound until the *'hiss'* of the water off the bow wave passes you. Then it's too late to do anything but hang on and hope that you don't flip over. Their boat must throw a three foot wake!"

"Bear, doesn't that sound just a little suspicious? I don't think that these are *'good guys'* in white hats. But, they could be undercover DEA, Coast Guard, Customs or even Florida Marine Patrol guys. You might be interfering in a covert operation and be in a dangerous spot. I'd find another place to fish if I were you."

"They must be able to see the channel markers in the dark because they never use a spotlight. Did I mention that they wear black clothes and ski masks?"

"No you didn't. A bell should go off in your head and tell you something before it's too late. As far as not using a light to spot the markers I'll bet that they are wearing night vision goggles. But, I'm concerned about your safety. What's happened so far?"

"I've been watching them come and go the past month or so."

"What do you mean come and go?"

"Usually when I'm going under the Roosevelt Bridge and heading for the North Fork about one-thirty in the morning' I pass them going the other way. They come running back up the North Fork *'balls to the wall'* about four-thirty when I'm getting ready to pick up my final set and head for home."

"It sounds like a regular schedule. Does this happen every night and at the same times?"

"I haven't been keeping a log, but I remember most nights. I saw them last night, the night before that and the night before that. I usually don't fish on Saturday or Sunday because there's too many drunk boaters out at all hours of the night. Plus, the boat cops are out heavy on the weekends looking for dopers. They might catch me by accident like they did with the manatee. But, I'm going fishin' tonight. I got me a whole bunch of fat silver mullet in *Kitching Cove* just waiting for me to catch 'em."

"Bear, I think that you have gotten yourself in deep shit. Have you told anyone else?"

"Nope. I ain't told nobody nothin'. I don't want nobody else knowing my business, or where I've been catching my fish and horning in for a share. Let them find their own spots."

"You better keep out of there before something serious happens to you. I mean much more serious than just getting your nets cut up. It could be you next! Do you remember what happened to Dave's brother last year and the missing sail boater in March? Have you gotten into conversations with them over you being there when they come through?"

"Usually they cuss at me, shoot me the *'bird'* and run over my float line. But, last night they got their props caught in my net and raised hell for twenty minutes while they cut it out. They were bitching that they were late and it was my fault. One of them told me that I would pay for it some day and that I'D be *'swimming with the fishes'*. I laughed and shot him a *'bird'* back."

"Then what did they do?"

"The one who shot me the *'bird'* shot me a *'double bird'*, spit in my direction and made a strange hand wave. He put his fingers under his chin and waved them up over his face and out towards me. I didn't know what it meant. So, I shot him back a *'double bird'* right back and spit at him. I was chewing 'bacca and shot a pretty good stream in his direction."

"Then what happened?"

"He made the same hand movement, kind of a backwards wave, and said, *'We'll meet again.'* His friend grabbed his hand, pulled it down and said something in a funny language that I didn't understand. It sounded like *Spanish* or *Italian* maybe?"

"Either one could spell big trouble for you."

"He sounded really mad, so I pulled in my net and took off for home. Before I left I spun around 'em at full throttle and waked them good just like they did to me. They were still working on cutting the cork line out of the prop and one of them fell out of the boat. Boy was he pissed! Then I turned the boat around and came home."

"Bear, I've got to talk to Mack about this and get his advice. I have the feeling that he might be a lot more prepared than you and I are to handle this. Promise me that you'll stay out of the North Fork tonight?"

"I can't promise nothing'. I have to fish to feed my family. Fishin' is in my blood. I can't do nothing' else. Plus, this is the prime weekend for silvers and I have to go. Then I'll stop."

"Bear, it's Saturday night and *Memorial Day* weekend to boot. Boat cops will be all over the place looking for drunks and dopers. They might run across you. Please don't go tonight!"

"I've got it all figured out. I've got a plan. If the boat cops pull me over I won't have any fish in the boat when I'm heading home. My little brother Bobo is going to meet me at the *River Gate Park* boat ramp in Port St. Lucie. We'll load the fish into his truck. That way I can come down the river empty. I'm going to throw in a fishing pole just in case they stop me. That way I can have two legal *'snuuks'* in the boat and I can say that I caught 'em with a fishing pole."

"What if the guys in the black speedboat show up? Maybe they mean business!"

"I got them figured out too. That's why I'm working on the gill net that they tore up last night. They ran through it like it was butter. They must have put on stainless steel props and rope cutters. Tonight I'm getting even. I've got me a quarter inch steel cable wove into the float line. They can't cut that! I'll stop 'em."

"Bear. You're not going to string a cable over the channel are you? At full speed that will decapitate them! You'll go to jail for murder. That's a lot more serious than killing a manatee!"

"No better than that. I'm threading the cable across the top of the net's cork line and tying on extra big, white Styrofoam floats to hold it up. They'll see the floats, think it's my net and go out of their way to hit it with their fancy, rope cutting, stainless steel, fancy props. The ends of the net won't be tied to nothin' solid so it'll wind up around their props and stop 'em dead. They won't be going anywhere for a long time. I'm sticking in a few pieces of barbed wire to snag their fancy manicured hands and fingers when they try to untangle the net from their prop."

"Then what are you going to do? Shoot them?"

"I'm not sure. But, I sure as 'hell' am going to laugh at them – just like they laughed at me last night. Nobody has laughed at me for a long time."

"Bear, please don't do this! I'm worried about your safety. Please stay home tonight."

"Ralph, a man's got to do what a man's got to do. If I don't do something I'm not much of a man in my own eyes. I've got to stand up for myself."

"Bear, think rationally. These people don't care who you are or how long your family has lived here. You are in their way and if you become to big a thorn in their side they might turn violent. I don't want to see you get hurt."

"My family has lived in the same house on Grouper Street ever since my grandfather built it with his own hands in 1923. My family has fished the Indian and St. Lucie Rivers and managed to make a living for three generations. Nobody is going to tell me that I can't fish where I want, when I want and how I want! Nobody!" Bear's voice rose to a high pitch. His face turned red when he realized that he had been shouting. "I'm sorry, Ralph. I didn't mean to get so excited. It's not your fault."

"It's okay. I understand. It's five-thirty and I'm going over to see Mack before he leaves to catch bait for tonight. I've got to talk this over with him and get his take on it. I'll get back with you. Please stay home tonight. These people might get nasty if you get in their way."

"See you tomorrow morning at the fish house about six o'clock? I'll have lots of fresh silvers."

"Maybe. But first I've got to talk to Mack."

Ralph tore out of Bear's driveway, raced down Grouper Street, turned right onto Salerno Road and got held up at the red traffic light at *Old Dixie Highway*. When the light turned green Ralph floored the aging pickup. The bald tires spun on the black asphalt and smoked before they finally caught traction. He turned North on Old Dixie, raced past the CITGO station, took a right at Indian Street, crossed *Willoughby Creek* and turned right onto Old Saint Lucie Boulevard. Just past *Whittaker's Boat Works* he made a right into the gravel drive leading to *Port Sewell Marina*.

Ralph's stomach rose up into his throat - Mack's truck was gone. He must be on the river catching bait for tonight's charter. But - where? Ralph sped out of the driveway in reverse. Brown pea gravel thrown up by the truck's tires flew in every direction and bounced off the windshield. Where was Mack?

Mack enjoyed the short walk from *Bath Tub Beach's* parking area, across *MacArthur Boulevard* and down the long, narrow wooden walkway to the aging dock. Gnarled outstretched limbs of Australian pine and red mangrove trees spread over the walkway and shaded it from the sun. It was peaceful and cool under the trees. He paused momentarily to watch the fiddler crabs scurry between the spindly mangrove roots in search of tasty, fleshy tidbits left by the falling tide.

The wooden dock, constructed in the early 1950's, extended more than 100 feet into the *Indian River*. When the sun heated up the weathered wood it oozed out the warm, pungent aromas of creosote and tar that melded together in the humid air. The rust-splotched tin roof at the end of the dock shaded him from the direct rays of the sun. The dock provided an excellent place to net mullet because the river bottom was white sand splotched with intermittent patches of green turtle grass.

Mack scanned the clear water watching for the dark outline of a school of mullet to appear against the patches of white sand - that's when he would throw his net in a wide circle over the school. His fingers caressed the smooth, elongated lead weights of the white nylon cast net draped across his lap. It was layered in neat folds ready for action. Mack could 'arc' the net in a perfect circle over a school of mullet twenty feet away with a smooth movement of his arms. Thought wasn't required. He acted on instinct and experience gained more than thirty years earlier.

The ebbing water, stained brown by 'tannin' in the mangrove

leaves, flowed under the dock with a soft *'whisper'*. The falling tide drained the *Indian River* of the cleansing saltwater, fresh from the *Gulf Stream,* that had labored for six strenuous hours to push in from the open sea. The shadows of mangrove trees along the western shoreline grew longer and their dark mirror images invaded the water's surface. The sun, tinted blood red by atmospheric pollution, slowly dropped lower in the western sky. Smoke from several smoldering piney-woods fires caused by lightening strikes southwest of town added to the haze.

Mack scanned the water's surface with his trained hunter's eyes watching for the tell-tale moving 'V' that would give away the location of a school of mullet scavenging for food in the knee-deep water. The mullet hugged the shallow water along the shoreline to evade predators such as marauding snook, tarpon and jacks. With a little luck he would catch a dozen eight to ten inch long *'finger mullet'* which are ideal snook bait. Snook candy!

Giant thirty-pound sow snook, ripe with roe and accompanied by precocious, anxious males, had begun their annual migration from the mangrove-shaded rivers, canals and brackish backwaters to the St. Lucie Inlet to spawn. Mack slowly shook his head as he thought. *"When June 1 comes the regulations change and we won't be allowed to keep any snook."* Tonight he had an important charter. He had fished these same clients the past two nights and they tipped big when they caught fish! If they landed a snook over thirty pounds they wanted to have it mounted and the thirty-four inch 'slot' size did not concern them. Mack would make an extra $100 as commission from the taxidermist. But, keeping a snook outside of the 'slot' limit was a serious risk. Mack had to think about it very carefully because he could lose his Coast Guard license - and his cover if he was caught.

He knew that it wasn't good to keep the big sows because they were the *'brood stock'* and the future of the species. That's why the Department of Natural Resources had established a twenty-six to thirty-four inch 'slot limit'. Anglers weren't allowed to keep a snook under twenty-six or over thirty-four inches in length and the season was closed from June 1 to August 31 to allow the fish to spawn. Mack didn't think that the 'book smart' biologists knew what they were talking about because he hadn't noticed any decrease, or increase, in the snook population compared to when he was a teenager on Florida's the west coast.

Mack supported the *'gill net ban'* because he was convinced that some of the commercial fishermen were catching and selling snook even though they had been declared game fish many years earlier. *'Striped mullet'* the poachers called them. Once carved into fillets few people could tell a snook fillet from any other fish. In order to successfully prosecute someone for illegally keeping snook the State would have to use DNA evidence, or some other scientific method, to determine if the fillet was snook. That was expensive and time consuming!

Maybe the commercial fishermen hadn't been catching as many snook before the net ban as the sport fishermen thought they were. But, then again maybe they were. Mack liked that idea because he could rationalize it - but he wasn't certain. During the peak of the *'gill net ban'* petition drive relations between the two groups almost became 'open war'. Radical members of each side delighted in tormenting the other.

When Mack attended school in Stuart to study for his Coast Guard captain's license several commercial fishermen were in class with him. The State of Florida paid their tuition under a program to provide retraining because of the loss of their livelihood as a result of the 'net ban'. Some of the commercial fishermen wanted to try their hand at guiding. At school they nodded to acknowledge each other's presence and 'almost' became speaking acquaintances. The commercial fishermen, distrustful of sport fishermen, kept their distance from them during the breaks from class. It was a 'silent' truce. During a break Bear sauntered over to the group of sport fishermen who were standing in the parking lot swapping 'big snook' stories.

He looked like a 'bear'. He was shoeless, squat and heavy set with a thick, bushy, black beard. He hid the nasty red line on his neck that stretched from ear to ear under his beard. It was a vivid reminder of a horrific 'booby trap' that he literally ran into during the gill net ban war. It was a 'strange' tale of woe. Commercial fishermen would often set their gill nets outside the end of several boat docks and run their boats at a fast clip 'in and out' between the docks. The engine noise panics the mullet and they race out of their safe haven into the gill nets. One moonless night Bear was herding mullet with his boat and hit a thin steel cable stretched between two docks and broke his neck. He would have died if Ralph hadn't been in another boat and called for help.

When Bear reached the group of shocked sport fishermen he addressed Mack. "Hey bud. Can you teach me how to catch *'snuuks'* with a fishing pole?" Bear pantomimed fighting a fish with an "imaginary' fishing pole cradled in his meaty paws. "I keep one in the boat in case I get stopped by the Marine Patrol and want to be able to explain how I caught 'em."

Anxious to please an old friend Mack responded. "Sure Bear. I'll take you out on my boat and teach you how to cast artificial lures and use live bait too. When do you want to go?"

Bear bent his right index finger at the first knuckle to form a hook, put it in the side of his mouth and jerked. Then he led himself away with his finger using his body to pantomime the actions of a hooked fish. The entire class erupted in laughter and Bear grinned from ear to ear.

Mack had taken the 'bait', hook, line and sinker. He was the 'hooked fish' and Bear was playing him for all he was worth. The blood drained from Mack's face when he realized that he was the butt of the joke. But, he joined in the laughter and acted as if he knew that it was a put on from the outset. He playfully slapped his tormentor on the shoulder. "Bear, I hope that you eat some bad manatee steaks and fart yourself to death." Several months later he would rue that remark.

KAPOW!

Startled by the noise of the pelican hitting the water Mack shook his head and opened his eyes. The white-headed brown pelican was treading water and washing down the meal that he caught when he hit the water from a steep dive. Mack checked his watch. 5:45 P.M. He still had time to catch bait, drive home for a bite of supper and meet his charter party at 8:30 P.M. The tannin-stained river water gurgled as it rushed past the oyster encrusted wooden pilings - the ebbing tide was picking up speed. Mack yawned and closed his eyes. He still had plenty of time.

The soft gurgle of the flowing water reminded of him of electronically generated *'white noise'* often used to mentally relax a resistant subject before the start of an intense interrogation session. Dentists began using *'white noise'* about ten years earlier to relax anxious patients. That was also when they began to use *Ketamine Hydrochloride* as an anesthetic. It causes a catatonic state, erases short-term memory and the blanks out the recall of any pain or discomfort experienced by the patient. Dentists lagged behind the intelligence community interrogators on both sides who began using *Ketamine Hydrochloride* in the 1960's.

As Mack listened to the moving water the warmth of the setting sun caressed his body and encased it in a warm cocoon. His head nodded, his chin fell to his chest, and his eyelids grew heavy and closed. The unseen sprites *'Darkness and Warmth'* enveloped him in their snug blanket. He stirred, shifted his position and tried to open his heavy lidded eyes. But, the warm sun and the softly gurgling water relaxed him. He dozed off.

Bear had completed mending his nets and was nestled in a soft hammock made of discarded gill nets strung between two palm trees. He smiled and admired his handy work with his one good eye. The other eye was shot out in a BB gun accident when he was a kid. Bear mulled over Ralph's words of caution and decided that he was a 'big boy' and could take care of himself. He had to 'get even', or he wouldn't be a man! What could these *Yankee mullet heads* do to him if their boat's propeller was fouled in steel cable and barbed wire? Were they going to swim over and kick his ass? Bear chuckled. He knew that when he pulled out the rusty twelve-gauge shotgun that they would plead for mercy. They didn't know that the firing pins were rusted off!

The quarter-inch stainless-steel cable strung across the top of the gill net's cork line gave off an ominous glint. Several eighteen-inch long strands of barbed wire were also interwoven in the net's nylon mesh. Bear was proud of his handy work, but equally disappointed that he it couldn't show it to anyone. *"What a mess this will make of their dainty fingers when they try to pull it loose."* He smacked his right fist into his open left palm with a loud *'whack'*. *"Tonight I'm going to kick some Yankee ass. Nobody is going to run me off the water!"* It was going to be a long night and Bear decided to take a nap. He relaxed in the hammock, closed his eyes and drifted off into dreamland. His unconscious mind drifted back to his roots on *Florida's West Coast* and the tragic accident that took place many years ago.

Bear had been on a snapper trip to the *Dry Tortugas* and didn't find out about the accident until he arrived home four days afterward. His first inclination of disaster came when he rounded *Punta Rassa Point*, lined up the red triangle and green square channel markers to head for the fish house dock and couldn't see the peaked tin roof of the fish house. There was nothing on the horizon except blue sky where the tin roof of the fish house should have been reflecting the morning sunlight.

Bear 'hailed' his family's fish house on Channel 16 of his VHF marine radio. *"Punta Rassa Fish House Punta Rassa Fish House Punta Rassa Fish House This is the fishing vessel 'SNUUK' on Channel 16. Do you copy? Over."*

Bear waited to hear his father's gruff voice respond. But, there was only static. He checked to be certain that the transmitter was not on the *'low power'* 1-watt setting, adjusted the volume and squelch levels and tried again. *"Punta Rassa Fish House Punta Rassa Fish House Punta Rassa Fish House This is the fishing vessel 'SNUUK' on Channel 16. Do you copy? Over."* Only bone-chilling static from the radio's speaker greeted him.

Bear's radio snapped into life! *"Fishing vessel 'SNUUK' this is the fishing vessel 'TARPON'. Do you copy? Over."*

Bear responded. "Fishing vessel *'TARPON'* this is the fishing vessel *'SNUUK'* we copy you loud and clear. Over."

"Fishing vessel *'SNUUK'* switch to Channel 68 and put your radio on 'low power'. Over."

"This is fishing vessel *'SNUUK'* on Channel 68. Mack is that you? Over."

"Yes. It's me. Bear I need to talk with you. I'm by the spoil island south of red day marker '14'. Do you see me? Over."

"Roger. I see you. Over."

"Pull over here I need to talk to you before you get in. The tides at a 'high stand' and you've got about two and a half feet of water. Can you make that? Over."

"It might be a little *'scrunchy'*, but the boat bottom needs a cleaning anyway. I'll give it a shot. I'm on the way. Over."

Bear almost went into shock when Mack explained to him

what happened. "Bear, we tried to reach you on the marine radio, but VHF radio only travels twenty-five to thirty miles on a good day and the *'Tortugas'* are almost one hundred-twenty miles away as the crow flies. We couldn't get in contact with you."

"Why? What's going on? What happened?"

"There was a terrible fire. They're all gone and so is the fish house. I'm sorry."

"What are you talking about?"

"There was a fire at the fish house. No one knows how it started. The Lee County Fire Marshal's report indicated that *'traces of an accelerant were found in the living room couch on the ground floor'*. Somebody set it after your folks went to bed."

"The fish house burned down? What about my folks, my sister and my brother?"

"The bedrooms were on the second floor and there was no hope. The house was seventy years old and a wooden tinderbox. It burned to the ground in less than thirty minutes. No one had a chance to escape. I'm truly sorry."

Bear's family was gone, he was eighteen and just out of *Fort Myers High School* with no where to go. His father's parents lived in *Port Salerno* on the East Coast. His mother's parents were killed in a car accident on *'Alligator Alley'* several years before. There was no one to guide him and he had a lot of thinking to do. After the memorial service for his family Bear took the commercial fishing boat to *Port Salerno* via the *Okeechobee Waterway* and left it at his grandparents. No one saw him after that. However, there were rumors that he had gone into the military and was killed in Viet Nam.

Bear gritted his teeth when he recalled the fire that took the lives of his father, mother, sister and brother in Punta Rassa over thirty years ago. Several developers had wanted that piece of land for a condominium. It was waterfront property and they didn't care that it had been in his family for several generations.

"Bear. Wake up. It's six-thirty. Are you going to sleep all day? Let's get loaded up." Bear's little brother Bobo had arrived in his brown, rusted-out pickup truck. Bear wasn't going to chance running the river at night with a gill net in his boat. He stuffed the sabotaged gill net and a good one behind the front seat. If the Florida Marine Patrol stopped Bobo they'll see two legal cast nets in the bed of the truck. They wouldn't bother to look in the cab, or behind the seat. Bear didn't tell Bobo about the 'special' net behind the seat. He didn't need to know.

"Bobo. Listen up. Here's the plan. I'll take the boat up river, you take the truck and we'll meet at the *River Gate Park* boat ramp in *Port St. Lucie* about twelve-thirty in the morning'. We'll load the gill nets in the boat and make the two-mile run down the North Fork to *Kitching Cove*. We'll make one good set, pick it up and run back to the boat ramp. We'll load the fish into coolers in the back of your truck, throw a couple of legal cast nets on the top of the coolers and you head for home. I'll meet you at the fish house at six o' clock in the mornin'. Do you understand?"

"Yes. But, . . .

"No ifs, ands or buts. You better have your furry butt waiting for me at the *River Gate Park* boat ramp when I get there at twelve-thirty. Now get going. I have things to do."

After Bobo left, Bear bolted down a dinner of cold fried chicken, cold french fries and a six pack of cold beer and traipsed off to bed to catch a couple hours of sleep. He needed all the rest that he could get because he was going to have a rough time on the *North Fork* tonight.

CHAPTER
14

"Bear. Wake up! It's ten-thirty and you've got to get your fat ass going. Bobo called to remind you that he would meet you at the *River Gate Park* boat ramp at twelve-thirty." Bear's wife Emogene bellowed from the living room. "Get your lazy butt out of that bed and get going. We need a couple dozen silver mullet for our cookout on Memorial Day. That's Monday - the day after tomorrow. You gotta' get your furry butt goin'."

"Hold your horses woman. I know what time it is. Call Bobo and tell him to bring his handheld radio and keep it on channel eighteen so we can talk back and forth."

"Call him yourself! He's your brother. Although I can't see why either of you would claim the other one. Lord knows you are both ugly and smell bad to boot! Both of you should be wearing a bright red warning banner that reads *'not allowed to breed'*."

"Yeah, yeah, yeah, but I know that you love me anyway. Get me some coffee for my thermos. I've got to go."

"Your thermos is already filled and is sittin'on the counter. I made you a couple of snappin' turtle sandwiches. They're in the brown paper bag in the refrigerator. Be careful lard ass. I'll see you in the mornin'."

"Thanks *'bourbon breath'* I love you too. I'll see you in the mornin' about six-thirty." Bear strolled out onto the front porch and slammed the screen door shut to let her know that he cared.

He took two steps, felt a roaring in his guts, paused to let his primeval male urge fill to it's maximum potential, lifted his right foot and let go a 'rip-roaring' wet fart. "Hey *'bourbon breath'* Do farts have lumps? Cause if they don't I just crapped in my pants!"

"What's so unusual about that? Your underwear is usually so full of greasy skid marks that the 'ass end' looks like a truck stop parking lot. Take off your skivvies and burn 'em before you come home. That'll make my job a lot easier."

Bear whistled and thanked his lucky stars that his wife hadn't been holding a lit cigarette lighter behind the crack of his butt. The resulting methane gas explosion would have rocketed him over the *Manatee Pocket* and halfway to the *St. Lucie Inlet.*

When he bent over to pull on his white rubber boots, a fixture of commercial fishermen, he let go another rip-roaring wet fart. He knew that his underwear would have to be humanely destroyed before he dared to come back into the house in the morning. A leather cord around his neck, threaded with two gigantic bear claws and a silver coin suspended from a three-inch piece of steel fishing leader, slipped out of his shirt. He tucked it back inside so that it would not reflect light - a habit leftover from his military training. The claws were a reminder of a near-death experience on Kodiak Island in Alaska where he underwent cold weather survival training. The coin was a poignant reminder of another bad experience that he blanked out of his mind long ago except for the man who gave it to him. Bear didn't know his name, but he would always remember what he did for him. Between the front feet of the *Springbok* stamped on the back of the *South African One Rand* coin was imprinted the numeral '1'.

Bear's blue commercial fishing boat was moored at the south end of the rickety, wooden fish house dock. He tossed in a rusty twelve-gauge 'double-barreled' shotgun and an ancient fishing rod equipped with an equally ancient broken reel. The rod was missing the top eye and the line was tangled into a massive bird nest on the reel spool. Bear held to a basic tenet. *"The law doesn't say that the rod and reel has to look pretty, or even work, to be legal. It just says that if an angler has a snook in his possession that he better have a rod and reel in the boat."* He didn't have a fishhook on the end of the line, but the law didn't specify that there had to be a hook on the line.

He squeezed the black rubber gas line bulb until it felt hard, hit the 'start' button and cranked over the ninety horsepower outboard. He glanced back, saw that it was pissing a stream of water out of the exhaust port, grunted his approval, cast off the lines and idled toward the mouth of the Manatee Pocket.

Three extremely soused, boisterous, loud-mouthed customers sitting at the bar in *Lobster's* waterside restaurant were happily demonstrating their obnoxious state of inebriation and having a rip-roaring good time. *"If they only knew what fun they're missing tonight."* Bear whispered to himself. When he passed Sailfish Marina he noted that the Florida Marine Patrol and Martin County Sheriff's Marine Unit boats were tied up for the night. Water was still draining from their outboard engines' exhaust ports so they must have recently come in. *"Guess they're getting a good night's sleep before the crazy holiday weekend."* Bear chuckled. *"I shouldn't have any law problems tonight."*

Unfortunately for Bear, he had no inkling of the series of dire events in store for him on this portentous night. When he rounded the entrance to *Port Sewell Marina* he looked for a sign of Mack being home. The cottage's lights were on, but the boat was not in the boathouse. *"Mack must have a snook trip tonight. If he was home I would stop and ask him if Ralph had told him about my problem and my plan."*

Bear rounded *Hell's Gate*, turned north and spotted green marker number "15" silently flashing 'green' at four second intervals. He cut inside of the marker to the west. The three boats anchored in front of the *'Bay Tree Lodge'* boathouse were fishing for snook. He didn't want to call attention to himself, so he ran far outside the channel and hugged the western shoreline. Mack's charter party, hooked up to a giant snook on the north side of the boathouse, didn't notice the commercial fishing boat on the west side of the channel because it wasn't displaying running lights.

Bear reached the *Evans Crary Bridge* at 11:05 P.M., scanned the top rail for anglers, saw none and silently slipped under the dark western end of the bridge unseen by the bridge tender. He kept tight to the shoreline and proceeded north towards *Woods Point*. He kept well to the west of unlighted green markers "21X" and "23X" and stayed at 'idle' speed until he rounded the point. He took his time because several unlighted boat docks extended 100 feet or more into the river. When he silhouetted the last dock against the background lights of the *Roosevelt Bridge* he felt secure enough to 'open her up' a little.

Bear had to make the three-mile run to the *Roosevelt Bridge* by 11:20 P.M. to be in position to wait for the black speedboat to pass through the bridge heading east. They usually passed each other about 11:30 P.M. on one side of the bridge or the other. It wouldn't do any good to set out his *'special net'* if his *'special friends'* weren't out tonight. Although it was Saturday, a night that the black speedboat usually didn't run, Bear figured that with *Memorial Day* being on Monday that they needed a lot of *'stuff'* to sell over the three day weekend. He was betting that they'd be out. He was greedy too and he was out tonight!

He passed Martin Memorial Hospital on his port side, pointed the bow of the boat at the railroad bridge tender's shanty and lined it up with the Roosevelt Bridge tender's shanty. His course took him west of green marker "23" that marked the shoal that runs from the south side of the river to the main channel. At low tide it was easy to tear off a lower unit. He pushed the 'tilt' button in with his thumb and raised the outboard lower unit up slightly. That gave him a little breathing room to pass over the bar, but it would be close! Fortunately for Bear the tide was at a high *'stand'* and hadn't started to ebb towards the *St. Lucie Inlet*. He held his breath, leaned forward to shift his weight and waited for the *'thumping'* of the prop against the sand bar. Somehow the boat skimmed over the bar without a bump. He lowered the motor back to a vertical position and pulled the throttle handle back to 'idle' speed.

Several people were fishing on the lighted concrete pier that jutted out from shore under the south side of the bridge. Bear saw no need to attract their attention. He changed course slightly to strategically position one of the massive concrete bridge pylons between himself and the fishermen. He avoided the main channel, idled under a span of the new *Roosevelt Bridge*, looked up at the sixty-five-foot center clearance span and wondered. *"Who could have a boat that tall?"* He kept the railroad bridge tender's shanty in line with the *Roosevelt Bridge* tender's shanty and quietly slipped alongside the wooden pilings on the south side of the railroad bridge. It was dark there and an easterly-bound boat could not see him. Bear's watch read 11:25 and he was right on schedule.

Just in case the Florida Marine Patrol stopped to check him he pulled out ten feet of line from the tangled mess on the antiquated spinning reel, tied a lead weight on the end and dropped it in the water. It looked good, but how would he explain why he had no hook or bait? He would worry about that if, and when, the time came. Peering under the railroad bridge and to the west Bear could see the opening under the Roosevelt Bridge perfectly and considered the possibilities. *"If they are smart they won't go under the bridge at full plane, but will slow down, putt through at idle speed and not call attention to themselves. But, they could bypass the main opening, slow to idle speed and pass under the south side of the bridge where neither bridge tender would be able to see them."*

The powerful throbbing of a super-charged, high horsepower outboard motor racing at full rpm, accompanied by the whisper of water rushing under a boat's hull, neared Bear's position. He didn't have time to react before the boat's ferocious wake arrived and violently rocked his boat. He grabbed the gunnels and hung on for *'dear life'* to keep from being tossed into the water. He glanced at his watch. It read 11:29. Bear smiled. *"He's right on time. We'll see him again about four-thirty in the North Fork."*

He wound in the twisted line, threw the useless fishing rod in the bottom of the boat, pulled up the chipped concrete block that served as an anchor and punched the starter button. The ancient outboard complained bitterly for a few revolutions then coughed into life. The fumes from the smoking exhaust almost smothered him before he could get the boat swung around and faced into the wind. Bear turned south and stayed back inside the shadow line so that the railroad bridge tender couldn't see him. At the pilings of an old boathouse he turned right and slipped under the railroad bridge. When he came out the other side he looked to his right towards the Roosevelt Bridge tender's shanty. *"I'm in his blind spot and he can't see me."* He slipped into the safety of the humid darkness beneath the bridge feeling confident that no one saw him. There would be no witnesses to his misdeeds, or fate.

Bear emerged from the shadows of the bridge and idled through the boats moored in the anchorage, He bumped into a sailboat, someone yelled a vile obscenity in his direction, but he didn't respond. When he knew for certain that he was out of the bridge tender's field of vision he made a right turn into the North Fork and hugged the western shoreline. After he passed the three long docks north of Dyer's Point he opened the boat up to it's full speed of fifteen knots. It was 11:45 and he had forty-five minutes to make the eight miles to River Gate Park and meet Bobo at twelve-thirty. Bear looked back at the new high rise Roosevelt Bridge and bitterly muttered aloud. *"How could people screw up the skyline with such an ugly concrete bridge?"*

Tiny bits of phosphorescence danced and sparkled in the 'prop wash' mimicking fireflies on a moonless summer night. Bright lights flickering along the shoreline reached out across the water and begged for his attention. *"It's amazing. I've made this trip hundreds of times and tonight I'm seeing things that I never saw before. Everything is so bright and clear."*

The fixed red light marking the entrance to *Club Med* stared down from its fourteen-foot high, creosoted wooden piling like the unblinking red eye of a Halloween goblin. He carefully threaded his way between unlighted day markers "6" and "7". If he got out of the channel he'd surely run into shallow water and go aground. He stayed in the narrow channel between the day markers and steered towards Kitching Cove.

"Bear. Are you there? Over." Bobo's timid southern drawl crackled over Bear's marine radio. The raspy sound startled him because his mind had drifted off to a far away place. He reached for the volume knob and turned it down a 'tad'. *"Bobo. I'm just passing Club Med. I'll be there in fifteen minutes. The silver mullet are jumping like crazy. I've never seen so many. I hit 'em with my spotlight and the water exploded. We'll make a good catch tonight. Over."*

"Hurry up, it's almost one o'clock. We have got to get going."

"Bobo. Hold your britches on son. I'll be there when I get there. Don't you fret none."

Bear glanced at his watch. 12:46 A.M. He had been so engrossed in looking at the lights along the shoreline that he forgot to keep the throttle lever pushed all the way forward. The throttle had a weak spring and slipped backward if he didn't keep his hand on it. He pushed it forward, held it in place with a meaty fist and the boat surged ahead. The overhanging branches of mangrove trees lining the sides of the narrow channel like dark leafy sentinels spread from bank to bank forming a green canopy over the water. Bear held his left arm up in front of his face to keep from being slapped in the mouth with leaves, raised the battered microphone to his mouth and keyed the marine radio.

"Bobo. I'm at the entrance to River Gate Park. Is everything cool? Over."

"It's okay Bear. Come on in. Over."

"I'll toss you my bow line when I reach the ramp. Be ready to catch it and wrap it over a cleat!"

Bear pulled into a slip alongside the concrete boat launching ramp, turned off the smoking outboard engine and slipped the eyes of the bow and stern lines around the steel cleats mounted to the floating wooden dock. He jumped out of the boat and shuffled up the concrete ramp to Bobo's truck. *A man can't run in rubber boots. Running spoils the image.*

"Bobo. Are you certain that you didn't see nobody?"

"A *Port St. Lucie* cop came by and asked what I was doing. I told him that I was waiting for you and that we were going out to catch some silver mullet with our cast nets. He asked me to show him how to throw a cast net and I spent a few minutes doing that. He left a good thirty minutes ago."

"Did you bring both big coolers and lots of chipped ice?"

"Yep. Both coolers are full. Let's go. I'm ready to catch fish!"

"Slow down a tad. Let's put one cooler in the boat to keep fish in and we'll transfer them to the other one when we get back."

The two anxious brothers loaded one of the large coolers in the bow of Bear's boat and tossed two fifteen-foot cast nets in beside it. Bear dragged the two gill nets out from behind the truck's seat and stuffed them into a black, plastic garbage can drilled full of one-inch diameter holes so that it would sink. A concrete block inside the can made sinking a certainty. If stopped by law enforcement Bear would slip the garbage can over the side of the boat sink it and retrieve it later. Bobo still didn't know about Bear's 'special' net.

"Bear. I ain't never seen so many mullet in one place before. Look at 'em jump! Let's get our set made and get out of here before somebody in one of them fancy houses sees us."

"Who's going to see us? They're all sleeping like babies. The only people that are gonna' pay any attention to what we're doing are the ones that you are waking up with your big mouth!"

They made their 'set' at the entrance to Kitching Cove. Bear ran the boat back and forth at full throttle along the shoreline and herded the frightened mullet into the gill net. It was a *'humongous'* catch! The cork floats were pulled completely under the water by the struggling fish.

"Bear. I ain't never seen so many fish in a net at one time in my life." Bobo gasped for air as he leaned his back into pulling the heavy float line towards the boat.

"That's 'cause you never spent enough time fishing with me. Let's get this net picked and get out of here. It's almost three o'clock. I got things to do and it's a long run back down the river to the *Manatee Pocket.*"

"Bear. Why are you in such a big hurry? The fish house don't open 'till six o'clock. We've got lots of time"

"Little brother, don't you worry yourself into a 'dither' about why. Just get busy picking them fish out of the net."

The excited pair dumped the ice out of the cooler into the bottom of the boat to make room for the fish. When the cooler was full of fish they tossed their flopping silver bounty into the bottom of the boat. Mullet covered the bottom and the net was still not picked clean. When they finally finished picking mullet out of the net fish filled the boat almost to the top of the gunnels. They only had only inches of freeboard to spare.

"Bear. Let's go back real slow. Just a little little-bitty wave could swamp us. Be careful."

"Bobo quiet down. I know how to drive a boat. I ain't sunk no boat yet. When we drop the nets off it'll help a little."

"I don't want to drown in a boat filled with dead mullet."

"Stop your whining and blubbering. I'm going to stash the net in a hole alongside that tree stump. It's about six feet deep there. You grab hold of the stump and hold us in place for a minute."

Bear tied six feet of thirty-pound test monofilament fishing line to a handle of the garbage can. He tied the other end to the stump and lowered the can into the water. It filled with water and sank to the bottom. A piece of red and silver tinfoil from a chewing tobacco wrapper twisted on a twig marked the cans location. Bear had to know where it was, and be able to find it, when he came back after he dropped Bobo off at the boat ramp.

"Okay cry baby. The net is over the side and we should have a little more breathin' room."

Bobo didn't know about the 'special' net that Bear had stashed in the bottom of the garbage can. When they reached the *River Gate Park* boat ramp a *Port St. Lucie City Police* car was waiting for them. The officer didn't look very happy. He leaned up against the hood of the car, his arms were folded over his chest and he held a long, black flashlight in his left hand.

"Bear. It's the cop that I showed how to throw a cast net while I was waiting for you."

"Little brother I hope that he likes you a whole lot."

"Hey there officer. Its sure nice to see ya' again. Did ya'll stop by to see how we did? We did real good!"

"Kinda'. Dispatch got a call that two commercial fishermen in a blue boat were gillnetting mullet in *Kitching Cove*. They were using their boat engine to scare the mullet into their net and the engine noise woke the people up. That couldn't have been you two clowns could it?"

"No sir! Not us! We were using cast nets." Bear made his case emphatically with a poker face while lifting a cast net filled with mullet from the bottom of the boat to reinforce his point. Sure, we made some noise because we used the boat to herd the school into shallow water between the channel and the cove so we could use cast nets. It could have looked like a gill net to somebody watching us because the fish were small and gilled themselves in the mesh. Just like these did! But, I assure you that we were using only cast nets and they're legal. Search our boat if you want."

"It makes sense if I put in my report that I searched your boat. Where's your boat trailer?"

"I ain't got no dern boat trailer. I ran the boat up here from *Port Salerno* 'cause I've been having fuel problems and wanted to run the bad gas out of the lines. Officer, can you wait a couple of minutes? We gotta' ice these fish down fast.

"No problem. I'll wait in my patrol car. Just let me know when you're ready."

Bobo backed the protesting pickup truck down the slanted concrete boat ramp. Bear dumped the ice out of the remaining cooler into the truck bed and started tossing in mullet. When the cooler was full Bobo shoveled chipped ice on top of the flopping fish and closed it. They filled up the other cooler with wriggling mullet and also covered them with ice. The remaining fish that they couldn't cram into the coolers they threw into the truck bed and shoveled chipped ice over them.

"Bobo. The fish in the back of the truck will keep 'till you get home. When you get there find a couple more coolers, throw in the fish and cover them with ice. It's three-thirty and you have a couple of hours before the fish house opens. You can be first in line and get the best price. Hold out a couple dozen for Emogene, drop 'em off in a cooler at the house and leave it on the front porch. Don't wake her up unless you want an *'ass-wupping'.*"

The young cop gingerly approached the boat. He hadn't been close to a commercial fishing boat before and didn't realize how bad dead fish could smell until now. He half-heartedly played his flashlight around the inside of the boat. He didn't see anything except two dingy life orange preservers, a red plastic bucket, a bailer fashioned from a one-pound coffee can, a couple of ropes and the two cast nets. He didn't know what safety items were required on a commercial fishing boat and felt uncomfortable about asking any questions about the rusty shotgun.

"Everything looks okay to me. The only nets that I see are those two cast nets. The people that called dispatch about the gill netters must have been mistaken. It certainly wasn't you guys. Thanks for letting me take a peek. See ya'll around." He 'beeped' his patrol car's horn twice as he pulled out of the parking area.

"Okay Bobo. We made it this far. Now you take off in your truck for Port Salerno and get the rest of these fish in coolers and iced down. I'll meet you at the fish house about six-thirty."

"How come so late? It should only take you an hour and a half at most to get back to Port Salerno if you go full speed. It's 'bout a quarter to four. You can be back at five-thirty easy. We could meet for breakfast before the fish house opens at six o'clock."

"Because I'm gonna' take one of them cast nets and catch me a few more silvers on the way back. They'll keep for an hour or so because it's still cool. I'll see you about six-thirty at the fish house. Then well go for breakfast. Don't forget Emogene's fish! Leave 'em iced down in a cooler on the front porch and don't wake her up unless you want her to kick your ass."

"Okay, if you say so. But I don't feel good about this. Keep your radio on channel eighteen so I can call you. Bear. Tell me for real. Are you having fuel problems?"

"Of course not. But it gave the cop a reason for us not having a trailer up here. Call me on the marine radio about five-thirty and I'll tell you where I am. Remember to call me on channel eighteen. You hear? Now scat!"

"Okay. But I have a funny feeling about all this. You aren't going to go back and set a gill net are you? People will be watching for you after all that ruckus and noise we made."

"Of course not. Now git! The ice is melting on them fish." Bear watched wistfully as Bobo pulled out of the parking lot and turned right towards *Port St. Lucie Boulevard*. Water flowed out of the rusted-out truck bed onto the pavement like a waterfall. *"I wouldn't be a bit surprised if an army of cats and dogs follows him down Highway One all the way to the fish house. No matter what some people say he's been a right good brother. Even if he's a little slow at times."*

The soft glint of light reflecting off metal from a dark corner of the parking area caught Bear's attention. He cupped his hands around his eyes and squinted to see in the dim light. He could make out the outline of a truck and boat trailer parked in the shadows far away from the launching ramps. He sauntered over to get a better look. The truck was a black *Dodge Ram Charger*. The truck windows were heavily tinted black and the camper shell mounted over the truck bed was also painted black. Strangely enough, so was the boat trailer.

Bear groped in his shirt pocket for something to write with

and found a stubby, yellow number two pencil that was missing the eraser, but no paper. He had a good memory for numbers and repeated the truck's tag number out loud over and over to himself on the way back down to the boat. He'd jot them down later. When Bear reached the boat ramp he glanced at his watch and shuddered with anticipation. *"It's three fifty-five. It's almost time for the black boat to come back through the Roosevelt Bridge and it'll only take him fifteen minutes to get here. I've got to act fast."*

He slipped into the boat, threw off the lines, hit the engine's starter button and 'nothing' happened. He held the starter button down with his thumb and jiggled the gearshift handle at the same time. The ancient outboard coughed twice, belched a cloud of blue exhaust smoke and came to life. *"Starter switch you are going to be the death of me yet."* he muttered. Bear backed away from the ramp, shifted into 'forward' shoved the throttle ahead as far as it would go and held it down. *"Time's a wasting. I've got to be ready for them. Let's go boat - balls to the wall."*

Bear made the two-mile trip to *Kitching Cove* in ten minutes, located the stump and retrieved the black garbage can containing his gill net 'surprise' package. He smiled and muttered, *"Now is the time for all good men to come to the aid of their country."* Somehow those words seemed appropriate for what he was about to do and he repeated them out loud once more, *"Now is the time for all good men to come to the aid of their country."* He softly repeated the phrase over and over out loud as he took to the task at hand. Bear had to be very quiet because earlier the noise from his ancient outboard engine woke up someone in one of the elegant waterfront homes. If he woke them up again they'd call the Florida Marine Patrol on him for gill netting for certain.

Bear's 'special' net was made of monofilament line and was fifty feet long by four feet deep. Eight white, Styrofoam balls, the size of softballs and spaced ten feet apart, were tied to the ¼ inch stainless steel cable that ran the length of the net. A short length of white cotton line strong enough to hold the net in place, but weak enough to break easily when struck, was tied to each end. Bear wanted the net to break loose instantly when hit by the boat so that the cable and barbed wire would wrap around the prop. That combination would stop a boat 'dead in the water' instantly.

Bear attached one end of the net to a mangrove tree root on the west side of the narrow channel. He pulled the other end across the channel with the boat and tied it to a tree limb. He backed off and looked at his handy work. The Styrofoam floats looked like white bowling balls on a pool table. They were very obvious! He smirked and muttered to himself. *"There is no way that they will miss seeing these and they'll go out of their way to hit 'em. Best of all, they'll know who did it. Now is the time for all good men to come to the aid of their country."* He hummed the melody as he pulled deep into the shadows of the mangrove trees lining Kitching Cove so that he could not be seen. He felt like a spider waiting for a fly to come into her sticky web. He glanced at his watch. 4:15 A.M. and almost 'show time'!

Bear reached down into the dark bottom of the boat and felt for the security of the ancient, rusty double-barreled shotgun. It was there. He thought, *"There's no turning back now, but what if they have guns too? Will they shoot at me while they're dead in the water with a fouled prop? It wouldn't be logical because gunshots would wake up the waterside residents only one hundred yards away. The Florida Marine Patrol would be there within ten minutes and the bad guys wouldn't be able to get away. But, what if they didn't think logically and did shoot at him? Then what?"*

Bear sensed its presence before he saw it! He felt the soft whisper of water racing against the slick hull and heard the soft drone of a muffled high-horsepower outboard motor racing at high rpm. When the black speedboat passed his hiding spot Bear heard a loud 'crunch' followed by a loud 'splash' and a lot of cursing. The black speedboat was caught in the net! But, the outboard engine still running wide open at 5500 rpm didn't realize that the propeller couldn't turn and stripped the gears off the drive shaft with a loud 'blam'! Without the load of the propeller to keep it in check the engine increased it's revolutions and threw a rod out the side of the block and stopped it cold.

The passenger went airborne over the bow and hit the water with a resounding 'splash.' The driver's face smashed into the steering console's instrument panel with a solid 'thud'. He was badly injured and in pain. The passenger was in the dark water splashing, groaning, coughing, spitting and cursing at the same time. *"I'm going to kill that son of a bitch dead! His ass is mine! I warned him last night. I think that my arm is broken."* The only noise that emanated from the boat's driver was a soft moaning and a 'bubbling' sound as he tried to breath through the blood welled up in his smashed nose and collapsed nasal passages.

Bear wanted to make certain that they knew that he was the cause of their pain and frustration. He laid the rusty, inoperative shotgun across his knees where it could be easily seen, started the engine and idled closer to the powerless boat. The severely injured passenger had managed to drag himself over the bow railing with his one good arm and was tending to the driver who was moaning and bleeding profusely from his nose and ears.

"Hello boys. I've been waiting for you. It's not nice to fool with Bear! I hope that you learned a valuable lesson tonight. Don't mess with us *'crackers'* because we will chew you up, spit you out and throw your bones to the fish. Consider yourself lucky that you didn't get yourself killed 'cause I could have done that too." Bear demonstrated his bravado and shock the rusty shotgun over his head to show that he meant business.

"Screw you hillbilly," screamed the pockmarked faced passenger with the broken arm. "I should have whacked you last night when I had the chance. Now you have really messed up good! You just don't know how deep you are in the shit, do you? Your fat 'hillbilly' ass is mine!"

"Who do you think you're talking to butt wipe? You're the one with the broken arm, the blown engine and no way to get home. Maybe I'll just shoot your lousy ass." For emphasis Bear pointed the shotgun in the direction of his adversary, sensed that someone was behind him and started to turn around.

Pfffffft!

Bear felt a sharp blow at the back of his head where it joined his neck and the blow was immediately followed by numbness. He felt his head go under water, but he couldn't lift his head to breath, or move his arms, or his legs. He tried to take a breath and the brackish water burned his nostrils and lungs. He gagged, coughed twice and then everything went black.

"Frankie! Why did you have to shoot the bastard? I wanted to do it myself." The pockmarked face man was screaming. "Look at my arm and Gino's nose. We deserved to be able to kill him ourselves. He was *'dead meat'* and his ass was ours!"

"Manny. Shut your face! He got both of you and good! Now he's dead and half of the people that live around here are awake and looking out their windows at us. Someone is going to call the Florida Marine Patrol. We have to get out of here right now! Throw me a line and I'll tow you to my place for the night. You can keep your boat in the boathouse until we get it fixed.

"Why are you here? What about my truck and trailer?"

"They're in my garage. I knew that something was wrong when I heard over the scanner that the cops had checked out two commercial fishermen in *River Gate Park* about three-thirty. I took the boat across the river and watched this guy go up to your truck and sneak around like he was looking for something. When he pulled out of the ramp I called Marco on the cell phone. He and Rico went over and picked up your truck and trailer."

"Frankie how did you sneak up on him without making any noise? We didn't see or hear you coming."

"This is an electric boat. It's powered by two car batteries and will run at ten knots for three hours. I was waiting for you at the *'007 Bridge'*. When I heard the yelling I slipped on down here. He didn't see me coming because of the mangroves.

Hey! It's almost five o'clock! Let's wrap this 'bozo' up in the net in the bottom of his boat, push him and his boat into that cove and get out of here. I want it to look like he got tangled in his net and drowned just like the other one did last year. Hurry up! The tide's coming in and it'll push him into the mangroves and hold him in there for about six hours until it turns and starts to ebb."

"Frankie, hold on for just a minute. I want a look at this guy's face." Manny, the man with the broken arm and pockmarked face, grabbed a handful of Bear's thick black hair and lifted his head out of the water. Bear's leather necklace holding the two bear claws and the *South African One Rand* coin fell out of his shirt. His tormentor grabbed it, tore it loose and dropped Bear's head back in the water. "Maybe I didn't get to kill him myself, but I have something to remember his ugly face by."

The trio wrapped Bear's body securely in the cast net and

forced his hands through the narrow mesh to make it appear that he got tangled up and drowned. They towed his boat and his body back into the secluded cove across from Kitching Cove and left them in a back corner that couldn't be seen from the main channel. The incoming tide would push Bear's boat and body even further into the vertical roots of the mangrove trees.

Three cotton ball shaped, pink tinged, fluffy cumulus clouds on the eastern horizon signaled the coming of sunrise and the beginning of a new day in Paradise. A lone female osprey circled overhead whistling a soft call of greeting to her long time friend floating face down in the murky, tannin-stained water below.

CHAPTER

15

It was 3:30 A.M. Sunday morning, the day before Memorial Day, when Mack entered the *'Cross Roads'* and met a brisk northerly wind. A wind-driven three-foot chop splashed over the bow, tepid, light green saltwater washed through the cockpit and ran out the scuppers. He couldn't run the boat any faster in the choppy water without snapping the taut length of thirty-pound test monofilament line that restrained the monstrous sow snook alongside the starboard side of the boat.

She looked up at him with unblinking yellow eyes and seemed to be asking, *"Why are you doing this? I have to spawn and guarantee the continuation of my species."*

If Mack was pulled over by a Florida Marine Patrol officer for a check, a quick 'jerk' would 'snap' the strained line and the trophy fish would drift away free. He recalled *Bear's* advice and suspended her off the boat's starboard side, *"The Marine Patrol cops keep those big, black, rubber boat bumpers on their starboard side and sneak up behind you on your port side."*

Mack made it through the *Cross Roads* and kept the bent, rusty iron 'dolphin' holding up marker number "4" on his starboard side. The marker's red light flashed on and off at four-second intervals and the numerals of the boat's compass also glowed ominously red. He steered 270 degrees on his magnetic compass and headed for the *Manatee Pocket*. He opted to pass the red, triangle-shaped, markers on his port rather than his starboard side because it was a more direct course than following the channel markers. Although the ancient mariner's adage was, *"Red right when returning from sea,"* the twenty-two foot *PURSUIT* only drew nine inches of water. Going aground was the least of Mack's worries tonight.

He passed red marker number "6" on his starboard side, turned north towards *Port Sewell Marina* and left the entrance to the *Manatee Pocket* on his port. Mack couldn't risk dropping his charter party and the giant fish there because Florida Marine Patrol officers might be monitoring the area. A $500 tip for bringing in the big snook was in the balance. He planned to drop the fish off at *Port Sewell Marina*, double back and drop his charter party off at *Sand Sprit Park* where he had picked them up at eight-thirty Saturday night. Later they would rendezvous for breakfast at the *Denny's* on US 1, about a mile south of Cove Road, and Mack would slip a cooler holding the fish into the back of their pickup truck.

It was less than a half-mile to the entrance to *Willoughby Creek* and the safety of *Port Sewell Marina*. Mack crept along at 'idle' speed, not wishing to draw attention to himself, and passed red day marker number "10" on his starboard side. Green marker number "11" was directly off his port bow and it's green light flashed on and off every four seconds

FLASH!

The 100,000 candle-power halogen spotlight caught Mack full in the face and blinded him. *"Captain. Stop right there and turn off your engine."*

Apparently the person behind the spotlight didn't know United States Coast Guard Inland Navigation Rule 36. *"If necessary to attract the attention of another vessel, any vessel may direct the beam of her searchlight in the direction of the danger, in such a way as not to embarrass any vessel."* Mack was taught at captain's school that *'not to embarrass'* meant not to shine a spotlight in the eyes of the other vessel operator.

Mack obliged, pulled the throttle handle back to 'neutral' and turned off the ignition. "I can't see. Can you turn off the damn spotlight?" The light went off and bright spots of white light danced before Mack's retinas.

The Florida Marine Patrol officer's boat was painted an ominous gray. A wide, black stripe ran down from each side from the bow and backwards toward amidships. Two large, black plastic boat fenders hung over the starboard side. The twin 250 horsepower outboards mounted on the transom purred like contented kittens. *"No outrunning this mother,"* Mack thought as the gray boat pulled along his port side.

The deep, authoritative voice barked out a second order from the darkness. *"Captain. Grab these lines and tie me off to the bow and stern cleats on your port side. I'll keep us in place with my engines. Hurry it up. The tide's running out hard and fast."*

Although he couldn't see the officer's face Mack knew who it was. He recognized the northern Michigander's 'twang'. Mack's right hand tightened on the taut length of thirty-pound test monofilament line that led over the starboard side. At this juncture a $500 tip was insignificant compared to a conviction for possessing a snook outside of the thirty-four inch 'slot' limit. He could lose his Coast Guard license, his livelihood and his cover.

Mack was very concerned because if he was arrested that his fingerprints would be run through the *Centralized Criminal Information System.* He couldn't allow that to happen. Too much was at stake. When he applied for his Coast Guard license and filed his fingerprints with the Miami Regional Examination Center - no negative reports came back. But that was Federal and could be handled internally. But, this was a State matter!

Mack 'yanked' on the monofilament line - it stretched, but it wouldn't break and sliced deeply into the soft flesh of his fingers. He gave it a second even harder 'yank' and it only cut deeper. Frantic, and filled with desperation, Mack yanked 'hard' and felt the line cut through his flesh 'to the bone' - the line popped with a loud *'crack'* similar to the sharp report of a .22 caliber pistol.

"What was that noise? Mack. Did you shoot a gun?" The Florida Marine Patrol Officer turned his powerful halogen spotlight towards Mack's boat and illuminated the entire cockpit.

Mack held his hand up, palm forward towards the officer, so that he could see the trail of blood streaming down his palm. "Sir, when I reached for your line I caught my hand on something. It startled me and I jerked. Now look at my hand! I'm bleeding like a stuck pig. I have to get to the marina and get this bandaged up before I bleed to death. I may have to go to the hospital"

"Mack! Look at that 'monster' snook floating 'belly-up' behind your boat!"

Mack swiveled around in his seat towards the spot where the dark, murky water was lit up by the bright spotlight. The thirty-five pound sow snook floated belly-up just behind the outboard motor. Her gill plates flared open as she labored in the swift current and attempted to assimilate enough oxygen through her swollen gills to activate her bladder and gain vertical stability. A three- foot length of clear monofilament fishing line trailed from her massive jaw as a reminder of her ordeal of the past hour.

"She must have been *'gut-hooked'* by someone using live bait. Look at the piece of mono coming out of her mouth. Live bait is bad this time of year because the fish swallow the hook. Get out your net and try to net it so that I take a look at her. Maybe the hook is only stuck in her throat and we'll be able to get it out."

The officer was playing 'coy'. He knew that it was no accident that the big fish had floated up behind Mack's boat. He was going to play this one to the 'hilt' and make him suffer. Maybe he couldn't prove possession of a snook in excess of the thirty-four inch 'slot' limit, but he sure could make Mack sweat bullets over it. The officer hoped that the Florida Department of Law Enforcement laboratory in Tallahassee would be able to verify that the mono in the fish's mouth matched the spool of *mono* in Mack's boat. But, the test could be made only if he could net the fish and get the *mono*. He had his camera out and prepared to shoot a photograph of the 'evidence'. A picture is worth 10,000 words and it could also mean a big fine for some one convicted of keeping a snook outside of the slot length limit.

Mack made an obviously half-hearted stab with the net and hit the fish in the head. She turned over on her left side and drifted away. Along with her went Mack's $500 tip, a possible $1,000 fine and the loss of his Coast Guard license. "Officer, I'm sorry, but the fish flipped over and sank. Should I hang around to see if she surfaces again? I might be able to catch her for you."

"Forget it Mack. It wasn't that important. But, this reminds me of the time that Bill Mason and I stopped a commercial fisherman, *Bear* I think his name was, for operating at night without having his boat's navigation lights on. Mack, I know that you were there too because I saw you sneaking around under the old *Roosevelt Bridge*. Running without navigation lights is the same reason that I stopped you tonight."

"I didn't have my running lights on? I must have blown a fuse. I took a lot of water over the bow coming through the *'Cross Roads'* and they probably shorted out."

"Mack. Do you recall how nervous that guy *Bear* was? That's because he had a bunch of snook hanging off the side of the boat strung on piece of mono. He almost cut his fingers off trying to break it when I wanted to put the cuffs him on for possessing a dead manatee. He was lucky. So were you. Check your fuses when you get back in. Toss off my lines and have a good night."

Warm sweat poured down Mack's neck and ran down the indentation of his spine. He turned the starter switch and the 250 horsepower *YAMAHA* outboard roared to life. He flipped the toggle switch for the red and green navigation lights and they instantly flashed 'on'. He still had to drop off his charter party and turned the boat toward the markers marking the entrance to the *Manatee Pocket* about fifty yards away.

After his party unloaded their fishing gear at the *Sandsprit Park* boat ramp the leader of the duo walked over to Mack and held out his hand. "That was close! Mack, we appreciate you trying to get that big fish for us. But, it wasn't worth getting caught over and we didn't need the notoriety either. Thanks! Here's the charter fee and a small token of our appreciation. We'd like to try to catch another big snook again next week. That is if you are willing."

Still shaken from the harrowing experience and holding his bleeding hand upright to reduce the flow of blood from the gash, Mack replied. "Thanks, but no thanks. I don't ever want to try that again. Mack shoved the thick wad of wet bills into his shirt pocket turned and walked down the dock to his boat. He threw off the lines, started the engine and gave a *'toot'* of his boat's horn as he backed out of the slip. He put the engine in 'forward' gear and motored at idle speed towards the mouth of the *'Pocket'*.

As he passed the last launching ramp a spotlight hit him 'full blast' in the face. *"Oh, no! Not again!"* The light switched off and a gruff, unfriendly voice boomed out of the darkness toward him. *"Mack. Come over here. I want to talk to you."*

When Mack pulled alongside the dock he saw that it was the same Florida Marine Patrol officer who pulled him over just a few minutes earlier. "Mack, I don't care who you were in your other life, or what you did before you moved to *Port Sewell*. But, now you are in my territory. You, and your commercial fishing buddies, will obey the fishing laws of the State of Florida, or I will take all of you in. Mason was transferred to Jacksonville and I'm 'the man' in town now. Do you understand me clearly?"

"Yes sir. I do. Can I go home now? I'm tired and my hand is still bleeding."

"Certainly. But, before you leave take a look at this 'baby'. She might be a state record." The officer held up a monstrous sow snook. A piece of thirty-pound test monofilament line hung from her mouth, her gill plates waved feebly as she gasped - she was drowning in the air. "I went back to the spot where I pulled you over and found her snagged on a channel marker piling by this line. It must have caught hold of it as the tide drifted her past it. I'd wager an educated guess that some commercial fisherman is up to his old tricks. I'm taking her into the office in Jupiter tomorrow as 'evidence'. I thought that just 'maybe' you would like to know. Pass the word along that I'm watching. Goodnight, Captain Mack." He placed a heavy emphasis on 'Captain.'

Mack's mouth was as dry as cotton. He restarted the engine, backed away from the ramp and turned toward the red and green day markers marking the mouth of the *Manatee Pocket*. When he passed the channel markers, he turned north, shoved the throttle forward and the boat almost jumped clear out of the water. Luckily he only had half a mile to go before he had to throttle back to ease into the mouth of *Willoughby Creek*. But, going at full speed, *'balls to the wall'* in the darkness helped to blow off the *'stink'* of what he had almost done that night. He idled through *North Lake* and headed for the boathouse. Totally exhausted, he didn't bother to rinse down the boat. He clipped the steel davit hooks on the 'fore' and 'aft' eye bolts, punched the

'Up' button and the electric hoist pulled the boat up and suspended it three feet above the water.

Mack felt it before he heard it! The vibrations of a powerful, super-charged outboard motor "throbbed' through the pilings of the boathouse and shook dust from the wooden rafters. He looked through the boathouse door and saw a black speedboat and its two occupants, make a sharp turn to the right at green marker "13A" and head for *Hell's Gate*. He glanced at his watch. 4:05 His 'ordeal' had lasted only a half hour. He was going to bed, not worry about tomorrow and forget about tonight! It would be daylight in two hours.

The hint of sunrise was on the eastern horizon, the shy summer sun peeked out from behind a pinkish tinged, puffy, white cumulus cloud and softly illuminated the mangrove tree lined cove in the *North Fork* of the St. Lucie River.

An anxious, pleading man's voice echoed across the water from a 'tinny-sounding' marine radio speaker interrupting the tranquil scene. *"Bear. It's five-thirty. Where are you? I'm waiting for you at the fish house dock. The fish are iced down and I'll be the first one in the door. Bear. Can you hear me? It's Bobo."* Again his frantic plea echoed across the dark waters of the remote cove directly across the *North Fork* from *Kitching Cove*. *"Bear. It's Bobo. If you can hear me say something."* There was no response - only eerie muted silence. *"I'll try you at six o'clock. You should be close enough to hear me then."*

The deep channel between *Fork Point* and *Club Med* provides prime tarpon fishing for early rising fishermen who get there at least an hour before sunrise. "Bill, did you hear something over there in the mangroves just a minute ago? It sounded like somebody hollering for a guy named 'Bear' on a boat radio. It came from over there where that crazy osprey is whirling around. Something must be wrong with that bird because it's not diving. It's just flapping around like it's trying to stay over the top of something in the water.

"Maybe one of her chicks fell out of the nest in that Australian Pine tree into the water."

"I heard something, but I don't pay attention to anything when I'm fishing. Don't worry about the damn bird. If her chick fell in the water it deserves to drown. That's *Nature's* way. Only the strongest survive. Look at al of those silver mullet jumping out of the water over there in that cove. I'll bet that there's a school of tarpon working them. Let's give 'em a shot."

"Bear. Are you there? It's a quarter to six. I'm getting worried about you. Over."

"Bill. There it is! I heard it again. It's coming from over there behind those mangrove trees. Somebody's got their marine radio turned on, but nobody is answering back."

"It isn't my problem. I'm worried about getting one of those tarpon to eat this tasty mullet that's running around on the end of my line like he's scared to death. Look at him go! Wow! Look at that tarpon jump! He's got a mullet hanging out of his mouth. Oh shit! He's got my mullet and he's running for the channel. Flip on the electric trolling motor and follow him."

The line *'sizzled'* off the reel. The metal spool began to show under the few remaining wraps of line and the fish kept running. The line reached the knot that tied it to the spool went *'ping' and* the trophy fish was gone. "I didn't have a chance. That *'big mother'* weighed at least one hundred pounds! May be even one seventy-five. It peeled off two hundred yards of line in less than ten seconds and *'ping'* it was over. I'm shaking so bad that I can't even hold the damn rod."

"Bear. Its Bobo are you there? It's six o'clock and the fish house just opened. I've got to get in and get these fish sold before somebody else beats me. Have you got any more silvers in the boat that you want me to ice down before you get here? I can meet you at Shepherd's Park, pick 'em up and carry them to the fish house. Bear are you there?" The now frantic, pleading voice echoed across the cove and through the mangrove trees.

"Bill. There it is again. It came from the other side of the channel back in those mangroves. It's the same area where that osprey keeps circling. Listen to her scream. She's really upset about something over there. Let's go over and check it out!"

"Yeah, I heard it. He sounds worried about somebody named *Bear.* I wonder what channel he's on? Let me get the scanner flipped on and we'll check out his channel and give him a call."

"Bear are you there?" The whining plea boomed out of the

fishermen's radio speaker and echoed across the channel into the mangroves. *"Bear, please answer me. I'm worried about you. Bear, where are you?"* The osprey screamed back in response.

"Fred, he's calling that guy *Bear* on channel eighteen. I'm going to give him a call back."

"Bobo. This is the *'WET DREAM.'* We're fishing up by *Club Med* and can hear you calling for *Bear*. Somebody else up here has got their radio set on channel eighteen and we can hear you calling for *Bear*. Can you hear me? Over."

"WET DREAM'. I hear you. I'm in *Port Salerno* and I'm trying to reach my brother *Bear*. I left him at *River Gate Park* about four o'clock. He was going to catch some mullet, bring the boat back and meet me for breakfast at the *Queen Conch* at six-thirty. Have you seen a blue commercial fishing boat up there? He might be broken down and need help. Over."

"We haven't seen any boats, but we can hear you calling him. I can hear my own voice coming out from behind a bunch of mangroves in that cove about a half mile north of *Fork Point*. We're going to run over there and find out what's going on. Stay on this channel and we'll call you back after we check it out."

"Roger *'WET DREAM'*. I'll stand by channel eighteen. Please hurry. *Bear* might be hurt and need help."

"Bill, I see it! There's a blue commercial fishing boat over there. It's pushed 'way back' in the mangroves. It'll be hard to get close to it without getting stuck. Tilt the motor up so that the water pump doesn't suck in mud."

"Bobo. Its *'WET DREAM'*. We found a blue commercial fishing boat wedged in some mangrove roots and we're trying to get up close to it." The fisherman's own voice echoed back at him from *Bear's* radio.

"WET DREAM'. Do you see *Bear*? Is he okay?"

"Bobo, hold your horses just a minute. We just got here and haven't had time to do anything."

"What do you see?"

"The boat's empty, except for a rusty old shotgun, a red, plastic bucket and a 'beat up' fishing rod. Hold on. I see a rope hanging off the bow into the water. Stand by while my partner Fred pulls it up. Holy Jesus!"

"What's wrong? Where's *Bear*."

"The damned osprey just about took my head off. Bobo, does your brother have a black beard?"

"Yes sir? Why?"

"Call the Florida Marine Patrol and get 'em up here 'pronto'. I'll call the Coast Guard on the radio. He's tangled up in a net and it looks like he drowned. There's an osprey up here that acts if she is guarding the boat. She keeps diving at us with her talons out. Ouch! She hit me in the head again!"

"How do you know for sure that he's drowned?"

"I don't want to give the details over the radio, but believe me he's drowned. Bobo, call the Florida Marine Patrol now! We'll stay close by him until they get here."

"What am I going to do?"

"I already told you twice! Call the Florida Marine Patrol! I'm going to call the Fort Pierce Coast Guard station then I'll switch back to channel eighteen. Tell the Florida Marine Patrol that we'll be standing by on channel eighteen!"

"You won't leave my brother will you?"

"No. We won't leave him. We'll stand by and wait for the Florida Marine Patrol to get here unless this damn 'crazy-ass' osprey kills us first. Fred! Duck! Here she comes again!"

"Fort Pierce Coast Guard, Fort Pierce Coast Guard, Fort Pierce Coast Guard. This is the vessel *'WET DREAM'* on channel sixteen. We have an emergency. Over."

"Vessel *WET DREAM*, Vessel *WET DREAM*, Vessel *WET DREAM*. This is Coast Guard Station Fort Pierce. Sir, do you have channel twenty-two alpha on your radio? Over."

" Yes, we have channel twenty-two alpha. Over"

"Vessel *'WET DREAM'*. This is Coast Guard Station Fort Pierce. Please switch to channel twenty-two alpha. Over."

"We're switching to channel twenty-two alpha. Out."

"Vessel *'WET DREAM'*. This is Coast Guard Station Fort Pierce on channel twenty-two alpha. Please give the nature of your emergency. Over."

"We were fishing in the *North Fork* across from *Cub Med* and we found a dead body in the water. We need the Coast Guard and Florida Marine Patrol to get up here 'pronto'. Over."

"Vessel *'WET DREAM'*. Coast Guard Station Fort Pierce. How do you know that the person is deceased? Are you medically trained? Over."

"There's no doubt - he's been dead for a while. Over."

"Vessel *'WET DREAM'*. Coast Guard Station Fort Pierce. Sir, are you a medical doctor?

"No. But, little brown crabs are coming out of his nose. Over."

"Vessel *'WET DREAM'*. Coast Guard Station Fort Pierce. Understood. Sir, will you stay in the area and monitor channel twenty-two alpha? Over."

"We'll stay for a while and be sure that he doesn't float away. We told his brother Bobo to tell the Florida Marine Patrol that we would monitor channel eighteen. Our VHF radio has a scanner and we will monitor both channels. Over."

"Vessel *'WET DREAM'*. Coast Guard Station Fort Pierce. Sir, we will notify the Florida Marine Patrol that they can reach you on channel eighteen or twenty-two alpha. Fort Pierce out."

"Bill, this is a hell of a mess that we've gotten ourselves into. I hope that we don't have to be witnesses in court or anything. I don't want to get involved. Let's just leave. They'll find him sooner or later. All they gotta' to do is call on channel eighteen."

"Fred, stop your damn whimpering. If you hadn't kept bitching at me that you were hearing something back here we'd have been long gone. We might have even been able to catch a fish or two. But, we've got about thirty minutes before the sun gets up too far. The tarpon 'bite' might still be going on over by *Harbor Ridge*. What do you say we give it a shot?"

"Screw it. Let's go fishing. That crazy bird will watch him until somebody gets here and pulls him out of the water."

The shy sun peeked out from behind the puffy, pink-tinged cumulus clouds on the eastern horizon and lit up the stately mangrove trees lining the tiny hidden cove in the *North Fork*.

CHAPTER
16

It was early Sunday morning. Mack had returned from last night's charter about 4:00 A.M. and went to bed His cut hand throbbed with a dull pain that pulsated up his arm with each heartbeat. He booked a $300 snook charter for tonight, but had refused several charters for Monday. It was *Memorial Day* and the one holiday that caused him anguish. There was nothing to celebrate just things to remember and he tried to blot out those memories. He didn't talk about his experiences and that kept most of them at bay. He felt that it was better that no one knew. The other members of his team could not celebrate Memorial Day – they were all gone.

It was called Memorial Day in order for people to remember and honor them. He couldn't understand why people wanted to party on Memorial Day. It wasn't a day for celebration. What was there to celebrate - the death of human beings? It was a day of remembrance, not celebration. He didn't look forward to it and preferred to be alone. No phones, no television, no beer, no hot dogs – only peace and quiet. That's what they deserved.

BRRRING BRRING BRRING

The unforgiving telephone wouldn't stop its relentless ringing. It pestered him until he had to answer it.

"Captain Mack here."

"Mack. Get up. It's Ralph. Bear's dead. A couple of sport fishermen found him about dawn floating next to his boat in the blind cove west of Kitching Cove. He was tangled up in a cast net and the Florida Marine Patrol figures he drowned. That doesn't sound right to me. A sliced up gill net floating nearby had a quarter-inch steel cable run through the float line. I saw him working on that same net yesterday afternoon and I warned him about trying to use it.

"This had better not be a sick joke!"

"It's no joke. Bears dead. I saw his body in the Florida Marine Patrol boat covered with a yellow tarp and again when they loaded it into the funeral home van. He's dead."

"Anything else?"

"Yes. His boat. There were five snook looped on a piece of thirty-pound test mono tied off to his starboard stern cleat and a rusty shotgun was lying in the bottom. It wasn't loaded and the firing pin was broken off. The Florida Marine Patrol called a meeting at the fish house for eight o'clock and they want you to be there. They checked your dock at three this morning and your boat was gone."

"I can't believe that Bears dead. I'll be there in five minutes."

Mack attempted to focus his blurry eyes on the dial of the alarm clock. The little hand was on the eight and the big hand was on the ten. He was still wearing his fishing clothes from the night before and didn't have time for a shower. He nuked a cup of instant coffee for one minute and fifty seconds and sipped it gingerly as he raced down the flight of wooden stairs to the boathouse on rubbery legs. He could get to the fish house faster by boat by cutting through *The Pocket* than by car. No one was going to stop him even if he threw a three-foot wake past the marinas. This was important!

He had known Bear since the fourth grade. His family was all long-time commercial fishermen and owned a fish house in Punta Rassa about fifteen miles southwest of Fort Myers. Bear's family was killed in a fire in the summer of 1960. Bear moved away shortly afterward to escape the pain of the loss of his family.

Mack managed to wedge his boat alongside the crowded dock and tie up between two commercial long-line boats. The ominous gray, black-striped Florida Marine Patrol boat was tied up at the end of the dock. The fish house parking lot was full and pickup trucks overflowed onto the vacant lot next door. Inside all work on icing down and packing fish had stopped.

The commercial fishing community stood as one group in front of the open overhead door facing toward the Manatee Pocket. The rising sun splashed their faces, but none of them squinted to avoid its harsh glare - they were looking far past it. Their white rubber boots formed a solid white line atop the gray cement floor. The rookie Florida Marine Patrol officer from Michigan, and Deputy Elmo from the Martin County Sheriff's Marine Unit, stood with their backs to the sun and faced the bedraggled group. The Florida Marine Patrol officer opened the meeting.

"All of you know why we called this meeting. Bear was found floating in the North Fork this morning with his hands and arms tangled in a cast net. It looks like he was trying to throw the net, got his hands tangled in the mesh, slipped, hit his head on the side of the boat and drowned. We figure it was an accident. But the coroner is doing an autopsy. We also found a gill net floating next to his boat that had a quarter-inch steel cable run through the float line. Do any of you know anything about Bear gill netting in the North Fork?"

There was a smattering of *"nope"* intermixed with the raspy shuffling of nervous white, rubber-booted feet on the wet cement floor. Every one of the commercial fishermen avoided eye contact with the officer and looked at the floor with a blank stare.

"If any of you knows anything about this, or why Bear was gill netting in the North Fork, I advise you to tell me right now. If I find out later that you hid anything from me I'll hang your butt for obstructing justice. Anybody want to say anything?" The room remained silent except for the muffled rasping of rubber boots on the cement floor. "You can all go now. But, if any of you are still gill netting up there, or know anything that you aren't telling me, I'll find out about it and see that you are prosecuted to the limit of the law."

The fishermen seemed to be in shock and filed out of the fish house as a group. Not one man spoke to another. They got into their trucks and left as silently as coastal fog lifting off the sea.

After the meeting Mack idled through the Manatee Pocket deep in thought over the events of the night before. *How could Bear have drowned in his cast net? It was impossible. No one can stick their hands through the mesh of a cast net. The net mesh is so small that a person's hands would have to be forced through by ripping holes in the net. How could Bear drown in three feet of water? He could have walked to shore.* There were many unanswered questions.

He looked at the boat's fuel gauge. He was down to less than half a tank and could use some fuel. He liked to keep the tank full just in case he had to go somewhere on short notice. When he passed Pirate's Cove he noted a seventy-plus foot *mega-yacht* hogging the fuel dock. *"How many gallons does it take to fill one of those monsters? One thousand? Two thousand? Maybe even three thousand gallons?"*

As he passed Mariners' Cay he waved at Jim the dock master who politely waved back. Its fuel dock was occupied by a *mega-yacht* at least eighty feet long. *"Where do people get the money to buy those things?"* he wondered.

Sailfish Marina's fuel dock was occupied by three sport fishing boats. Mack decided to postpone fueling until later. He had things to do that couldn't wait. He kept a full, five-gallon container of gasoline in the boathouse in reserve - just in case.

He washed the boat down and watched to see that the bilge pump was working. After the wash down, he hooked the electric davit's steel hoist cables to the boat's bow and stern eye bolts and pushed the 'up' button. The five-horse electric motor hummed, the gears turned and like 'magic' the boat slowly rose up, stopped and hung three feet above the water.

Shaking his head in disbelief, Mack climbed the wooden stairs to the cottage. 'Sparky' the cat was sitting at the screen door meowing and demanding that he open the door for him. When the door cracked open just a 'tad' the brazen cat dashed through, ran directly to the kitchen and sat down directly in front of the refrigerator door.

Meow

"What a place. It comes with a built-in cat."

Mack dug a can of cat food out of the fridge, spooned some out onto a saucer, nuked it for fifteen seconds and placed it on the floor. The apparently famished cat bolted it all down in seconds. Mack took the opportunity to slump in the closest green recliner to catch his breath.

BRRRING BRRING BRRING

Mack tried desperately to ignore the obnoxious telephone hoping that the answering machine was on and would catch the call. But, it kept on ringing. He considered the options of either answering it, or ripping it off the wall, but he elected to answer it.

"Hello. Captain Mack here."

"Mr. Captain. We want to go snook fishing tomorrow. The people at the tackle store told us you were the best guide in town. What's it going to cost for two of us." The caller sounded like a teen-aged kid.

"Young man, tomorrow is Memorial Day and it's a sacred day to me. Thirty years ago I defended your freedom to celebrate it. Go out and celebrate your personal freedom by eating too many hotdogs and puking your guts out."

"I'm sorry, sir. You don't have to be so nasty about it. I was just asking."

Mack realized that it wasn't the kid's fault. He didn't know how he felt. "Sorry young man, but I don't fish on Memorial Day. There's too many drunks on the water It's not safe."

He hung up, switched on the answering machine and turned the volume down so that he couldn't hear who was calling. It was 9:15 A.M. He had to make a call. Thirty years was a long time, but he remembered the number. The phone rang twice and then there was a 'click' and a recording. *"We are very sorry. This is not a working number. Please check the number and try again."* He tried the number three more times. He knew it by heart - it wasn't wrong. What had happened? He had to go over there now! Memorial Day weekend or not, he had to go. It was about 160 miles to Fort Myers. He needed some answers. Now!

He stripped off his tan, cotton shorts and blue, sailcloth cotton guide's shirt. When he turned the shirt pockets inside out three $100 dollar bills fell out onto the floor - the charter fee for last night. There was also a wad of damp five $100 dollar bills. The tip! But they didn't get to keep the fish. Why a tip for nothing?

After he shaved and showered, he tossed his shaving kit, a change of underwear, a clean shirt and a towel into a plastic bag - just in case he had to stay overnight. He slipped the little *Beretta,* and a full seven shot clip, into the shaving kit - just in case.

He was going to check on a high school friend who lived on Sanibel Island. They played football, basketball and baseball together during the school year and in the summer they played Babe Ruth League baseball at Terry Park in Tice. But, sports had to be fit in between fishing trips. His friend's family, like Bear's, owned a small marina and commercial fish house in Tarpon Bay on Sanibel. His friend, like himself, didn't talk about his military experience. But, Mack thought that he might have answers to some of his questions because he also grew up with Bear. After he came home from the military he started a fishing guide service out of his family's marina in Tarpon Bay.

He glanced at a Florida map. The shortest route to Fort Myers was via Route 76 to Port Mayaca then Route 441 south through Pahokee. At Belle Glade he would cross over to Routes 80/27, take it to Clewiston. Ten miles north of Clewiston, where Routes 80 and 27 split, and he would take Route 80 into Fort Myers. He topped off the tank at the *CITGO* station next to the Fire Station in Port Salerno. At 9:41 A.M. he crossed over the railroad tracks onto Salerno Road and was off for Fort Myers and hopefully some answers.

The drive down Route 76 towards Port Mayaca, was a lesson in local politics. Run-off water from the orange groves, laced with fertilizer phosphates and poisons from weed and insecticide sprays, was polluting the St. Lucie River. Both sides of the highway were lined with orange trees almost the entire way to the Indiantown cutoff road. There were hundreds of acres of orange trees and only a few houses in the twenty-three mile stretch. He thought, *"It was obvious that the runoff from the insecticides and excess fertilizer had to go into the river. Why couldn't the county commissioners see that and take action to stop it? The source of the pollution was blatantly obvious".*

Several concerned Martin County activists had formed a citizens' advisory group with the mantra of *'Save the river - stop the pollution.'* Certainly, the concerned Martin County residents had the power of the ballot box behind them, but the citrus growers had the bucks for political donations. *What counts more – votes or money? You can buy all the votes you need - if you have enough money.*

'Old Florida' and any concern for the environment was long gone. It had died when the citrus industry was frozen out of Lake and Orange counties in the freeze of 1988. The big companies bought up land in St. Lucie and Martin County and quietly went about the business of planting orange trees. Now, just a few short years later, the St. Lucie River shared in the same pollution by chemicals, nitrates and insecticides as the St. John and Kissimmee River chains.

In Port Mayaca, at the deserted train station next to the tracks, stood an ancient, silver water tower that was at least fifty years old. He pulled off onto the side of the road to savor the moment. Then, the image of 'old Florida' faded. Alongside the water tower stood a recent addition of 'visual commercial pollution' - an ugly, silver cell phone tower.

Bobby Vinton singing *"Lonely Boy"* over the local 'oldies' station brought back a flood of memories, some good, but mostly bad. The line, *"I am a soldier, a lonely soldier away from home and I want to go home"* brought a tear to his eyes. There were so many poignant memories, some of them were good, but most of them were not.

At Canal Point, a dozen black and Hispanic migrant workers were fishing off the bridge *'brim'* and *'specs'*. He recalled seeing the same scene forty years before on a trip across from Fort Myers to see an uncle in West Palm Beach. It hadn't changed. The actual fishermen had certainly been 'recycled' several times. While passing through Belle Glade, a town occupied by migrant cane field workers he thought, *"There but for the grace of God and the color of my skin go I."* A sobering thought.

Clewiston however had grown up! New business development was everywhere. The *Jolly Roger Marina* looked like it was doing well and so did *Robbie's Restaurant*. He had eaten many good meals at Robbie's in years long past. The *Clewiston Inn* looked exactly as it had when he had stayed there in the 1960's.

"Was sweet potato pie still on the menu?" He considered stopping for a few minutes a *Roland Martin's Marina* to chat with the Lake Okeechobee fishing guides that he had known for years, but time was precious. He had a mission to accomplish in Fort Myers and he wanted to get back to Port Sewell before darkness fell.

Along Route 80 the roadside drainage canals looked the same. White cattle egrets prowled the shore looking for tasty frogs. He wondered if they knew how lucky they were that their species was no longer hunted for their white feathers for use in ladies' hats! Ortona whizzed by, then Alva, then Olga, then he was passing over the Orange River. His grandfather owned five acres of waterfront on the Orange River back in the 1950's long before the first trailer was parked, or house built, along it's banks.

He clearly recalled the day he was there with his grandfather Mack and shot a blue jay with a .22 caliber rifle so that he could take it home and mount it. His grandfather chewed him out for the dire event, but the bird made a beautiful mount. What followed later, *equine encephalitis*, twenty-nine days in a coma, and three months of total body paralysis might have been the dire payback for the deadly sin against such a beautiful creature.

East Fort Myers and Tice had not changed at all, at least in his memory bank. He pulled over at a chain restaurant in a shopping center at 12:12 P.M. A ravenous after-church crowd had just arrived for brunch and there looked to be about thirty of them. *"Some of them could well do without eating anything and could live off the 'fat of the land' indefinitely."*

Aggravated at himself for being late he snorted at the hostess. "I'm in a big hurry and need a table fast. I've got an appointment in Fort Myers at 1:00 P.M. I want to get my order into the kitchen before the 'grazing herd' from the church does. They're apt to eat the whole place in one sitting."

The waitress got the message, rushed him to a window table and with a canned, plastic smile said, "Sir. Your server will be with you shortly."

"Does my server have anything to do with that church group? I told you that I was in a hurry. If my server is also waiting on them I'm leaving now. I must get my order in ahead of them because the kitchen will run out of food and fodder!"

"I'll take your order, *sir*. What would you like, *sir*." There was marked emphasis on '*sir*'. It was a game to her. She figured that she would catch him off guard and that he would have to study the menu before he could make a selection. Thus, his order would get in behind the church group and he would be held up. She would win! 'Check mate' in the first degree. Without opening the menu, or cracking a smile, he retorted. "I would like an omelet with all the crap in it, whatever you may call it, an All American, Granny's or Country omelet. I don't really care. White toast, lots of coffee and a glass of water with a lemon slice. Thank you."

His 'brick' cell phone stood upright as a vertical sentry next to the plastic half-empty catsup bottle. Mack took out his pen and began to make notes of the clues he had regarding Bear's death and his open questions. He didn't ask to be involved, but this was something he had to do - for Bear. He didn't know what he could do, but he had to do something. He had a hunch that major clues rested in Fort Myers, Sanibel, Punta Rassa, or St. James City on Pine Island. It shouldn't take him long to find 'something' that would lead him to 'something' else. He was trained to sniff out the 'non-obvious'. Uncle Sam had spent his money well and had gotten his money's worth. That debt was repaid long ago and he could use those talents towards solving Bear's murder, finding his killers and seeking a form of justice that fit the dirty deed. Personal satisfaction ranked in his priorities and controlled rage burned in his guts.

"Was everything to your satisfaction, *sir*?" The snotty waitress placed the emphasis on '*sir*' with a flippant lilt to her tone of voice. "Is there anything else that I can get for you, sir?

"Just a check please, *ma'am*." He responded in a cool, polite tone. "Ma'am the next time a customer is seated at your station a big dose of attitude adjustment on your part might go a long way. Have a good day."

The waitress 'threw' the grease-spotted check on the table, spun on her right foot, flounced her apron and stomped off in the general direction of the kitchen. He gave her a parting shot. "Who are you on the way to torture next - the cook or the dishwasher?" He threw a 'five-spot' on the table. Not a bad tip for a seven-buck meal. His attitude wasn't the best today either and he'd share the blame with her. Besides, she wasn't bad looking and he might stop by again on his way back.

He drove down south U.S. 1, turned right onto Colonial Boulevard and swung into the cemetery. He found the Masonic Garden section and walked directly to his grandparents' plots. He stood silently between them and felt that they knew he was there. But, there was something missing! His grandfather was a World War I Navy veteran and there was no American flag on his grave to mark his service to his country. Mack spotted a golf cart occupied by an pasty-faced, overweight middle-aged man and a kid that looked to be all of eighteen and flagged them down. They both wore a long-sleeved white shirt and cheap necktie.

"Who is in charge of placing the flags on veteran's graves? My grandfather was a World War I Navy veteran and there is no American flag on his grave. I want one there in five minutes, or there'll be hell to pay." The pasty faced middle-aged man responded. "Flags aren't the cemetery's responsibility. The American Legion puts them up." Mack grabbed his tie and lifted him off the golf cart seat. "It's yours now! Do you understand?" The man's faced turned beet red. "Yes sir. There'll be a flag there in five minutes. You can count on it."

"I'll wait." Mack knelt and picked at the *dollar weed* invading the bronze marker that fit flush with the ground. Minutes later an American flag flew proudly after it was placed in its holder.

The drive down Royal Palm lined McGregor Boulevard was surreal. Mack recalled the names of families that had lived on each side street and even spotted the palm tree that he had hit with a rental car in the midst of a hurricane. It was a bizarre tale.

Mack had concluded a business meeting in Jacksonville and the airlines had canceled all flights into Fort Myers because of an approaching hurricane. He wanted to get home so he rented a car in Jacksonville and promised the girl at the rental agency that he would stop in Orlando and not continue on to Fort Myers until the hurricane had passed.

Mack left Jacksonville at 8:00 P.M. and was driving down McGregor Boulevard in Fort Myers towards home at 2:00 A.M. The wind was blowing eighty miles an hour in gusts, the rain was coming down in horizontal sheets and he could only see about ten feet past the hood of the car. Mack was traveling twenty miles an hour when a Royal Palm tree toppled over front of him.

The car stopped abruptly when it hit the chunky palm tree, the hood flew up and yellow antifreeze from the ruptured radiator splattered the windshield. Mack took a healthy 'swig' from the almost empty bottle of *Jim Beam* resting on the seat beside him and walked the rest of the way home in the driving rain. When he got home he reported the rental car stolen from his hotel in Orlando and went to bed. Mack never heard what happened to the rental car, but the rental car company canceled his credit card.

Realizing that he had drifted off Mack shook his head and snapped out of the fog back into reality. He turned onto Route 869, Summerlin Road, and headed for *Punta Rassa* two miles further down the road. He paid his toll and went over the high-rise bridge to *Sanibel Island*. When he lived there a car ferry ran back and forth every hour on the hour. Visitors who didn't make it off the island by dark spent the night there - often sleeping in their cars. When he got to the other side he was amazed as to how much *Sanibel* had changed. There were marinas everywhere! He drove down *Periwinkle Way* and turned right on still dirt covered *Tarpon Bay Road*. When he reached the end of the dusty road his stomach cringed - the marina and fish house were gone. *"That's why no one answered the telephone."*

Mack parked the truck in the parking lot of the fisheries research station, got out and walked around. The blackened creosoted wooden pilings of the fish house dock jutted out of the water about fifty feet from the sea wall. The four oyster-encrusted concrete pilings of the fish house stood upright beside the sea wall and appeared to be scorched and smoke damaged.

"Hey there bud. Can I help you with something?"

Mack turned around and saw a middle-aged, slightly balding, paunchy police officer sitting in his squad car. He had been so engrossed in the scenery that he hadn't heard the crunch of gravel under the car's tires as it came down Tarpon Bay Road. "What happened to the fish house and marina that were here years ago?"

"Son, I reckon that you haven't been here for quite some time. It burned down about five years ago. There was some talk about allowing a developer to build condos here, but it got squashed in the re-zoning hearing. Are you looking for somebody special? Maybe I can help you?"

"Yes I am. I grew up in Fort Myers and left over thirty years ago to join the military. This is my first trip back. I'm looking for a guy that grew up here. His name was Eugene Sethman. He came back to Sanibel after he got out of the military and became a fishing guide."

"I knew him. By the way, my name's Billy O'Dell. I came down from Cleveland in nineteen-seventy and got a job as a patrolman. Now I'm police chief. Gene was a fishing guide and he lived in the marina all by himself. He never got married. One morning, about five years ago, they found him floating face down in Tarpon Bay all wrapped up in his cast net and drowned. They figure that he slipped and hit his head while he was throwing his net. A week later the marina and fish house caught on fire and burned down to the water. He didn't have any 'kin that we could find, so the state took over his property. Are you 'kin to him?"

"No. I was just a very good friend of his, but we went back a long way. What happened to his personal effects?"

"We have them locked up at the station. Nobody has ever come by to claim anything. If you can prove that you knew him, and that he was your friend, you're welcome to whatever you want. You'll have to sign a release that you got it. Follow me."

When they arrived at the station the police chief brought out a metal box, about the size of a cigar box, opened it up and laid it on his desk. "Mack, take a look through there and see if there's anything that you want. You can have that newspaper article about his death and the marina fire. I have another one here somewhere. Is there anything special that you're looking for?"

"Yes. Did you see a small silver coin? It's called a *Rand* and it comes from South Africa. It has an animal that looks a lot like a deer stamped on one side."

"Oh yeah, I remember that coin. Nobody could figure out why he would be carrying around a coin from South Africa. Here it is. There's the deer and there's a little number one stamped above its head. What could that mean?"

"It was a secret club that we both belonged to. Here is mine."

"Yours has a number one stamped on it too, but it's between the deer's front feet. Does that mean something special?"

"Yes. But, it's a secret and I can't tell you what it means."

The police chief smiled, "Is this something like Mission Impossible? If you told me what it means you'd have to kill me?"

"Yes. So, please don't ask me again. May I please have the damn coin? That's all I want."

"Take it. I was just joshing you about what it meant. It must be a college thing. Right?"

"Yeah, you're right. Wait a minute. Did you find his *ZIPPO* lighter in his things? His name is inscribed on it like a signature."

"Yep. Here it is. I was keeping in my desk's top drawer just for safekeeping. Here take it too."

Mack left the police station and drove back across the bridge towards *Punta Rassa*. He pulled off into the sandy parking lot on the north side of the second causeway and parked the truck where he could look across *Pine Island Sound* towards *Tarpon Bay*. Mack turned off the engine and closed his eyes. He had some serious thinking to do before he left town.

This wasn't the Florida that he knew as a teenager growing up here in the 1950's. The pristine, unmarred Florida landscape had disappeared by the middle 1960's. Developer's greed changed the virgin face and pure soul of South Florida forever. Virgin pinewoods and palmetto-studded flatlands were sacrificed for inexpensive tract housing.

Land development companies got a firm grip on the scrub pine forests and palmetto lands. Clanking draglines and gigantic, snorting, pollution-belching bulldozers operated unchecked all day and often into the night under the harsh glare of floodlights to rape the land. Diesel-powered, earth ripping, unfeeling steel draglines tore the soft, virgin surface sand from its limestone base to form canals. Soil from the freshly dug canals was used to build up the new waterfront lots. Bulldozers scraped the palmetto fields clean of foliage so that lots could be marked off, roads built and foundations laid. It was easier to build tract houses if everything that grew naturally was cut down and scraped off the land.

Builders threw up walls of cold, concrete blocks and dressed them with exterior green shrouds of cheap landscaping. 'CBS' construction they called it. The cold concrete block walls enclosed cold terrazzo floors that are unyielding to the feet, legs and spine. The fringe of sparse vegetation planted alongside the concrete block walls was usually *croton* interrupted by scrawny red or pink *hibiscus* bushes. A couple of palm trees in the front yard completed the meager landscaping and the *'dream home'* was ready to snare an unsuspecting buyer.

Fast-talking, high-pressure salesmen used maps to point out the location of each lot because they couldn't take prospective buyers out to see the property. Buyers were told that it was in the 'pre-construction phase'. That meant that no roads were built within five miles of it. Most of the 'prime' lots were so far back in the scrub and wetlands that dirt construction roads wouldn't be built near them for ten years. But, prospective lot purchasers were provided with a free weekend in Florida, including air transportation, hotel rooms and meals, in exchange for sitting in on a short 'overview' of the "planed' development.

The sales pitch was planned as strategically as a military exercise. Once the prospects were in the sales room it was too late for them to turn back. The trap was 'sprung' and there was no escape! Maps, site plans, paintings of homes and artists' conceptions of the planned community lined the walls. They had to buy and buy they did! The sales pressure was not subtle. The facilitator spoke into a hand-held microphone at a frantic pace while walking around the room urging the attendees to buy a lot.

"The prime lots are going fast. Place your bid before all the prime lots are gone. Don't miss out on your dream of Florida retirement. Only $100 down and $15 a month buys you a prime lot where you can build your Florida dream home when you retire," the pitchman cried. *"Bid as high as you can or you'll miss out for sure! You sir. How much are you willing to bid?"*

Red pins marked 'sold' lots and more red pins were added to the site plan during each session.

"Landscaping? Don't worry about that. Plants in Florida grow so fast that before you know it they'll take over the house. Just stick a trimming from a shrub in the ground and it'll grow like a weed," promises the sweating salesman wearing a cheap, brown and white checked, polyester sport coat. *"We sprigged the*

yard with St. Augustine grass. Keep it watered and it will fill in the whole yard by next summer." In the backyard of a model home tufts of brown, lifeless grass poke above the sandy soil and fried in the hot sun as a single portable plastic lawn sprinkler slowly arcs back and forth providing them with life-giving water.

Friends and neighbors who traveled to south Florida together, on what they thought was a free vacation, found themselves bidding against each other for lots that they couldn't even get out to see. It was war and they all lost in the end!

BRRING BRRING BRRING

The cell phone's insistent ringing roused Mack from his slumber. The salt air, warmth and light breeze coming off the Gulf of Mexico had gotten the best of him. He glanced at his watch as he picked up the phone. 3:45 P.M. "Mack here."

"Mack. It's Ralph. You've got to get back here fast! All hell's apt to break loose. My uncle finished the autopsy on Bear and he was shot with a small caliber weapon, most likely a twenty-two caliber rifle - just like Dave's brother was last year."

"Shot? The Florida Marine Patrol officer said that he was tangled up in a cast net and drowned."

"Yes. In fact he did drown. My uncle said that his lungs were filled with water which indicated that his face was in the water and that he was alive and conscious for maybe as long as three minutes trying to breath. He was shot in the back of the neck, at the point where the spinal cord attaches to the brain and he was paralyzed from the neck down. He knew that he was drowning, but he couldn't lift his head out of the water to breathe."

"That's a horrible thought. What else did your uncle say?"

"He said that there were no powder burns on the skin which indicates that the gun was at least two feet away from his neck. But, the entrance wound had an *'abrasion ring'* around it. Do you know what that means?"

"Yes. It means that the weapon was small caliber and fired from a significant distance away from the entrance wound.

Did your uncle recover the bullet?"

"Not yet. They were taking X-rays to try to locate it,"

"Did he recover a bullet from Dave's brother last year?"

"I don't know. I'll ask him when he calls me back. Oh, I

almost forgot. There was a red mark on the back of Bear's neck, like somebody tried to strangle him. But, there were no red marks on the front side of his neck, except for the red scar from when he hit the wire cable last year. My uncle said it was strange."

"Tell your uncle to keep the news about the gunshot wound quiet. He should be able to list 'drowning' as the cause of death on the death certificate. If he recovered a bullet from Dave's brother's body ballistics tests will be able to determine if the bullets were fired from the same gun. If he locates the bullet tell him to hang onto it. I'm leaving *Sanibel* now. Get a copy of the autopsy report from your uncle and meet me at your house at eight o'clock tonight. Where's Bear's boat?

"It's tied up to the dock behind my house. Emogene asked me to store it for her until she can get things sorted out."

"Cover it with a tarp and keep everyone away from it."

"Why? There's nothing in it except a red plastic bucket, a beat up fishing rod, a bailing can and an old, rusty shotgun."

"Don't worry about why. Just cover the boat up and do it fast before it rains, or the dew falls."

"Okay. You got it."

"Good. I'll meet you at eight tonight at your house. Don't go anywhere near Port Sewell Marina."

"Roger."

Mack hung up and dialed '6-6-6' on his cell phone. When the digital pager answered he keyed in '9-9-9'. He was 'shooting in the dark' hoping for a break. It was a 'long shot' and a 'crap shoot', but it was his only option. He tore out of the sand covered parking area, leaving a cloud of dust behind him, headed for San Carlos Boulevard and the shortest route to Stuart. It was 4:03 P.M.

Mack wanted to make it back to Stuart by 7:00 P.M. He needed that extra hour real bad.

CHAPTER
17

Mack pulled up in front of Ralph's house on Flounder Street at 8:02 P.M. and 'beeped' the horn twice to let Ralph know that he was there. Ralph came to the front door. "Mack! You're right on time and I'm impressed. But, where's your truck."

"Actually Ralph, I'm two minutes late and I apologize for my tardiness. I had truck trouble coming back from *Fort Myers*."

"Why are you driving a car? Where's your truck?"

"It overheated just this side of *Port Mayaca*. I limped in about a quarter to eight, dropped it off at a gas station at ninety-five and *Kanner Highway* and got this rental car. They're going to replace the water pump on Tuesday. They can't do it tomorrow because it's Memorial Day and the parts stores are closed.

"You could have called me. I'd run out and picked you up."

"You had enough things to worry about. Let's take a look at Bear's boat. Did you cover it up with a tarp like I asked?"

"I sure did. Come on. It's in the canal behind the house."

"Has anyone been by to look at it?"

"Before I called you two crime scene investigators from the Martin County Sheriff's Department came by, took a few photos and poked around for awhile. Mel stopped by to take some swabs and paint samples for analysis at a laboratory. He said that he wants to meet with you tomorrow.

Oh, I almost forgot. Two reporters from the *Port St. Lucie*

News came by for a look. They were really strange ducks."

"What do you mean strange ducks? Did they have feathers, waddle and quack?"

"No, they didn't quack. But, they asked a lot of questions, but didn't write anything down."

"What kind of questions did they ask?"

"They asked if I thought that Bear had any enemies that would want to kill him, or if he ever talked about having any run-in's with anyone in the North Fork when he was gill netting up there."

"Why would they ask questions like that? The police report said that he got tangled up in his nets and drowned. Nothing indicated that he was killed, except what your uncle told you."

"How am I supposed to know why? They're reporters. Maybe they have a good source."

"What did you tell them?"

"Not much. I can be really stupid at times."

"What did they look like? Can you describe them?"

"One of them was tall and thin and had pock marks on his face. The other one was short and fat. They both had olive complexions, talked like New Yorkers and were real pushy."

"Did they give you a business card, or a phone number?"

"No. They both said that they left their wallets in the office."

"Did anyone get in the boat?"

"Mel did because he had to take the swabs and paint samples. But, I didn't pay attention to anyone else. I just asked them to let me know when they left. Oh, I almost forgot about Dave. He stopped by right after you left. He wanted to stand here and just look at Bear's boat for a few minutes. He said that it was his way of saying goodbye to him."

"Did he get in the boat?"

"I don't know. I didn't hang around. I went over to help Bobo and Emogene with Bear's arrangements. Then I drove up to Fort Pierce to pick up the autopsy report that you asked me to get when you called me the second time. Here it is."

"Thanks. Are the plastic bucket, fishing pole and shotgun still in the boat?"

"They were there when I put the tarp over it about four-thirty."

Mack picked up his black valise and walked down the short

incline to the canal. Bear's boat drifted slowly back and forth in the light wind. It gently tugged at the white nylon tether that kept it from escaping with the outgoing tide. A light rain that fell earlier randomly deposited silver water droplets that beaded up on the dark canvas cover. When Ralph pulled back the end of the tarp the beads rolled off and splashed into the dark water.

"Ralph, I want you to pull the tarp back over me and the boat. I can see better with this flashlight if it's totally dark under here." Mack began to examine the interior of the boat with the aid of a four-cell, flat black, metal flashlight.

"Mack. There's not much to see there except a plastic bucket and that rusty old shotgun." Mack grunted in the affirmative and continued to poke and prod at every nook and crevice of the boat. He found a piece of thirty-pound test monofilament fishing line wrapped around the stern cleat on the starboard side, a paper chewing tobacco package outer wrapper and a stubby, number-two, yellow pencil that was missing the eraser.

"What are you looking for so hard?"

"I'm not exactly sure. I'm just looking." Mack lifted the rusty, double-barrel twelve-gauge shotgun out of the bottom of the boat and pushed the metal tang over to the right with his thumb. The receiver broke open and exposed the two empty shell chambers. He raised the gun to eye level, pointed it towards the streetlight and looked through the barrels. He grunted, snapped the shotgun shut and turned toward Ralph.

"Bear couldn't have shot this gun under any circumstances. The firing pins are rusted tight and both barrels are plugged. I can't see any light through them. Do you think that Emogene would mind if I took it back to the marina and cleaned it up? It's an old *Remington Model 1900*. She might be able to get a hundred bucks for it at a gun shop."

"She'll be tickled pink. But, I won't tell her that Bear had a gun in the boat with him. Are you done looking?"

"I suppose. I can't imagine how he was going to react if they called his bluff. The gun wasn't capable of firing because of the rusted firing pins and the plugged right barrel. Maybe he planned to spit chewing tobacco juice at them and spit them to death like a grasshopper."

"He was pretty darn mad. I don't think that he realized that they were playing for keeps."

"I wish that he would have asked for help before he did something that stupid. Did your uncle find anything unusual in his clothing?"

"Nothing unusual. Two unopened packages of chewing tobacco, a yellow, plastic-handled pocketknife, three one-dollar bills and forty-two cents in change. My uncle said that he had dried 'crap streaks' in his underwear. You know. 'Skid marks', like he had been farting several hours before he died. Oh, my uncle said that there was one strange thing."

"What was that?"

"One of the packages of chewing tobacco had the outer paper wrapper missing, but the tin foil inside wrapper was intact. Maybe he had started to open it, but changed his mind."

"Most likely that's it. Maybe he got busy pulling in his nets and didn't have time to finish opening the package. I don't think that it's relevant to his death. What did your uncle do with the packages of chewing tobacco?"

"There're both right here in a plastic bag with his money and knife. I was going to give it all to Emogene tomorrow."

"Does Emogene chew tobacco?"

"No."

"Then she won't miss the chewing tobacco. Can I have it?"

"I didn't know that you had the habit. Sure. Here it is."

"Thanks." Mack stuffed the two small packets of chewing tobacco into his right shirt pocket and fastened the pearl button.

"Ralph. I'm pooped. I only got three hours of sleep last night and I drove 350 miles today. It's past ten o'clock and I have to get some shuteye. I'll catch up with you tomorrow. Let's meet for breakfast at the *Conch* at seven. Bring Bobo with you."

"Why do you want Bobo there?"

"He was the last person that we know that saw Bear alive. He might know something."

"Okay. I'll try to get him there."

"Good. I'll both of you at seven at the *Queen Conch*."

Mack left Ralph's house and drove back towards *Port Sewell Marina*. The instant that he made the right turn off of *Old Dixie*

Highway onto *Old St. Lucie Boulevard* his pager vibrated, a car flashed its high beams in his rear view mirror and turned on it's right turn signal. Mack immediately pulled off onto the right hand side of the road and turned on his 'emergency' flashers.

He looked in the side view mirror and saw a person walking up the road towards his car. He reached under the front seat for the little *Berretta,* pulled it close and cradled it in his lap. He pointed the barrel upward, at a forty-five degree angle, directly at the driver's side window.

"Hey there *Yankee Boy.* It's about time ya'll got your scrawny butt back from *Fort Myers.* What were you doing over there? Looking up some old high school girl friends? They're all grandmothers several times over by now and are wrinkled up like old prunes."

"Tina! You got my message. Did you drive the *Beamer* up from West Palm?"

"Heck no. When I got in from DC this evening I got a good deal at the airport on renting a *Lincoln Town Car* for a week. I'm going to drive it while the *Beamer's* in the shop. Here's the report you asked me to get for you. I hate to admit it, but you were correct on both counts. How about if I stop by the marina for a nightcap with you before I drive back to West Palm?"

"It's not a good idea. It's past ten-thirty and I've been driving all day. I'm beat and I've got to get some sleep. I have to meet Ralph and Bobo for breakfast at seven in the morning. Tomorrow is *Memorial Day* and it will be a busy day around the marina. Plus, there are a lot of loose ends left to pull together. Don't drive the *Beamer* - leave it where it is – and don't call me on the marina telephone. If you need me, page me and leave a 'secure' number. I'll get back with you. Do you understand? "

"Yes. But, why breakfast with Ralph and Bobo?"

"They're the last persons that we know of that saw Bear alive. Ralph saw him yesterday afternoon at the house working on his nets. They might have some ideas on what happened."

"You're right. I'm tired myself. It was a long flight back here. Call me tomorrow. Bye."

"Bye." He listened to the *'click, click, click'* of her spike heels on the asphalt as she strode briskly back to her car. Tina 'tooted' her horn twice, flashed her headlights, made a wide 'U-turn' directly in the middle of *Old St. Lucie Boulevard* and headed towards *Old Dixie Highway*. When Mack arrived at the marina the cat was impatiently waiting for him at the front door.

"*Meow*"

"Come in you mangy ball of fur. I'll fix you some dinner and treat you to a 'cat shower'. What do you say to that?"

"*Meow*"

After the cat finished his dinner Mack threw him outside, poured himself a glass of Merlot and settled down in the green recliner to mull over the events of the past twenty-four hours.

BRRRING BRRRING BRRRING

When the phone rang the third time Mack's first inclination was to ignore it, but on second thought he realized that it might be an important call about Bear's death.

"Hello. Captain Mack here."

"Mack. It's Dave. I've been trying to reach you for a couple of hours. Are you okay? I saw your truck parked at a gas station down by Interstate 95 and *Kanner Highway* when I drove by there about nine-thirty or so. Did you break down somewhere?"

"Hi Dave. Thanks for calling. I'm just fine. The truck heated up on me coming back from West Palm and I dropped it off at the gas station. They're going to replace the water pump on Tuesday. They can't do it tomorrow because its Memorial Day and the parts houses are closed. I've been over at Ralph's house shooting the 'bull' for the past couple of hours."

"Mack, how about meeting me at the *Queen Conch* for lunch tomorrow? I'll stop by and pick you up. You can fill me on your trip to *Fort Myers*. It sure has changed over the years."

"How did you know that I went to *Fort Myers*?"

"Ralph told me when I stopped by to look at Bear's boat. He said that you even went out to *Sanibel* and met the police chief. Isn't Billy O'Dell a crusty old fart right out of the textbooks?"

"He sure is. Okay Dave. I'll meet you for lunch at the Queen *Conch*. Don't bother to pick me up because I've got some running around to do. Plus, I have to check on my truck."

"Okay. Have it your way. I'll meet you at the *Queen* about a quarter to twelve."

"A quarter to twelve it is. Bye." Mack returned to his green recliner and his glass of warm Merlot. It tasted good and he poured himself another glass, sat down and pulled the lever to allow the chair to slip backwards to the full 'recline' position. He had a lot to think about. *"Why was Bear carrying a rusty shotgun with a plugged barrel? Who were the two unidentified reporters from the Port St. Lucie News that stopped by to interview Ralph? How did they know that Bear's boat was behind Ralph's house? Why did Bear have a packet of chewing tobacco missing the outside paper wrapper in his pocket? Why would someone shoot him and then wrap him up in his own net? Why did Mel stop by to take paint samples and test swabs? Why was the Sanibel Police Chief so willing to give him the coin and newspaper article?" How could Mack's friend of thirty years get tangled in his own cast net and drown? Why did his marina on Sanibel Island burn down?"*

There were many vague, unanswered questions in his mind, plus he was very sleepy and overtired. The room began to spin around him. The familiar whirling orange spiral, with the black center, appeared and burned its image into his brain. It was coming back and there was nothing that he could do to stop it.

WHUP WHUP WHUP

The rotating metal blades of three olive drab, unmarked helicopters chopped away at the thick night air in an eerie, rhythmic, almost calming musical sonata. However, the familiar sound did not betray the true nature of what was ahead.

The sun peeked through pink-tinged, puffy cumulus clouds on the eastern horizon as Mack and his team members checked and rechecked their gear and weapons. The 'touchdown' on the remote mountaintop in northern *Laos* was scheduled for 0615 hours. The first chopper landed and dispersed eight young soldiers who formed a circle around the designated drop area. Mack's chopper, loaded with 'top-secret' electronics gear, followed it down. The third chopper waited in line with another eight man 'insertion team' and two civilian 'observers'.

It would take less than thirty minutes to unpack and set up the sophisticated sensing and radio transmitting equipment that would direct the jet fighters and B-52' to their targets along the

Ho Chi Mien Trail. At the completion of the 'insertion' the choppers would take off and radio their base that 'Observation Station Baker Three' was in full operation. But, it was a 'suicide mission' and everyone knew it. The expected life span of the two civilian observers was less than twenty-four hours. That's all the time it would take for the VC to pinpoint their mountain top position with radio direction finders and dispatch a team of *'killer commandos'*.

Too often the VC knew in advance exactly when, and where, the forward observation teams were being placed and would be waiting for them in the surrounding jungle morass. When the helicopters attempted to land they would be blown out of the sky with rockets and anti-tank rounds.

Other times, they would allow the choppers to land because they wanted to capture the observers and torture them to extract their security codes and transmit false position reports. If the false transmissions were accepted as genuine the dispatched B-52's dropped their devastating payloads harmlessly in the jungle far from any meaningful intended target. A lot of innocent water buffalos were blown up.

Often the VC allowed an observation team to land and set up their equipment only to blow the site to pieces with mortar rounds after the departing helicopters passed behind a nearby mountaintop out of radio range. The site would be listed as 'active' but no transmissions would ever be sent or received. The helicopter pilots learned to swing around the mountaintop for a look back at the site. Rising black smoke was a good indication that it had been overrun and destroyed.

Mack was extremely apprehensive. The day before, two *Air Force/CIA* 'insertion teams' were blown out of the sky as they attempted to land on their designated site. It was obvious that there was a 'mole' somewhere inside the planning organization.

In an attempt to provide additional security for this mission Mack's best friend, Eugene Sethman, led the team in a third chopper. The first chopper landed without incident, discharged its occupants, took off and hovered nearby while the young soldiers formed a wide circle around the perimeter of the observation site. The squad leader on the ground gave a '*thumb's up*' signal and the pilot of Mack's chopper set down in the tall grass. Mack led his team off the 'bird' and they began to unload the gear while the third chopper hovered nearby waiting it's turn to land the observers.

BLAM!

The 'horrendous' explosion rocked the ground and a young man on the far edge of the landing zone's perimeter disappeared in a ball of flame. The shock wave threw dirt clods in all directions. Chunks of black earth rained down on the chopper nicking the fragile rotor blades. Stunned by the violent blast, Mack shook his head and looked in disbelief at the smoking combat boot that had landed at his feet. A red stump oozed blood from the gaping hole in the boot where a foot used to be. He circled his hand around his head three times. It was the signal for his team to board the chopper and get out.

The first team that landed was bombarded with mortar fire. As the frightened men sought cover from the mortar rounds they were driven further into the heavily mined area on the outer edge of the 'landing zone'. Explosions rocked the mountaintop. Clods of black earth and bloody body parts flew through the air.

The waiting helicopter that had dispatched the team on the ground had its tail rotor blown off by a rocket. It drifted slowly down the mountain towards the green, heavily wooded valley below in a 'spiral of death' and crashed in a ball of orange fire. The other two teams had to depart as quickly as possible as there was no hope for the men left on the ground. As his chopper lifted off Mack saw six men dressed in black pajamas scramble over the top of the mountain top and spray the survivors on the ground with automatic weapons fire.

BRRING BRRING BRRING

Mack's clouded mind didn't correlate the shrill sound with the telephone for a second or two. "Captain Mack here."

"Mack. It's Ralph. You were supposed to meet me, and Bobo, for breakfast at the *Queen Conch* at seven o' clock. It's past seven-thirty and you're still in the sack. Get your butt up and come on over. We're waiting."

"Give me a couple of minutes. I have to take a shower and

shave." Mack hung up the phone and realized that he still wore the clothes that he had put on the day before. He had fallen asleep in the recliner and slept there all night.

He shaved, took a shower with the cat and left for the *Queen Conch*. He needed a hot cup of coffee desperately. When Mack entered the restaurant Ralph, Bobo and Mel, the *'narc'*, were all sitting together in a corner booth at the rear of the restaurant. They motioned for him to join them. Ralph opened the conversation. "Good morning sleepy head? Did you get enough shuteye or do you need a nap before lunch?"

"I'm okay. I fell asleep in the chair and spent the night there. Thanks for calling me."

"No problem. Mel was already here and asked to join us because he has a few questions that I can't answer."

"Mel? I have questions too and don't know where to get the answers. How can I be expected to tell you anything?"

"Mack, I took four *swabs* on the interior of Bear's boat yesterday and ran them through an *ion detector*. Three of them indicated 'positive' traces of cocaine. Do you think that Bear was running drugs? He spent a lot of time on the water at night."

"I don't think so. If he had been involved in drug running he would have been able to afford a better boat and house. I think that he was just in the wrong place at the wrong time. Who ever killed him might have accidentally spilled cocaine while they snorted up to celebrate drowning him, or just wanted to throw you off of their trail."

"Mack, did you find anything when you went through the boat that I should know about?"

"How did you know that I searched the boat?"

"Ralph told me."

"Thanks a lot Ralph. Mel, I didn't find anything except a plastic bucket, a twelve-gauge shotgun with rusted firing pins and a clogged barrel. There were also a couple of chewing tobacco wrappers in the bottom of the boat."

"I saw the same stuff. That shotgun was really a mess. But, it might be 'evidence'. What are you going to do with it?"

"I don't think that it's 'evidence' of anything except Bear's stupidity. He might have been killed because he threatened someone with it. I'm going to clean it up, sell it and slip the money to Emogene. She's going to need it and a lot more."

"Mack, just what makes you think that Bear was killed? The autopsy report says that he drowned and that it was an accident. The coroner feels that Bear hit his head with the lead weights of his cast net when he was throwing it, hit his head on the side of the boat, fell overboard, got tangled in the net and drowned."

"That's a good theory and probably the most likely one. But, I don't think that he could hit his head with the lead weights, plus he could have stood up and walked to shore. The water where they found him was less than three feet deep"

"What if the weights knocked him unconscious? Then he wouldn't be able to stand up."

"Anything's possible. I'm not a detective – you are. I'm a fishing guide and he was my friend. I'm not involved in the case, but I want to help if I can. I'm sorry if I caused a problem."

"Mack. Please, don't take personal offense at my questions. I've got a job to do. I have to check out every lead. Oops, I almost forgot. Where were you between midnight and six o'clock yesterday morning?"

"I had a night snook trip. My charter party and I pulled out of the *Sandsprit Park* boat ramp about nine o'clock Saturday night and I got back about four in the morning. You can ask that young Florida Marine Patrol Mystery officer. He pulled me over about three-thirty. I went straight home after that."

"Where were you between nine o'clock yesterday morning and eight o'clock last night?"

"I drove over to Fort Myers to see an old friend of mine."

"Would you mind giving me his name and phone number so that I can call him and verify that you were there?"

"Wouldn't do you any good. When I got there I found out that he died five years ago."

"How did he die?"

"He hit himself in the head with the leads of his cast net, fell over the side of his boat and drowned."

"Just like Bear. It must be a common thing for fishing guides. Mack, how do you know all of those details?"

"I met the Sanibel Island Chief of Police. He told me about it.

His name is Billy O'Dell."

"Okay. I'll call him and check out your story. Meanwhile, don't you leave town."

"I'm not planning on going anywhere. Mel, can I see you outside for a minute?"

"I guess so. I'm done with my questions for you at least for now. Ralph and Bobo. Don't either one of you leave town."

Mack and Mel left the table together, walked outside the restaurant and around the corner. "Mack. What do you want? You're a suspect until you're cleared. Don't ask me for any special treatment just because he was your friend."

"Why did you 'ambush' me in front of Ralph and Bobo? Don't you have any feelings? Bobo lost his brother yesterday and Bear was Ralph's best friend."

"Listen here Mack. When it comes to money and drugs, family ties and friendship go right out the window. They are both suspects, just like you are, until they're cleared."

"You can't be serious! Neither one of them would hurt Bear."

"I'm as serious as a heart attack. Money and drugs do strange things to people. I've seen it time and time again. Blood relationships mean nothing in the drug racket."

"Mel, tell me the truth about what happened to your brother. Was his disappearance drug related?"

"How do you know about my brother missing? He wasn't into drugs. He was straight!"

"How do you know he was straight and not dealing cocaine on the side? Didn't you just tell me that money and drugs are thicker than blood? Where is your brother anyway?"

"Him and his sailboat both disappeared back in March. Nobody knows what happened to him."

"Perhaps he made enough money and wanted to disappear to another country. Maybe, and just maybe, he felt that someone was getting close to him and the drug action? Maybe you?"

"My brother wasn't into drugs. Don't you think that I would know if he was? I've been a 'narc' here for four years. I know who is doing what, where they're doing it and when."

"Then why didn't you know about Bear's dealing? Why aren't you catching his killer?"

"Okay. That's enough out of you. Now, you stay out of the way of my investigation. Do you understand? No more poking around. No more questions. And, don't leave town."

"Yes sir. Can I go back inside and finish my breakfast now?"

"Get out of here. Don't you dare say a word to Ralph, or Bobo, about our conversation."

Mack went back inside and rejoined Ralph and Bobo. Ralph was curious. "What did Mel say to you outside?"

"Ralph, we just discussed the weather and the Florida Marlin's summer schedule. That's all."

"Come on Mack. You can tell us."

"We just talked about the weather and the Marlin's schedule. Ralph, can you get several of the commercial fishermen over to your house for a fish fry this afternoon about four-thirty?

"Of course. What do you want them for?"

"I just want to ask them for a favor. Nothing important. Tell them that I'll bring the beer." It was almost nine-thirty when Mack left the *Queen Conch*. He had a lot of things to do and he had to be back there by 11:30 A.M. to meet Dave.

Mack got back fifteen minutes late and Dave was waiting for him in a corner booth. "Hey there Mack. You've been a busy, busy boy the last couple of days. I'm so glad that you could meet me for lunch. It's too bad about Bear. Got any ideas about who killed him?"

"Who killed him? It's my understanding that the coroner feels that he hit his head with the weights of his cast net, knocked himself unconscious, fell over the side and drowned."

"Come on. Let's be reasonable. How could an experienced fisherman like Bear hit himself in the head with his net weights? He'd been throwing a net for more than thirty years. I think that somebody knocked him on the head, robbed him and held him under the water until he drowned. Then they tangled him up in that net to make it look like it was an accident."

"Anything's possible. We'll just have to wait and see what other information comes out of the investigation. That Martin County 'narc', Mel Mangini, was waiting for me this morning when I came over here for breakfast. He ordered me to not ask any questions, or get in the way of his investigation. He sounded real serious about it too. Do you have anything on him?"

"He's basically a 'country hick'. He's really pissed off because his brother disappeared without a trace and he can't solve the caper. I think that his brother was involved in bringing in drugs from the *Bahamas*, pulled a double-cross and someone whacked him. I told you about him."

"Yes, you did. Nobody knows where he went. Maybe he was in drugs over his head and wanted to get out of town before he got caught? Maybe he's holed up somewhere in the *Bahamas*?"

"It could be, but I seriously doubt it. Something will turn up. Mack, tell me about your trip to Fort Myers. Did you have a good time?"

"My trip over there to was to take care of some personal things. It had nothing to do with Bear's death, except that it lit a fire under me to get over there and get what I had to do done."

"What did you think about the place? It's really changed."

"*Tice* and *East Fort Myers* were about the same as I remembered them, but Fort Myers has really changed. Thirty years makes a big difference. There are housing developments, condos and strip malls everywhere."

"What do you think about the development along the road to *Punta Rassa* and the *Sanibel Causeway*?"

"Quite truthfully, I got lost. I had to pull in at a convenience store and ask where I was."

"It's a mess. The last time that I went over there I decided that there was just too many people there for me. Did you see all of the new marinas on *Sanibel*?"

"I was literally blown away when I was crossed the causeway. Everywhere I looked on the *Pine Island Sound* side of Sanibel I saw marinas. It's unbelievable!"

"I understand that you met Sanibel's Police Chief, old *Billy* O'Dell. He's a real 'hoot'? We go back away together."

"How did you know him?"

"He was a pilot for '*Air America*' and we were stationed together in *Laos*. When I got out he talked me, and a couple of other guys into buying condos on *Sanibel*. I lived there for almost five years. I lease it out as a 'timeshare'. I may go back there someday."

"When did you leave *Sanibel*?"

"A little more than five years ago. I lived there before I moved to *Stuart*."

"When I lived in *Fort Myers*, and was in high school, I knew several guys from *Sanibel*. They rode the school bus into town everyday. They were upset because they couldn't go out for sports because the ferry stopped running at six o'clock. Football practice usually lasted until six-thirty. They couldn't practice and get back in time to catch the ferry back to *Sanibel*."

"I heard that one of your friends, Eugene Sethman, was a fishing guide on *Sanibel*. I was living there when they found him drowned in *Tarpon Bay*. The newspaper said that his body was tangled up in his cast net. Right after that the place where he was living, it was a little marina and a fish house, burned to the ground. It was a shame. He was a good man."

"He and I went back a long way and that's one reason that I went over there. I had to see for myself. Dave, it's getting late and I still have some things to do over at the marina. Plus, I'm going to a fish fry at Ralph's tonight. Most of the commercial fishermen are coming and I promised to buy the beer."

CHAPTER
18

It was Monday - one full week after Memorial Day. The late afternoon sun had slipped almost below the western horizon when Mack eased into the entrance of *Willoughby Creek* and pointed the boat's bow up the narrow channel towards *Port Sewell Marina*. Ralph, Bobo, Robert, Rufus, Tiller, Fred, Goose, Tiny, and Fred saluted him as they piloted their commercial fishing skiffs past *Hell's Gate* on their way back to the *Manatee Pocket* and home for dinner.

"Mack, I'll meet up with ya'll about one-thirty at *Coconut Point*," Bobo hollered across the water. Mack waved, but didn't try to yell back at them because he knew that they couldn't hear him over the roar of their outboard motors. They knew that he had heard and that he'd be there.

'Mackie' the six-month old 'liver and white' male *Brittany Spaniel* pup that Mack rescued at the dog pound three days earlier had already become a 'boat dog'. *'Gun-shy'* it stated on the admittance card as the reason for committing the freckle faced pup to certain death. *"Gun shy my ass,"* Mack said as he pulled out a damp twenty-dollar bill to pay for the frightened pup's bail. *"Who wouldn't jump and run away from the sound of a shotgun fired off ten feet away from his ear?"* It only took one wet lick across Mack's cheek with the pup's long tongue for the bond between man and dog to be made! Although the pup was

initially hesitant to jump into the boat, his first wide-open romp on the *Clam Island* sand bar chasing sea gulls turned him on to boating. He even had his own International orange life vest.

Mackie whined anxiously as Mack guided the boat into the boathouse. The instant the boat nudged the wooden dock the anxious dog jumped off and started 'watering' a dock piling as Mack made a round turn, two figure eights and a half hitch on the metal cleats to secure the bow and stern lines. *"If I could whiz on the pilings without getting busted by the cops I'd do it too."* The pup tried to understand what Mack had said and looked at him with an inquisitive look on his freckled, white hairy face. He seemed to be in a trance as urine gushed out of his little pecker onto the piling. *"Maybe I could rent you out to the fire department,"* Mack added as he rose to his feet.

Mackie looked at him, cocked his head to the right, scratched the wooden boathouse floor with all four feet and loose wood flew everywhere. Satisfied that he had thoroughly 'marked his turf' the pup ran up to Mack, sniffed his pants leg and started up the twelve steps to the cottage above. The pup 'froze' on the third step. His head didn't move, the hair on his back rose straight up, his eyes rolled to the left towards Mack and a low, 'primeval' guttural growl came from somewhere deep in his throat.

"Whoa boy. Hold it right there. Whoa. Whoa. Whoa." Although Mack had not started to train the pup for hunting *Mackie* understood and held his position. Mack scanned the boathouse for a weapon that he could use to defend himself if there was someone in the cottage. He spotted a metal gaff hook mounted on the end of a wooden pole about four feet long. If nothing else, he could keep an assailant four feet away from him. *"Okay boy. Let's go upstairs and find out if we have a visitor."* Mack said softly as he put his right foot on the first step. The pup eased forward in a hunter's crouch - his belly touching the step. One cautious step at a time they crept steadily upward. Suddenly, *Mackie* broke, raced to the top of the boathouse steps, leaped on the door that led to the front porch and began to bark frantically.

BANG!

The front door slammed shut and Mack could hear the 'crunching' footsteps of a person running down the loose pea gravel driveway towards *Old St. Lucie Boulevard.* Mack's left hand turned the doorknob at the same time as his beefy shoulder hit the door - nothing happened. The door was locked from the inside and the dead bolt was solidly in place. *Mackie* barked frantically at the sound of the footsteps 'crunching' in the loose gravel driveway - he wanted to get through the locked door and chase the person. *"Hold it boy. That guy just might have a gun. Let's go around the front and see if he left the door unlocked."*

The duo slowly eased back down the steep wooden steps to the boathouse. *Mackie* strained to pull away as Mack held the edge of the dog's collar tightly in his left hand. Once on the boathouse dock they stepped across the narrow walkway to the powerboat dock. *Mackie* stared up the open steps in the direction of the driveway, barked and struggled to get loose from Mack's vise-like grip on his collar. But, it was to late – the roar of a truck's engine and the squeal of tires on the road made it clear – their visitors hadn't stuck around to pay their respects.

"Okay boy. Let's go upstairs and see what's up."

The cottage's front door was left wide open, but the spring-activated screen door was closed. The inside lights were off. The glowing red eyes of the outside video cameras were 'lit' indicating that they were activated by the motion detectors along the driveway. *"Maybe, just maybe, we got lucky and got some good video shots of our visitors. Let's go take a look."* Automatically activated into high gear by the key word 'go' *'Mackie'* began barking thinking that he was going for a ride in the truck or the boat. *"No boy. I meant go inside."* Mack opened the screen door and coaxed the growling dog to follow him into the dark cottage.

The heavy brass padlock mounted on the outside of the electronics room was intact, but someone had tried to cut it in two with a hacksaw. Mack sat down at the video multiplexer console, hit the 'selector' button for camera 'one' and a full frame view of the driveway appeared on the color monitor. *"The camera is working okay. Let's see who we've got on video tape."* He pushed 'rewind' ran the digital recorder back to 8:20 P.M. and pushed 'play'. The time displayed in the top left hand corner of the monitor was 8:20 P.M. But, the screen was blank.

Mack allowed the video to run. At 8:22 P.M. the monitor 'jumped' into life - a black pickup truck coming east on the south side of Old St. Lucie Boulevard came to a stop in front of the marina. A tall man wearing a black, long sleeved shirt and black ski mask, jumped out of the passenger's side door. He left the door open in case he had to make a hasty retreat. Holding an automatic pistol in his right hand and down alongside his right leg he crept along the edge of the gravel driveway. *"The bastard is wearing a mask so I can't identify him."*

When the 'motion-activated' floodlight came on the man raised his hand and aimed the pistol at the camera. There was a soft *'pffft'* followed by a puff of white smoke. The light went out and the night vision lens kicked in. The landscape and man appeared in shades of green, but the masked figure went out of frame when he reached the front porch.

"This is where camera two takes over." Mack pressed the camera 'two' button on the multiplexer console and just like 'magic' the intruder appeared on the front porch. The pistol was sticking out of his waistband and he held a 'snap-gun' lock-picking tool in his right hand. He slipped the lock pick into the keyhole, pulled the trigger of the 'snap-gun' tool several times and twisted the doorknob with his left hand - the door swung open. The time on the monitor was 8:25 P.M. *"It didn't take him long to get in. He must have known that I was gone. Let's see if we can find him in 'real time.' He can't be far away and I'll bet that we can pick him up on the Global Positioning System tracker."* The dog whined and wagged his four-inch stump of a tail in an attempt to agree with his master.

Mack flipped on the GPS tracker and punched 'real time - play'. A street map of Martin County appeared on the screen in brilliant hues of red, green, yellow and blue. The number '002' flashed beside a yellow dot on the red line that marked Federal Highway. The dot was north of Indian Street, south of Monterey Road and moving north on Federal Highway.

Mack hit 'trace' and 8:20 P.M. appeared in blue in the top left corner of the screen. A yellow line traced south on Federal Highway, turned east on Indian Street, passed over the Willoughby Creek Bridge, turned right onto Old St. Lucie

Boulevard and stopped in front of the marina. The time on the monitor read 8:22 P.M.

Mack punched 'real-time - play' and turned his attention back to the yellow dot with the blinking '002' beside it. The yellow dot continued moving north on Federal Highway, at Port Saint Lucie Boulevard it turned west, continued over the Florida Turnpike, made a left turn on Darwin, made a right turn onto a side street and stopped. *"Got cha!"* "Mackie. It's about time that we got to know our boys a little better. What do you think boy?" The anxious dog wagged his docked four-inch stub of a tail, looked Mack in the eye and responded. *"Woof."* In dog talk that meant, *"I don't have the foggiest notion of what you said, but if I act like I understand you might take me for a walk, or at the least give me a biscuit."*

Mack decided that he needed a nap after all of the excitement because he planned to be very busy later that night. He kicked off his deck shoes, tilted the green recliner backwards as far as it would go and dozed off to the muted sounds player of *Kenny G.* playing *'Sentimental'* coming from the CD player in the corner.

BRRING   BRRING   BRRING

Mack tried to ignore the phone, but it wouldn't stop ringing and the answering machine was turned off. It was a nine-foot journey to reach the wall phone in the kitchenette. That's a long way when you are bone tired. Mack glanced at the Caller ID unit on the countertop. It read, *'BLOCKED CALL.   9:17 P.M.'* He picked up the receiver. "Captain Mack here."

"Hey Yankee! Did ya'll get the message yet, or do you need a repeat lesson? Don't stick your nose in where it doesn't belong. Stay out of the North Fork of the St. Lucie River. Stupid people get hurt up that way all the time. Do you remember what happened to your buddy Bear last week?"

Click

Mack punched *69 hoping to get a phone number. *"We are sorry, but the calling number cannot be identified from your telephone."* There was a 'rap' on the front door and *'Mackie'* began to bark. Mack opened the drawer and slipped the *Berretta* out of its holster into the palm of his right hand. In the same movement he pulled back the slide with the thumb and index finger of his left hand, jacked a round into the chamber and flipped the safety 'off' with his thumb - he might not be a second chance. He aimed at the darkened front door and began to slowly squeeze the trigger . . .

"Mack. Are you in there? It's Ralph. We've got to talk."

"Yeah. I'm here. You almost got your furry head blown off."

"What do you mean furry head? I'm almost bald."

"I had some visitors waiting for me upstairs when I pulled into the boathouse. They called a few minutes ago to stress that I should stay out of the North Fork. When you knocked on the front door I thought that they were back. I'm a little edgy."

"I'm sure as hell glad that you didn't blow me away. Mack. We've got to talk about tonight. Right now. Are you certain that we can get away with this? I don't want to get shot."

"I can't be absolutely certain about anything, except that I am going to be there."

"Ralph, how about you? Are you with me on this, or is my butt hanging out on a limb?"

"I'll be there and so will all of the boys. We promised you that we would and we will. Let's go over what you want us to do."

"Do you have the cast nets loaded? How about the gill nets?"

"Yes. The gill nets are stashed in garbage cans in the hole by the old cypress stump."

"How about the shark net?"

"It's already hung and ready for business."

"Did you get the four nylon boat tie-down straps, two rolls of duct tape and one hundred feet of black polypropolene rope?"

"Yes. It's all in a black trash bag under the boat seat."

"Did you get the flashing yellow lights for the nets?"

"Yep."

"How about the two battery-powered halogen spotlights?"

"They're both mounted on top of the bridge and the battery-operated garage door opener control is set up on the south side."

"How about the quarter-inch diameter stainless steel cable?"

"It's already in place. We'll adjust the height just before they come through."

"Did you get the meeting set up for seven-thirty in the morning at the fish house?"

"Yes. Everyone will be there. The boots are ready to go."

"Do you have someone with a marine radio stationed at every point that we discussed?"

"Yes. They'll be at *The Crossroads, Hell's Gate,* the *Evans Crary* and *Roosevelt Bridges, Dyer's Point, Light House Point, Bessey Creek, Harbor Ridge* and *Club Med.* The toughest ones who have the stomach for this will be waiting in *Kitching Cove."*

"Do they all know to fall in behind and follow them up the river with their running lights turned off?"

"Yes. We went over the chart, the details of the operation and everyone's position at my house right after dinner."

"Ralph, where will you be?"

"At the north side of the '007' Bridge. I'm handling the two spotlights and the shark net."

"Did you top off the gas tanks in Bear's boat?"

"Yes. Plus, there's an extra five gallons in a plastic container in the bait well. The key is in the ignition."

"It sounds like everything is just about ready. I'll be up there a little before four-thirty. I'll flash a green light twice so that you know that I'm in position."

"Roger. I'm going home and get some sleep before it's time to leave for the North Fork."

"Good idea. I'm going to try to get a little sleep myself. It is going to be a long night. Mack, I'll see you about two-thirty. Good luck." Ralph left at 9:32 P.M. Mack decided to take a nap, went to bed and set the alarm for 1:30 A.M.

After he woke up, and gulped down three cups of 'nuked' instant coffee he went into the electronics room, inserted a video CD into the multiplexer and pushed the 'play' button on the control console. Mack went to his bedroom, 'rummaged' around in the closet and pulled out a pair of 'night vision' glasses and a matte-black electronics control box equipped with several lights and buttons. He tossed them in his black phyisian's valise along with the *Berretta,* an extra full clip, a black Navy watch cap, a black ski mask and a pair of 'lead-loaded' leather gloves. He donned black jeans and a black turtle neck sweater with sewn-in thick leather elbow patches. He caught a glimpse of himself in the full-length mirror - he looked like a very tall crow!

Mack 'double-locked' the front door and dropped the Bahama hurricane shutters into place, but he left enough of a gap so that light from the inside of the cottage could be seen through them. He dialed *72 and transferred the marina calls to his cell phone. If someone called to check on him he wanted them to think that he was at home. When Mack left the cottage he didn't turn the tiny nail head over the front door to the 'up' position to engage the marina's security system. He walked to Ralph's house because it was only a ten-minute walk from the *Port Sewell Marina* and he needed the exercise.

At 4:18 A.M. Mack was snuggled far back into the mangroves at *Fork Point* with the boat's stern cleat tied off to a mangrove root. A black tarp covered his boat from bow to stern. He could see everything coming upriver, but he couldn't be seen. Several dark, innocuous-appearing commercial fishing boats drifted past west of his position on their way up the North Fork. Others softly motored north past *Club Med* towards Kitching Cove. Mack's marine radio spoke to him through an earphone in his right ear, *"They passed under the Roosevelt Bridge, turned right and are heading towards Dyer's Point."*

"It's okay. We're ready for 'em" responded a deep, gruff, male voice. The voice sounded full of anticipation.

Mack aimed his night-vision glasses downriver to the opening between *Dyer's Point* and the *Roosevelt Bridge*. A small boat was coming up the river *'balls to the wall'* throwing a huge rooster-tail without it's red and green running lights turned on. That was dangerous. Someone could get seriously hurt if they hit a submerged object in the water, or were struck by another boat.

A faint green light flashed three times from the entrance to *Light House Point*. Ten seconds later, a green light flashed three times from just south of the *Harbor Ridge* boat docks. Eight seconds after that a green light flashed three times from behind the oyster bar between Har*bor Ridge* and the *Five Fingers*.

Mack monitored the progress of the speeding boat headed his way through the night-vision glasses. It hugged the darkened western shoreline of the St. Lucie River. When it reached *Harbor Ridge* the boat made a sharp turn northeast towards the channel markers at *Club Med*. Without slowing down the speeding boat made a hard right turn into the channel, sped past *Club Med* throwing a huge wake.

Mack threw off the line securing the boat to the mangrove root hit the starter button and the ancient, four-cylinder outboard motor awkwardly coughed to life. He eased the throttle forward, felt the gears mesh and put the 'pedal to the metal.' He swung south, far outside *Fork Point*, to avoid the buildup of mud and sand that ran along the southeastern edge of the point. The black boat's wake left the moored boats at the *Club Med Marina* rocking at the dock. Mack ran the tired outboard motor at full-throttle and tried to keep the racing boat in sight.

The white *'pickin'* lights mounted in the stern area of the commercial fishing boats lining each side of the narrow channel were lit and Mack could make out some of the men's gaunt, shadowy faces. They cursed vehemently as their flat-bottomed boats were rocked back and forth. The racing boat slowed down to 'idle' speed and picked it's way through the maze of flashing yellow lights obviously marking gill nets. The occupants were in a hurry, but they didn't want to risk getting their propeller tangled in the nets. When it reached *Kitching Cove* the boat veered left into the narrow mangrove-lined channel that led behind the island, to the *'007 Bridge'* and exited south of *River Gate Park*.

After they passed the commercial fishing boats and their flashing yellow net lights the black boat sped up. The narrow channel was dangerous enough during daylight hours and doubly so at night. The mangrove branches spanning the ten-foot wide channel almost touched the dark water in some spots. Apparently oblivious to any possible danger the operator of the black boat did not use a spotlight. Obviously he knew the area well and didn't want to attract anyone's attention to his position.

Mack recalled that there was a 'dead-end' pocket at the end of the channel. A boat that missed the sharp right turn at the cypress stump would be trapped in the pocket. The dead-end was straight ahead of the speeding black boat – if it didn't make a hard right turn at the stump it would be 'trapped'.

The 'flash' of a brilliant spotlight lit up the night and an agitated voice rang out of the darkness, *"Gino! There it is! Turn right now or you'll miss the channel!"*

"Got it. Hang on tight Manny. I can make it easy!" growled a guttural voice. The boat made a hard right turn and the operator, seemingly confident of his position, pushed the throttle forward. The boat surged ahead on full plane and threw a huge wake into the narrow channel. The boat had to continue going forward and could not turn back because eight commercial fishing boats followed along behind closing off any possible escape route. As the speeding black boat passed them each of the commercial fishing boats pulled their anchors and fell in line behind it – without displaying their red and green navigation lights.

Mack followed close along and when he saw that any escape route for the speeding boat was blocked he decided to run up the other side of the island. He had to travel about a quarter of a mile back down the narrow channel to *Kitching Cove* and a half a mile to *Fork Point*. Mack made a hard left turn at the cypress stump, crammed the throttle full forward, the boat did it's best to leap ahead and almost got up on 'plane'. Mack switched on the red and green navigation lights. He was concerned that he might not see something ahead of him in the darkness and flipped on the 100,000 candle-power halogen spotlight and went 'full bore' down the narrow channel.

When Mack came out of the channel into *Kitching Cove* he didn't slow down – he had to get around Fork Point and back to the '007 Bridge' before something 'bad' happened. But, Club Med's *Marina* was directly ahead on his port side. Mack fearing that he would cause wake damage to the moored boats, swung over to the starboard side of the channel and held as close as he could safely get to the mangrove trees lining the bank. Although the boat only drew nine inches he was concerned about hitting a submerged stump. At *Fork Point* he swerved sharply to 'port' to avoid hitting the sandbar, cleared the green marker, made a sharp turn to 'starboard' and headed north up the *North Fork*. It took him four minutes to reach the northern end of the island and the *'007' Bridge*. Four commercial fishing boats blocked the channel exit leading to *River Gate Park*. Mack pulled the throttle back and the boat settled down in the water alongside Ralph's boat.

"What 'cha catching tonight?" Mack said in a soft voice.

"Just waiting for the right time to nail a couple of 'skunks' that will be coming under the bridge real soon," Ralph responded in a whisper. He smiled smugly, "Mack be real quiet. Too much noise scares 'skunks'." Mack glanced into Ralph's boat and noticed the metallic 'glint' of metal among a pile of netting.

FLASH!

The two halogen spotlights mounted on the top railing of the *'007' Bridge* lit up the night sky. Simultaneously, a large-mesh shark net dropped down from the top railing covering the opening of the bridge and sealing off any possible escape route up the North Fork. The black boat's driver panicked, shoved the throttle forward and the boat surged ahead. Ten feet before the low bridge it 'paused' then 'flew' backwards like an airplane caught on the catapult of an aircraft carrier. The quarter-inch stainless steel cable strung across the channel, and suspended eighteen inches below the surface, snagged the outboard motor's lower unit. The steel cable wrapped up in the propeller and the drive shaft sheared off. The super-charged 250 horsepower outboard motor with no load to restrain it revved up to its maximum rpm's and exploded. Six twenty-foot diameter nylon cast nets arched in the air and settled over the boat and its two dazed occupants.

Mack and Ralph carefully lifted up the edge of the shark net and slipped under the bridge to take stock of the carnage.

Gino, the boat's operator, had smashed his face on the boat's plastic windshield. He was moaning and hopelessly clawing at the nylon mesh covering him from 'head to toe'. Manny, the pockmarked faced antagonist, was still full of fight. All six foot four inches of him stood up in the glare of the spotlights as he lifted the nets and their heavy lead weights with him. Manny screamed at Mack. "What the hell's going on here? What do you idiots think you're doing?"

"Welcome to the party Manny. You are the guests of honor."

"Who are you? What do you want?"

"Who we are isn't really important at this point in time. Do you remember *'Bear'* and what you did to him last week?"

"We didn't do nothin' to nobody. Who's *Bear*?"

"*Bear* was the commercial fisherman that you harassed by running over his gill nets. Last week you shot him in the back of the head and drowned him in *Kitching Cove*. He was our friend."

"We didn't shoot him. Frankie did."

"Who's Frankie?"

"He's our boss. He lives in that big house right straight across the river from here."

"Why did Frankie shoot him?"

"That crazy fisherman had a shotgun. He was going to shoot us because we messed up his nets. Frankie saved our lives."

"Why was he wrapped up in a cast net?"

"Frankie wanted to make it look like he drowned. Believe me - we didn't do nothin' to him. Frankie did it! Not us."

Mack idled alongside the black boat so that he could look Manny directly in the eye. He spotted Bear's leather necklace with the bear claws and the *One Rand* coin around Manny's neck.

"Where did you get that necklace?"

"I found it on the ground at the *River Gate Park* boat ramp."

"Do you know who it belonged to?"

"No. Do you want it? Let us go and you can have it."

"Manny, what do you have stashed in these coolers?"

"Fish. Just fish! Is that against the law here? We were bottom fishing for snapper. We gotta' get 'em on ice before they spoil."

"I must be blind. I don't see any fishing poles in your boat."

"We dropped them off at a friend's place in *Hobe Sound*."

Mack lifted the lid off the white fiberglass cooler in the bow. It was filled to the top with flat, rectangular packages wrapped in brown paper. He slit open one of the packages with his fillet knife and a white powder resembling the fine white sand in an hourglass ran out onto the deck.

"This is strange looking snapper. It appears that you've been very bad boys and need to be taught a lesson. But, spanking you is out of the question. First, hand me that necklace. I'll see that it's returned to its rightful owner."

"Here. Take it. You can have it. Just let us go. You can have the boat and the 'stuff' too."

Two stocky commercial fishermen pulled their boats alongside each side of the black boat to insure that the net-covered 'bad boys' wouldn't fall over the side and drown. Mack cinched a four inch wide black nylon boat 'hold down' strap around Manny and Gino's torsos and pulled it tight pinning their arms to their sides.

"Ralph. Can you put these two very 'bad boys' in your boat and take care of them?"

"No problem. Come on over guys. Be careful that you don't slip and fall overboard. You might drown yourselves."

"How about these nets? We can't move our arms."

"That's the whole idea." Mack carefully placed the leather necklace in an inside pocket of the black leather valise and snapped it closed. "Ralph. I'll see you for breakfast at the *Queen Conch* about six-thirty. Take real good care of these guys."

"Don't worry Mack, we'll take real good care of them." Ralph wrapped two layers of silver duct tape over Manny and Gino's mouths. They shook their heads from side to side and attempted to voice their objections, but only grunts and muffled sounds could be heard through the sticky tape. Ralph pushed the protesting pair down onto the bottom of his boat and threw a black canvas tarp over them. "Mack. Are you certain that you won't need some more help from us?"

"No. I don't need any help. Rat should have everything in hand by now. I just have to mount this electric trolling motor on the black boat. Then I'll be on my way. Don't forget to get that cable and shark net out of here. Make sure that each of these bad boys has a package of this excellent cocaine inside his shirt."

"No problem. I'll see you at six-thirty for breakfast. I'll be monitoring channel seventeen for you. Call me if you need help."

"Thanks, but I'm certain that I won't require any assistance."

After he had completed mounting the electric trolling motor on the bow Mack took the black boat in tow and slipped into the darkness of the St. Lucie River under the *'007 Bridge'*. He turned off his boat's red and green navigation lights.

Ralph turned his boat down the narrow channel leading to *Kitching Cove*. The other eight commercial fishermen's boats parted for him and formed an aisle as he passed by them. They fell in behind and formed a long column. Not a word was spoken. There was no need to talk.

CHAPTER

19

Mack, with the black boat in tow alongside, slowly headed towards a large house located on the canal directly across the river from River Gate Park. Thirteen softly glowing white lights mounted along the top of the sea wall cast ghostly images on the dark water. Security lights at each corner of the main house lit it up like a national monument.

Mack could make out the outlines of two men standing on the sea wall next to a boathouse. They couldn't see him because he was in the black shadow line. One of the men, Marco, was short and squat. The other man, Guido, was tall and thin.

Mack tied off one end of a one hundred-foot length of quarter-inch, black polypropolene line to his boat's bow cleat and tied the other end to a stern cleat on the black boat in tow beside him. He slipped into the black boat, gave his own boat a push backward and watched it disappear into the darkness of the shadow line. He pressed the 'on' switch of the electric trolling motor mounted on the bow and the black boat silently inched ahead. He pulled the black ski mask down over his face and was ready. The black boat slowly edged out of the shadows toward the men on the sea wall.

The short man spotted him first "Manny. Where the hell have you been? You're an hour late and the boss is worried. He was tracking you on the plotter and you stopped by the *'007' Bridge* for almost thirty minutes. What happened? Where's Gino."

"We hit something in the channel north of *Club Med* and sheared off the prop. I had to come in the rest of the way with the electric trolling motor. I dropped Gino off at the *'007' Bridge*. He's walking to the boat ramp at *River Gate Park* to pick up the truck and the trailer. Marco, how about giving me a hand?" Mack brought the boat alongside the sea wall and stretched out his right hand. When Marco leaned over to grasp his hand Mack took it and simultaneously swung the boat away and jerked on his hand. Marco flew off the sea wall and landed in the water with a style similar to a pregnant female walrus diving off an ice floe.

"Manny! Help me. I can't swim."

"The boat got away from me and I can't steer very well with this electric motor. Guido, can you come down and help Marco? I can't steer and I'm afraid that I might hit him with the prop."

"Guido! Hurry up! Get over here quick, I'm drowning!"

"Marco you're an idiot! Why don't you just stand up? The water is only four feet deep and you can walk out."

"I'm short and I can't touch the bottom. Ouch! Something is trying to eat me! Guido, hurry up! I don't want to die this way."

Mack pulled the black speedboat further out from shore and back into the shadow line. "Guido. You've got to help him out. I can't steer this thing. The battery is just about shot."

"Marco, just hold on. I can't swim either. I gotta' find a rope or something to throw to you. Nothing is going to eat you." Guido walked into the boathouse, but he didn't come back out.

A thin, long-haired, naked, bearded figure wearing a fluorescent orange helmet slithered out of the boathouse and snaked along the top of the sea wall. "Pssst. Mack. It's me. Rat. Everything is okay. That one won't wake up for at least an hour."

"Guido! Where are you? I'm drowning. Help me. Please!"

Mack guided the boat behind the drowning man, grabbed him by the hair pushed his head under water and pulled it out, "Shut your mouth, or you're a dead man. Do you understand me?"

"Who are you? What do you want?"

"Shut up." Mack directed the mist from a tiny aerosol can into his face, the man went silent and Mack held his face out of the water by his hair. Mack guided the boat alongside the sea wall and tied it off to the two metal cleats mounted in the cement.

"Mack. Pull into the boathouse. We can drag him out of the water in there and tie him up with the other one."

"Rat. You're naked! Where the hell are your clothes?"

"I never wear clothes when I'm on a raid. Didn't you know that dogs don't bark at a naked man? That's a *Senaca Indian* trick that my Indian grandfather taught me. Indian scouts went out on raids naked so they could sneak in and out of an enemy's camp at will. Indian braves slept naked because they didn't want to have to get dressed when they went outside to take a whiz in the middle of the night. And, he didn't want his neighbor's dogs barking at him and waking up the rest of the camp. So, the dogs were trained not to bark at a naked man. It works."

"How do you know it's true?"

"Did you hear any dogs barking when you came up?"

"No. I didn't. Were there any dogs here?"

"Oh yeah. There were two big guard dogs in the compound. A grumpy German Shepherd and a very nasty Rottweiler. They were surprised to see me, but they didn't bark. I don't think that they had ever seen a naked man before. I sprayed them with that aerosol can that you gave me. They fell right over dead as 'door nails' and never even whimpered. What was in it?"

"It's called '*Black Leaf Forty*'. Where are the dogs now?"

"They're upside down in the shopping cart on the front of my motorbike. Mack, the timing of this raid was absolutely perfect. We're having a cook out at *Shepherd's Park* tomorrow night. They will be plenty of meat. Do you want to come?"

"I don't think so. I already have plans for tomorrow night. Where's this guy's buddy?"

"He's hanging off a hook on the wall of the boathouse. That place is chock full of cocaine."

"You didn't kill him did you? We need them both alive to take the fall for this caper."

"Of course not. I just put him to sleep for an hour or so."

"Good. Let's get this one in there too." After the second man was hog-tied, and gagged, Mack had to catch up with Rat to find out what had transpired so far.

"What's going on in the house? Who's there? What have you done so far?"

"I've got individual explosive charges set up around the house that match buttons 'one' through 'six' on your control box. It's wired just like you drew on the sketch. Push button 'one' and all of the outside security lights blow out."

"Is there any time delay in the charges?"

"No. They are all instantaneous. Push the button and *'boom'*."

"How about the security system?"

"It's cut off at the phone jack on the outside of the house. You can activate it by dialing the security company's code number with your cell phone."

"Excellent. Who's in the house? Any women or children?"

"Not that I could see. There are only two guys in the house. They were sitting in the den drinking brandy and smoking big *'cheroots'* the last time I looked. One of them is called *Frankie*, just like you said. I couldn't pick up the other one's name, or see his face. He had his back to the window. They were tracking the boat on a big color plotter video screen. They got real worried when you stopped for so long down there by the *'007' Bridge*. How did that go down?"

"It all went just fine. Ralph's giving the two *'goombas'* a ride they will never forget."

"A ride to where? They're drug dealers and deserve to go 'down the river' with the big boys."

"Don't let it bother you. The two in the house are the ones that I want. I know that one of them killed Bear, Thatch's brother and Mel's brother. They are going to pay big time."

"What are you going to do to them?"

"You don't want to know - it's very personal. Get dressed and take off for home. I'll stop by *Shepherd's Park* in the morning on my way back to the marina and fill you in on everything."

"Don't you need help" Those two probably have guns."

"Don't worry about me. I told you that it's personal. Now get going. You have a big dinner party to worry about."

"Okay. I'm goin'. But, I don't feel good about it."

"I do. Now get going before it starts to get nasty around here. The cops will be here in about ten minutes. You don't want them to see you running around Port St. Lucie naked as a jay bird with two dead dogs in your motorbike's basket."

"How about the Florida Marine Patrol? Do you think that they are going to show up?"

"I don't think so. At least not right away. The last I heard they went on a distress to *Nettle's Island*. But, they have a big problem because their props got tangled up in an illegal gill net. They won't be out of there for at least a couple of hours."

"How about the Martin County Sheriff's Marine Unit?"

"They're working a big drug bust in *Hobe Sound*. Tina's down there coordinating the whole thing."

"You're all alone?"

"I certainly hope so. Rat now get going. When I'm done I'm going to trip the security system and you had better be long gone because the place will be swarming with cops in ten minutes."

"Where will you be when the cops get here?"

"Hopefully between *'Club Med'* and the *Roosevelt Bridge*."

"What are you going to do with their boat?"

"I'm not sure at this point. But, I'll think of something. Do you want some of this cocaine for the party?"

"No! That's the last thing that those guys need. Aftershave and canned heat are just fine for them."

"Now get out of here before they come out of the house looking for these two bozos. Get dressed. You don't want to be caught riding your motorbike through *Port St. Lucie* and *Stuart* 'buck-ass naked.' This state has laws against public nudity."

"There's no state law against taking dogs for a ride in a supermarket cart is there?"

"I don't think so. But, those dogs are dead. At least put a blanket over them just in case you are stopped."

After Rat left Mack pushed button number 'one' on the matte black electronic control box and the outside security lights blinked out. Rat did his job. Mack pulled the black ski mask over his face, grabbed his black valise and ran for the house. He crept up to the den window and attached a clear, plastic suction cup to the glass. The suction cup contained a sensitive acoustic coupler and fiber optic cable that fed video and audio signals to a digital CD recorder in the black valise. A monitor jack provided audio output to Mack through an earphone. The quality was so good that it sounded like he was in the room with them.

"Frankie. Where the hell are Manny and Gino? They disappeared off the GPS tracking unit after they left the *'007' Bridge*. They should have been here by now."

"Don't worry so much. Marco and Rico are down at the dock watching for them. Where's that stupid fishing guide Mack? Are you tracking him?"

"Of course. We've had that hick 'wired' since the day he got here. There's a GPS satellite transmitter in his truck and also one in his boat. We know exactly where he is at all times. Yesterday afternoon he was fishing in the *North Fork*. He got home about eight-thirty last night and he hasn't left the place since."

"How do you know that for sure?"

"Motion detectors at the marina tell us when he's moving and television cameras track him constantly. He's at home. I'll pull up the remote marina transmitters on the screen. Look. His truck is still in the marina parking lot and his boat is in the boathouse. I'll hit the 'live' video feed button. See. He's in bed and sleeping like a baby. Do you want to hear his snoring?"

"No. That's not necessary. I'm worried that he's getting too close to us. That trip that he made to *Fort Myers* really concerns me. He didn't know that his buddy had 'bitten the bullet.' I think that he might be on to us. *Billy O'Dell* said that he was asking too many 'smart' questions."

"He can't ask any smart questions. He's pretty darn stupid."

"Isn't he the same guy from *Air Force OSI* that was watching us at *Phuong Hoang*? We had a good connection back to the states and Billy was flying back two tons of heroin a week on Air America until he screwed it up."

"Yep. That's him. After the SOG team picked him up at that VC compound and brought him back to *Lon Bien* I debriefed him with *Ketamine Hydrochloride* mixed with *Diazepam*. He was a real tough cookie and I had to resort to *Scopolamine* to get what I wanted out of him. I had an Air Force shrink diagnose him as 'neurotic' and 'hallucinogenic.' We transferred him to *Bethesda* for deprogramming. It took almost a month, but he finally responded to a combination of electroshock and drug therapy."

"Any chance of him remembering what went on in *Laos*, or *Fort Myers*, when you were there? Billy gave him that damn coin and newspaper article! They could trigger a flash back."

"I don't think so. Tina's very concerned about him and monitors him closely. If he reports any dreams, or displays any sign of even minor memory recall, we'll get him down to the VA Hospital in West Palm for a mental tune-up. We still have the option of terminating the project if he catches on to us."

"How about that red-headed, smart-mouthed broad? Does she remember anything?"

"Do you mean Tina? She's not a broad. She's a classy lady."

"She's a broad. Does she know that the two of you were married in Maryland?"

"No. She doesn't remember anything. After her breakdown she was totally reprogrammed back at *Bethesda*. She's okay now and I can handle her just fine."

"Speaking of the broad - where is she now?"

"She's been on a special assignment in DC since April. I don't know when she's coming back. I've got a satellite transmitter installed in her car and it's still parked at her condo."

"What if that Mack guy starts snooping around Manny and Gino during their runs?"

"If he tries to stop them they'll wipe him out just like they did that Bear guy."

"They didn't wipe him out - I did. After they got their props tangled in his nets three nights in a row I had them put on stainless steel props and rope cutters. I told them to run through the damn net and cut it to pieces. But, they got stuck again last week because that damn "cracker" had strung a steel cable in the damn net. Fortunately, I'd been tracking them on the GPS plotter and saw that they had stopped in *Kitching Cove*. I cranked up the electric boat and snuck down the back way.

When I got there I saw that he was going to wipe them out with a shotgun. So, I popped him in the back of the head from fifty yards away. A damn good shot, even if I say so myself. I used the old .22 caliber *High Standard HD noise-suppressed pistol* that I brought back from Laos. I installed a night vision scope and laser sight on it. It works great."

"The newspaper article said that he drowned. The coroner's report and didn't say anything about a gunshot wound."

"Those yokels can't tell a gunshot wound from a pimple. As far as they are concerned if a body is found in the water the person drowned. The entrance wound of a .22 caliber slug is so small that it's almost impossible to see it in thick hair. That's why I shot him in the back of the head.

There wasn't any exit wound because of the bullet's low muzzle velocity. A .22 long-rifle slug travels at 1,255 feet per second, but the impact is only 140 foot-pounds. The bullet didn't kill him - it just knocked him out. He fell face first into the water and drowned. The boys held his head under water for a couple of minutes to make sure that he drowned. He didn't even wiggle."

"I didn't know that you had a *High Standard* twenty-two. I've still got mine too. That's what I used on that nosy sail boater that snuck offshore to try to catch the boys making a pickup. When he left the *Manatee Pocket* at two in the morning I followed him out. He was surprised to see me and even invited me onboard. But, he begged me to shoot him after I wrapped him up in his boat's anchor chain. He thought that I was going to throw him over the side and drown him. First, I shot him in both knees. Then I 'nailed' him right between the eyes. He never moved a muscle."

"Wasn't he that Martin County Sheriff's *narc's* brother?"

"Yeah. He doesn't have any idea about who is doing what."

"How come nobody found a trace of him or his sail boat?"

"The captain of the mother ship towed the sailboat thirty-five miles out, just past the center of the Gulf Stream, and set in on fire. It burned to the waterline and sank in less than five minutes. There was nothing left to find. Even if something did happen to float off the boat it was picked up by the Gulf Stream and was seventy-five miles north of there within twenty-four hours."

"What about his body? That would float."

"Not when it's wrapped in a couple hundred feet of one-inch anchor chain and stuffed in the chain locker. End of story."

"What are you going to do with that guy Mack? He's been around for three months and he's getting very curious. The boys are very nervous because he's asking all the right questions."

"Don't worry. I'll take care of him when the time comes.

We almost had him 'nailed' good the other night. Marco and Guido booked him for snook trips three nights in a row and convinced him to bring in a big 'sow' snook over the thirty-four inch 'slot' limit. We tipped off the young Florida Marine Patrol guy that Mack was going to be sneaking in an oversized snook and he pulled us over right on schedule. But, before he could find the snook tied off on the back cleat Mack managed to break the monofilament with his hand. The mono cut his hand up pretty good because the boys had switched the line on him. He had a piece of thirty-pound test mono tied on the back cleat. When he went in the tackle shop to buy some hooks the boys cut it off and substituted fifty-pound test. No one can break fifty-pound test mono with their hands. He was very lucky. We might try to book him again for a snook trip up here to the *North Fork* and 'whack' him there. *Kitching Cove* would be just about the right place."

"I agree. That's where they found that Bear guy and the 'other guy' last year. It would be perfect and a 'three peat' for us."

"What 'other guy' last year?"

"Do you remember that nosy commercial fisherman who was found drowned up there in his nets last year? He was a FDLE agent and was making a case against the boys. I popped him with the old *High Standard* 'twenty-two' at about forty yards. The boys finished him off in his net.

"You bastard! That was my brother! You didn't have to kill him. He wasn't an agent!"

"How was I supposed to know that he was your brother? You never told me."

"Why should I tell you? I never figured that you would hurt a commercial fisherman."

"He might have been your brother, but he definitely wasn't a commercial fisherman. He was an FDLE undercover agent, just like that guy 'Bear'. I got the word from the inside. Didn't you know that? You are supposed to be our 'inside' guy. That's why we pay you the big bucks every month. Find out yourself."

"Honest. I really didn't know. He never told me. Maybe I told him too much about our operation."

"Duh. That's why they call them 'undercover' agents. Now that we got rid of that 'Bear' guy the FDLE will send in another agent in a month, or so. Keep your eyes peeled for him."

"My poor brother. You shot him. Wait a minute. The autopsy

report said that he drowned. There wasn't anything in the report about a gunshot wound. Something isn't right about that. They couldn't miss two gunshot wound victims in a row."

"Why not?"

"Because I have attended a lot of autopsies. They always cut the scalp loose and peel it back over the skull to look for indentations, cuts, etc. They had to notice a bullet entry wound. Something smells rotten about this whole situation."

"Hold on a minute. I just got 'beeped'. The boys must be back. Let's go down to the boathouse and meet them. I want to know why they spent so damn much time stopped by the '007' Bridge."

Mack dropped his head below the windowsill, snapped off the suction cup and tucked it in an inside pocket of the black valise along with the cell phone. He removed a small, black aerosol can and the *Berretta*. He held the matte-black control box in his left hand and waited for the two men to come through the front entrance of the house into the front yard.

"Frankie! It's dark as hell out here. Where are the frigging security lights?"

"Maybe we blew a fuse. Marco! Rico! What the hell's wrong with the lights? Where are you? Manny! Gino! Are you guys at the boathouse yet?"

Mack pressed button number 'two' on the black control box.

KABOOM!

The explosion detonated in the entryway and the shock wave threw both men forward and flat onto the ground. Mack pounced on top of the first man, put his right knee in the middle of his back and sprayed his face with the contents of the black aerosol can - he went limp. Mack then turned his attention to Frankie.

Frankie was on his hands and knees towards the burning house and attempted to get to his feet when he saw Mack. Mack allowed him to get onto his knees and sprayed him in the face with the aerosol can - he went limp. Mack secured the two men's arms to their sides with black nylon boat tie-down straps and ran two wide strips of silver duct tape over their mouths. When they awoke thirty seconds later Mack was in their face.

"Gentlemen. I'm glad that you both remember me because I certainly remember the two of you. I thought that I gave the *Air*

Force Office of Special Investigation an 'air tight' case against you for running heroin out of Laos on government aircraft. I should have watched my back and my associates a little closer.

Which one of you two 'smarmy' slime balls alerted *'Charlie'* that my team was coming in that day? They knew exactly where we would be and at what time - you set us up good. But, that Special Forces SOG team messed up your plans when they brought me back alive didn't they? You sent them in to rescue your own guys, not me, because you were being double-crossed and your supplier was holding your men as ransom. But, they all drowned in the river. You killed all of them with your greed."

The two tightly-bound men frantically shook their heads from side to side in unison and attempted to scream through the silver duct tape over their mouths to no avail. Their wide-open eyes mirrored the image of fear that an animal senses, but does not comprehend during its walk from the livestock hauler's truck and 'up' the inclined ramp to the slaughterhouse.

"Yes Dave my friend. Tina remembers everything and so do I. She was pulled back to Langley in April for a full evaluation and then to Bethesda for 'reprogramming'. She's been back about a week. You couldn't track her because I found the 'bug' in her *Beamer* last week and it's sitting on a shelf in her garage. But, she's been driving a rental car since she got back. Right about now she's taking your cohorts in *Hobe Sound* into custody."

"Now, the three of us are going for a short boat ride before the cops get here and spoil our party plans. I've got Bear's boat with me because I thought that it would be very appropriate under the circumstances. You stand up." Mack prodded Dave with his foot, but he sat back down on the ground, shook his head vehemently from side to side and refused to move. "Dave. I'm really pleased that you want to play 'hard ball.' I am going to enjoy hurting you." Mack placed a 300,000-volt stun gun under Dave's chin and pressed the 'energize' button. Dave's head snapped back and a muffled scream 'roared' through the two layers of duct tape.

"Are you both going to be good boys and walk down to the boathouse, or shall I do it again? Frankie. Maybe you would like some motivation? This works very well as a convincer." Both men immediately leaped to their feet and started walking toward the boathouse. Tears streamed down Dave's face and he appeared to be wailing under the two layers of silver duct tape.

When the trio arrived at the boathouse Mack tugged on the black polypropolene rope. Bear's blue, 'rag-tag' commercial fishing boat eased out of the darkness of the shadow line and ominously glided towards the seawall. Mack helped Dave and Frankie into Bear's boat, pushed them down onto a pile of old nets covering the bottom and threw a black canvas tarp over them. He pulled the black speedboat alongside, tied the black line to its bow and shoved it towards the stern of Bear's boat. He cranked up the ancient outboard motor, put it in gear and pulled away from the sea wall towing the black speedboat behind him.

Mack brought the boat to a stop at the edge of the dark shadow line. He unsnapped the top and opened the black valise, removed his cell phone and the black control box. He activated the Caller ID 'calling number blocking' feature of the cell phone, activated the 'identifier code' for Frankie's security system and dialed the telephone number of the security firm to report a break-in. After the call to the security company was confirmed he calmly dialed '666.' When the pager answered he punched in '999' and replaced the cell phone in the valise.

Mack turned his attention back to Dave and Frankie who were still under the black canvas tarp, trussed up like hogs on the way to market and whimpering like punished children. He pulled back a corner of the tarp so they could see Frankie's house. "Okay boys - watch the 'fireworks'. Mack pressed button 'three' on the control box and the front security gate of the mansion blew off its hinges. He pressed button 'four' and the rear entrance of the house disappeared in a ball of flame. He pressed button 'five' and the four-car garage exploded. He pressed button 'six' and the guesthouse rose up at least ten feet off the ground, blew up in a huge ball of fire and settled over what remained of the garage.

Mack formed a circle with the thumb and index finger of his left hand and placed the control unit back into the black valise with his right. The pager on his belt vibrated – he glanced at the lit digital readout - '666.' Everything was okay and on schedule.

As Mack steered across the river toward the *'007' Bridge* he could see two sets of flashing blue lights coming up the main channel towards him at high speed. But, it didn't matter. The boat operators couldn't see him because his running lights weren't turned on. When the Florida Marine Patrol and Martin County Sheriff Marine Unit boats arrived at the burning house Mack and his treacherous cargo were almost to *Kitching Cove.*

Mack could hear the 'screaming' wail from the sirens of approaching fire trucks. It didn't matter if the house burned to the ground because the drugs were in the boathouse with Marco and Guido. They'd both be awake by now, but very confused. Mack made certain of that because he sprayed them with *Ketamine Hydrochloride.* He untied them before he shoved away from the sea wall and they would take the 'rap' for everything. There wouldn't be anyone else left around for the police to charge.

Mack pulled into the hidden cove directly across the channel from *Kitching Cove* just as the sun was tinting the fluffy cumulus clouds in the eastern sky a light pink. Ralph, and several other commercial fishermen, waited patiently for him in a far corner of the cove. Their boats were drawn into a tight circle around two floating bodies tangled in white nylon netting.

"Hey Ralph. Looks like you boys came across a really bad boating accident. I'd wager a guess that those two guys fell out of their boat, got tangled up in some nets and drowned. That's funny because I found this black boat that I'm towing behind me floating loose up the river a couple of miles. Maybe it's theirs? If so they should have it. I've also got some really dirty nets in the bottom of this boat that need to be washed out. Would a couple of you hefty guys help me lift them up and dump them over the side? Be careful. They're very heavy."

The sun was peeking over the eastern horizon as the somber procession of commercial fishing boats rounded *Dyer's Point* and headed towards the *Roosevelt Bridge.* Mack was in the lead followed by Ralph and Bobo. Mack waved the other boats ahead and steered through the anchorage towards the opening in the limestone breakwater at *Shepherd's Park.* He glanced over his right shoulder towards the North Fork and saw the thick, black smoke from an uncontrolled fire billowing skyward.

There was just enough daylight to see and Mack opened his tightly closed right hand to look at the two silver coins nestled between the bulk of his thumb and the curve of his palm. He flipped them over with his left index finger to look at the backsides. One of the coins had the numeral '1' stamped to the left of the *Springbok's* hind leg. The other coin had the numeral '2' stamped in the same place. Mack smiled smugly and slipped the two coins into the right pocket of his black jeans. He pulled alongside Rat's sailboat and beat on the starboard side of it with his fist hoping to wake Rat up. But, there was no response.

"Hey Mack. I'm over here. Pull into the park and tie up at the seawall for awhile."

Mack steered through the narrow opening that led into the park and the boat launching ramps. There were at least a dozen bearded, long-haired men standing in a circle around an open fire and long, metal spit that held what appeared to be two 'suckling' pigs. Most of the men wore the shirt, or pants, from an Army uniform. Several of the concrete picnic tables were covered with newspapers and set with paper plates and plastic silverware.

"Mack. Come on over and meet the boys. We decided to get an early start on dinner. It'll be ready in a couple of hours. Pull up a seat and join us. The boys went shopping last night and we made up a fresh batch of liquid nourishment. We've got lots of hot coffee and 'dumpster' donuts. Just dip a cup of java out of one of those white bait coolers."

"No thanks. I had a late dinner last night and my stomach feels a little queasy. Rat. I need to talk to you about something real important. Can you come over here for a minute?"

"Sure can. Freddy! Grab hold of this spit and keep turning it real slow. We want these 'shoats' crispy on the outside, but we don't want to burn 'em. They gotta' brown evenly all over."

Mack motioned Rat over to the concrete walkway that jutted out into the river and circled the western side of *Shepherd's Park* in a curving arc. "Thanks for letting me use your kayak last night. Hey, those are pigs on the spit aren't they?

"Of course. One of the boys picked up a couple of shoats last night at a farm on the *Palm City loop road*. The farmer will never miss 'em. He's got plenty of 'em left. What'cha want Mack?

"Rat. Jump on your motorbike and meet me and Ralph at the *Queen Conch* in *Port Salerno* for breakfast. It's important."

"Mack. Look over there! That's one really big fire up 'yonder' in the North Fork. Wonder what it could be?"

"Rat. Look at this. It's Bear's necklace."

"Where did you find it?"

"Found it on a skunk that got caught in a net and drowned in the North Fork last night."

"I knew that you'd find it. It's a shame about the poor skunk. But wasn't there two skunks?"

"Yes. There were. Plus, there was some terribly filthy garbage floating in the river too."

"It's amazing how people can just throw their garbage in the water. That's pollution."

"Did anyone see you leaving the *Manatee Pocket* last night?"

"There was nothin' going on anywhere in the North Fork last night that I saw. I was here all night fixing them two shoats. Ask Freddy. He's the one turning the spit and he'll tell ya' straight."

"Thanks. I owe you one, bud."

"The name is Rat. Spelled R-A-T. You don't owe me nothing.' I owe you." He patted Mack on the shoulder, winked, turned and limped down the concrete walkway towards the crowd of anxious, hungry, bedraggled men gathered around the spit.

A middle-aged, balding fisherman, clad in blue Bermuda shorts, a flowered Hawaiian shirt, black socks and brown sandals stood on the concrete seawall with his fishing rod bent almost double struggling vainly with an unseen underwater foe. Mack decided to watch him for a few minutes just to see what he would pull in – 'if' he won the battle with the underwater denizen.

When the exhausted fisherman leaned over to dip his landing net into the water his straw hat fell off as he jumped back in surprise. "What the hell is that? Jesus Christ! It's a dog's head! It's a German Shepherds head! Mable! Come over here quick! I caught a frigging dog's head!"

Mack smiled and walked back to the green kayak. After all, Rat said it best. *"Meat's just meat after it's cooked."*

CHAPTER
20

At the meeting at the *Port Salerno* fish house the two white rubber boots that were passed around to benefit Bear's wife Emogene were filled to the top with cash.

After the meeting a few of the boys gathered at the *Queen Conch* for breakfast. Mack sat with his back to the wall and Rat sat next to him on his left side. Opposite Mack sat Deputy Elmo from the Martin County Sheriff's Marine Unit. To Elmo's right sat Mel Mancini of the Narcotics Unit. Ralph sat to Rat's left at the end of the table facing the front door where he could watch everyone coming and going.

"Mary, I'll get the check for everyone and give them anything they want." Mack smiled, "Each one of you deserves much more than a breakfast for what you did for Bear's wife. I wish that I could have done more that I did."

"Anything we want?" asked Rat sitting up straight in his seat. "I sure am hungry for some scrambled loggerhead turtle eggs with a slab of turtle meat on the side."

"I meant anything on the menu. And absolutely no manatee or Rottweiler steak."

Rat blushed as best he could, slipped on his sunglasses, slumped back in his seat and stuck out his lower lip in a fake pout. "Mary, I'll have a Western omelet with everything. Feel free to add any goodies that you find leftover on anybody's plate when it comes back to the kitchen. You can't waste perfectly good food. Meat's 'meat' after it's been cooked."

"Mack. You took care of things that none of us could have ever done in a million years. You have lots of contacts to call on for help and I sure hope that you didn't use up all your favors."

"Thanks for your thoughts Ralph. But, it was a team effort all the way. All of you saw it through to the end."

"Mack, I just can't figure out how you knew where the drop in *Hobe Sound* would be and when. We staked out that house for weeks and never saw anything suspicious. How come your intelligence sources are better than ours?" Mel asked with a smug grin. "Oops!" he added with a wink of his left eye. "I don't really want to know do I? You'd have to kill me if you told me, right?"

"Mel, it just took some dumb luck and a little perseverance. Nothing special that you couldn't have done if you had the time and the proper resources." Mack said with a smug grin and a wink of his left eye towards Ralph. "I guess that maybe I knew someone that you didn't know. I had a lot of outside help."

"Bear told me that he had seen two guys in a black speedboat speeding up the *North Fork* right past *Kitching Cove*. They ran over his nets, fouled their props and threatened to kill him if it happened again. He decided to carry a shotgun in the boat with him and he knew that it didn't work. The firing pins were rusted tight. After fouling their props several times they switched to razor sharp stainless steel props and they sliced right through the net like it was warm butter. Bear told me that he was tired of having his nets cut to ribbons and he replaced the cork line with a quarter-inch stainless steel cable. He figured that would teach them some manners. It didn't." Ralph added with a wistful sigh.

"Why didn't he call us or the Florida Marine Patrol for help?" asked Deputy Elmo. "We could have set up a surveillance team and nailed them cold."

"Elmo, why would he report anything to you? He was gill netting! That's against the law and it wouldn't have been very smart of him now would it? Plus, everybody knows that the Sheriff's Department and Florida Marine Patrol don't work past eleven o'clock at night." Ralph slammed his fist on the table, water jumped out of the full glasses onto the plastic tabletop. "Do you really think that anyone who is doing something illegal only does it when you are on duty so that you can catch them?"

"No. But if we knew we could have asked for extra overtime and we might have caught them."

"Hold it guys. Let's not quibble. The point is that the bad guys were caught. It doesn't matter who caught them or how," Mack added. "Now Emogene has a few bucks and can move to *Pine Island* and be with her family in *Bokeelia*. All's well that ends well and breakfast is here. Let's eat."

"Mack. Is Tina back from DC yet?" asked Ralph with a sly wink of his right eye.

"I don't know. Hey, it's nine o'clock and time for the local news. Let's see what's going on in town. Mary, would you please turn on the television set over the counter? Thank you."

A 'talking head' appeared on the television screen.

"Good morning everyone. I'm John Betts and this is a special live report from action news. Ms. Tina McShay, a spokesperson from the Florida State Attorney's West Palm Beach Office, wishes to give a statement about a significant drug bust that took place in *Hobe Sound* last night. Ms. McShay, please go ahead."

"Thank you John.

Early this morning a task force of agents from the Florida Department of Law Enforcement, the Palm Beach County State Attorney's Office, U.S. Federal Marshals, Drug Enforcement Administration, Coast Guard and the Martin County Sheriff's Office raided a home in *Hobe Sound* and arrested four men for narcotics trafficking. The multi-agency task force confiscated two black speedboats, a cabin cruiser and a sailboat. They found fourteen kilos of cocaine and $44,000 in cash in the home. The men's identities have not been revealed.

Another incident involving drug trafficking, not thought to be related to the *Hobe Sound* bust, took place in the North Fork of the St. Lucie River and left six men dead. At 5:15 this morning St. Lucie County fire fighting personnel were dispatched to an estate on the shore of the North Fork of the St. Lucie River after a report was received of a series of explosions and fire.

A private security company received a call from the estate's alarm system at 5:10 A.M. indicating that the home's security outside perimeter had been penetrated. The security company notified the appropriate law enforcement agency and several patrol cars were dispatched to the scene.

Fire fighters arrived on the scene and found the house, garage and guesthouse engulfed in flames. When law enforcement personal arrived at the scene several shots were fired at them from the boathouse. They returned fire and killed two men in the boathouse. Each of the gunmen was armed with a 9-millimeter automatic pistol and a noise suppressed twenty-two caliber pistol of unidentified origin. Both gunmen's names are being withheld pending investigation and notification of their next of kin. The estate owner was known to have kept two extremely vicious guard dogs on duty, a German Shepherd and a Rottweiler, neither animal was found on the premises. It is assumed that the dogs were in the house and killed in the fire.

Just before dawn this morning two sport fishermen found the bodies of four men floating in a small cove directly across from *Kitching Cove*. Two of the men were apparently riding at a high rate of speed in a black speedboat and hit a gill net held in place by a stainless steel cable. The men were thrown out of the boat, broke their necks and drowned. The speedboat had three large coolers onboard each filled with packages of cocaine.

The other two men found ion the cove were bound with nylon boat tie-down straps, gagged with two layers of silver duct tape and shot execution-style in the back of the head. Their feet were tied together at the ankles, their bodies were draped over opposite sides of a recently stolen commercial fishing boat and their heads were suspended under the surface of the water.

We suspect that the two gunmen killed by law enforcement personnel in the estate's boathouse snuck into the main house, subdued the two principals, dragged them into the stolen commercial fishing boat, towed it to Kitching Cove and executed them. Afterwards they strung the gill net 'booby-trapped' with the steel cable across the channel to ensnare the black speedboat.

The two men returned to the estate, set fire to the house, garage and guesthouse in an attempt to destroy any evidence. They were unable to escape in the battery-powered boat found inside the boathouse because the wire leading from the battery's positive terminal to the boat's ignition switch had been cut. With their only means of escape cut off the two gunmen elected to shoot it out with law enforcement. They died in the gun battle.

We feel that this incident was an attempt by a rival group from out of town to silence the local competition. This case was already under investigation and law enforcement was poised to make an arrest. However, because the principals in the case are deceased and the narcotics seized we consider the case closed.

Thank you for your patience. There will be no questions."

"Mack. Why didn't you tell us that Tina was back?"

"Come on Ralph. How was I supposed to know that she was back? I'm not her keeper."

"I thought that you two had something going on. Guess that I was wrong."

"You were. But, thanks for thinking of me."

After breakfast each man went his own way. But, when Mack pulled into *Port Sewell Marina* Deputy Elmo was waiting for him. His green and white-striped catamaran patrol boat was moored to the powerboat dock. The gold star painted on the side was very conspicuous. Mack tied off the bow and stern lines of his boat to the dock's cleats with a round turn, several figure eights and a half hitch. "Deputy Elmo. What can I do for you?"

"Mack. I need to talk with you for just a few minutes. It's not 'official' business. It's just that I have to know how you pulled this off. Can you spare me a few minutes and fill me in a little bit? I know that you can't tell me everything, but just a little. Please? My curiosity is killing me."

"Elmo, I didn't do anything special. I'm just a fishing guide. From what I just saw on television some bad guys did some very bad things to someone we all knew. The bad guys are dead or on their way to jail. End of story." Mack's right hand slipped into the pocket of his shorts and he rubbed the two coins between his thumb and forefinger. He began to recall things best forgotten, shuddered, took a deep breath and pushed the thoughts far back into his subconscious - at least temporarily.

"Okay, Elmo. You deserve better. Please understand that I can't tell you everything because I don't want to wind up in court as a material witness. I can't do that under any circumstances.

Much of what happened the other night is best forgotten and I already have. I have a very poor memory."

"Ten-four on the poor memory. Okay, Mack I'm pledged to secrecy. How did you know that they were running cocaine right past our noses almost every night? How did you know who they were? How did you know where they were going? How did you know they would be there last night?" Elmo was left somewhat breathless after sputtering out his last 'rapid fire' question.

"Elmo, I'm not sure what question came first, but I'll try to answer them as best I can. I didn't know for certain that they were running cocaine until about two weeks ago. An old friend of mine, from many years in the past, had been watching them for months. He was curious and began logging the days and times that they came down and went back up the North Fork. They only ran Monday through Thursday between 1:30 A.M. and 4:30 A.M. That is a very 'specific' three-hour window and they never ran on Friday, Saturday or Sunday.

The cocaine was brought over from the Bahamas on a large 'mother-ship'. Several small speedboats would rendezvous with it about fifteen miles off shore and make the transfer. The whole deal took less than ten minutes. Take a look at these logs."

"Wow! It's right there in black and white. Even us and the Florida Marine Patrol boats are logged in. Why didn't they run on the weekends?"

"There's far too much surveillance on Friday and Saturday by the Coast Guard, Marine Patrol and you guys. You are all out there day and night over the weekend. There's too much chance of getting caught."

"You're right. We go home at about eleven o'clock most weeknights. But, we watch the inlets real close during the weekends. How did you track them? You even tracked our boats? You seemed to know where we were most of the time."

"All of the time," Mack corrected him with a grin.

"Who kept the logs? It couldn't be you! Look at these times! You had to sleep sometime."

"That was the easy part. The *Roosevelt Bridge* tenders change shifts at eleven at night and seven in the morning. A cup of hot coffee and a couple of donuts at the eleven o' clock shift change go along way towards cooperation. A scrambled egg, bacon and cheese sandwich with hot coffee at six in the morning makes a tired bridge tender a very happy camper."

"Wow. Such detailed logs. I'm surprised that you don't have pictures too."

"I do. Would you prefer a video tape, CD or black and white eight by ten inch photos for your files?"

"Both! How did you get pictures in the middle of the night?"

"Film based cameras require a flash. But, a video camera equipped with a thermal imager and night-vision lens that is tied into a CD multiplexer and VCR recorder does wonders."

"A thermal imager? Night-vision video cameras? You've got stuff that we don't even have! Where'd you get it?"

"Where I got it isn't important - only the output is. Do you want the video tape? Don't you tell anyone where you got it."

"Yes, I want it, but now my curiosity is really peaked. I have a lot more questions."

"You asked four questions. I am going to give you only four answers. You can figure out the rest by yourself."

"But, there's so much more to know."

"Sorry, Elmo. You asked four questions and you will only get four answers. No more! Understood? You know too much already. Do you remember what I told you about my concern about being called as a material witness? It can't happen. I will not let it happen under any circumstances! Understood?"

"Yes, I understand, but . . .

"No buts! The next question was, 'How did I know that they were dealing drugs?'

First of all, the black speedboat was running up and down the river between 1:30 A.M and 4:30 A.M. That's well after all local law enforcement personnel were off the water and snoring peacefully in bed. Second, the boat didn't ever display its red and green running lights. Third, the two occupants were dressed in black. That was more than just a 'tad' suspicious. Fourth, the boat had a large cooler in both the bow and stern areas, plus another one in the middle. But, there were no fishing poles onboard."

"Mack, you should be a detective. Did you ever consider becoming a private investigator?"

"No. But you aren't making this easy. Now just sit there and listen. I'm handing you this case on a silver platter. All you have to do is write it up. Do you want the details or not?"

"Yes. I'm sorry. I'll keep quiet, but it's very hard to do."

"Elmo, one more interruption and out you go. Then you can try to figure out what happened by yourself and explain to your sergeant and lieutenant why you blew it. Understood?

"Yes! Don't stop now. I'm all ears."

"The black speedboat had to be making a pickup of something heavy because it sat lower in the water when it returned back up river than when it went down three hours earlier. It should have been lighter, and drawn less water, because it had been running at high speed for at least two hours. At twenty-five miles per hour a two hundred-fifty horsepower outboard uses twenty-five gallons of fuel an hour. In two hours that would be fifty gallons or about three hundred pounds. Something very heavy was added during that three hour round trip to and from the *Roosevelt Bridge*."

"How did you know that it sat lower in the water when it came back up river?"

"It had to pass under the *Roosevelt Bridge* and the bridge tenders aren't blind!

"How do you know that they hadn't fueled up somewhere along the way?

"No marinas are open that time of night."

"How did you figure out where they were going?"

"Basic mathematics. It's a sixteen mile round trip from the *Roosevelt Bridge* to the *St. Lucie Inlet* and back. At twenty-five miles per hour the trip takes thirty-eight minutes. The boat was gone for about three hours from the time it passed under the *Roosevelt Bridge* and returned. It wasn't sitting still during those three hours. Assuming that it took thirty minutes to load the boat we are looking at a two and one-half hour round trip running time. At a speed of twenty-five miles per hour two and one-half hours equates to a round trip distance to and from the *Roosevelt Bridge* of sixty miles. *Jupiter* is forty miles round trip and *Fort Pierce* is fifty miles. That made *Fort Pierce* the most likely pickup point. But, the black boat never went under the *Stuart Causeway Bridge* according to the bridge tender. If they slowed down for the mantee zones in the *Intracoastal*, and that's a big if, it added an extra half hour to their round trip time. The pick up point had to be near *Jupiter*."

"Mack, you had all the bases covered."

"The boat's fuel capacity was also a big factor. That model is equipped with a built-in seventy-gallon gas tank. A two hundred-fifty horse outboard, running at twenty-five miles per hour would use at least twelve gallons for the twelve mile round trip from the *North Fork* to the *Roosevelt Bridge*. That left eight gallons to spare. They weren't going past *Jupiter* because they didn't have enough fuel."

"But, they could have added fuel in *Jupiter*!"

"They could have, but that would have also added weight. They had the fuel usage figured right down to the gallon. They had some to spare, but not much. I felt that they weren't going past *Jupiter* because the trip would use too much fuel. They had to be meeting another boat in the *Intracoastal* and transferring the drugs, or slipping into a canal and picking them up at a residence below the *Hobe Sound Bridge*, but above *Jupiter*."

"How did you know that they were running to below the *Hobe Sound Bridge*?"

"The *Hobe Sound Bridge* tender likes donuts and coffee in the morning and Rat supplied them." Mack added with a grin as he handed him a second blue spiral ring notebook. "It's all in here."

"The black speedboat passed under the *Hobe Sound Bridge*, that's fourteen miles away, about an hour after it passed under the *Roosevelt Bridge*. A round trip accounted for two hours of travel time. The boat came running back northbound under the *Hobe Sound Bridge* about an hour later. Allowing thirty minutes to load up and 'shoot the bull' it left thirty minutes for round trip travel time to and from the *Hobe Sound Bridge*.

At a speed of twenty-five miles per hour for thirty minutes the round trip distance would be about twelve miles. One half of twelve is six. I estimated the pickup point to be within six miles of the *Hobe Sound Bridge*. That put it in the *Jupiter Sound* vicinity, south of *Rolling Hills*. Two hours from the *Roosevelt Bridge* to the *Hobe Sound Bridge*, a half hour to load up, plus a half hour run time and you get three hours round trip from the *Roosevelt Bridge*. It was easy. Basic math skills and lots of luck."

"Mack, were you a detective before you moved here?"

"No. But, I read a lot of 'who dunnit' *mystery* books. Maybe I just have a curious mind."

"You know far too much."

"Let's talk about 'who'. It wasn't Colonel Mustard in the dining room. One night when the black speedboat slowed down to pass under the *Roosevelt Bridge* a kayak slipped out from under the shadows and bumped into it with it's bow. It wasn't a big bump - just a slight tap. The kayak operator excused himself, backed off and disappeared into the shadows. But, there was a lot of verbal 'pissing and moaning' before the black speedboat's operator hit the throttle and took off like a bat out of hell."

"It was Rat! He has a green kayak!"

"A miniature GPS satellite transmitter attached to the bow of the kayak with double-sided waterproof tape was transferred to the black speedboat's hull by the contact. I was parked in a strip mall north of the *Roosevelt Bridge* and tracked the boat with a portable GPS receiver equipped with a video plotter. When the boat turned into the launching ramps at *River Gate Park* I was waiting across the street in the Post Office parking lot.

The boat was loaded on a trailer behind a black pick up truck. I followed it down *St. Lucie Boulevard*, watched it turn left onto *Tulip* and then right onto a side street. After the truck stopped I used the plotter to home in on the address, waited fifteen minutes and drove past the house. The boat was parked beside the house and covered with a tarp. I wrote down the boat's FL numbers, the trailer and truck's tag numbers. I removed the transmitter that was held on with tape and reattached it with epoxy inside the steering console. I also attached a transmitter under the truck's front bumper."

"What made you suspect that they were delivering narcotics?"

"It didn't take a genius! The suspicion was already there - I just needed confirmation. I swabbed the inside of the coolers and passed the two swabs through a portable *ion detector*. They both tested positive. I also swabbed a cotton ball in each area and put them in plastic FDLE evidence bags. The three coolers were dry on the inside which meant that there hadn't been any ice, or fish in them."

"How did you get the FDLE evidence bag?"

"You ask too many questions. Will you please just accept what I'm telling you and run with it? Here's the report from the Florida Department of Law Enforcement. The results indicate that all three samples tested positive for high grade cocaine."

It was easy to run down the owner of the house, boat, trailer and truck. It was Manny. A records check indicated that he had two convictions for narcotics trafficking in New Jersey and served eighteen months. He was sentenced for a misdemeanor in Florida three years ago for marijuana possession and only got one-year probation. His brother Gino also lived in Port St. Lucie and also had a felony conviction in New Jersey for trafficking cocaine. He did twelve months hard time plus another five years on supervised probation. They both looked very suspicious."

"Why didn't you contact us for assistance?"

"This was more important than another minor drug conviction and one day's headlines in the newspaper. Let's just say that it was a personal matter that had to be settled."

"What did you do next?"

"Based on where Manny lived, and his life style, I didn't figure him to be the main dealer. I felt that he was the 'mule' and only delivering the stuff. When I tracked the boat on the GPS plotter it made a detour across the river to the west after going under the *'007' Bridge*. It stopped for about ten minutes and then took off for *River Gate Park*. When I stopped at the house the outboard was still draining water, but the boat and coolers were empty. So they had dropped the drugs off somewhere. That was another trail to follow."

"Where did they drop the stuff?"

"Don't you listen? I told you that they made a jog to the west after they passed under the *'007' Bridge*, stopped for ten minutes and then took off for *River Gate Park*."

"Could you identify who lived there?"

"No. It's a gated community and I couldn't get an address off the GPS. I took another route. That's where Rat played a significant role. He can get in anywhere! He took care of the two guard dogs and bypassed the electronic security system. It was hilarious to see because he was buck-ass naked!"

"Why was he naked?"

"His Senaca Indian grandfather told him American Indians believed that dogs will not bark, or growl, at a naked man. When he was in Laos doing 'snatches' he always snuck into a village naked. It worked because the two dogs on guard duty in the compound never made a peep."

"Why didn't you clue us in? We could have helped?"

"I told you that this was a personal matter. I didn't need law enforcement involved at that point. They would just screw things up and get in the way. You got to be in on the collar didn't you?"

"Yes, but we didn't get to do any of the surveillance and investigation work. That's the 'fun' part, at least for me"

"You'll get over it. If you are asked tell people that it was a long and detailed undercover operation conducted over several months that involved several different agencies. Everyone will get to take some of the credit and will all look good."

"How did you identify the location of the main supplier in *Hobe Sound*?"

"GPS is a wonderful thing, especially if you have a receiver and plotter that interfaces with a VCR. I can record and replay everything at any time of day or night. I didn't have to follow them around at night. That might have blown the whole thing. When I had time during the day I replayed the tape at high speed and was able to lock in on their exact location.

"How did you find the exact house?"

One day I took a run down to *Hobe Sound* and took a few digital photos for reference. I used my GPS to get the exact longitude and latitude of the house and dock. I mounted a GPS satellite transmitter in their black 'go fast' boat that I figured was used to make 'off-shore' pickups from the mother ship. I installed a solar-powered, motion-activated video camera equipped with night-vision in the mangrove tree directly across the canal from the house. The video signal was transmitted to the marina via a digital cell phone equipped with a high-speed modem.

I tapped their phone lines to get their phone and pager numbers, plus the pager codes used to signal a pickup. I cross-referenced the phone and pager numbers directly to their owners and their addresses. It was simple."

"Where did you get all of that electronics stuff? Can I see it?"

"No. You know too much already. That's the end of the story. Elmo, get out. I've got to get some sleep."

"But Mack, I . . ."

"No ifs, ands or buts. Mr. Deputy, what did you say your name was? My memory is fading fast and I can't recall."

"I get the picture and I'm out'ta here. Bye."

CHAPTER

21

BRRING BRRING BRRING

The damn phone was as persistent and relentless as the hungry female mosquito that darted in and out from behind Mack's right ear in an attempt to snatch a delicious tidbit of hemoglobin. He swatted at her and the 'buzzing' stopped momentarily. At least there was some respite from the 'buzzing', but the persistent telephone would not stop ringing. Mack swiped at it with his eyes closed and knocked the clock off the nightstand onto the floor.

BRRING BRRING BRRING

The phone kept ringing unmercifully.

"Captain Mack here. I'm trying to get some sleep. Call me back tomorrow."

"Mack. It's Ralph. It is tomorrow. It's nine-thirty Wednesday morning and you've been sleeping since yesterday morning. That's almost twenty-four hours. There's been a lot going on that you should know about. Can I come over?"

"Sure. Give me time to jump in the shower and shave."

"Okay. Put on some coffee I'm bringing over some donuts."

"Ralph? You didn't get the donuts from Rat did you?"

"No. But, last night he brought over some great barbequed ribs. They really hit the spot."

"Please don't tell me any more. Bring the donuts, but no ribs."

Mack stumbled into the bathroom and somehow managed to

drag himself into the shower stall.

"Meow"

The pair of pleading, round yellow eyes looked up at him from the floor of the dry shower stall. "Kitty, hang on just a minute. Let me get the water the right temperature for you."

The elevated deck made an ideal location for early morning coffee and donuts. The sun peeked through a mantle of puffy, white cumulus clouds and the silver mullet in the shallow *North Lake* basin repeatedly leaped out of the water in search of whatever it is mullet look for in the 'alien' air environment.

"Mack. About five-thirty yesterday afternoon Rat stopped by with the barbequed ribs and I tried to reach you on the phone to invite you to dinner. You didn't answer and I came over to check on you. When I got here your truck was gone. I figured that you had woke up and gone out for something to eat. I called you again about midnight and you didn't answer. So, I came over again. Your truck was still gone and I was worried about you."

"Ralph, I'm fine. I went to bed after the meeting at the fish house and woke up about three-thirty in the afternoon. I was hungry and went out to get something to eat. It was such a nice day that I decided to take a ride and wound up in *Fort Pierce*. I sat around at the marina *Tiki Bar* watching the boats go by until closing time. I got back here a little after two o' clock."

"I'm sure glad that you're okay. I was really worried about you after the shenanigans the other night. Those guys might have mean friends."

"Those types of people don't have any friends - just enemies. Anything on the news?"

"Tina's face was on all the local news broadcasts last night and there's a big article in today's *Stuart News* about it. I left the newspaper on your coffee table."

"Thanks. I'll read it after I wake up. Anything new?"

"No. Everyone figures that the *Hobe Sound* group brought in a couple of *New York* 'hit men' to take care of their *North Fork* competition. Mack. How did you pull all of this together?"

"Ballistics tests on the bullets that your uncle removed from Dave's brother and Bear showed that they were fired from the same gun. It was a *CIA issue High Standard, noise-suppressed, twenty-two caliber pistol.* Ballistic tests will prove that Frankie and Dave were both killed by the gun that killed Mel's brother. And, strangely enough it was found in the boathouse with the two 'hit men' thus the 'hit men' must have killed all three of them!"

"Even Mel's brother? How could that be possible? You said that Dave shot him and that his boat burned to the waterline and sunk in the Gulf Stream."

"Dave did shoot him and the boat did burn to the waterline. But, the hull went aground on the *Bahamas Bank* the next day. We had a tracking transmitter on the sailboat and located it at *White Sand Ridge* twelve miles north of *Memory Rock.* The water there is less than three feet deep at high tide. Mel's brother's body was recovered and your uncle did the autopsy."

"He never told me anything about it."

"Why should he tell you? You might inadvertently say something to the wrong person."

"Does Mel know about it?"

"I told him yesterday morning, before we met for breakfast."

"How did you figure out that Billy O'Dell, the Sanibel Police Chief, had something to do with all this?"

"First of all, he knew that I was there and snuck up on me at the marina. Somebody called him and told him to watch for me.

The biggest clue was when at lunch Dave mentioned that I had met the police chief and asked what I thought of him. The only way that he could have known that detail was by talking to the police chief himself. You told Dave that I was going to *Fort Myers* about ten o'clock in the morning. But, I didn't talk to you again until four o' clock in the afternoon after I left *Sanibel.* Dave was quoted in the newspaper clipping as saying that he was stationed with Gene in Laos. I knew right then and there that Dave was involved in this drug trafficking operation."

"Billy O'Dell was flying heroin out of Laos for Dave and Frankie on *Air American* planes. We had an airtight case against him until you disappeared. He must be in this right up to his ears. I'll bet that the pilots in *Fort Pierce* are buddies of his. Did he recognize you when you stopped on *Sanibel?*"

"Of course he did. Dave called him and told him that I was coming. Dave was testing me to see how well the reprogramming had worked on me. That's why Billy O'Dell gave me Gene's coin, his *ZIPPO* lighter and the article about his death.

Dave hoped that I would have a serious 'flashback' that would give him a good reason to have me committed to the VA Hospital for treatment under his supervision. Dave knew that I was getting close to him. He shot Gene in the back of the neck and wrapped him in his cast net to make it look like an accident."

"How do you know that?"

"I called your uncle to find out the Lee County coroner's name and phone number. I was lucky because I went to high school with him. He confirmed that Gene was shot and faxed his autopsy report to your uncle. That's the reason why you made a second trip to *Fort Pierce* in the same day. The ballistics test showed that it was the same gun that killed Mel's brother."

"What made you think that Dave installed a tracking transmitter in your truck?"

"On my way back I called a friend who runs an electronics lab in *Stuart* on *Kindred Street*. He met me in *Port Mayaca*, swept the truck with a multi-frequency scanner, and found it. That's why I dropped the truck off at the gas station and rented a car.

Then we went to Tina's condo in *West Palm* and he found a tracking transmitter in her *Beamer*. He took it out and left it on a shelf in her garage. I called Tina and advised her to rent a car at the airport when she came in from DC because her car had 'problems.' But, I didn't tell her what the 'problems' actually were. She checked into the *Breakers Hotel* under an assumed name and stayed away from her condo because Dave had it wired with sensors and cameras."

"How could you get in to her place?"

"She gave me the key to her condo and asked that I start the *Beamer* up once a week."

"Dave tracked your truck to the gas station, got suspicious when it sat there for so long and went out to check on you."

"That's why I slit the radiator hose where it enters the water pump. He saw the water and antifreeze puddle under the truck and was satisfied that I had a problem. But, he was frustrated because he couldn't track me. One of his flunkies installed a transmitter in the rental car when I met him for lunch at the

Queen Conch. I drove over to Kindred Street and my friend used a portable frequency scanner to find it."

"What did you do about it?"

"I called the car rental agency and told them that I wanted another car. I insisted on the same make, model and color so that Dave wouldn't get suspicious. They brought it over and we swapped cars. The last I heard the rental car was on it's way to *Key West* with a vacationing couple from Des Moines, Iowa."

"Why did you tell me to cover Bear's boat with a tarp and not bring it to the marina?"

"Did it rain before I got there to go over it?"

"Yes."

"I wanted to protect any palm or finger prints that might have been there and the tarp kept people out of it. I didn't want you to bring the boat to the marina because I figured that Dave had installed a tracking transmitter in it. I didn't want to alert him that I was 'on' to him. Plus, when I inspected the boat I didn't want anyone to see me in it. I had a lot of things to do under there."

"Did you get any useable prints?"

"Yes. I got Frankie's, Manny's and Gino's. Tina ran them through the FBI and they were confirmed as theirs."

"Did you find a tracking transmitter too?"

"Yes. Dave planted it in Bear's boat after his goons reported that Bear was hanging around the North Fork. I removed it and stuck it to the bottom of your dock. Count backwards three pilings from the end and look underneath. It's still there.

Dave thought that he was safe because he had tracking transmitters in my truck and boat, Tina's car, plus Bear's truck and boat. Whenever the ignition key was turned to start the engine it activated the tracking transmitter and it sent a signal to Dave's monitoring station that one of us was on the move. He knew exactly where each of us was twenty-four hours a day."

"Did you check out the two reporters from the *Port St. Lucie News?*"

"Yes. They were Manny and Gino. Dave sent them down to retrieve the GPS tracking transmitter, but they couldn't find it."

"What did you do with the old shotgun?"

"I cleaned it up, sold it and put a hundred bucks in the boot yesterday for Emogene. But, she doesn't need to know that Bear had a gun in the boat."

"What was plugging up the barrel?"

"Do you remember that stubby, yellow, number two pencil that was in the bottom of the boat?"

"Of course."

"Do you recall that one of the chewing tobacco packages was missing the paper wrapper?"

"Yes. So what?"

"Bear wrote down two tag numbers on the paper wrapper and stuffed it inside the gun barrel. Tina ran the tag numbers. They were for a truck and boat trailer registered to Manny. Bear saw Manny's truck and trailer somewhere that night. It wasn't on the highway because Bear was in the boat. It had to be at the *River Gate Park* launching ramps. Bear identified his killers himself. The stubby yellow pencil was the key that he had written a note."

"Dave had the marina wired with video cameras. Why didn't he know that you had left?"

"The marina's security system had an 'alert' feature that notified Dave if I left. But, it had to be activated by turning the head of a nail over the front door so that it pointed 'up'. I didn't turn the nail 'up' when I left. The system was not activated."

"Couldn't he check on you with the inside video cameras to be sure that you were there.

"Yes. He could. But, the cameras' signals pass through the video multiplexer's recording heads a tenth of a second before they are transmitted. My friend on Kindred Street made a 'real time' video that I slipped into the video multiplexer before I left. It ran a pre-recorded, continuous image of me in bed and added 'real time' and date signatures. If Dave tuned in the marina the camera would show me in bed asleep. The time and date on the monitor would be current."

"Weren't you worried that Dave was going to catch on the other night?"

"No. He was too busy monitoring what was going on in *Hobe Sound*. He was willing to let his partners go down for the count. Then, he and Frankie wouldn't have any competition. During the investigation Tina's investigator will find a link between the two groups and rationalize that the *Hobe Sound* group put out a 'contract' on Dave and Frankie. She'll prosecute and convict the *Hobe Sound* group for drug distribution, racketeering and four counts of homicide. Case closed."

"How much does Tina know about what went on here?"

"Not much. I had her called back to DC for a complete evaluation and reprogramming. In her mind I'm a fishing guide and Dave was the bad guy."

"Does she know that she was married to Dave when they were stationed at Langley?"

"No. In her mind both of her husbands were drunks and she divorced them."

"Does she know that you and I were in the *Air Force Office of Special Investigation* and put together the heroin smuggling case against Dave and Frankie in Laos?"

"Of course not. And, she'll never find out if you just keep that coin in your shirt."

"Do you mean this one?"

Ralph pulled a silver chain out from under his shirt which contained a single *South African One Rand* silver coin with the numeral '2' stamped between the *Springbok's* front feet."

"That's the one. It almost matches the two others that I found the other night." Mack put his right hand into his pocket, rummaged around and pulled it back out. When opened his closed hand three *South African One Rand* coins glistened in his sweaty, open palm.

"Mack. You've got three *Rand* coins. Not two. Where'd you get the third one?"

"I guess that I can't count very well. There were only two coins in my pocket when I went to bed yesterday morning. You didn't really think that you saw three coins in my hand. Do you?"

"No. Now that you pointed it out to me I only see two."

"Good. I thought that you would understand. Now, where were we?"

"I asked you how much, if anything, Tina knew about what was going on here. Does she have any inkling that Dave shot her parents and faked the car accident five years ago when he came over here from *Fort Myers*?"

"No. Dave did that for his own protection because her parents recognized him. He tried to burn down the marina, but he only got the house. Her parents' deaths caused her to have a breakdown. That's when Dave, as her ex-husband, took charge of her treatments. Actually, it was reprogramming."

"Why did Dave get involved in running cocaine? He owned an electronics business."

"He needed money. He had massive gambling debts and there was a big drop in his company's profits because military spending is down. He was in 'hock' to Frankie for thousands of dollars and Frankie had him under his 'thumb'.

Dave's company manufactured the communications and surveillance equipment used by local law enforcement agencies for 'covert' operations. He had scanners tuned in on all of the radio frequencies used by law enforcement personnel. He was able to monitor all of the agencies twenty-four hours a day. Plus, I think that he liked the excitement."

"You were sent here because *the company* knew that Dave was up to something and Tina couldn't handle it. Right?"

" I came here to become a fishing guide. Period!"

"What are you going to do now? Are you going to leave?"

"Not if I can help it. I like it here. Besides, somebody has to watch out for those two baby ospreys out in that old Australian pine tree - and Tina. It might as well be me."

"One last thing. Bear was working for the FDLE as an undercover agent, wasn't he?"

"I think so. There was an FDLE supervisor's business card stuffed in the gun barrel."

"Mack. Thank you for everything that you have done for Bear, Bobo and Emogene."

"No thanks are necessary."

"Don't forget the cat. The last I saw him he was heading for the bathroom. That was about fifteen minutes ago and he was running full tilt – 'balls to the wall.' He was in a very big hurry."

After he had rousted the cat out of the clothes hamper and used a full can of 'Garden Lilac Mist' spray to freshen up the bathroom, Mack sat down to read the newspaper. The twenty-eight point, bold face type headline read:

FOUR MEN FOUND DEAD IN THE
NORTH FORK OF ST. LUCIE RIVER

Local law enforcement officials are baffled over finding four bodies in the North Fork of the St. Lucie River. The four included two convicted drug dealers from the New York area, a prominent real estate developer whose name is being withheld and Dave Thatch the CEO of Thatch Electronics.

At 5:10 A.M. yesterday morning a security system alarm alerted local law enforcement that the real estate developer's estate's perimeter had been penetrated. Several neighbors had called '911' to report that several explosions had come from the estate. When law enforcement personnel arrived they were met with gunfire from a boathouse. Police returned fire and killed two armed men who were hiding in the boathouse.

Each man was armed with a 9-millimeter automatic pistol and an unusual .22 caliber pistol equipped with a noise suppressor. Ballistics tests confirmed that they were the weapons used to kill Thatch and the real estate developer. FDLE officials are baffled because the particular model of .22-caliber pistol found at the scene was a unique type issued only to 'covert' military units operating in Southeast Asia during the 1960's.

The boathouse contained ten kilos of cocaine and a battery-powered boat. Spokesperson Tina said that the men were going to use the electric boat to travel across the North Fork to River Gate Park where their rental car was parked. The boat was inoperative because the cable from the battery to the ignition had been cut.

The bodies of Thatch and the developer were found in a commercial fishing boat in a cove opposite Kitching Cove. The boat's identifying numbers were painted over fueling speculation that it had been stolen. The men's arms were bound to their sides with plastic straps. Their feet were tied together and they were hanging off opposite sides of the boat with their heads in the water. Both men had several electrical burn marks on their neck indicating the use of a powerful electric stun gun to torture them. The men were shot execution style with a small caliber bullet at the base of their skull. However, an autopsy indicated that both men drowned.

The St. Lucie County coroner said, "Who ever shot these men had an excellent knowledge of the human nervous system. They were shot with a .22-caliber weapon at a distance of greater than three feet because no powder marks were found at the entrance wound. The bullet severed the spinal cord resulting in paralysis from the neck downward. The men were conscious when their heads were immersed under the water and it took them at least five minutes to expire. They must have suffered terribly."

The bodies of two other men were found tangled in nets and floating next to a black speedboat containing three coolers filled with packages of cocaine. Their necks were broken and they had drowned. The boat's propeller was tangled in a net and a steel cable. The FDLE spokesperson said that the obvious executions were meant to send a message and speculated that the two incidents took place as follows:

"The black speedboat was delivering cocaine after rendezvousing offshore with a mother ship that brought the drugs over from the Bahamas. The mother ship serviced several local drug distributors and one of them got jealous over the competition and wanted the entire market. Two professional hit men were brought in from New York who monitored the activities of the black boat to determine its schedule and route. Last

evening they set a gill net, buoyed by a steel cable, across the channel. The black speedboat traveling at a high rate of speed hit the cable and stopped suddenly. The boat's occupants were catapulted into the water, broke their necks and drowned. The 'hit men' used the electric boat to tow their bodies and boat into the cove where they wrapped them in nets and set them adrift.

They went back to the estate about 4:00 A.M., disabled the two men inside with a stun gun, bound them with plastic boat tie-down straps and placed duct tape over their mouths. They placed them in the stolen commercial fishing boat and used the electric boat to tow it to the cove. They made the men lean over opposite sides of the commercial fishing boat, with their legs tied together, so they could not slip over the side, and shot them in the neck. Their faces fell into the water and they drowned.

They used the electric boat to return to the estate and set explosive charges to destroy the house, garage and guesthouse. When they returned to the boathouse their only means of escape, the electric boat, would not operate because the battery cable had been cut. When law enforcement personnel arrived the two men were trapped between the water and the burning house and they decided to shoot it out and were killed.

Although four people lost their lives a major cocaine distribution ring was eliminated and we consider the case closed."

Inside on page twelve Mack found a much smaller item.

SANIBEL CHIEF DIES IN ACCIDENT

Late Tuesday evening Sanibel Island Police Chief Billy O'Dell's body was found floating in Tarpon Bay tangled in a cast net. It appeared that he had attempted to throw the cast net over a

*school of mullet, slipped, hit his head on the
concrete sea wall and drowned. He had been
Sanibel Police Chief since 1975 and served in the
Air Force in the Far East in the late 1960's.'*

Mack tore out the article and placed it in a small teak wood box with the three *South African One Rand* coins. The latest addition to his growing collection had the numeral '3' stamped slightly to the left of the *Springbok's* hind leg.

Mack looked at his watch. It was almost 10:30 A.M. and he had to meet Tina for lunch at *The Breakers* in Palm Beach at eleven-thirty. She would not be happy if he was late. But, before he could leave he had to fill the rental car with gas, clean the 'Love Bugs' off the windshield and vacuum the obvious traces of white *Sanibel Island* beach sand out of the trunk.

It was a long drive over and back in the dark, but it had been a very worthwhile trip. Mack was satisfied and had evened the score for Bear.

CHAPTER
22

It was the week of the Fourth of July, just over a month since Bear's violent death in the North Fork of the St. Lucie River. Mack's dreams had become more frequent and violent. Two nights ago he woke up screaming and drenched in sweat. He decided to find help and made an appointment for today at the Veterans Hospital in West Palm Beach. He didn't have much hope because he had explained his dreams to disinterested VA doctors many times before. They passed them off as 'figments of his imagination'. *"Too many war movies."* they told him.

Thursday wasn't out of the ordinary. It was 'just another day in Paradise', but it felt portentous and Mack sensed an omen in the air. The monotonous drive down I-95 felt 'strange' - there were no birds flying. The normally heavy traffic was minimal - very odd for 8:10 A.M. It was 'rush hour' and the cars should be almost bumper-to-bumper. Mack felt 'something', but didn't know what, and it made him feel uneasy.

He recalled the 'mental concentration' training sessions on Okinawa guided by a white-bearded Indian yogi. Mack was told to 'imagine' the sound of two hands softly clapping together in five-second intervals. He concentrated on the sound of the two palms coming together until he could anticipate and 'hear' it. After perhaps two hours of concentration on the imagined sound, the yogi suggested that one of the hands stopped moving, but the other hand bridged the open gap to maintain the clapping – all by itself. Mack could 'hear' the sound that the one hand made!

He pulled into the parking lot in front of the VA Hospital and was amazed at the large number of luxury cars in the parking spaces. Big Lincoln's, Buick's and Cadillacs filled almost every space. Mack wondered if these people really needed VA medical care. It seemed to him that if they could afford a big luxury automobile that they could afford to pay for private medical insurance. But, the VA was free. Perhaps they could afford the fancy car because they didn't have to worry about health insurance premiums.

Mack watched intently as white-haired elderly men, our nation's warriors from a previous era, limped through the front door. Many of them had to be assisted by their wives. Inside the doorway several apparently helpless old men sat in plastic-backed wheelchairs with their eyes closed and wore clear plastic tubes in their noses that provided them with life-giving oxygen.

Mack felt fortunate that wasn't there for any physical ailment, at least that he was aware of, but the continuing heavy, portentous feeling in the air concerned him. He often developed a mental picture of tragic events several days before they actually came to fruition. He didn't have a corn that ached, or a joint that throbbed, it was simply an ominous awareness that 'something eventful' was going to happen and he could often see it unfold.

He was still able to clearly recall experiments that required that he attempt to guess the suit of a single playing card laying face down on table covered in green felt. The statistical odds were one in four because there are four suits in a deck of playing cards. Mack initially scored below thirty percent, but after some practice he increased his score to above seventy-five percent.

The experiments advanced to reading the headlines of a newspaper. Initially the newspaper was held at arm's length - close enough to read easily. But, on the next day, and each succeeding day thereafter, the newspaper was moved six inches further away. It reached the point where he had to squint to read it. Finally it was moved to a distance when he could not make it out at all visually. At that point he was asked to close his eyes and imagine slowly creeping closer and closer to the newspaper until he could turn it right side up read the headline. After several weeks he was able to read a newspaper upside down and fifty feet away. Those highly developed sensory skills came in handy later.

Snap! Reality check! Mack's mind had drifted off to the distant past. This was now and he had an appointment to make. The waiting room was filled with white-haired old men most of who were accompanied by obviously anxious wives. He printed his name on the sign-in sheet, noted the time as 9:12 A.M., sat down and waited to be called for his 9:30 A.M. appointment. And wait he did. It wasn't until 10:18 A.M. that a sweet young nurse came into the waiting room, pointed at him, crooked her finger, smiled and breathlessly gushed, "Sir. It's your turn. Please follow me." He followed her into the hallway and waited for directions.

"Your X-ray will be done in examination room number Four. It's right down the hall - the second door on the left."

"I'm not here for an X-ray. Please check my file."

"It says X-ray right here on this slip of paper, Mr. Ledbetter. See for yourself."

"My name is not Ledbetter, it's MacArthur!"

"Mr. MacArthur, I'm so sorry. It appears that we might have made a slight mistake. You're here for a general checkup."

"I'm certainly glad that you caught the mistake. I might have walked out of here missing a leg and the wrong one at that."

"We don't make those kind of mistakes here."

"If you don't make those kind of mistakes here, then exactly what kind of mistakes do you make here?"

"Mr. MacArthur that wasn't funny. Let's go. Follow me."

"Yes it was. At least I thought so. Now where are we going?"

"To the 'neutering' room. Mr. MacArthur your testosterone level is obviously a little high!"

"Thanks, but no thanks. I already gave at the office."

"Mr. MacArthur get in there so that I can take your vitals."

"That's what you said two minutes ago. I'm attached to both of them and I'd like to keep them if you don't mind."

"Mr. Funnyman, I'm talking about your height, weight and blood pressure. Get in there! Now!"

"I'm coming. I'm coming. I'm right behind you."

"Very funny Mr. Funnyman. But I'm not laughing. Sit down

on this stool and let me take your blood pressure while you can still walk without assistance and open your big mouth to talk."

"Yes ma'am. I'll be good. I can be real good when I want to be. Ouch! Isn't the blood pressure cuff a little tight? My arm has turned white from the elbow down."

"One-twenty over eighty. Pulse sixty-eight. You're okay. Get on the scales."

"Yes, boss lady."

"Seventy-six inches and 228 pounds. Okay. Get down off the table and follow me. I'm are going to find an examination room for you."

"Not a rubber one I hope. I'd like a single room with a king size bed and view of the ocean."

"Mr. MacArthur I'm warning you. Don't get smart mouthed with me. I can 'neuter' you before you can blink your eye and you won't feel a thing until it's all over. Here we are. Go in, take off your shirt and lay face down on the examination table."

"Am I going to be physically violated?"

"No smart Mr. Smart Mouth. I am going to take an EKG to check your heart. That is if you have one."

"It looks like an electroshock therapy machine. If you put a rubber headband on me I'll cry."

"It's an EKG machine and it won't hurt you. But, if you don't shut up and be good I will!"

"Do you have a sister named Tina? If you do, tell her that she needs to see an exorcist!"

"No I don't! My sister's name is Elizabeth."

"Thank God. I thought that I was in Purgatory and I'm not even Catholic."

"Okay 'Mr. Smarty Pants. I'm done with you. You can get up and put your shirt back on. The doctor will be in soon." The nurse slipped out of the room and closed the door behind her.

Mack sat down and scanned the tiny examination room. How 'sterile' it was with its flat-white walls. The white plastic, round faced clock on the wall above the door read 10:44 A.M. Three dog-eared magazines of ancient vintage were neatly arranged on top of the tiny wooden desk. Each magazine had the address label neatly snipped out of the cover. The tiny room was perhaps all of eight feet wide and ten feet long. An ugly plastic tree sat in a wicker basket beside the desk and its fake plastic base was surrounded by equally fake, and ugly, plastic mulch.

A single lithograph print, perhaps three feet by three feet hung on the wall above the tiny desk. It was a strange scene of a white stucco house covered with a mottled tiled roof consisting of orange, blue and brown curved tiles. A single 'bedraggled' palm tree with its fronds whipping in the imagined breeze graced the front yard – if it could be called a 'yard.' What made the print exceptionally 'tacky' was the flat white wooden frame. It didn't make much of an impression on a white wall.

The far end of the room, on the opposite end from the door, contained the obligatory 'fake tile' counter top and sink. The color scheme was utterly obscene. The three cabinet doors above the counter top were painted white, the counter top itself was blue and the three cupboard doors on the bottom were fake wood with glued-on plastic fronts.

Five tall glass containers sat on the left side of the counter top. They featured domed, chrome tops with a cute chrome knob mounted on the top. From left to right they were neatly labeled; *Swabs with Cotton Tips, Gauze Pads, Cotton Balls, Tongue Depressors* and *Bandages*. On the blue counter top in front of the glass containers lay an ominous, extra-large size tube of *K-Y Jelly*. The large depression in the center of the tube clearly indicated that it had been 'squeezed' often. The presence of the tube didn't concern Mack very much until his eyes focused on the rectangular orange box next to it labeled *'Latex Examination Gloves - medium.'* He knew that he wasn't pregnant and certainly didn't need a 'Pap smear' taken. The sight of the tube of *K-Y Jelly* helped him to make up his mind to leave.

Mack decided that he had waited long enough for the doctor. He was certain that there was nothing wrong with him and he was out of there! He stood up to leave and was trying to figure out what he was going to say to 'Attilla the Nurse' on his way out when the door cracked open. 'She' was back! "The doctor is running a little late. She'll be with you in a minute. Just hold on."

"Hold on my ass. I'm out of here. I don't need a female doctor checking me out much less trying to dig for oil in my butt!"

"Hold it right there buddy boy! You're not going anywhere. You're here and you might as well stay. She's not going to check your prostate. At least she's not supposed too, but then again in your case - she just might. Sit down."

'Fear' crept up from somewhere below his feet, crawled slowly up the inside of his legs and lodged at the point where his neck joined his spine He was trapped like a rat and couldn't get out! He had no choice, but wait there for the doctor and decided to entertain himself by checking out the room in detail. The pale yellow waste can had a large red sticker on the lid and another one the canister itself. The plastic sticker read, *'BIOHAZARD'* in gigantic, bold, black capital letters on a bright red background. Biohazard? Should he even be in the room?

On the floor, alongside the examination table, sat a small chrome-plated stool. It was cute in a way with its four chrome legs and topped off in ridged black rubber. The chrome legs even had little black rubber 'booties' on them. The four-foot long fluorescent light fixture over the examining table contained four bulbs and two of them were burned out. There were several long, vertical gouges in the white plasterboard wall directly above the examining table. Mack shivered. He wondered if the deep gouges had been made by the fingernails of a frantic, screaming male patient climbing the wall during a prostate examination.

The door opened. She was finally there! "Good morning Mr. MacArthur. I'm sorry to be so late, but we had an emergency patient and are running a tad behind schedule. I apologize for the inconvenience. How did we treat you?"

"The nurse needs an exorcist! She's an evil woman and she wants to hurt me!"

"Mr. MacArthur be serious. What can I do for you today?"

"Just let me out of here! I'm just fine."

"First let's go over your vitals. Your blood pressure and pulse are just fine and your EKG was normal. Do you currently take any medications?"

"Nothing. Just a glass of red wine before I go to bed for cholesterol reduction."

"Are you certain that you take nothing? How about an aspirin a day for blood pressure?"

"Nothing. Can I go now?"

"Hold on. Not just yet. Why did you make an appointment if you don't feel that anything is physically wrong with you?"

"It was time for my annual checkup and I've been having some bad dreams recently."

"I see in your file that you have been complaining about the bad dreams for several years. Do you want me to put you on medication to help your depression and mood swings?"

"What do you mean depression? I'm certainly not depressed."

"According to your records you have been reporting severe nightmares for several years. The VA Hospitals in Chicago and Bethesda both indicated that you suffered from mood swings and should be on *Paxil* or perhaps *Prosac*."

"I don't have mood swings just damn scary nightmares. I don't know if they are from real events, or just my imagination. That's why I'm here - to find out why. No one will tell me."

After a cursory examination she told him that the violent dreams, 'flashbacks' as she called them, would become less frequent as time passed. But, there was a caveat! "Wait here for a few minutes. I need to get someone more qualified than I am in that field to talk to you about your dreams and suggest treatment for them. Hold on for a minute. I'll be right back."

After the doctor left the room Mack flipped open the brown cover of his thick medical file and scanned the top page.

"Diagnosis: Severe Post Traumatic Stress Disorder. Specific additional treatment undetermined.

Ketamine Hydrocloride, Mescaline and Diazepam have shown to be totally ineffective. If necessary suggest use of electrotherapy and permanent institutional setting. If patient becomes physically violent, or relates severe nightmares, immediate project termination may be necessary. For approval contact M."

Mack got up from the table, put on his clothes and left the room in a trot. The bored nurse at the front desk doing her nails looked up at him when he walked past and raised her eyebrows in disbelief. "Where do you think you are going buster?"

"Out! You dumb ass people don't understand anything. None of you do! I quit. It's over. I'm leaving!"

The shocked nurse scurried down the hall screaming. "Doctor! Doctor! Doctor! He's leaving!"

Mack glanced down the hall. The female doctor was talking to a tall, red headed woman dressed in a gray, striped business suit. The red head smiled at him and gave him a 'thumbs' up'.

He dashed out the front door and headed for the parking lot. Mack wanted to get out of there as fast as he could and on the road. The day was only half over and he still had plenty of time to drive back to Stuart, snare a few silver finger mullet in his cast net and catch the last two hours of the afternoon outgoing tide. There might just be a snook sleeping under the mangrove-lined banks just west of the *"Hole in the Wall."* Bear would like that too. Mack made the trip in 'record time' – twenty-nine minutes!

Mack enjoyed the walk from the *Bath Tub Beach* parking lot, down the oak and mangrove shaded walkway to the long wooden dock that jutted more than one hundred feet out into the Indian River. It was late afternoon, the shadows of the mangrove trees lining the western bank of the river were growing longer by the minute and the western sky was tinged light pink. He sat down on the warm, creosoted, wooden planks to soak up what was left of the waning sun and watch the floating debris drift down river on the outgoing tide.

The warm sun felt good on his face and the ebbing water flowing past the wooden pilings gurgled softly like a country brook. Mack closed his eyes and drifted off into nothingness. He had left his problems in the examination room of the VA Hospital and he was resolved to never going back. His peaceful interlude with *'Mother Nature'* was interrupted by the sound of pounding footsteps that shook the rickety, wooden dock. The footsteps were accompanied by loud, panic-stricken screaming.

"Mack! It's Ralph! Wake up! There are three really mean-looking guys in town looking for you! They've been asking a lot of questions and they're snooping around the marina right now. They said that they were from *Chicago* and knew you. But, I don't think that they're your friends. Mack, you better hurry up."

EPILOGUE

"Those who didn't cannot comprehend why."

"Those who did cannot forget."

The author

ACKNOWLEDGEMENTS

I am deeply indebted to the many gracious people who loaned me their expertise, their ideas, their time, their experiences, their hopes, their fears, their anxieties, their dreams and even parts of themselves to enable me develop these unique characters.

Perhaps in some small way each of us can recognize some of our own traits in Mack, Tina, Rat, Bear, Dave, Ralph, Elmo and Mel. Do they exist? Of course they do, at least to me, and I am deeply honored that they permit me to enter their world and share in their experiences. I am but a simple scribe that is permitted to record their trials, tribulations and experiences for your pleasure.

As I write this conclusion to the first book in the planned series of many *TREASURE COAST MYSTERIES* Rat is pulling at my leg urging me to go 'cat-snapper' fishing under the Roosevelt Bridge. The tide will be 'dead low' in a couple of hours and he has a bucket filled with chicken necks. I think I'll go with him.

But, before we leave I wish to thank a person who nudged and nurtured me along from the beginning of an idea almost two years ago. She directed my efforts through many hours of tedious research and shared the exhilaration of sending out inquiry letters and the sharp, negative pangs of callous rejection. But, she never allowed defeat. She wants to remain anonymous and I respect that. Thank you J. Let's open that bottle of warm Merlot now.

ORDER FORM

☐ Please send me ___ copy(ies) of **TREASURE COAST DECEIT**
I am enclosing $18.45 plus $2.50 postage for each copy.
Florida residents please add 7% Sales Tax ($1.30)

☐ My check for $_____ is enclosed (or)

☐ Please charge my ☐ Visa ☐ MasterCard

_____

Account number   Expiration date

_____

Signature

_____

Please print your name

_____

Street or Box   City   State   Zip

_____

Daytime phone   Fax   Email address

Please make check or money order payable to TREASURE COAST MYSTERIES or email this form to MTALLPAUL@AOL.COM. Please allow 4 weeks for delivery. Send order with payment to: TREASURE COAST MYSTERIES, 43 Kindred St. Stuart, FL 34994

RAT - one of the colorful characters in TREASURE COAST DECEIT

Paul McElroy is president of Charter Industry Services, Inc. headquartered in Stuart, Florida. The company specializes in conducting professional maritime training courses. He founded *Charter Industry* a trade journal for professionals in the marine charter industry in 1985. He has extensive writing experience in magazines and newspapers with more than 200 published articles to his credit.

Captain McElroy received his first United States Coast Guard license in 1983 and operated a sport fishing charter business in the Chicago area for several years. He currently holds a Merchant Marine Officer's MASTER - Near Coastal license He served in the United States Air Force, spent a two-year tour in the Far East and specialized in electronics. He speaks Japanese and Spanish.

Mr. McElroy received his Bachelor of Science Degree in Business Administration from Florida State University. Prior to joining the maritime industry he was an executive in the headquarters of a major telecommunications corporation. He lives in south Florida with his wife Michi, is a member of the Mystery Writers of America and the National Association of Maritime Educators. This is his first novel.

Contact him at: www.TreasureCoastMysteries.com